AWESOME ATHLETES!

The *Sports Illustrated For Kids* HALL OF FAME

A *SPORTS ILLUSTRATED FOR KIDS* BOOK

BANTAM BOOKS

NEW YORK • TORONTO • LONDON • SYDNEY • AUCKLAND

AWESOME ATHLETES!

A Bantam Book/December 1995

SPORTS ILLUSTRATED FOR KIDS books are published in cooperation with Bantam Doubleday Dell Publishing Group, Inc. under license from Time Inc.

Cover and interior design by Pegi Goodman
Computer graphics by John Grimwade
Illustrations by Darryl Collins

For information address: Bantam Books

ISBN 0-553-48316-1

Published simultaneously in the United States and Canada

Bantam Books are published by Bantam Books, a division of Bantam Doubleday Dell Publishing Group, Inc. Its trademark, consisting of the words "Bantam Books" and the portrayal of a rooster, is Registered in the U.S. Patent and Trademark Office and in other countries. Marca Registrada. Bantam Books, 1540 Broadway, New York, New York 10036.

PRINTED IN THE UNITED STATES OF AMERICA

CWO 10 9 8 7 6 5 4 3 2 1

Front cover photographs by (clockwise, from top): Otto Greule/AllSport, Andrew D. Bernstein/NBA Photos, UPI/Bettmann. Back cover photographs by (from top): Heinz Kluetmeier/Sports Illustrated, Richard Mackson/Sports Illustrated.

CONTENTS

SHAQUILLE O'NEAL
PAGE 196

BILLIARDS

BOWLING

BOXING

CYCLING

DIVING

FIGURE SKATING

FOOTBALL

TROY AIKMAN
PAGE 12

GOLF

GYMNASTICS

HOCKEY

HORSE RACING

RODEO

SKATEBOARDING

SKIING

SLED-DOG RACING

SOCCER

SOFTBALL

SPEED SKATING

SHANNON MILLER
PAGE 176

Welcome to the Sports Illustrated For Kids Hall of Fame!

Awesome Athletes! is a jam-packed *Sports Illustrated For Kids* Hall of Fame. It is filled with the stories of 284 of the greatest athletes of today and all time. It includes many of your favorite players as well as legends from the past. These legends set the amazing records that today's stars are trying to break!

How does an athlete get to be called "awesome"? It can happen in several ways. We included many athletes because they played a sport better than anyone had ever done before. We included others because they played with such imagination that they changed the way their sport would be played forever. There are players here who took a new sport and made it popular. And some who inspired others by overcoming great obstacles on their way to greatness.

The athletes in this book come from different sports. There are men and there are women. Some are big, like 7' 1", 310-pound Shaquille O'Neal, and others are small, like 4' 11", 93-pound Shannon Miller. But all these athletes have one thing in common — they are awesome!

— The Editors of *Sports Illustrated For Kids*

HOW IT WORKS

There are different ways to read *Awesome Athletes!* If you want to thumb through the book, the athletes are presented from *A* to *Z*, from front to back. If you want to read about athletes in your favorite sport, you can find them listed by sport on the Contents page. If you want to find a specific athlete, you can can look him or her up in the Index. In some profiles, you'll see the name of another athlete in type that looks Like This. It means *that* athlete is also written about in the book. Find out where by checking the Index.

HANK AARON

On a rainy April evening in Atlanta, Georgia, in 1974, 40-year-old Hank Aaron stepped into the batter's box against Los Angeles Dodger pitcher Al Downing. Hank was one swing away from breaking one of the greatest records in sports — BABE RUTH's all-time major league record of 714 career home runs. The pitcher delivered, and Hank swung with his powerful wrists. He smacked the ball into the left-field bullpen! It was home run number 715 for the man nicknamed "Hammerin' Hank."

Henry Louis "Hank" Aaron grew up in Mobile, Alabama, at a time when black players were not allowed to play in the major leagues. He started his career in the Negro leagues, with the Indianapolis Clowns.

INFO-BOX

BIRTHPLACE: Mobile, Alabama
CAREER: 1954–1976
CLAIM TO FAME: Hank is major league baseball's all-time home run king, with 755 career homers.

Hank was a shy, soft-spoken 20-year-old when he broke into the major leagues with the Milwaukee Braves in 1954 (later, the team moved to Atlanta). He remained a humble person throughout his career. All the while, he steadily produced run after run. Hank averaged about 33 home runs per season for his career. He hit 40 or more homers eight times.

An All-Star in each of his 23 seasons, Hank wasn't just a slugger: He won two batting titles and three Gold Gloves for his play in right field. He led the Braves to National League pennants in 1957 and 1958.

In addition to his best-known record (755 home runs), Hank set 11 other career marks, including most RBIs and extra-base hits. He is second all-time in runs scored (a tie with Babe Ruth) and ranks third in hits.

Hank retired from baseball in 1976. In 1982, he was inducted into the National Baseball Hall of Fame. He now works as an executive in the Atlanta Braves' front office.

As he closed in on Babe Ruth's record, Hank received a lot of hate mail from racists. They did not want to see an African-American hold the record. Since he retired as a player, Hank has spoken out often for more opportunities for African-Americans in major league baseball management.

Family Ties

There have been many brother combinations who have played in the big leagues: trios such as the DiMaggios (Dom, Joe, and Vince) and the Alous (Felipe, Matty, and Jesus) and duos such as the Waners (Lloyd and Paul) and the Niekros (Phil and Joe). Here's a trivia question: Of all these great brother combinations, which family has hit the most home runs? And how many? We'll give the totals first: 768 homers hit by two brothers. Yes, of course, the answer is the Aaron brothers, Hank and his younger brother Tommie, who played seven years in the majors. Hank hit 755 home runs, Tommie hit 13.

WHEN HE WAS A KID Hank Aaron was 16 when he first began playing organized baseball, with the semi-pro Black Bears, in his hometown of Mobile. He also played halfback for his high school football team.

For several years, Hank, a right-handed batter, hit cross- handed (he put his left hand on top of his right hand when he gripped the bat). He got away with this "wrong" hitting style only because his wrists were so strong. But he soon realized how much *more* power he could generate if he gripped the bat correctly.

KAREEM ABDUL-JABBAR

No one in NBA history scored more points than Kareem Abdul-Jabbar. A 7' 2" tall center, Kareem played in the NBA for 20 seasons, longer than any other player. He collected six NBA championships and a record six MVP awards.

Kareem was born Lew Alcindor, in New York City. As a 6' 8" tall teenager, he led Power Memorial High School to a record of 95 wins and only 6 losses. In college, Kareem played for the University of California at Los Angeles (UCLA) Bruins. His teams won 88 games while losing only twice in three varsity seasons. Kareem was such an unstoppable scorer that, in 1967, the NCAA outlawed dunking to slow him down. (The dunk was legalized again nine years later.) Kareem led UCLA to three national titles. He won two College Player of the Year awards and was a three-time NCAA tournament Most Outstanding Player.

Kareem was the first pick in the 1969 NBA draft. He was taken by the last-place Milwaukee Bucks. In the 1970–71 season, Kareem averaged 31.7 points per game, and teamed with OSCAR ROBERTSON to lead the Bucks to an NBA title. At that time, he changed his

Time Capsule

Here are a few of the changes that took place in the United States while Kareem was scoring all those points:

1970: The first Earth Day was held.

1975: The last U.S. troops left Vietnam, ending the long U.S. involvement in the Vietnam war.

1976: The U.S. celebrated the 200th anniversary of its independence.

1981: MTV came on the scene as the first 24-hour music channel.

1989: George Bush became the last of five presidents to hold office during Kareem's career. The others were Richard Nixon, Gerald Ford, Jimmy Carter, and Ronald Reagan.

name to Kareem Abdul-Jabbar.

In 1975, Kareem was traded to the Los Angeles Lakers. Four seasons later, MAGIC JOHNSON joined the team. The combination was awesome, and the Lakers won five NBA titles.

In 1984, Kareem broke the NBA career scoring record, set by WILT CHAMBERLAIN, of 31,419 career points. He finished his pro career with 38,387 points in 1,560 games. His greatest scoring weapon was his "sky hook." When Kareem threw the hook shot down toward the basket from high in the air, it was almost impossible to stop.

INFO-BOX

BIRTHPLACE: New York, New York

CAREER: 1969–1989

CLAIM TO FAME: Kareem is the NBA's all-time leader in points scored and games played.

Kareem is the NBA's all-time leader in points, games played, minutes played, blocked shots, field goals attempted, and field goals made. Kareem retired in 1989. In 1995, he was admitted to the Naismith Memorial Basketball Hall of Fame.

A CLOSER LOOK In addition to being the all-time points leader, Kareem was probably the most consistent scorer in NBA history. From 1977 to 1987 — more than a decade! — Kareem scored 10 points or more in 787 straight games. The end of that streak came against his old team, the Milwaukee Bucks. Even the greats have off days.

TROY AIKMAN

Troy Aikman is one of the hottest quarterbacks in the NFL today. His strong arm and leadership skills led his team, the Dallas Cowboys, to two straight Super Bowl victories. But Troy's journey to the championship wasn't an easy one.

Troy played high school football in his hometown of Henryetta, Oklahoma. There he was named all-state and earned a scholarship to the University of Oklahoma. By his sophomore year, Troy was Oklahoma's starting quarterback. His season was cut short, however, when he broke his ankle in the fourth game. After that season, Troy transferred to the University of California at Los Angeles (UCLA).

His booming passes made Troy an outstanding quarterback at UCLA. He led his team to 20 wins over two seasons. As a senior, he passed for 24 touchdowns, made 228 completions, and threw for 2,771 yards — all UCLA records.

The Dallas Cowboys chose Troy with the first pick in the 1989 draft. Troy started 11 games in his first season with the Cowboys, and they lost them all. The team finished the season with 1 win and 15 losses.

The Dallas coaches didn't give up on Troy. In 1992, he went from being one of the NFL's lowest-rated quarterbacks to being a champion.

When He Was a Kid

Growing up, Troy knew he wanted to be a professional athlete, but his first choice wasn't football. It was baseball! Several scouts for major league teams wanted to draft him straight out of high school. But Troy didn't want to skip college to play a sport. His only problem was telling that to the baseball scouts!

The night before the draft, Troy got a call from a scout. He wanted to know what it would take to get Troy to play baseball. Troy said it would take a lot . . . of money! He asked for an amount that was so large nobody would pay it. And that was the end of his baseball career.

(NFL quarterbacks are rated according to how well they pass.) He led the Cowboys to Super Bowl XXVII, where he completed 22 of 30 passes for 273 yards and threw four touchdowns to defeat the Buffalo Bills.

INFO-BOX

BIRTHPLACE: West Covina, California
CAREER: 1989 to the present
CLAIM TO FAME: Troy led the Dallas Cowboys to two straight Super Bowl championships.

The following season, Troy led his team to another Super Bowl. The Cowboys beat the Bills again to become only the fifth team to win the Super Bowl two years in a row.

Troy has been a great clutch performer. In post-season play, he has the second-highest quarterback rating ever (103.8) and is number one in average gain per pass attempt (8.56 yards) and completion percentage (68.9 percent).

DID YOU KNOW?

- When Troy was in high school, he entered a typing contest. Troy was the only male contestant, and he won!
- If he couldn't be a pro athlete, Troy might have become a doctor. He thought about studying medicine in college but, because of football, didn't have time to take the classes.
- In 1991, Troy helped raise $225,000 to build a health-and-fitness center for kids in his hometown. He also sponsors a college scholarship for financially needy kids.

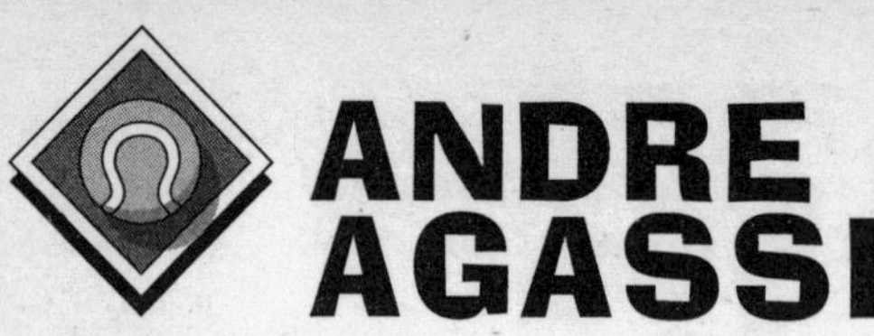

ANDRE AGASSI

Andre Agassi first became famous for his long hair and flashy clothes. Now he is known as a great tennis player, too.

Andre turned pro in 1986, when he was 16. His style on the court — he would blow kisses at the crowd or throw his shorts and shirts to spectators after victories — got him noticed right away. But after a winning start, he began losing. He got so upset he thought of quitting tennis.

INFO-BOX

BIRTHPLACE: Las Vegas, Nevada

CAREER: 1986 to the present

CLAIM TO FAME: Andre has become one of the top male tennis players in the world today.

Andre's early career was a roller-coaster ride. In 1987, he won his first tour title, and by year's end he had moved up to Number 25 in the world tennis rankings. In 1988, he won six tournaments and moved up to Number 4. By October, he was Number 3 in the world! But in 1989, Andre again went into a slump and slipped to Number 7. In 1990, he reached the French Open finals and bounced back to Number 4. In 1992, Andre won Wimbledon, his first Grand Slam title. But in 1993, an injury sent him tumbling to Number 24.

Andre decided to make some changes in his life. He hired a new coach. He stopped eating junk food and spent more time working out. He prepared harder for tournaments.

It worked! In 1994, Andre won another Grand Slam event, the U.S. Open. He beat every player in the Top 10 and shot up to Number 2.

Then Andre cut his hair! In April 1995, he passed Pete Sampras to become the Number 1 male player in the world.

When He Was a Kid

Andre started tennis training early. When he was a baby, his father hung a tennis ball over his crib to develop his eye movement. When Andre could sit up, Mr. Agassi had him use a Ping-Pong paddle to hit a balloon.

MICHELLE AKERS

Michelle Akers is the Michael Jordan of women's soccer. She has taken U.S. soccer to new heights. In 1991, she led the U.S. women's team to its first World Cup championship. It was the first World Cup title for any United States soccer team, male or female, in the 128 years of U.S. soccer history.

Michelle began playing soccer when she was 8 years old. By the age of 10, she was an excellent ball handler. In high school, she became a well-known player and received college scholarship offers.

In college, Michelle was named to the All-America team in each of her four years at Central Florida University. She also won the first-ever women's Hermann Award, given to the best collegiate soccer player in the country.

Michelle scored 10 goals in the 1991 World Cup tournament, and was awarded the Golden Boot as the tournament's leading scorer. She was named U.S. Soccer's Female Athlete of the Year in 1990 and 1991. In the 1995 World Cup tournament, Michelle tried to play with an injury, and the U.S. finished third.

INFO-BOX

BIRTHPLACE: Seattle, Washington

CAREER: 1985 to the present

CLAIM TO FAME: Michelle led the U.S. women's soccer team to the World Cup championship in 1991.

As a member of the U.S. women's team, Michelle has scored a goal in almost every game in which she has played. In 89 games, she has scored 82 goals!

ANOTHER SIDE In 1988, Michelle attended a football clinic run by the Dallas Cowboys' kicking coach, even though she had never kicked a football before. At the clinic, she made several 50-yard field goals! Still, she decided not to switch sports, even though one football agent was trying to get her interested in becoming the first female player in the history of the National Football League. She preferred to spend her time playing the one sport she loved — soccer.

MUHAMMAD ALI

Muhammad Ali is the only boxer to win the heavyweight championship three different times (1964, 1974, and 1978). A great showman and a great boxer, he became the best-known athlete on the planet.

Muhammad was born Cassius Clay in Louisville, Kentucky. People called him "The Louisville Lip" because of the way he bragged. But he backed up his boasts in the ring. He had a brilliant amateur career, highlighted by his winning the light heavyweight gold medal at the 1960 Olympics.

After turning pro, Muhammad challenged champion Sonny Liston for the heavyweight title in 1964. Muhammad was the underdog, but he attracted attention by making up poems about what he would do to Sonny in the ring.

At 6' 3" and 215 pounds, Muhammad was big and strong, but he was also lightning fast. He won the heavyweight title with a technical knockout in the seventh round and proclaimed himself "The Greatest."

Muhammad had been deeply interested in the Muslim religion. After winning the title, he changed his name from Cassius Clay to Muhammad Ali .

After nine title defenses, Muhammad was drafted

Amazing Feat

After splitting their two previous matches, Muhammad Ali and Joe Frazier met in 1975 in a fight that Muhammad called the "Thrilla in Manila" (Manila is the capital of the Philippines). The bout was one of the most exciting in history. Muhammad controlled the early rounds, then Joe dominated the middle rounds. But in the 12th round, with both warriors nearly exhausted, Muhammad somehow regained the edge, battering Joe through the next two rounds. When "Smokin' Joe" couldn't answer the bell for the final round, Muhammad was declared the winner. The faces of both fighters were badly beaten. Later, Muhammad said of the fight, "It was like death. Closest thing to dyin' that I know of."

INFO-BOX

BIRTHPLACE: Louisville, Kentucky
CAREER: 1960–1981
CLAIM TO FAME: Muhammad was probably the greatest heavyweight boxer in the history of the sport.

into the U.S. military in 1967. But Muhammad refused to enter the military on the grounds that he was a Muslim minister. He was sent to prison briefly, and boxing officials took away his title. In 1970, Muhammad was found innocent of violating the draft law and was allowed to box again.

Muhammad had been away from the sport for more than three and a half years. In his first attempt to regain the heavyweight title, he lost to the new champion, Joe Frazier, in 1971. It was Muhammad's first defeat in 34 pro bouts.

He got another chance at the title in 1974, against the new champion, GEORGE FOREMAN. Muhammad knocked George out and was again the heavyweight champion of the world.

Muhammad kept the title for three more years before losing a decision to Leon Spinks, on February 15, 1978. But Muhammad won back his title in a rematch. In all, Muhammad made 19 successful title defenses. When he retired, in 1981, his career record was 56–5, with 37 knockouts.

It has been more than a decade since his last fight, but today Muhammad Ali is still one of the most-recognized people in the world.

FOOTBALL

MARCUS ALLEN

Marcus Allen ranks among the Top 10 rushers in NFL history. He's also a fine receiver and a solid blocker.

At Lincoln High School, in San Diego, Marcus played several positions. As a safety, he once made 30 unassisted tackles in one game. In his senior year, he quarterbacked the team to the city championship.

At the University of Southern California, Marcus became the first college running back to top the 2,000-yard mark in a season, rushing for what was then a record 2,342 yards in his senior year. He won the Heisman Trophy as the nation's top collegiate player.

In 1982, as a rookie with the Los Angeles Raiders, Marcus led the NFL in scoring and was named Rookie of the Year. Three years later, he again topped the league in scoring. In 1985, his 2,314 total yards from scrimmage set an NFL record.

Marcus is the only NFL player to rush for 100 yards in 11 straight games. In 1993, he joined the Kansas City Chiefs.

INFO-BOX

BIRTHPLACE: San Diego, California

CAREER: 1982 to the present

CLAIM TO FAME: Marcus has been one of football's greatest all-around running backs.

Amazing Play

Marcus's greatest game was Super Bowl XVIII, in 1984. On one play, Marcus took the handoff and tried to run a sweep toward the left sideline. No good. Washington Redskin tacklers grabbed at him from all sides. He reversed field and ran toward the right sideline. By avoiding five would-be tacklers, Marcus ran for 74 yards and the touchdown that clinched the game for the Raiders. In all, Marcus rushed for what was then a Super Bowl-record 191 yards. (Timmy Smith of the Washington Redskins rushed for 204 yards in Super Bowl XXII, in 1988.) He was named the game's MVP.

MARK ALLEN

In the triathlon, competitors must swim up to 2.4 miles, bicycle up to 112 miles, and run up to 26.2 miles — in the same day. No one does it better than Mark Allen.

Mark won the World Triathlon Championship 10 times in his first 10 tries. He also won the Ironman competition five consecutive years.

INFO-BOX

BIRTHPLACE: Glendale, California

CAREER: 1982 to the present

CLAIM TO FAME: Mark is the top male competitor in the triathlon, one of the world's most grueling sports.

Mark had been an All-America swimmer in college. He became interested in the triathlon while watching the 1982 Ironman competition on televison. He was impressed by Julie Moss, who finished the race even though she had collapsed earlier from exhaustion.

Mark began competing in triathlons later in 1982. And in 1989, he married Julie Moss!

LANCE ALWORTH

Wide receiver Lance Alworth looked as sleek as a deer when he leaped into the air for a catch. A teammate nicknamed him "Bambi."

Lance played most of his career with the San Diego Chargers of the old American Football League (AFL). He set what was then a record by catching at least one pass in 96 consecutive games. He was the only AFL player to gain more than 1,000 yards receiving for seven straight seasons.

Lance went to the Dallas Cowboys in 1970. When he retired, he ranked fourth among pro receivers in career catches. In 1978, he became the first AFL player to enter the Pro Football Hall of Fame.

INFO-BOX

BIRTHPLACE: Houston, Texas

CAREER: 1962–1972

CLAIM TO FAME: One of the all-time great wide receivers, Lance was the best pass catcher in the old American Football League.

MARIO ANDRETTI

Mario Andretti was one of the few auto-racing drivers to compete successfully in all three major types of racing — Indy car, stock car, and Formula One. He is the only driver ever to win the Formula One championship, the Indy-car championship, and the Daytona 500 stock-car race!

Mario fell in love with racing as a small boy in Italy. He and his twin brother, Aldo, raced for a while on a junior circuit in their early teens.

The family moved to the U.S. in 1955 and settled in Nazareth, Pennsylvania. Mario went to work in a garage, where he learned more about cars. In 1961, Mario quit his job to pursue a racing career. Over three years, he won more than 20 stock-car events.

Mario joined the U.S. Auto Club (USAC) in 1964. In 1965, he was Indianapolis Motor Speedway Rookie of the Year. That year he won the USAC championship for the first of four times.

Mario was named Driver of the Year in three decades: the 1960s, '70s, and '80s.

INFO-BOX

BIRTHPLACE: Montona, Italy
CAREER: 1964–1994
CLAIM TO FAME: Mario was a champion in three different kinds of auto racing: Indy car, stock car, and Formula One.

How It Works

There are three major types of professional auto racing: stock cars, Indy cars, and Formula One cars.

Stock-car racing gets its name because the cars used are common brands of cars, such as Plymouth, Chevrolet, and Ford. Indy cars have rear engines and open cockpits. Formula One cars are the smallest in size and made to handle the tough curves and hills of the Grand Prix courses.

Each type of car requires a special skill to drive it, which makes Mario Andretti's achievements that much more remarkable.

EARL ANTHONY

With a bowling ball in his hand, Earl Anthony was a one-man wrecking crew. He won 41 tournaments on the Professional Bowlers Association (PBA) tour, including a record six national championships.

Growing up, Earl had wanted to be a big-league baseball pitcher. He received an offer from the Baltimore Orioles to play in the minors, but instead he went to work in the grocery business. His company started a bowling team, and Earl became its star.

In 1970, Earl joined the PBA tour. In 1971, he set a record with 42 straight games of 200 or better, and in 1974, he had four 300 games.

Earl was the first bowler ever to win more than $1 million in prize money.

INFO-BOX

BIRTHPLACE: Tacoma, Washington

CAREER: 1970–1991

CLAIM TO FAME: Earl won six PBA championships and was bowling's first million-dollar man.

BOWLING

NATE ARCHIBALD

At 6' 1", Nate "Tiny" Archibald played among tree-tall NBA players for 13 seasons, averaging 18.8 points and 7.4 assists.

Nate was drafted by the Cincinnati Royals (now the Sacramento Kings) in 1970. In his third season, the team moved to Kansas City, Missouri, and Omaha, Nebraska, splitting home games between the cities. Nate averaged 34 points and 11.4 assists per game, becoming the first player to lead the league in those categories in the same season.

In the 1980–81 season, Nate won a championship with the Boston Celtics. After he retired, he became recreation director of a center for homeless people in New York City.

INFO-BOX

BIRTHPLACE: New York, New York

CAREER: 1970–1984

CLAIM TO FAME: Nate is the only player ever to lead the NBA in scoring and assists in the same season.

BASKETBALL

ARTHUR ASHE

Arthur Ashe was the first African-American tennis player to win the men's singles title at the U.S. Open and at Wimbledon. He won the U.S. Open as an amateur, in 1968, and Wimbledon as a professional, in 1975. He also won the Australian Open, in 1970.

Arthur learned to play tennis as a boy, in Richmond, Virginia. During his high school years, he moved to St. Louis, Missouri, so that he would have better tennis competition. In his senior year of high school, he won the national interscholastic championship and earned a college scholarship to the University of California at Los Angeles (UCLA). In 1965, Arthur won the NCAA singles championship.

During his pro career, Arthur won 51 tournaments and was the world's Number 1–ranked player in 1975. He often represented the U.S. as a member of the Davis Cup team (which competes against other countries). From 1981 to 1985, Arthur was the non-playing captain of the Davis Cup team.

In 1979, Arthur had a heart attack and was forced to retire. After his career, he became well known for his views on racial equality and justice for all people. During a heart operation, Arthur became infected with HIV, the virus that causes AIDS. He died in 1993.

INFO-BOX

BIRTHPLACE: Richmond, Virginia

CAREER: 1969–1980

CLAIM TO FAME: Arthur was the first male African-American player to win tennis's biggest tournaments.

HOBEY BAKER

Hobey Baker was the first U.S.-born player to be elected to the Hockey Hall of Fame. Yet he never played in the NHL.

Hobey was born in 1892, near Philadelphia, Pennsylvania. When he was 11, he went to St. Paul's School in Concord, New Hampshire. St. Paul's had just adopted a new sport from Canada called ice hockey.

Hobey fell in love with hockey. He would practice on frozen lakes long after dark to learn to control the puck without seeing it. His team often beat squads from Harvard and Princeton universities.

Hobey later became captain of the Princeton hockey team. During his college career, the team lost only seven times. The ice arena at Princeton now bears Hobey's name. He was also a great football player, as a kicker and punt returner.

After college, Hobey joined the St. Nicholas amateur hockey team in New York City. (The NHL wouldn't be formed until 1917.)

Hobey's life came to a sudden end just after World War I, when he was killed test-flying an airplane. Each year, the best college hockey player in the U.S. receives a trophy in his name.

INFO-BOX

BIRTHPLACE: Wissahickon, Pennsylvania

CAREER: 1911–1917

CLAIM TO FAME: Hobey is the only athlete elected to both the hockey and college football halls of fame.

More Stars!

The first Hobey Baker Memorial Trophy was presented in 1981, to Neal Broten of the University of Minnesota.

Neal had been a member of the U.S. Olympic hockey team that won a gold medal in 1980. He later became an NHL All-Star.

Other Hobey Baker award winners include Robb Stauber (University of Minnesota), Kip Miller (Michigan State University), Scott Pellerin (University of Maine), and Paul Kariya (University of Maine).

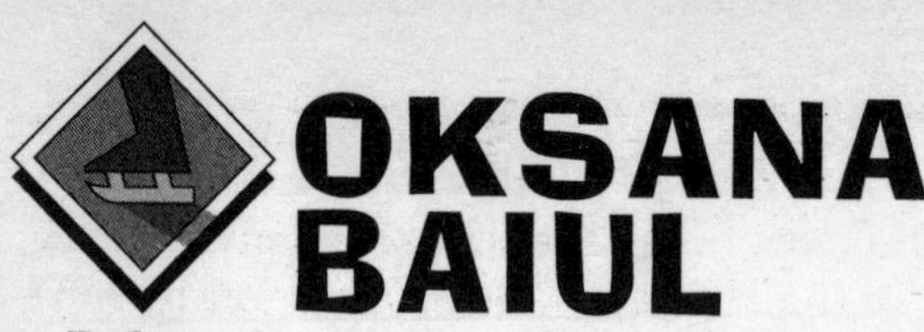

OKSANA BAIUL

Before she starts a figure-skating performance, Oksana Baiul *[AHK-zan-ah bye-OOL]* says she listens to the blades of her ice skates. She doesn't begin her program until she gets the okay from them. So far, Oksana and her skates have made a winning combination. Entering the scene in 1993, Oksana became the youngest female world figure-skating champion since 1927, and won an Olympic gold medal in 1994.

INFO-BOX

BIRTHPLACE: Dnepropetrovsk, Ukraine
CAREER: 1993 to the present
CLAIM TO FAME: By age 16, Oksana was already a world champion and an Olympic gold medalist.

Oksana's life now is filled with excitement, but it hasn't always been that way. Her father abandoned her and her mother when Oksana was a baby. In 1991, her mother died of cancer. Oksana didn't have any relatives. Her coach and a friend of her mother's were the only people she had left. Then, a year after her mother died, when Oksana was 14, her coach took a job in Canada and moved away.

But soon Oksana's luck started to change. In 1992, another coach, Galina Zmievskaya *[zim-YEV-sky-ya]* invited Oksana to live with her and also be coached by her.

When She Was a Kid

Oksana, who is now 5' 4" tall and weighs just 95 pounds, was chubby when she was 3½ years old. Her mother and grandfather wanted to sign her up for ballet school to help her lose that baby fat, but the school wouldn't take any students under the age of 7. So Oksana's grandfather bought her a pair of skates and suggested she try figure skating, a popular sport in Ukraine. Oksana had fun skating and even won some local skating competitions. When she was old enough, she took ballet lessons, which helped her become the graceful skater that she is today.

Oksana moved from her hometown of Dnepropetrovsk *[NEP-roe-puh-TROFSK]*, Ukraine, to Odessa, Ukraine.

Coach Zmievskaya also worked with Viktor Petrenko, the 1992 Olympic men's figure-skating champion. (Oksana and Viktor now do most of their training at a rink in Simsbury, Connecticut.) After training with her new coach for six months, Oksana became the world champion. She was just 15 years old!

Oksana was still inexperienced in international competition when she arrived in Norway, for the 1994 Olympic Games. Because she was still new to this kind of pressure, she was not a sure bet to win the gold medal. During practice — the day before she was to compete — Oksana crashed into another skater and hurt her leg and back. But she was determined to perform. Oksana thrilled the audience with her graceful moves and won the Olympic gold medal.

DID YOU KNOW?

- Oksana's favorite food is a candy bar.
- Her favorite skater is Jill Trenary, a three-time U.S. champion and the 1990 world champion.
- Viktor Petrenko used to buy skate blades for Oksana because she couldn't afford them.
- Oksana's homeland, Ukraine, used to be part of the Soviet Union. Ukraine is about the size of Texas.

ERNIE BANKS

Ernie Banks had a hard childhood growing up in Dallas, Texas. He was picking cotton at age 10. One of 12 children, Ernie sometimes had to skip meals because there wasn't enough food to go around.

Yet if there was any major league baseball player known for his sunny personality, it was Ernie. He became famous for saying, "What a great day for baseball. Let's play two!"

Nicknamed "Mr. Cub," Ernie played his entire career with the Chicago Cubs. He hit 512 home runs, making him one of only 14 big-leaguers to hit more than 500 home runs.

INFO-BOX

BIRTHPLACE: Dallas, Texas
CAREER: 1953–1971
CLAIM TO FAME: Ernie was one of baseball's great sluggers and, through his personality, a "goodwill ambassador" for the game.

Ernie played shortstop early in his career. In 1955, he hit 44 homers, then a record for shortstops. He once hit five grand slams in a season, which set another record.

Ernie won the National League MVP Award two years in a row: 1958 (when he hit a league-high 47 home runs, breaking his own record for homers by a shortstop) and 1959 (when he belted 45 homers). The Cubs never won a pennant during his career. Ernie was elected to the National Baseball Hall of Fame in 1977.

A Closer Look

Most fans think of Ernie Banks as a home-run-hitting shortstop. But he actually spent more of his career playing first base than short. Even though Ernie led all National League shortstops in fielding in 1960 and 1961, leg injuries had cut down on his range. So, in 1962, he agreed to move to first base if it would help his team. He became as good a fielder at first as he was at short. In 1969, Ernie won the league's fielding title. He also led all N.L. first basemen in assists five times.

ROGER BANNISTER

On May 6, 1954, England's Roger Bannister ran a mile in 3 minutes 59.4 seconds. It was the first time anyone had ever run a mile in less than four minutes.

Until Roger's run, most people thought it was impossible for a person to run a mile in less than four minutes. (The record that Roger broke — 4 minutes 1.4 seconds — had been set in 1945 by Sweden's Gunder Haag.) Later in 1954, Roger ran the mile in less than four minutes for a second time. He beat Australia's John Landy in a race known as the Mile of the Century.

When he ran his miracle mile, Roger was a 25-year-old medical student at England's Oxford University. While most of his competitors focused on running, Roger focused on becoming a doctor.

Roger became nearly as famous a doctor as he had been an athlete! In 1971, he was named chairman of the British Sports Council. Then, in 1975, for his work in medicine, Roger was knighted by the queen of England and became known as Sir Roger Bannister. Today, he is retired as a doctor and works on medical journals.

More Stars!

John Walker, from Auckland, New Zealand, was the first person to run a mile in less than 3 minutes 50 seconds. In 1975, John ran a mile in 3:49.4. He was also the first person to run a mile in less than 4 minutes 100 times.

Today, Noureddine Morceli is the best miler in the world. Noureddine is from Algeria, a country in northern Africa. In 1993, he lowered the world record in the mile to 3:44.39.

INFO-BOX

BIRTHPLACE: Harrow, England

CAREER: 1946–1954

CLAIM TO FAME: Roger was the first person to run a mile in less than four minutes.

CHARLES BARKLEY

Think of someone who does not look like a basketball player. Maybe he's too short, or on the heavy side, or both. Then imagine that person becoming a basketball *superstar*. Some people in Leeds, Alabama, had trouble believing it when a short, chubby boy named Charles Wade Barkley predicted that he would make it to the NBA.

Not only did Charles's friends laugh at him, but his high school coach told him that the only way he would make the varsity team was if he grew taller. Between his sophomore and senior seasons, Charles sprouted from 5' 10" to 6' 6" tall! He moved from guard to center for the varsity team. With his speed, power, and ball-handling skills, he averaged 19.1 points and 17.3 rebounds per game as a senior. Charles also earned a scholarship to attend Auburn University.

When He Was a Kid

Charles did not just "grow" into a great high school player; he worked hard at improving his skills. Charles didn't get much court time in his first varsity season. Because of his weight (220 pounds on a 5' 10" body), he was much slower than the guards on other teams. To make up for his size, Charles practiced rebounding, many nights all by himself. He made his legs stronger by jumping over a fence that surrounded his house. The fence was five feet high. Today, Charles's great leaping ability and quickness are two important parts of his game.

At Auburn, Charles led the Southeastern Conference (SEC) in rebounding for three straight seasons. He was later chosen SEC Player of the Decade for the 1980s.

Following his junior year, Charles tried out for the 1984 U.S. Olympic Team. He did not make the final cut, but he impressed the NBA scouts. The Philadelphia 76ers selected Charles with the fifth pick of the

first round of the 1984 NBA draft.

Charles became a starter for the Sixers toward the end of his rookie year. In his second season, 1985–86, he averaged 20 points and 12.8 rebounds per game. Charles led the NBA in rebounding in 1986–87, and the next season averaged a career-best 28.3 points per game.

Charles has been an All-Star selection eight straight times since the 1986–87 season and was MVP of the All-Star Game in 1991.

Before he starred for the Dream Team at the 1992 Olympics, "Sir Charles" was traded to the Phoenix Suns. In his first season, he led the Suns to the NBA Finals, losing to the Chicago Bulls in six games. That season, Charles was voted the NBA's MVP.

INFO-BOX

BIRTHPLACE: Leeds, Alabama

CAREER: 1984 to the present

CLAIM TO FAME: Although he's only 6' 6" tall, Charles is one of basketball's all-time great power forwards.

A CLOSER LOOK On his 22nd birthday, Charles showed the NBA why the word *power* belongs in *power forward*. That day, he dunked the ball so hard, he moved the 2,240-pound basket support six inches to the right! A 76er team official later said, "The last time that support was moved, it was by a forklift." The next season, in a game against Portland, Charles went on a one-man fast break that ended with a dunk so powerful that he pulled down both the rim and the collapsible backboard at Philadelphia's Spectrum arena.

RICK BARRY

A sweet shooter, Rick Barry could score from all over the court. He also made 90 percent of his free throws — shooting underhand!

BIRTHPLACE: Elizabeth, New Jersey

CAREER: 1965–1980

CLAIM TO FAME: Rick was one of basketball's greatest scoring forwards and free-throw shooters.

In his senior season at the University of Miami (Florida), Rick led the nation in scoring. In 1966, he was NBA Rookie of the Year, with the San Francisco (now Golden State) Warriors. The following season, he led the NBA in scoring.

In 1968, Rick jumped to the new American Basketball Association (ABA). There he became the only player to have led the NCAA, NBA, and ABA in scoring.

In 1972, Rick returned to the Warriors. In the 1974–75 season, he led them to the NBA championship.

SAMMY BAUGH

When Sammy Baugh joined the NFL more than half a century ago, teams played mostly a running and defensive game. The forward pass was first allowed in pro football in 1933, but few teams used it. "Slingin' Sammy" changed that.

Sammy cracked his wrist like a whip and slung the ball hard. He was the first overhand passer. More teams followed his example and began passing the ball.

INFO-BOX

BIRTHPLACE: Temple, Texas

CAREER: 1937–1952

CLAIM TO FAME: A quarterback and a tailback, Sammy was the father of pro football's modern passing game.

As a rookie, Sammy helped the Washington Redskins win the 1937 NFL championship. He led the Redskins to five division championships and another NFL title, in 1942. Sammy led the NFL in passing for six seasons, a record that still stands.

ELGIN BAYLOR

Elgin Baylor was the first player to "fly," in the way that Michael Jordan would years later.

The 6' 5" forward was a great scorer, with an NBA career average of 27.4 points per game. He scored more than 60 points in a game three times, including a 71-point performance in 1960.

In college, Elgin led Seattle University (Washington) to the finals of the NCAA tournament. He was drafted first overall by the Minneapolis (now Los Angeles) Lakers in 1958.

The Lakers had finished in last place the season before. But as a rookie, Elgin averaged 24.9 points and 15 rebounds per game and led them to the NBA Finals.

In the 1961–62 season, he played in just 48 games yet averaged 38.3 points. The next season, Elgin played a full schedule and averaged 34 points.

Elgin spent his entire career with the Lakers but never won a championship. Knee problems forced him to retire during the 1971–72 season — the season the Lakers won the NBA title for the first time since 1953–54.

INFO-BOX

BIRTHPLACE: Washington, D. C.

CAREER: 1958–1971

CLAIM TO FAME: A Hall of Fame forward, Elgin was basketball's first high-flying scorer.

More Stars!

In 1960, rookie guard JERRY WEST joined Elgin Baylor and gave the Lakers one of the greatest one-two scoring punches in basketball history. Elgin and Jerry both averaged more than 30 points per game for the Lakers during the 1961–62 season.

In 1968, WILT CHAMBERLAIN joined Elgin and Jerry on the Lakers. In the 1968–69 season, Elgin averaged 24.8 points per game, Jerry 25.9, and Wilt 20.5. But despite having three future Hall of Famers in their starting five, the Lakers lost to the Boston Celtics in seven games in the NBA Finals.

FOOTBALL

CHUCK BEDNARIK

"Concrete Charlie," as Chuck Bednarik became known, was the last of the 60-minute players. He played center on offense and linebacker on defense for the Philadelphia Eagles. A hard-hitting blocker and tackler, he was chosen All-Pro at both positions.

After high school, Chuck became an Army Air Corps pilot and flew combat missions in World War II. At the University of Pennsylvania, he won the Maxwell Award as the nation's best college player.

Chuck helped the Eagles win the NFL title in 1949 and in 1960. He was inducted into the Pro Football Hall of Fame in 1967.

INFO-BOX

BIRTHPLACE: Bethlehem, Pennsylvania
CAREER: 1949–1962
CLAIM TO FAME: Chuck was the last of pro football's great two-way players, starring on offense *and* defense.

HOCKEY

JEAN BELIVEAU

Jean Beliveau led the Montreal Canadiens to 10 Stanley Cup championships in the 20 seasons he played in the NHL.

At 6' 3", 205 pounds, Jean *[zhan]* was a big man. Everyone marveled at how effortlessly he could move on skates. Defensemen bounced off Jean as he made his way down the ice. His size and skills made him nearly impossible to slow down.

When he retired, Jean was the highest-scoring center in NHL history, with 1,219 points. (WAYNE GRETZKY now holds that mark.) He twice won the Hart Trophy as league MVP.

Jean was also admired for his modesty. He always gave credit to his teammates and coaches.

INFO-BOX

BIRTHPLACE: Trois Rivieres, Quebec, Canada
CAREER: 1951–1971
CLAIM TO FAME: One of the NHL's great centers, Jean played for 10 Stanley Cup champions.

COOL PAPA BELL

James Bell could hit like Ty Cobb and run like Rickey Henderson. Everyone called him "Cool Papa" because he was so calm under pressure. But because in his day only whites were allowed to play big-league baseball, Cool Papa was one of the greatest players never to play in the majors.

INFO-BOX

BIRTHPLACE: Starkville, Mississippi
CAREER: 1922–1946
CLAIM TO FAME: Cool Papa, a star in the Negro leagues, was probably the fastest runner in baseball history.

For 25 years, Cool Papa starred in the Negro leagues (which were formed in 1920 to give blacks the chance to play organized ball). Statistics weren't always kept, but Cool Papa is known to have batted .300 or higher 13 or more times and over .400 twice. His lifetime average was about .350. He recalled stealing 175 bases in around 200 games in 1934.

But perhaps Cool Papa's greatest moment was choosing not to play at all. On the final day of the 1946 season, the 43-year-old outfielder was hitting .402 and needed just a few more at-bats to win the batting title. Instead, he decided not to play and let young Monte Irvin win the crown.

It was rumored that the major leagues were going to let in black players. Cool Papa wanted Monte to be noticed by scouts. Three years later, Monte made his big league debut with the New York Giants.

A Closer Look

Negro-league fans created a lot of myths about Cool Papa's speed:

- They said he could turn off the light and be in bed before the room got dark.
- They said he once rounded second base and got hit with his own ground ball.
- They said he once scored all the way from first base on a sacrifice bunt.
- They said he once caught his own throw from center field and tagged a runner out at third!

JOHNNY BENCH

During spring training of Johnny Bench's rookie season, the great TED WILLIAMS gave the young catcher an autographed baseball. On it, Ted had written: TO JOHNNY BENCH, A HALL OF FAMER FOR SURE.

That season, 1968, Johnny set a record for catchers, with 40 doubles, and became the first catcher to win the National League Rookie of the Year award. Two years later, Johnny was named MVP after leading the league with 45 home runs and 148 RBIs. He also led the Reds to the pennant.

Before he retired in 1983, Johnny had hit 389 home runs and led the league in RBIs three times. He had a rifle arm and won 10 straight Gold Glove awards for fielding.

INFO-BOX

BIRTHPLACE: Oklahoma City, Oklahoma

CAREER: 1967–1983

CLAIM TO FAME: Johnny was one of the best all-around catchers in baseball history.

Johnny's career had its low points, too, but each time he quickly bounced back. For example, in 1971, Johnny's batting average fell to .238 (from .293 the previous season). But in 1972, he led the league with 40 homers and 125 RBIs. He won his second MVP award and the Reds won the pennant. In 1976, Johnny again batted just .234, with 16 homers. But in the World Series, he hit .533 and was named MVP.

True to Ted Williams's prediction, Johnny was elected to the National Baseball Hall of Fame in 1989.

MORE STARS! Johnny Bench batted fourth or fifth in the lineup for one of the greatest hitting teams in baseball history — the Cincinnati Reds' "Big Red Machine." The team ruled the National League in the 1970s, winning six division titles, four pennants, and two World Series. Other Red greats who played for manager Sparky Anderson during those years included PETE ROSE, Hall of Famer JOE MORGAN, George Foster, Dave Concepcion, and Tony Perez. From 1970 to 1977, Red players won six of eight N.L. MVP awards.

PATTY BERG

Patty Berg did a lot to help build the Ladies Professional Golf Association (LPGA). She was the LPGA's first president. As a player, she won 57 LPGA tournament titles. That ranks her third on the all-time list.

Patty was a terrific all-around athlete when she was growing up in Minnesota. She was the quarterback on a boys' football team. When she was 13, she took up golf. Three years later, she won the 1934 Minneapolis City Championship!

Patty won 29 amateur championships over a seven-year period. In 1940, she turned professional. She then served in the Marine Corps during World War II, from 1942 to 1945.

After helping to launch the LPGA in 1948, Patty made the LPGA Hall of Fame in 1951, its first year. She brought power and aggressive play to the women's game. She won 15 major titles, including the first U.S. Women's Open in 1946.

Patty led the LPGA in victories four times and was its leading money-winner three times. During the 1959 U.S. Women's Open, she became the first woman to get a hole-in-one in official competition!

In 1978, the LPGA established the Patty Berg Award. It is given each year to a golfer who has done a lot for women's golf. Patty herself won the award in 1990.

INFO-BOX

BIRTHPLACE: Minneapolis, Minnesota

CAREER: 1940–1980

CLAIM TO FAME: Patty helped start the LPGA and won 57 LPGA tournament titles.

YOGI BERRA

Lawrence "Yogi" Berra was one of the best catchers to play the game of baseball.

Yogi was 21 when he played his first game with the New York Yankees, late in the 1946 season. He started as an outfielder, but the Yankees felt his future was behind the plate. The great Yankee catcher Bill Dickey, in his final year in the majors, worked with Yogi on his defensive skills.

The young backstop didn't need much coaching in hitting, though. Yogi set American League records for home runs by a catcher in a season (30 in 1952 and in 1956) and over a career (313). (Lance Parrish broke Yogi's single-season record in 1982. Carlton Fisk broke the career record.)

Yogi was named to the A.L. All-Star team 14 times. He won the league's MVP award a record-tying three times.

Yogi always performed best when the pressure was on. He played on more World Series-winning teams (10) than any other player in history. He holds several Series records, including games played (75), at-bats (259), and hits (71).

As a manager, Yogi's teams won pennants in both the A.L. (the Yankees) and the N.L. (the New York Mets). In 1972, he was elected to the National Baseball Hall of Fame.

INFO-BOX

BIRTHPLACE: St. Louis, Missouri

CAREER: 1946–1963, 1965

CLAIM TO FAME: A great catcher, Yogi played on more World Series championship teams than any other player.

A CLOSER LOOK Yogi Berra has a funny way with words. His quotes are called "Yogi-isms," and here are just a few:

- When Yogi was a manager, he had this to say about letting a player steal a base: "He can run anytime he wants. I'm giving him the red light."
- After a fan told Yogi that he looked cool despite the heat, he said, "Thank you, ma'am. You don't look so hot yourself."
- When describing the skills it takes to be a good ballplayer, Yogi said, "Baseball is ninety percent mental. The other half is physical."
- After his Mets came from behind to win the 1973 pennant: "It ain't over till it's over."

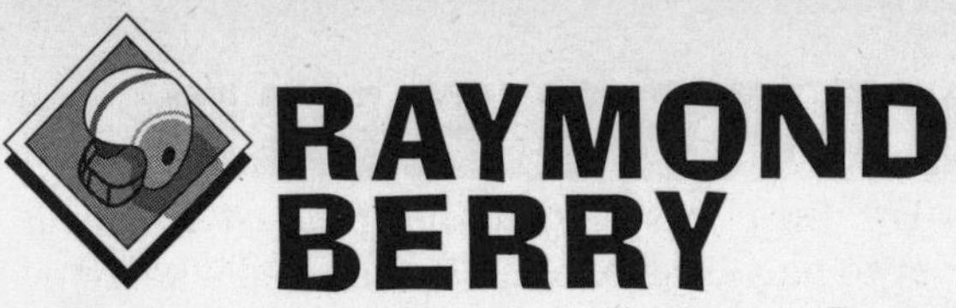

RAYMOND BERRY

The passing combination of receiver Raymond Berry and quarterback JOHNNY UNITAS was one of the best in NFL history. It helped the Baltimore Colts win NFL championships in 1958 and 1959.

INFO-BOX

BIRTHPLACE: Paris, Texas
CAREER: 1955–1967
CLAIM TO FAME: This Pro Football Hall of Famer was the receiving half of one of the greatest passing combinations in NFL history.

Raymond led the NFL in receiving from 1958 to 1960. He played in five Pro Bowls. When he retired, his 631 career receptions stood as an NFL record for five years.

Those accomplishments came from determination and hard work. A student of the game, Raymond came up with 88 possible pass patterns he could run, and he practiced every one of those moves. He fumbled the ball only once in his pro career!

Raymond's father was his Paris (Texas) High School football coach, but Raymond didn't make the varsity team until his senior year. He played college football at Southern Methodist University (also in Texas).

When He Was a Kid

When he was growing up, Raymond was a skinny kid whose eyesight was so bad that he couldn't read the big *E* on the eye chart. He wore thick glasses off the field and contact lenses on it. He also wore a canvas back brace, and one of his legs was longer than the other. But he overcame his physical challenges to become an NFL great.

Raymond was a 20th-round draft pick by the Colts in 1954. But he practiced hard in the off-season and recruited everybody he knew to throw him passes.

One of his best performances came in the 1958 NFL title game. Raymond made 12 catches, then a post-season record.

LARRY BIRD

Larry Bird was one of the greatest forwards ever to play basketball. He combined a keen understanding of the game with hard work and a sharpshooter's touch to become one of the game's greatest all-around players. For his NBA career, Larry averaged 24.3 points, 10 rebounds, 6.3 assists, and about 2 steals a game. He led the Boston Celtics to three NBA championships in the 1980s.

Larry grew up in the small town of French Lick, Indiana. In college, Larry averaged 30.3 points a game in three seasons with Indiana State University. He led the Sycamores to the NCAA championship game in 1979. They lost that game to a Michigan State team led by MAGIC JOHNSON. It was the first matchup in what would become a great rivalry.

Both players joined the NBA for the 1979–80 season. Larry went to the Boston Celtics and Magic went to the Los Angeles Lakers. Their dramatic East Coast–West Coast rivalry helped increase NBA basketball's popularity.

The Celtics had managed only a 29–53 record the year before Larry joined the team. But behind Larry's Rookie of the Year effort, the Celtics turned those numbers around, finishing at 61–21. The next year, Larry led Boston to the NBA title.

Larry fit in well with the Celtics' team game and helped form their "big three" front court of Larry, fellow forward KEVIN

Amazing Feat

You might remember the television commercials in which Larry Bird and MICHAEL JORDAN try to outduel each other with impossible shots — pretending to make shots by bouncing the ball over highways, off buildings, and so on. On April 20, 1986, Larry and Michael had a real duel in a playoff game between the Celtics and the Bulls. Michael scored a playoff-record 63 points, while Larry scored 36. Michael won the duel, but Larry and the Celtics won the game.

McHALE, and center Robert Parish. At 6' 9" tall, Larry ran the offense from his forward spot, and his feel for the game made it seem as if he knew where all the players were on the court at all times. He showed that with full-court lobs and behind-the-back passes.

INFO-BOX

BIRTHPLACE: West Baden, Indiana

CAREER: 1979–1992

CLAIM TO FAME: A great all-around player, Larry was the NBA's Most Valuable Player three seasons in a row.

In the 1986–87 season, Larry became the first player ever to shoot more than 50 percent from the field and more than 90 percent from the free-throw line. Perhaps his greatest weapon was the three-point shot. For his career he made almost 4 of every 10 three-point shots he attempted.

Larry led the Celtics to two more titles, in 1984 and 1986. He won three straight Most Valuable Player awards between 1984 and 1986. Larry retired in 1992, after being co-captain of the gold-medal-winning U.S. Olympic basketball Dream Team.

A CLOSER LOOK As great a basketball player as Larry Bird was, he never won an NBA scoring title. In fact, no member of the Boston Celtics has ever won a scoring title! The Celtics have one of the greatest winning traditions in all of sports, but they have always won by playing team ball and spreading the points among more than one or two star players.

BONNIE BLAIR

At the 1994 Winter Olympics, Bonnie Blair skated her way into history. She won two gold medals in speed skating to go along with the three gold medals she had won at earlier Olympics. Bonnie became the first U.S. woman ever to win five Olympic gold medals.

Bonnie began skating when she was 2 years old. She wore ice skates and hobbled around the rink near her home in Illinois. When any of her five older sisters and brothers tried to hold on to her, she'd take off. She wanted to skate on her own.

Bonnie took up speed skating and excelled at it. She tried out for the 1980 Olympic team. When she didn't make it, she decided to go to Europe to train against the best speed skaters in the world.

In 1984, Bonnie made the U.S. Olympic Team and competed at the Olympics in Sarajevo, Yugoslavia. She finished eighth in the 500 meters. But it was only the beginning.

Bonnie went on to compete in the 1988 Olympics, in Calgary, Alberta, Canada. There she won her first gold medal and set a world record of 39.10 seconds in the 500 meters. She also won a bronze medal in the 1,000 meters.

In 1992, Bonnie reached the Olympics again — this time in Albertville, France. She won gold medals in the 500 meters and

Fun Fact

In 1982, Bonnie decided to leave her home in Champaign, Illinois, and go to Europe to train for the Olympics. There was only one thing standing in her way: money. She didn't have any!

Bonnie needed $7,000 to make the trip. She tried to raise the money by asking local businesses to sponsor her. It didn't work. But a local policeman heard about her problem and got the Policemen's Benevolent Association involved. The police held bake sales and candy drives and even sold bumper stickers to raise money for Bonnie's trip. The bumper stickers referred to Bonnie as CHAMPAIGN POLICEMEN'S FAVORITE SPEEDER.

1,000 meters, becoming the first female skater to win the 500 meters in back-to-back Olympics. Later that year, Bonnie won the Sullivan Award as the best amateur athlete in the United States.

In Lillehammer, Norway, in 1994, she won two more Olympic gold medals — again in the 500-meter and 1,000-meter races. Less than a month later, Bonnie skated in a 500-meter race in Calgary, Canada. She finished in 38.99 seconds, breaking the world record.

Sports Illustrated named Bonnie its Sportswoman of the Year for 1994. She then went on to win the 1995 world championship in the 500, breaking her own world record with a time of 38.69. It was her final race. She then retired, ending an amazing career.

INFO-BOX

BIRTHPLACE: Cornwall, New York

OLYMPIC CAREER: 1984, 1988, 1992, and 1994

CLAIM TO FAME: Bonnie won five Olympic gold medals.

DID YOU KNOW?

- Bonnie comes from a speed-skating family. Four of her brothers and sisters have won national speed-skating titles. The day Bonnie was born, her father dropped her mother off at the hospital and went on to the skating rink where his other children were competing.
- Bonnie ate a peanut butter and jelly sandwich before every competition.
- Bonnie always planned to finish college when she retired from speed skating. She has already taken classes in physical education and business.

GEORGE BLANDA

George Blanda was a quarterback and a kicker for 26 pro football seasons. He played in 340 games and didn't stop playing until he was 48 years old — both NFL records!

George played his first 11 pro seasons in the NFL, then joined the Houston Oilers in the new American Football League (AFL). George helped Houston win the first two AFL championships, and was Player of the Year in 1961.

In 1967, George was traded to the Oakland Raiders. In 1970, he came off the bench in the final minutes to help the Raiders win four big games — at the age of 43!

INFO-BOX

BIRTHPLACE: Youngwood, Pennsylvania

CAREER: 1949–1975

CLAIM TO FAME: George played in more pro football games than anyone in history.

JEFF BLATNICK

Jeff Blatnick won a gold medal in Greco-Roman wrestling at the 1984 Summer Olympics, becoming the first American ever to win a medal in the super heavyweight division. But he also won a different battle — against cancer.

In 1982 Jeff learned he had Hodgkin's disease, which is a cancer of the lymph nodes, spleen, and liver. He underwent radiation treatment and had his spleen and appendix removed.

After the treatment, Jeff trained himself back into shape, and he made the Olympic team. At the Olympics, he advanced to the championship match. Although his opponent outweighed him by 35 pounds, Jeff won!

INFO-BOX

BIRTHPLACE: Schenectady, New York

OLYMPIC CAREER: 1984

CLAIM TO FAME: Jeff beat cancer and then became an Olympic wrestling champion.

CAROL BLAZEJOWSKI

Carol Blazejowski was nicknamed "The Blaze." Her fireworks on the basketball court in college produced a scoring average of 31.7 points a game.

Carol was a three-time All-America at Montclair State College, in New Jersey. As a senior, she averaged 38.6 points a game and was named Collegiate Woman Basketball Athlete of the Year.

After college, Carol played professionally for the New Jersey Stars of the Women's Basketball League. In 1993, she was named to the Naismith Memorial Basketball Hall of Fame.

INFO-BOX

BIRTHPLACE: Elizabeth, New Jersey

CAREER: 1977–1985

CLAIM TO FAME: In the 1970s, Carol's scoring ability helped make women's basketball popular.

BRIAN BOITANO

Brian Boitano was one of the greatest jumpers and spinners in figure-skating history. He is best remembered for an exciting performance at the 1988 Winter Olympics, where he edged out Brian Orser of Canada for the gold medal. Their exciting showdown was known as "The Battle of the Brians."

Brian was the first U.S. skater to land a triple Axel jump in competition *(see page 57)*. He was also the first skater to land six triple jumps in one competition. He was the U.S. champion from 1985 to 1988 and the world champion in 1986 and 1988.

When Brian was 30 — old for a figure skater! — he made his third Olympic team and finished sixth at the 1994 Winter Games.

INFO-BOX

BIRTHPLACE: Mountain View, California

OLYMPIC CAREER: 1984, 1988, and 1994

CLAIM TO FAME: Brian was one of the most athletic skaters of all time.

BARRY BONDS

Barry Bonds has been the best player in the National League in the 1990s. In that time, Barry has won three Most Valuable Player awards and five Gold Glove awards (for fielding excellence) and led his team to three divisional pennants.

Barry's father, Bobby, played for the San Francisco Giants until Barry was 10 years old. Barry grew up in and around Candlestick Park, the Giants' home field. While the team warmed up for games, Barry got to practice in the outfield. Out there, he received plenty of pointers from his father and from his godfather, Hall of Famer WILLIE MAYS.

In high school, Barry was a three-sport athlete — playing football, basketball, and baseball — but baseball was his true love. Over three varsity seasons, he batted .404. In his senior season, Barry hit .467 and was a high school All-America.

In his three-year college career at Arizona State University, Barry hit .347, blasted 45 home runs, and

INFO-BOX

BIRTHPLACE: Riverside, California
CAREER: 1986 to the present
CLAIM TO FAME: A three-time MVP, Barry is the best all-around player in the National League today.

When He Was a Kid

As a kid, Barry could hit a Wiffle Ball hard enough to shatter glass. When he started hitting baseballs, no window was safe. He broke so many windows at his house that his mom, Pat, became a regular customer at a nearby glass store.

Barry started his habit of choking up on the bat when he was a kid. His father, Bobby, who was a big-league star from 1968 to 1981, used to bring home major league bats for his son to play with. The bats were so big and heavy that Barry had to choke up when he swung. He still chokes up on the bat today.

drove in 174 runs. He tied an NCAA record with seven consecutive hits in the College World Series.

The Pittsburgh Pirates drafted Barry in the first round in 1985. In 1986, his rookie season, Barry led all first-year players in home runs, runs batted in, stolen bases, and walks. He led the Pirates to the National League Eastern Division championship three years in a row (1990–92). During that time, he also won two MVP awards. When his Pirate contract expired after the 1992 season, Barry signed with the Giants.

In his first at-home at-bat with the Giants, Barry hit a home run! He went on to win his third MVP award, finishing the 1993 season with a .336 average and 46 home runs. He also starred in the field, winning his fourth Gold Glove.

Barry cooled off a bit in the strike-shortened 1994 season, but he finished strong, batting .312, with 37 home runs.

FAMILY TIES Barry had a lot to live up to when he joined the major leagues. A lot of people knew him only as "Bobby Bonds's son." His dad combined power and speed by hitting 30 home runs and stealing 30 bases in a single season five times!

But in 1990, Barry accomplished his own major league first. While leading the Pirates to the championship of the National League's Eastern Division, Barry became the first player in major league history to hit .300, drive in 100 runs, score 100 runs, hit 30 homers, and steal 50 bases — all in the same season. Since then, a lot of people know Bobby Bonds as "Barry Bonds's dad."

BJÖRN BORG

Björn Borg is the only professional tennis player in history to win the Wimbledon singles title five straight years. Wimbledon, along with the French Open, the Australian Open, and the U.S. Open, is one of tennis's four Grand Slam tournaments *(see page 71)*. Björn won Wimbledon from 1976 to 1980.

In addition to his victories at Wimbledon, Björn won the French Open a record six times. Although he reached the final of the U.S. Open four times, he never won. It was the biggest disappointment of his career.

Björn, who grew up in Sweden, was not an attacking player who liked to charge the net. Instead, he defeated his opponents by staying back at the baseline and using a powerful forehand and backhand. He was known for hitting his groundstrokes very hard and with amazing topspin, which causes the ball to drop as it crosses the net.

INFO-BOX

BIRTHPLACE: Sodertalje, Sweden

CAREER: 1973–1981

CLAIM TO FAME: Björn dominated men's tennis until he decided to retire, at the age of 25.

Unlike some of today's stars, Björn never lost his cool on the court. That helped him win 62 titles, including 11 Grand Slam singles victories — tying for second place with ROD LAVER. In 1975, Björn helped Sweden win its first Davis Cup (a team competition among countries). He was the Number 1–ranked player in the world in 1979 and 1980. When he retired, he was just 25 years old.

AMAZING FEAT One of Björn Borg's most memorable matches was the 1980 Wimbledon final against JOHN MCENROE. The match was a seesaw event, with John winning the first and third sets, 6–1 and 7–6, and Björn winning the second and fourth sets, 7–5 and 8–6. In the final set, neither competitor would allow himself to lose. The final set lasted 34 games! Björn ended up winning, 18–16, taking the Wimbledon championship in one of the greatest matches in tennis history.

MIKE BOSSY

Mike Bossy was a sharpshooting right wing for the New York Islanders when they won four straight Stanley Cups. He scored more than 50 goals in a season nine times in a row. He scored more than 60 goals in five of those seasons.

INFO-BOX

BIRTHPLACE: Montreal, Quebec, Canada
CAREER: 1977–1987
CLAIM TO FAME: Mike's goal-scoring helped the Islanders win four straight Stanley Cups.

It seemed that Mike could always score. In his first game, at age 6, he scored 21 goals. As a teenager, he scored 308 goals in four years at the junior-league level. Amazingly, when he was eligible to be drafted by the NHL, 12 teams passed.

Mike was determined to show he belonged in the NHL. He promised himself and his teammates that he would score 50 goals in his first season. He did that and more, setting a rookie record of 53 goals. (Teemu Selane of the Winnipeg Jets broke that record by scoring 76 in the 1993–94 season.)

Mike never stopped scoring. After only 10 seasons, he was second on the all-time scoring list for a right winger, behind GORDIE HOWE. Mike set the record for assists for a right winger in a season, with 83.

Mike's career was cut short by back problems. He retired at the beginning of the 1988–89 season. At the time, he was the sixth-leading scorer of all time.

A Closer Look

It is not unusual for there to be fights and scuffles during pro hockey games. But Mike refused to participate in them. He believed that fighting took away from the game. Mike's rule was to keep his mind on hockey and scoring — no matter what anybody did to distract him. And that he did very well. Mike won three Lady Byng trophies for gentlemanly play. He also had an 11-year total of 210 penalty minutes, which is half the single-season total for some players.

BILL BRADLEY

Bill Bradley was a great college basketball player at Princeton University and later an important member of two NBA championship teams with the New York Knicks. These days he is best known as Senator Bill Bradley. He represents New Jersey in the U.S. Senate.

As a kid, Bill was just an average athlete, but he practiced hard. He became an outstanding basketball player and student in high school. He decided to attend Princeton, a great school for learning but not for sports.

Almost by himself, Bill made Princeton a basketball power. A 6' 5" tall forward, he averaged 30 points and 12 rebounds per game, and was named an All-America twice. As a senior, in 1965, Bill was named College Player of the Year and led his team all the way to the semi-finals of the NCAA tournament. He scored a tournament-record 58 points in his final game.

INFO-BOX

BIRTHPLACE: Crystal City, Missouri

CAREER: 1967–1977

CLAIM TO FAME: Before he became a U.S. senator, Bill was one of college basketball's all-time greats.

After college, Bill studied as a Rhodes scholar at Oxford University in England. In 1967, he joined the Knicks. His unselfish team play helped the team win NBA titles in 1970 and 1973.

Meanwhile, Bill prepared for his next challenge. He talked to people about their concerns and worked on election campaigns. He was first elected to the Senate in 1978.

More Stars!

A number of retired athletes have become politicians:

- Jack Kemp. A former AFL quarterback, Jack has been a congressman and was a cabinet member under President Bush.
- Steve Largent. Oklahoma voters elected the former Seattle Seahawk wide receiver to Congress in 1994.
- Jim Bunning. This former major league pitcher represents Kentucky in the House of Representatives.

TERRY BRADSHAW

FOOTBALL

Terry Bradshaw led the Pittsburgh Steelers to four Super Bowls — and four victories — in six years.

Terry grew up in Shreveport, Louisiana, where he quarterbacked his high school varsity football team his senior year. He also set a national high school javelin record.

After playing college football at Louisiana Polytechnic Institute, the 6' 3", 215-pound quarterback was drafted by the Pittsburgh Steelers with the first pick of the 1970 draft. With Terry in charge, Pittsburgh took home Super Bowl trophies in 1975, 1976, 1979, and 1980! In 1978, Terry won the NFL Player of the Year award. He threw four touchdown passes in Super Bowl XIII (in 1979), and was the MVP of his last two Super Bowls.

Terry was tough. With 3:02 left in Super Bowl X, in 1976, he was knocked unconscious on a blitz — just after he threw a long pass for a touchdown. Terry woke up after the game was over. Thanks to his pass, Pittsburgh had won, 21–17.

Terry was inducted into the Pro Football Hall of Fame in 1989.

INFO-BOX

BIRTHPLACE: Shreveport, Louisiana

CAREER: 1970–1983

CLAIM TO FAME: Terry was the first quarterback to lead his team to four Super Bowl victories.

BASEBALL

GEORGE BRETT

George Brett played 21 years in the major leagues. Considering the start of his pro baseball career, however, it's surprising that he lasted more than two pro seasons.

In 1972, playing in his second year of minor league baseball, for San Jose, 19-year-old George led the California League in errors at third base. The next season, in a brief call-up to the Royals, he hit just .125. But George knew that hard work would pay off. And did it ever!

In 1975, he batted .308, leading the league in hits and triples. From there, he never looked back. George won three batting titles, hitting .390 in 1980. He compiled a .305 career batting average, 3,154 hits (11th on the all-time list), 665 doubles (5th all-time), and 1,119 extra-base hits (10th all-time).

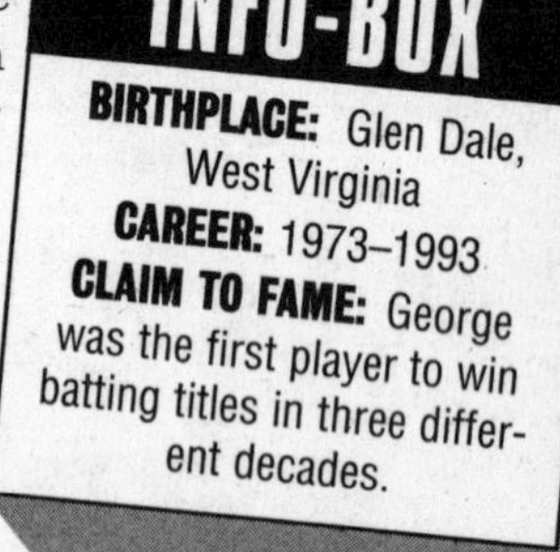

INFO-BOX

BIRTHPLACE: Glen Dale, West Virginia

CAREER: 1973–1993

CLAIM TO FAME: George was the first player to win batting titles in three different decades.

George is one of only four major leaguers (along with HANK AARON, WILLIE MAYS, and DAVE WINFIELD) to have at least 3,000 hits, 300 homers, and 200 stolen bases in a career. He is the *only* player to have more than 3,000 hits, 300 homers, 600 doubles, 100 triples, and 200 steals. George will be eligible for the National Baseball Hall of Fame in 1999.

A CLOSER LOOK In 1983, at Yankee Stadium, George hit a homer in the ninth inning to give the Royals the lead in a game against the New York Yankees. Yankee manager Billy Martin said George's bat had too much pine tar on it (pine tar is a sticky substance used by hitters to help them grip the bat better). The umpires agreed and would not allow the homer. George was so angry he had to be held back by his teammates. A few days later, league officials ruled that the home run *was* legal, and the end of the game had to be replayed (the Royals won).

LOU BROCK

Lou Brock is the National League's single-season and all-time stolen-base champion. He stole 118 bases with the St. Louis Cardinals in 1974 and retired with 938 career steals. (RICKEY HENDERSON now holds both *major league* stolen-base records.)

INFO-BOX

BIRTHPLACE: El Dorado, Arkansas

CAREER: 1961–1979

CLAIM TO FAME: Lou stole more bases in a season and in a career than any other National Leaguer.

Lou was dangerous at the plate, as well as on the base paths. After joining the Cardinals during the 1964 season, he batted .315, with 111 runs scored, 200 hits, 30 doubles, 11 triples, and 43 stolen bases.

The Cards, who were in fourth place when Lou came on board, won the N.L. pennant in the last week of the season and topped the New York Yankees in the World Series.

In 1966, Lou won the first of his four straight stolen-base crowns. (He would win eight in all.) His best year was 1967, when he led the league in runs scored (113) and stolen bases (52), and had 21 homers and 76 RBIs. St. Louis again won the pennant, and they beat the Boston Red Sox in the World Series. Lou batted .414 and stole seven bases in the Series.

Another Side

Lou broke into the major leagues with the Chicago Cubs in the early 1960s. In those days, he was known as much for his power as his speed. In fact, he once hit a 460-foot home run. It was one of only four ever hit into the center-field bleachers at the Polo Grounds, then the home of the New York Mets.

Lou stole a total of 14 bases in his two World Series. That tied a Series record. A smart base runner as well as a fast one, Lou set his single-season stolen-base record in 1974, at the age of 35. He was elected to the National Baseball Hall of Fame in 1985.

FOOTBALL

JIM BROWN

Jim Brown was nearly unstoppable when he was running with a football. It took at least two people to tackle Jim . . . if they could catch him. Even then, the 6' 2", 228-pound Cleveland Brown fullback often dragged his defenders right over the goal line. He ran over tacklers if he couldn't get around them. He never ran out-of-bounds to avoid a hit.

Many people consider Jim the greatest running back in football history. Thirty years after he retired, in 1965, Jim still holds five NFL rushing records. He led the NFL in rushing for eight of his nine professional seasons, which is an NFL record. So too is his average of 5.22 yards gained every time he ran with the football.

Jim was an outstanding athlete in football, basketball, baseball, and lacrosse at Manhasset High School in New York. At a North-South lacrosse all-star game, several coaches called Jim the best lacrosse player the country had ever produced.

At Syracuse University, in New York, Jim received All-America honors in both football and lacrosse. He participated in track and field, placing fifth in the national decathlon championships. In 1956, he set a major-college football record when he scored six touchdowns, kicked seven extra points, and ran for 197 yards in one game. His 43 points scored is still a record.

No wonder Jim was the Cleveland Browns' number-one draft pick in

A Closer Look

Though other players sometimes hurt Jim when they tackled him, he never let them know it. Even if Jim was flattened on a play, with several players piled on top of him, he just picked himself up slowly, showing no emotion, and ambled back to the huddle. Opponents would think he *must* have been hurting. But on the next play, Jim would barrel down the field again. In 122 regular season and championship games, Jim missed just one quarter of play due to an injury.

1957. That first season, he led the NFL in rushing and set a single-game record when he carried the ball 31 times for 237 yards (and four touchdowns). (The current record is held by WALTER PAYTON.) Jim was named the NFL Rookie of the Year. In 1963, when the NFL season was only 14 games long, he set what was then an NFL record by rushing for 1,883 yards in a single season. In 1964, Jim's 114 yards rushing helped the Browns win the NFL Championship Game.

INFO-BOX

BIRTHPLACE: Simons, Georgia

CAREER: 1957–1965

CLAIM TO FAME: An awesome blend of power and speed; Jim was the greatest running back in NFL history.

Jim did not miss a game or a Pro Bowl in nine years. He retired in July 1966 to become an actor and to help African-Americans improve their economic situation. Currently, he works to rehabilitate gang members in Los Angeles, California. He was elected to the Pro Football Hall of Fame in 1971.

HOW IT WORKS How did Jim manage to blast through defensive linemen? From lacrosse, he had learned to cradle the ball in one arm while attacking opposing players with the other arm. He also used a trick called the "limber leg." As he ran he would move a leg to tease a defensive player into grabbing for it. When the opposing player lunged, Jim pulled in his leg and took off down the field. Jim included in his running a "high step" maneuver, in which he lifted his knees to keep a tackler from grabbing both of his legs at the same time.

SERGEI BUBKA

Since 1984, Sergei Bubka has set 35 world records in the pole vault. Between 1983 and 1990, he won every major championship in the sport except the gold medal at the 1984 Olympics (at which he did not compete).

In 1991, Sergei became the first pole vaulter to clear 20 feet. Sergei is still the only vaulter who has cleared 20 feet, and he has done it nine times! He holds the world records of 20' 1$\frac{3}{4}$" outdoors and 20' 2$\frac{1}{8}$" indoors.

Sergei was born and raised in Ukraine. He began vaulting seriously when he was 15 years old. Four years later, in 1983, he surprised everyone when he won the pole vault at the first-ever outdoor track-and-field world championships. He won the worlds (which were held every four years and are now held every two years) again in 1987, 1991, and 1993.

Sergei was the favorite to win the Olympic gold medal in 1984, but the Soviet Union boycotted the Games, which were held in Los Angeles, California. He won the gold in 1988, but did not win any Olympic medals in 1992.

Sergei combines a sprinter's speed with great acrobatic ability. No athlete has dominated a track-and-field event the way Sergei has ruled pole vaulting.

INFO-BOX

BIRTHPLACE: Voroshilovgrad (now Lugansk), Ukraine

OLYMPIC CAREER: 1988, 1992

CLAIM TO FAME: Sergei is the greatest pole vaulter in history.

HOW IT WORKS Sergei's home country is Ukraine. But until 1991, he competed for the Soviet Union. Ukraine was then part of the Soviet Union. In 1991, the Soviet Union broke up into 15 independent countries. At the 1992 Olympics, 12 of those countries, including Ukraine, competed together as the Commonwealth of Independent States, also known as the Unified Team. Since then, the former Soviet republics have competed as separate countries.

SUSAN BUTCHER

The Iditarod Trail Sled Dog Race is a 1,157-mile race from Anchorage, Alaska, to Nome. It is one of the toughest races in sports. Susan Butcher has won it four times!

INFO-BOX

BIRTHPLACE: Cambridge, Massachusetts
CAREER: 1978 to the present
CLAIM TO FAME: Susan has won the grueling Iditarod sled-dog race four times.

The Iditarod is held every March. To compete, racers and their dogs must cross two mountain ranges, ice-covered rivers, the frozen Bering Sea, and a burned-out forest covered with stumps. They must brave temperatures that reach 50 degrees below zero and winds that reach 140 miles per hour.

Susan competed in her first Iditarod race in 1978. At the time, many people thought a woman wouldn't be strong enough to finish the race. Susan proved them wrong, finishing 19th. The next year, she was 9th.

After the first day of the 1985 Iditarod, Susan was in the lead, but her team was attacked by a wild moose. The moose killed 2 of her dogs and hurt 13 others. Susan had to drop out. (That year, Libby Riddles became the first woman to win the Iditarod.)

Susan finished first in 1986, 1987, 1988, and 1990. She came in second 4 times and in the top five 12 times. The Women's Sports Foundation named her Professional Sportswoman of the Year in 1987 and 1988.

A Closer Look

Susan begins training her dogs as soon they are born. Her voice is the first voice they hear and her face is the first face they see. Once they are old enough, Susan takes the puppies on three- to four-mile walks. At age 1, each dog gets a doghouse and a special diet. Susan then takes them on daily runs, sometimes 25 miles or more. Unlike many trainers, Susan treats her dogs like pets.

FOOTBALL

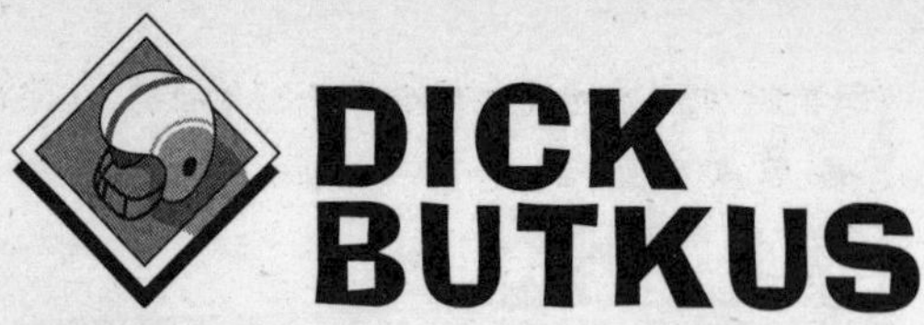

DICK BUTKUS

The Chicago Bears have always been a tough defensive football team, and middle linebacker Dick Butkus was their toughest player. "When I hit a guy," Dick said, "I wanted him to know who hit him without his ever having to look around and check a number."

INFO-BOX

BIRTHPLACE: Chicago, Illinois

CAREER: 1965–1973

CLAIM TO FAME: A fierce defender, Dick was one of the greatest linebackers in football history.

Dick grew up in Chicago and played center and linebacker at the University of Illinois, where he was an All-America. He captained Illinois to a 1964 Rose Bowl victory and was a first-round draft choice of the Bears in 1965.

At 6' 3" tall and 245 pounds, Dick was a fierce tackler and a superb pass defender. In a typical game, he'd make 15 unassisted tackles, assist on 10 more, and leave the quarterback dazed. He made 22 career interceptions. He recovered 25 opponents' fumbles, which ranks third on the NFL all-time list. He played in nine Pro Bowls (1965–73).

The other NFL teams were probably relieved when a knee injury forced Dick to retire in 1973, after nine pro seasons. An award honoring the outstanding linebacker in college football each year is named after him.

DICK BUTTON

Dick Button changed the sport of figure skating by inventing new jumps and inspiring other skaters to be more athletic and acrobatic.

Dick grew up in Englewood, New Jersey, where he began figure skating when he was 12. He loved to skate but often had trouble staying on his feet. At practice, he would fall so much that he had to bring dry clothes to change into! Dick went on to become a five-time world champion and seven-time U.S. champion. He also won two Olympic gold medals.

> **INFO-BOX**
>
> **BIRTHPLACE:** Cambridge, Massachusetts
> **OLYMPIC CAREER:** 1948 and 1952
> **CLAIM TO FAME:** Dick started a new athletic and acrobatic style of skating.

Two days before the 1948 Olympics, Dick completed the first double Axel *(see below)* in skating history. He performed it perfectly at the Games and won the gold medal. Dick was the first U.S. figure skater to win a gold medal in the men's singles event.

Four years later, Dick was a senior at Harvard University, in Massachusetts. He still made it to the Olympics and showed off another new jump: the triple loop *(see below)*. He became the first skater to perform a triple jump in competition. All nine judges awarded him first place.

Later, Dick became a professional skater. He also went to law school and became a sports commentator and author.

HOW IT WORKS

Axel: An Axel is the only jump that the skater launches going forward. He leaps into the air off one foot, spins around one and a half times, and lands on the opposite foot, skating backward. It is named after its creator, Axel Paulsen. In a double Axel, the skater spins two and a half times. Today, skaters perform triple Axels.

Loop: In a loop jump, the skater slides backward on a curve, takes off on one foot, and lands on the same foot, continuing the direction of the curve. In a triple loop, the skater spins around three times before landing!

BASEBALL

ROY CAMPANELLA

Roy Campanella was one of the best — and smartest — catchers ever to play the game. Many people expected him to become the first black manager in the major leagues.

In 10 years with the Brooklyn Dodgers, Roy was named National League Most Valuable Player three times (1951, 1953, and 1955). In 1953, his best season, he batted .312, scored 103 runs, and set big-league records for a catcher by hitting 41 homers and driving in 142 runs.

Roy's career was cut short by a car accident that left him unable to walk. He was elected to the National Baseball Hall of Fame in 1969.

INFO-BOX

BIRTHPLACE: Philadelphia, Pennsylvania
CAREER: 1948–1957
CLAIM TO FAME: One of baseball's greatest catchers, Roy won three MVP awards over five seasons.

FOOTBALL

EARL CAMPBELL

One of the greatest running backs ever to play professional football, Earl was the first player to lead the NFL in rushing in his first three seasons. He also was the first to win the league's MVP award in each of his first three seasons.

At the University of Texas, Earl won the Heisman Trophy in 1977. He rushed for 4,444 yards in his college career.

Earl was drafted by the Houston Oilers with the first pick of the 1978 NFL draft. He rushed for 1,450 yards as a rookie, tops in the NFL, and won the Rookie of the Year Award as well as his first MVP.

Earl was traded to the New Orleans Saints in 1984, and he retired two years later.

INFO-BOX

BIRTHPLACE: Tyler, Texas
CAREER: 1978–1985
CLAIM TO FAME: Earl was the NFL's top rusher and its Most Valuable Player in each of his first three seasons.

ROD CAREW

Rod Carew was born on a train in the Panama Canal Zone. Later, he and his mother moved to New York City. At age 18, one day after graduating from high school, he signed with the Minnesota Twins.

After three years in the minors, Rod made it to the big club in 1967. He batted .292 and was named the American League Rookie of the Year. Two seasons later, he led the league with a .332 batting average. That was the first of 15 straight years in which he hit .300 or more!

In 1977, his best season, Rod batted .388 — more than 50 points higher than anyone else. He was named American League MVP.

INFO-BOX

BIRTHPLACE: Gatun, Panama
CAREER: 1967–1985
CLAIM TO FAME: Rod won seven American League batting titles and hit .300 or more for 15 seasons in a row.

Rod won seven batting crowns during his career, but he wasn't known as a power hitter. In 1972, he was the first major leaguer to win a batting title without hitting a home run. He was known as a great runner, though, and many of his more than 3,000 hits were bunts or infield singles. He also holds the American League record for stealing home the most times in a single season (seven, which also ties the major league mark).

Rod joined the California Angels in 1979. After he retired, both of his former teams retired his uniform number — 29. He was elected to the National Baseball Hall of Fame in 1991.

More Stars!

Rod is not the only Hall of Famer not born in the U.S.:

- Luis Aparacio (Venezuela). A slick-fielding shortstop, Luis played from 1956 to 1973.
- Roberto Clemente (Puerto Rico). The Pittsburgh Pirate outfielder had 3,000 career hits.
- Ferguson Jenkins (Canada). The pitcher won 284 games over a 19-year career.
- Juan Marichal (Dominican Republic). Juan won 243 big-league games.

BASEBALL

STEVE CARLTON

For most of his career, Steve Carlton didn't talk to sportswriters because he didn't like certain articles that had been written about him. Instead, he let his pitching speak for him.

"Lefty" Carlton is Number 2 on baseball's all-time win list for left-handers, behind WARREN SPAHN. Steve won 329 games in his career. He struck out 4,136 batters, second only to NOLAN RYAN. He won more Cy Young Awards (four) than any other pitcher.

INFO-BOX

BIRTHPLACE: Miami, Florida
CAREER: 1965–1988
CLAIM TO FAME: One of the greatest left-handed pitchers of all time, Steve won four Cy Young awards in his major league career.

Steve started his big-league career with the St. Louis Cardinals but was traded to the Philadelphia Phillies. (With the Cardinals, he once struck out 19 batters in one game — and lost!) In 1972, as a Phillie, Steve led the National League with 27 wins. That same season, he also led the league in earned run average, strikeouts, complete games, and innings pitched. Steve accounted for nearly half of his team's wins!

From 1976 to 1982, Steve was the best pitcher in the N.L. He led the Phils to three straight division titles (1976–78) and to a World Series victory in 1980.

In 1994, the sportswriters Steve had avoided during this career voted him into the National Baseball Hall of Fame.

A Closer Look

Steve really hit his stride as a pitcher after he began a special exercise program. Most athletes did not train that hard in the early 1970s, and Steve's program was unusual. He trained by using isometric exercises and kung fu (a Chinese martial art) and by twisting his hands in buckets of rice. His great conditioning allowed him to make 30 or more pitching starts in each of 16 major league seasons.

JoANNE CARNER

JoAnne Carner won major championships as an amateur and as a professional. She is the only golfer to have won the U.S. Golf Association Girls Junior, the U.S. Women's Amateur, and the U.S. Women's Open titles.

She won the U.S. Women's Amateur five times. She was the last amateur to win a tournament against pro golfers.

JoAnne has won 42 Ladies Professional Golf Association (LPGA) tournaments, including two U.S. Women's Opens and two du Maurier Classics. She has been named Player of the Year three times, and joined the LPGA Hall of Fame in 1982.

INFO-BOX

BIRTHPLACE: Kirkland, Washington

CAREER: 1970 to the present

CLAIM TO FAME: JoAnne is the only female golfer to win her sport's junior, amateur, and pro championships.

DON CARTER

Don Carter dominated bowling in the 1950s and 1960s the way Babe Ruth dominated baseball in the 1920s.

As a teenager in St. Louis, Missouri, Don worked as a pinsetter in a bowling center. He liked the game so much that he built a bowling alley in his basement.

From 1950 to 1964, Don was named Bowler of the Year six times. He was the first bowler to win the Grand Slam of bowling, winning the top four tournaments of his time in the same year. Don rolled a total of 23 perfect (300) games in his professional career.

In 1970, the Sportswriters of America voted Don the greatest bowler of all time. He joined the Professional Bowlers Association Hall of Fame in 1975.

INFO-BOX

BIRTHPLACE: St. Louis, Missouri

CAREER: 1952–1964

CLAIM TO FAME: In the early days of professional bowling, Don was known as "Mr. Bowling."

WILT CHAMBERLAIN

Before there was SHAQUILLE O'NEAL, there was Wilt Chamberlain — only Wilt was harder to stop on the court. A powerful slam-dunker, he was called "The Big Dipper." The 7' 1", 275-pound center was also known as "Wilt the Stilt."

BIRTHPLACE: Philadelphia, Pennsylvania
CAREER: 1959–1973
CLAIM TO FAME: Wilt combined size, strength, and grace to dominate games the way no one ever had before.

Wilt's career scoring average of 30.1 points per game is second only to MICHAEL JORDAN's 32.3. Wilt once scored 100 points in a game! His 31,419 points still rank him second in lifetime scoring, behind Kareem Abdul-Jabbar. Wilt's average of 22.9 rebounds per game remains an NBA record.

After Wilt attended the University of Kansas, he played a year with the Harlem Globetrotters. He began his NBA career with the Philadelphia Warriors, in 1959. Wilt averaged a record 50.4 points per game during the 1961–62 season. He finished with 4,029 points, making him the only player ever to score more than 4,000 points in a season.

Wilt was famous for his offense, but at the time, there was a player just as famous for his defense: Boston Celtic BILL RUSSELL.

Another Side

He was an awesome slam-dunker. He is one of the all-time greatest rebounders. But Wilt just couldn't shoot free throws. In his career, he was a .511 shooter from the stripe, and in the 1967–68 season, he shot a dreadful .380 from the line. Chris Dudley of the Portland Trail Blazers has shot .451 in his career, and he is known at the worst free-throw shooter ever. Wilt, who isn't far behind, once said, "I'm not paid to shoot free throws." Sure enough! He missed 5,805 attempts.

Wilt and Bill had one of the most famous rivalries in NBA history. In 1960, Wilt set the all-time NBA record of 55 rebounds in a game in a contest between his Warriors and Bill Russell's Celtics.

Wilt left the NBA's Eastern Division when the Warriors moved to San Francisco in 1962, but he returned in 1965 to play for the Philadelphia 76ers.

In the 1966–67 season, Wilt led the Sixers to 68 wins (then a record) and the NBA title. The next season, Wilt focused on his passing and became the first center ever to lead the league in assists.

Wilt was traded to the Los Angeles Lakers for the 1968–69 season and stayed with the team until his retirement. His final triumph came at the age of 35: Wilt led the NBA in field-goal percentage and rebounding, and he helped lead his team to a record 69 wins and the 1972 championship.

AMAZING FEAT March 2, 1962, was a good night for offense, a bad night for defense, and a historic night for Wilt Chamberlain. The Big Dipper poured in 100 points that night as his Philadelphia Warriors beat the New York Knicks, 169–147. Wilt hit 36 of 63 field goals. Usually a horrendous free-throw shooter, he even made 28 of 32 free throws! He scored his 100th point on a slam dunk in the final minute of play. No one else has ever come close to Wilt's amazing record. (Here's a little-known fact: The game was played in Hershey, Pennsylvania!)

JULIO CESAR CHAVEZ

Julio Cesar Chavez, of Mexico, has been called the best pound-for-pound fighter in the world because of his strong yet small body. At 5' 7" tall and 140 pounds, Julio holds the super lightweight title. (Boxers compete against each other according to their weight.) He has also won world championships in two other weight categories: super featherweight (130 pounds) and lightweight (135 pounds).

In his 14-year career, Julio has fought more than 90 times and lost only once. He also fought to one draw (a tie).

INFO-BOX

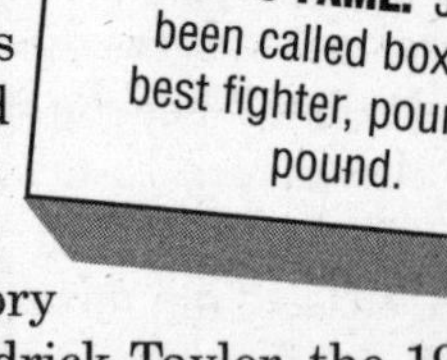

BIRTHPLACE: Ciudad Obregon, Sonora, Mexico
CAREER: 1980 to the present
CLAIM TO FAME: Julio has been called boxing's best fighter, pound for pound.

Perhaps Julio's greatest victory came in March 1990 against Meldrick Taylor, the 1984 U.S. Olympic gold medal winner. In the final round, with Julio trailing on points, he rallied to knock out Meldrick with just two seconds left in the bout.

Julio was undefeated until January 1994, when he lost a fight — and his title — to Frankie Randall in a split decision. The two fought again three months later. Julio won the bout and won back his title. He plans to retire after an even 100 fights.

A Closer Look

Julio Cesar Chavez is a hero in his country of Mexico. Before a 1993 bout with Greg Haugen, a crowd of 25,000 people (including Mexico's President Carlos Salinas de Gortari) watched Julio train in the parking lot of Estadio Azteca (Aztec Stadium), in Mexico City, Mexico. That's more people than attend most fights! Then 136,274 people watched Julio beat Greg in their bout on February 20 in Estadio Azteca. That was the biggest crowd ever to see a boxing match in person!

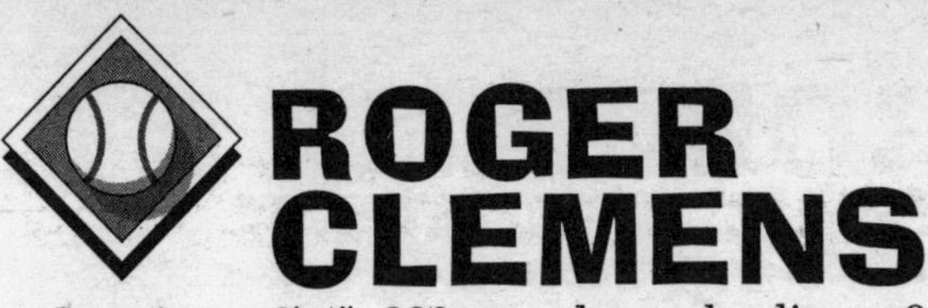

ROGER CLEMENS

Imagine a 6' 4", 220-pound man hurling a 95-mph fastball at you, and it's easy to see why so many batters have been struck out by Roger Clemens.

INFO-BOX

BIRTHPLACE: Dayton, Ohio
CAREER: 1984 to the present
CLAIM TO FAME: Roger has been one of the most dominating pitchers in baseball for the past 10 years.

Roger grew up in Texas and had his first taste of success when he led his high school team to a state championship. He attended the University of Texas and helped Texas win the 1983 College World Series.

Drafted by the Boston Red Sox, Roger was a big-leaguer by 1984. His best season so far came in 1986. He set a major league record by fanning 20 batters in one game. He also won his first 14 games of the season. Roger finished the year with a record of 24–4 and an earned run average of 2.48. He led the Red Sox to the 1986 American League pennant. He also won the Cy Young Award, the All-Star Game MVP, and the American League MVP, making him the first pitcher ever to win all three awards in one season.

Roger went on to win another Cy Young Award in 1987. He has already passed CY YOUNG himself as the all-time Red Sox strikeout leader.

AMAZING FEAT On April 29, 1986, Roger Clemens set a major league record that will probably stand for a long time: He struck out 20 batters in a nine-inning game. The old record — 19 strikeouts — had been shared by STEVE CARLTON, NOLAN RYAN, and TOM SEAVER. Roger didn't walk a single batter during the game. Just 29 of his pitches connected with a bat, and only 10 were hit into fair territory. He gave up three hits and got the win as the Red Sox defeated the Seattle Mariners, 3–1. To this day, Roger's record remains one of pitching's greatest accomplishments.

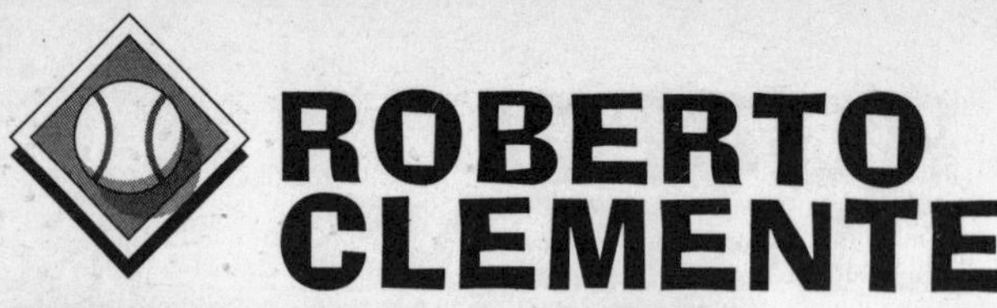

ROBERTO CLEMENTE

As a boy in San Juan, Puerto Rico, Roberto Clemente would do anything to play baseball. Whenever his mom sent him on errands, he would return hours later — all dirty from playing ball!

During his 18-year major league career, Roberto hit .300 or more 13 times and won four batting titles. He also won 12 straight Gold Glove awards for his play in right field. He was National League MVP for the 1966 season.

INFO-BOX

BIRTHPLACE: Carolina, Puerto Rico

CAREER: 1955–1972

CLAIM TO FAME: Roberto was the first Hispanic player elected to the National Baseball Hall of Fame.

In 1971, Roberto's team, the Pittsburgh Pirates, beat the Baltimore Orioles in the World Series. He hit .414, and was named the Series MVP.

On September 30, 1972, Roberto hit a double in Pittsburgh's Three Rivers Stadium. It was his 3,000th career hit, a great career achievement. It was also his last. Three months later, Roberto died in a plane crash. He had been delivering supplies to earthquake victims in Nicaragua (a country in Central America).

SWEETWATER CLIFTON

In 1950, Nat "Sweetwater" Clifton made history as the first African-American player ever signed by an NBA team. Sweetwater got his nickname because he carried around a jar of water and sugar to drink (he liked sweet soft drinks, but when he was young he couldn't afford to buy them). He also made sweet moves on the court.

INFO-BOX

BIRTHPLACE: England, Arkansas

CAREER: 1950–1958

CLAIM TO FAME: Sweetwater Clifton was a pioneering African-American basketball player.

Sweetwater played basketball at Xavier University of Louisiana. At the time, no NBA team would sign a black player. One outlet for talented black players was the Harlem Globetrotters, who entertained fans by using fancy moves in exhibition games throughout the world. Sweetwater became one of their stars.

In 1950, the NBA opened its doors to black players. Sweetwater, a 6' 7" forward, became the first African-American to sign a contract with an NBA team. He soon began playing for the New York Knicks.

Sweetwater averaged 10 points and 8.2 rebounds a game during his NBA career. He brought along some flashy moves from the Globetrotters that livened up the NBA, and he helped open the door for other great black players.

A CLOSER LOOK The year 1950 was a breakthrough year for African-American basketball players. Shortly before Sweetwater Clifton became the first African-American to sign a contract with an NBA team, two other black players were selected in the 1950 NBA draft. Chuck Cooper of Duquesne University was selected by the Boston Celtics with their second pick. Earl Lloyd was then selected by the Washington (D.C.) Capitols. Because Washington played its first game before either Chuck's Celtics or Nat's Knicks, Earl made history, on October 31, 1950, as the first African-American to play in an NBA game.

TY COBB

Ty Cobb has been called the greatest major league baseball player in history. He was aggressive in everything he did. To scare his opponents before games, he would sharpen his spikes on the top step of the dugout. He often fought with managers, opposing players, umpires, and fans. He had few friends. But even those who disliked him respected and admired his skills on the field.

"The Georgia Peach" (a nickname he was given because he came from Georgia, a state famous for peaches) was not a power hitter. Yet he dominated the game with his hitting and baserunning. He would reach first on a single, then steal his way around the bases.

When he retired, in 1928, Ty held dozens of major league records. Many of those marks remain today, including most runs scored in a career (2,245) and highest career batting average (.367). He ranks second all-time in hits (4,191) and triples (297), and fourth in games played (3,034), at-bats (11,429), doubles (724), and stolen bases (892). He held the records for most stolen bases in a season (96) and in a career for more than 50 years. Ty remains the all-time leader in steals of home, with 35.

INFO-BOX

BIRTHPLACE: Narrows, Georgia

CAREER: 1905–1928

CLAIM TO FAME: Ty was the greatest hitter in baseball history.

In his 24-year career (spent mostly with the Detroit Tigers), Ty led the American League in batting 12 times. He hit at least .320 for 23 straight years. And he's the only A.L. player to hit .400 or better three times. His best season was 1911, when he had a career-high .420 batting average. That season, he led the league in every offensive category except homers.

Fun Fact After Ty Cobb died in 1961, Lefty O'Doul, a great pitcher from Ty's day, was asked how he thought the Georgia Peach would hit against modern-day pitchers. Lefty guessed that Ty would bat around .340. Ty played in an era when the ball was not as lively as it is today. Lefty's questioner asked why such a great hitter wouldn't hit even better today. "Well," Lefty answered, "you have to take into consideration that the man would now be 78 years old!"

As a member of the Tigers, Ty was part of American League pennant-winning teams from 1907 to 1909.

From 1921 to 1926, Ty was the player-manager of the Tigers. He spent the last two seasons of his career as a player with the Philadelphia A's. In 1927, he batted .357. In 1928, at the age of 41, he batted .323!

Even though he was probably the least-liked man in baseball, Ty got the most votes when the National Baseball Hall of Fame opened and chose its first five ballplayers, in 1936.

A CLOSER LOOK Ty Cobb was one of the cleverest players in baseball. A born right-hander, he taught himself how to bat left-handed. He figured that way he would be closer to first base after he hit the ball.

Ty also discovered that if he swung three bats while he was on deck, the one he swung at the plate seemed a lot lighter. He was probably the first person to practice that baseball warm-up routine.

Another secret to Ty's batting success was his split-handed grip (keeping a space between his top and bottom hands as he held the bat). He said the grip helped him control the bat better when he tried to hit a pitch.

NADIA COMANECI

In 1976, Nadia Comaneci *[coe-man-EECH]* became the first gymnast ever to earn a perfect score in Olympic competition. The 4' 11" tall 14-year-old from Romania scored two perfect 10's during the team competition. She earned five more in the individual events. In all, Nadia won three gold medals (including one in the all-around competition), a silver, and a bronze at the 1976 Games.

Nadia began training for the Olympics when she was 6 years old. Her coach, Bela Karolyi, later coached U.S. champions Mary Lou Retton and Kim Zmeskal.

The 1980 Olympics were held in Moscow, capital of what was then the Soviet Union. Nadia had grown much bigger, but she still was a fierce competitor.

Nadia missed winning a second all-around gold medal by a tiny margin. She needed a 9.9 score in the final event, the balance beam. After a long debate, the judges scored her near-perfect routine a 9.85. The next day, Nadia won gold medals in the beam and floor-exercise individual events.

INFO-BOX

BIRTHPLACE: Onesti, Moldavia (now part of Romania)
OLYMPIC CAREER: 1976 and 1980
CLAIM TO FAME: Nadia was the first gymnast ever to score a 10 at the Olympics.

MAUREEN CONNOLLY

In 1953, Maureen Connolly became the first woman, and only the second tennis player ever, to win the Grand Slam. The Grand Slam is made up of the sport's four most important tournaments *(see below)*. Maureen won all four in the same year!

> **INFO-BOX**
>
> **BIRTHPLACE:** San Diego, California
>
> **CAREER:** 1951–1954
>
> **CLAIM TO FAME:** Maureen was the first female player to win the Grand Slam of tennis.

Maureen, who grew up in California, didn't begin playing tennis until she was about 10 years old. By age 15, she had won 50 tournaments and become the youngest girl to win the National Junior Championships. In 1951, at 17, she became the second youngest player to win the U.S. National Championships (now called the U.S. Open; *see page 74.*)

Maureen was just 5' 4" tall, but she hit powerful ground strokes from the baseline. Sports reporters nicknamed her "Little Mo." (At the time, one of the biggest battleships in the country was called "Big Mo.")

How It Works

The Australian Open, French Open, U.S. Open, and Wimbledon are the Grand Slam events of tennis. Wimbledon is played on grass. The Australian and U.S. Opens are played on hard courts — a fast surface that is best for serve-and-volley players *(see page 72)*. The French Open is played on clay, a slow surface that favors players who hit good ground strokes and play by the baseline.

Maureen won a total of nine Grand Slam singles titles. Between September 1951 and July 1954, she lost only once. In 1954, at age 20, Maureen broke her leg in a horseback riding accident. She never played competitive tennis again.

She was inducted into the International Tennis Hall of Fame in 1968.

JIMMY CONNORS

During his career, Jimmy Connors won a record 109 tennis tournaments. He also finished the year ranked Number 1 in the world five straight times, from 1974 through 1978.

Jimmy grew up in California and learned the game from his mother, Gloria. She was a tennis instructor. Later Jimmy was coached by Pancho Segura, who was a great player in the 1940s and 1950s.

In 1970, Jimmy entered the University of California at Los Angeles (UCLA). In 1971, he won the NCAA men's singles title. Jimmy turned pro in 1972.

Early in his career, Jimmy was known as the "bad boy" of tennis because of his rude behavior on the court. He would argue with officials and taunt opponents. But he also played great tennis.

> **INFO-BOX**
>
> **BIRTHPLACE:** Belleville, Illinois
>
> **CAREER:** 1972–1992
>
> **CLAIM TO FAME:** Jimmy won more tennis tournaments than any other male player in history.

Jimmy's best year was 1974, when he won the Australian Open, Wimbledon, and the U.S. Open. He would win the U.S. Open four more times, and Wimbledon once more. As he grew older, Jimmy matured and grew more popular with tennis fans, who enjoyed his fiery will to win. He retired in 1992, but still plays in tournaments once in a while.

HOW IT WORKS In the years before Jimmy turned pro, men's tennis was dominated by "serve-and-volley" players — aggressive players who try to end points quickly by serving and then charging the net to volley. But Jimmy changed the way people thought the men's game should be played. Using both his forehand and two-handed backhand, Jimmy proved that players could win by rallying from the backcourt. Today, serve-and-volley players, such as Boris Becker of Germany and Pete Sampras of the U.S., are changing tennis back to the way it was before Jimmy Connors's day.

JIM CORBETT

In 1892, "Gentleman Jim" Corbett became the first boxer to win the heavyweight title wearing boxing gloves. Before Jim's title fight, boxing matches had been bare-knuckled brawls. But an English sportsman, the Marquess of Queensbury, helped come up with a set of boxing rules. Those rules set rounds at three minutes long and required boxers to wear gloves.

On September 7, 1892, Jim faced JOHN L. SULLIVAN in New Orleans, Louisiana, to decide the heavyweight championship under the new rules. John L., as he was called, was the last and the best of the bare-knuckle champions. John L. was expected to win because he outweighed Jim 212 pounds to 178. But Jim announced before the fight, "I can lick him without getting my hair mussed." And he did.

Jim knocked out John L. in the 21st round. He kept the bigger man off-balance by using a new punch he invented, called a jab. The jab was a short, straight punch used to keep the opponent away. It was the same jab that boxers use today.

Jim remained the heavyweight champion until 1897. He lost his title when he was knocked out by Bob Fitzsimmons on St. Patrick's Day.

INFO-BOX

BIRTHPLACE: San Francisco, California

CAREER: 1884–1903

CLAIM TO FAME: "Gentleman Jim" was the first boxer to win the heavyweight title wearing boxing gloves.

MARGARET COURT

Margaret Smith Court was one of the best female tennis players of all time. In 1970, she became only the second woman in tennis history to win the Grand Slam — she won the Australian Open, the French Open, Wimbledon, and the U.S. Open all in the same year *(see page 71)*. During her career, she finished the year as the top-ranked player seven times.

Margaret won more Grand Slam singles titles than any other player, 24. Including doubles and mixed doubles matches, she won 62 Grand Slam titles.

INFO-BOX

BIRTHPLACE: Albury, New South Wales, Australia
CAREER: 1959–1977
CLAIM TO FAME: Margaret won more Grand Slam singles titles than anyone in the history of tennis.

Margaret, who was from a small town in Australia, worked hard in the gym when she was young. She was tall and strong and very athletic, which made it easy for her to serve and volley *(see page 72)*. Her success helped make women's tennis more athletic.

In her Grand Slam year, Margaret won 21 of the 27 tournaments she entered and had a record of 104–6. In four other years, she won three of the four Grand Slam events.

Margaret was elected to the International Tennis Hall of Fame in 1979.

HOW IT WORKS Until 1968, tennis players had to be amateurs to compete in tournaments such as Wimbledon and the U.S. Open. That meant that they earned no prize money. But in 1968, the big tennis tournaments were opened up to professionals as well as amateurs, and most of the top players turned pro. The period of tennis since 1968 is known as the "Open era." Before the Open era, the major tournaments were known as the U.S. National Championships (now the U.S. Open), French Championships (French Open), Australian Championships (Australian Open), and All-England Championships (Wimbledon). The arrival of the Open era changed tennis.

BOB COUSY

Bob Cousy was perhaps the best playmaker the sport of basketball has ever seen. He was the first NBA player to use fancy dribbling moves and make perfect no-look passes. While Bob ran their offense, the Boston Celtics won six NBA championships, including five in a row.

In college, Bob was a three-time All-America at Holy Cross, a Massachusetts school. Celtic coach Red Auerbach was under a lot of pressure to sign the local hero for his team. But Red didn't think the 6' 1" guard was good enough. Bob joined the Celtics only after another NBA franchise folded.

In Boston, Bob's great speed, ability to see the whole court, and brilliant passing proved to be the key to the Celtic fast-break offense. The addition of shot-blocking and rebounding star Bill Russell, in 1956, completed the championship team.

"The Cooz" led the league in assists eight times, and he often led the Celtics in scoring as well. For his career he averaged 18.4 points, 7.5 assists, and 5.2 rebounds per game.

Bob retired in 1963, but later came back as a player-coach. At 41, he was the oldest player ever to appear in an NBA game.

INFO-BOX

BIRTHPLACE: New York, New York

CAREER: 1950–1963, 1969–1970

CLAIM TO FAME: Bob was one of basketball's greatest playmaking guards.

DAVE COWENS

At a height of 6' 9", Dave Cowens was smaller than most centers. What he lacked in size he made up with speed, rugged play, and non-stop hustle.

Dave played college basketball at Florida State University, where he was named to the All-America team. The Boston Celtics picked him in the first round of the 1970 draft.

Dave was a memorable sight on the court. He often played with a crazed look on his face that would scare his opponents! He was always in motion.

Because he was small for a center, Dave's style of play was a little unusual. Instead of posting up near the basket, he would sometimes set up 20 feet away. Instead of overpowering opponents, he would shoot over them or drive around them.

In his 11 seasons in the NBA, 10 of which were with Boston, he averaged 17.6 points, 13.6 rebounds, and 3.8 assists a game.

Dave helped lead the Celtics to NBA championships in 1974 and 1976.

INFO-BOX

BIRTHPLACE: Newport, Kentucky

CAREER: 1970–1980, 1982–1983

CLAIM TO FAME: Dave was a hustling center who led the Celtics to two NBA titles.

Time Capsule

Here are some other events that happened in 1976, the year Dave Cowens won his second NBA championship with the Celtics:

- The U.S. celebrated its bicentennial (200th birthday).
- Dorothy Hamill won the Olympic gold medal in women's singles figure skating. Her short haircut became a fashion trend.
- Jimmy Carter was elected President by a narrow margin over Gerald Ford.
- A U.S. robot spacecraft made the first successful landing on Mars.
- The first *Rocky* movie premiered.

LARRY CSONKA

Larry Csonka, a 6' 3", 237-pound running back, led the Miami Dolphins to back-to-back NFL championships.

A first-round draft pick in 1968, Larry rushed for more than 1,000 yards each year from 1971 to 1973. In 1972, he led the Dolphins to the only undefeated season in NFL history. Miami won back-to-back Super Bowls in 1973 and 1974, and Larry won the MVP award in 1974.

Larry later played in the World Football League and then with the New York Giants. He returned to the Dolphins in 1979, his last season, and led the team to a division title.

INFO-BOX

BIRTHPLACE: Stow, Ohio
CAREER: 1968–1979
CLAIM TO FAME: A punishing fullback, Larry led the Miami Dolphins to the only undefeated season in NFL history.

BOB DAVIES

Bob Davies was basketball's first ballhandling wizard. He brought new moves to the game and was the first to regularly use the behind-the-back dribble.

Bob was a magician with the ball even as a 5' 5" high school freshman. At Seton Hall University, in New Jersey, his ball-handling and passing skills made him a two-time All-America.

In the pros, Bob led the league in assists in 1948–49 and was always among the leaders in his other seasons. In 1951, the 6' 1" guard led the the Rochester Royals (now the Sacramento Kings) to their only NBA title.

Bob was also known for his gracious personality. He was the model for Chip Hilton, the hero of a series of books for boys by Long Island University basketball coach Clair Bee.

INFO-BOX

BIRTHPLACE: Harrisburg, Pennsylvania
CAREER: 1945–1955
CLAIM TO FAME: A great dribbler and passer, Bob was basketball's first great ball-handling guard.

DIZZY DEAN

His name was Jay Hanna Dean, but everyone called him "Dizzy." For a brief time, he was one of the best pitchers in baseball.

From 1932 to 1936, Dizzy dazzled hitters with his fastball and fast curve (which he called a "crooky"). Pitching for the St. Louis Cardinals, he led the National League in strikeouts for four years.

In 1934, Dizzy's younger brother Paul joined the Cards. Between them, they won 49 games that year. Dizzy himself had one of the greatest seasons of any pitcher in history, winning 30 games while losing just 7. He also led the league in strikeouts, shutouts, and complete games and was named the league's Most Valuable Player.

INFO-BOX

BIRTHPLACE: Lucas, Arkansas

CAREER: 1930, 1932–1941, 1947

CLAIM TO FAME: Dizzy was one of baseball's best pitchers and wackiest characters.

Family Ties

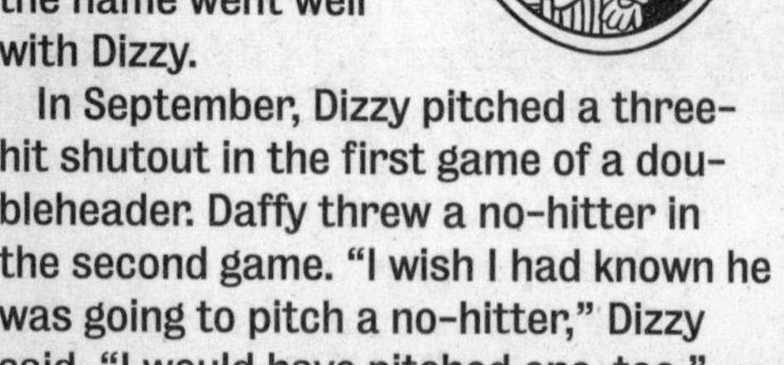

When Paul Dean joined his brother Dizzy on the Cardinals in 1934, there was nothing daffy about him. Yet people called him "Daffy" because the name went well with Dizzy.

In September, Dizzy pitched a three-hit shutout in the first game of a doubleheader. Daffy threw a no-hitter in the second game. "I wish I had known he was going to pitch a no-hitter," Dizzy said. "I would have pitched one, too."

Together, the Deans won 49 games in the regular season that year. They each won two games in the World Series.

Three years later, Dizzy was pitching in the All-Star Game when a line drive broke the big toe on his left foot. After that, he was never as successful a pitcher as he had once been. He played just three more full seasons.

After his retirement, Dizzy became a popular radio and TV sportscaster. In 1953, he was elected to the National Baseball Hall of Fame.

ERIC DICKERSON

In 11 seasons, Eric Dickerson established himself as one of the greatest running backs in NFL history. Eric holds the record for most yards gained rushing in a season (2,105) and is second on the all-time rushing list with 13,259 career yards. (The all-time leader is WALTER PAYTON.)

In his senior year at Sealy High School, in Texas, Eric was the country's top high school running back. As a college player at Southern Methodist University, also in Texas, he rushed for 4,450 yards, the most in Southwest Conference history.

Eric joined the Los Angeles Rams in 1983. As a rookie, he led the league in rushing with a record 1,808 yards that season, earning NFL Rookie of the Year honors.

On his way to setting the rushing record for a single season, in 1984, Eric averaged 5.6 yards per carry. He set an NFL record with twelve 100-yard rushing games.

In 1986, Eric led the league in rushing again. The next year, he was traded to the Indianapolis Colts for eight players. He finished his career with the Los Angeles Raiders and Atlanta Falcons.

INFO-BOX

BIRTHPLACE: Sealy, Texas

CAREER: 1983–1993

CLAIM TO FAME: Eric Dickerson rushed for more yards in one season than any other player in NFL history.

JOE DiMAGGIO

When Joe DiMaggio hit safely in 56 straight games during the 1941 season, he set a major league record that may never be broken. The closest anyone has come is 44 games, and two National Leaguers share that mark: Wee Willie Keeler (in 1897) and PETE ROSE (in 1978).

The 1941 streak is famous, but Joe's first hitting streak, in 1933, was also spectacular. As a 19-year-old minor leaguer, he hit in 61 straight games for the San Francisco Seals. That set a Pacific Coast League record that remains to this day.

"Joltin' Joe" enjoyed at least two other great streaks during his career: He played his entire 13-year career with one team, the New York Yankees, and he was named to the American League All-Star team in each of his 13 seasons.

A complete ballplayer, Joe had one of the best combinations of hitting and fielding skills ever found in a major leaguer. He was a strong defensive outfielder, with a very powerful and accurate throwing arm. In 1947, he made only one error in the entire season! His skill and grace in the field earned him the nickname "The Yankee Clipper." (A Yankee clipper is a type of sailing ship.)

Joe had a lifetime batting average of .325 and hit 361 home runs. Although he hit a lot

Amazing Feat

Joe's streak of hitting in 56 consecutive games began on May 15, 1941. Over the next two months, he had at least one base hit in every game in which he played. During that time, he batted .408, with 15 home runs and 55 runs batted in — good enough stats for a whole season for many players.

The streak finally ended on July 17, 1941, in a game against the Cleveland Indians. Joe hit the ball hard, but two outstanding plays by third baseman Ken Keltner kept Joe from recording a hit. However, Joe remained hot. He hit safely in the next 16 games, making his streak 72 out of 73 games.

of homers, he rarely struck out. In his entire career, he fanned 369 times.

During his career, Joe led the Yankees to nine World Series titles. He was named A.L. MVP three times (1939, 1941, and 1947).

In 1969, 18 years after he retired from baseball, Joe was named the game's greatest living player. He might have accomplished even more, but his baseball career was interrupted when he served in the armed forces in World War II.

Joe was elected to the National Baseball Hall of Fame in 1955.

INFO-BOX

BIRTHPLACE: Martinez, California

CAREER: 1936–1942, 1946–1951

CLAIM TO FAME: Joe was an awesome all-around baseball player.

FAMILY TIES First there was Vince, then there was Joe, and finally there was Dom. All born within six years, the DiMaggio brothers each played in the major leagues for at least 10 seasons. Vince, the oldest, was a good fielder and a fast runner. But he was never a strong hitter. In fact, he once set the record for the most strikeouts in a season! Vince played for five different teams. Dom, on the other hand, was a good hitter. After 11 big-league years, he had a lifetime batting average of .298. He was also a great leadoff hitter and a talented outfielder for the Boston Red Sox. His only problem was that he was constantly being compared to big brother Joe!

TONY DORSETT

The letters *TD* may stand for Tony Dorsett, but they also stand for touchdown! Tony lived up to his initials in a big way, scoring 91 TDs in his 11-year professional career.

At the University of Pittsburgh, Tony became the first college player to gain more than 6,000 rushing yards. He broke or tied 14 NCAA records, and his record of 6,082 career rushing yards still stands. He helped Pittsburgh win the national championship in 1976. A four-time All-America, he won the 1976 Heisman Trophy as the nation's most outstanding football player.

INFO-BOX

BIRTHPLACE: Rochester, Pennsylvania

CAREER: 1977–1988

CLAIM TO FAME: Tony is the all-time leading rusher in college football history and third all-time in NFL history.

In 1977, Tony joined the Dallas Cowboys and was named NFC Rookie of the Year. He rushed for more than 1,000 yards in a season eight times and set the NFL record for the longest run from scrimmage — 99 yards. He helped the Cowboys reach two Super Bowls.

Tony ended his career ranked third all-time in rushing yards and second in combined rushing and receiving yards. He played his final season with the Denver Broncos. In 1994, he was elected to the Pro Football Hall of Fame.

Amazing Feat

In a 1983 game against the Minnesota Vikings, the Dallas Cowboys had the ball inside their own 1-yard line. The coaches called for a straight-ahead run by Ron Springs, the Cowboy fullback. But Ron thought they had called a different play and went to the sideline. When the ball was snapped, Tony Dorsett alertly took the handoff. He ran 99 yards for the score! It's the longest touchdown run from scrimmage in NFL history.

KEN DRYDEN

Ken Dryden is the only player to star in the playoffs one season and win the Rookie of the Year award the next!

Ken started playing in the NHL very late in the 1970–71 season. He made goaltending history that year. He had only played six regular season games before he led his team, the Montreal Canadiens, into the playoffs.

INFO-BOX

BIRTHPLACE: Hamilton, Ontario, Canada
CAREER: 1971–1979
CLAIM TO FAME: In his brief career, Ken proved himself to be one of the best goaltenders in NHL history.

With Ken in goal, the Canadiens beat the defending-champion Boston Bruins, the Minnesota North Stars, and the Chicago Black Hawks to win the Stanley Cup. Ken won the Conn Smythe Trophy as the MVP of the playoffs. The following season, he won the Calder Trophy as Rookie of the Year.

During his eight seasons with Montreal, Ken led the league in shutouts four times, made the All-Star team five times, and won or shared the Vezina Trophy *(see page 265)* five times. He helped the Canadiens win six Stanley Cups!

Because he was tall (6' 4") and as quick as a cat, Ken was very difficult to score against. For his career, he gave up an average of 2.24 goals per game, one of the lowest goals-against averages in NHL history.

Ken retired from hockey at the age of 31. He was elected to the Hockey Hall of Fame in 1983.

ANOTHER SIDE Ken was one of the smartest goalies ever to play hockey. He graduated from Cornell University, in New York State. Then he took his earnings from pro hockey and put himself through law school. He even took the 1973–74 season off to get some experience working for a law firm. Ken retired from hockey while he was still in his prime because he wanted to put his education to work. He has practiced law, written a book about his hockey experiences, and worked as a TV commentator for NHL games.

FOOTBALL

JOHN ELWAY

John Elway, quarterback for the Denver Broncos, is famous for leading his team to thrilling come-from-behind victories.

Growing up, John excelled at football and baseball. He was a two-time All-America quarterback at Stanford University, in California. In 1982, he batted .318 for a New York Yankee farm team.

With John's help, Denver has won five AFC Western Division titles, three AFC championships, and made three Super Bowl appearances (all losses). John had passed for more than 3,000 yards in a season nine times through 1994 (second only to DAN MARINO). In 1993, John was the AFC's Most Valuable Player.

INFO-BOX

BIRTHPLACE: Port Angeles, Washington
CAREER: 1983 to the present
CLAIM TO FAME: Through 1994, John had led the Denver Broncos to 34 come-from-behind victories.

SWIMMING

KORNELIA ENDER

Kornelia Ender could swim — and fast! At age 13, the swimmer from East Germany (now part of Germany) won three silver medals at the 1972 Olympics. In 1973, at the world championships, she broke the world record in the 100-meter freestyle. She set 23 world records in her career.

At the 1976 Olympics, Kornelia became the first female swimmer to win four gold medals at one Olympics, setting world records in each event (the 100-meter and 200-meter freestyle, the 100-meter butterfly, and the 4 x 100-meter medley relay). She added a silver in the 4 x 100-meter freestyle relay.

Kornelia helped make East Germany a swimming power.

INFO-BOX

BIRTHPLACE: Plaven, East Germany (now Germany)
OLYMPIC CAREER: 1972 and 1976
CLAIM TO FAME: Kornelia won four gold medals in swimming at one Olympics.

JULIUS ERVING

Julius Winfield Erving II was known to the basketball world as “Dr. J.” He was one of the most amazing athletes, and one of the most popular people, ever to play the game. He combined power and grace in a way no one had before. Before Dr. J, no one had ever seen a player take off from the free-throw line, soar 15 feet through the air, and slam the basketball through the net.

Dr. J played three great seasons for the University of Massachusetts, averaging 26.3 points and 20 rebounds a game. He was drafted by the NBA, but he signed with the Virginia Squires of the American Basketball Association (ABA), in 1971.

In 1973, Julius was traded to the ABA's New York Nets. He led the Nets to two ABA championships and was named the league's Most Valuable Player three times.

The ABA and the NBA merged in 1976, and Dr. J went to the NBA's Philadelphia 76ers. During his 11 seasons with Philadelphia, he averaged 22 points, 6.7 rebounds, and 3.9 assists a game. In 1983, “The Doctor” led the 76ers to their first NBA championship in 16 years.

INFO-BOX

BIRTHPLACE: Roosevelt, New York

CAREER: 1971–1987

CLAIM TO FAME: Julius's high-flying moves helped turn the dunk into an art form.

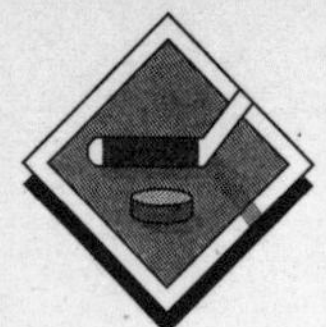

PHIL ESPOSITO

Phil Esposito was one of hockey's greatest centers. In 1970, his scoring helped the Boston Bruins win their first Stanley Cup in 26 years. Phil and the Bruins won it again in 1972. With Bobby Orr backing up Phil on defense, the Bruins became an NHL powerhouse.

At 6' 1" and 205 pounds, Phil was famous for planting himself in front of the net, eager to take a pass, nab a rebound, or deflect a shot for a goal. In his more than eight seasons with the Bruins, Phil won five scoring championships. He scored more than 50 goals five times. He was the first player to score more than 70 goals and to tally more than 100 points in a season. He won two Hart Trophies, as league MVP, in 1969 and 1974.

In the 1975–76 season, Phil was traded to the New York Rangers. He led the Rangers to the Stanley Cup finals in 1979. When Phil retired in 1981, he was the second-highest scorer in NHL history.

INFO-BOX

BIRTHPLACE: Sault Ste. Marie, Ontario, Canada
CAREER: 1963–1981
CLAIM TO FAME: Phil was a great scorer for the Boston Bruins and New York Rangers.

FAMILY TIES Phil grew up in Ontario, Canada, playing hockey with his younger brother, Tony. Tony always played goalie and Phil tried to score. Little did they know that years later, Phil would be trying to score on his brother during the Stanley Cup playoffs.

In the 1970 Stanley Cup semi-final playoffs, Phil played center for the Boston Bruins and Tony was in goal for the Chicago Black Hawks. Unfortunately for Tony, Phil led the Bruins to a four-game sweep of the Black Hawks. The Bruins then went on to beat the St. Louis Blues for the NHL championship.

Tony never played for a Stanley Cup champion, but both Phil and Tony were elected later to the Hockey Hall of Fame.

JANET EVANS

Swimmer Janet Evans won four gold medals at two Olympic Games and has her sights set on winning more in 1996.

Janet began swimming at age 1 and learned the butterfly and breaststroke as a 3-year-old. At 15, she broke long-standing world records in the 800-meter and 1,500-meter freestyle events.

At the 1988 Olympics, Janet, then 17, won gold medals in the 400-meter and 800-meter freestyle and the 400-meter individual medley. When she won the 400-meter freestyle, she set another world record!

After the Olympics, Janet became a national hero. In 1989, she won the Sullivan Award as the nation's top amateur athlete. She attended Stanford University, in California, until she left to concentrate on training for the 1992 Olympics. She made the team and won a gold medal in the 800-meter freestyle and a silver in the 400.

After the 1992 Olympics, Janet stopped swimming briefly, but then decided to try to make the U.S. Olympic team for 1996. At the 1994 national championships, she won all three distance events and raised her total of national titles to 42.

INFO-BOX

BIRTHPLACE: Fullerton, California

OLYMPIC CAREER: 1988, 1992

CLAIM TO FAME: Janet is the best female freestyle distance swimmer of all time.

More Stars!

Only Tracy Caulkins has won more national swimming titles (48) than Janet Evans. From 1978 to 1984, Tracy set five world records and more than 60 U.S. records. In 1978, she won the Sullivan Award. Unable to compete in the 1980 Summer Olympics *(see page 213)*, Tracy waited four more years to win an Olympic championship. Finally, at the 1984 Games, she won three gold medals, in the 200-meter and 400-meter individual medleys and the 4 x 100-meter medley relay.

CHRIS EVERT

Chris Evert was a champion on the women's tennis tour for 17 years. Between 1972, when she turned pro, and 1989, when she retired, Chris was never ranked below Number 4 in the world. During that time, she won 157 singles titles. Only Martina Navratilova won more.

Chris grew up in Florida and began playing tennis when she was 6 years old. Her father, Jimmy, a tennis instructor, was her only coach. Chris was not a natural athlete, so she worked hard to develop her game.

A baseline player *(see page 72)*, Chris hit powerful and accurate ground strokes. She rarely went to the net to volley.

During the first 10 years of her career, Chris had a record of 792–67. She won a total of 18 Grand Slam singles titles in her career. Her winning play and gracious personality made her a fan favorite.

INFO-BOX

BIRTHPLACE: Fort Lauderdale, Florida

CAREER: 1972–1989

CLAIM TO FAME: A consistent winner, Chris was one of the greatest female tennis players of all time.

Chris retired as a player in 1989. She was inducted into the International Tennis Hall of Fame in 1995.

BOB FELLER

Bob Feller combined a nasty curveball with one of the greatest fastballs of all time.

Bob made his first big-league start with the Cleveland Indians in 1936, when he was just a teenager. The 17-year-old pitcher struck out 15 batters! In 1938, he led the American League in strikeouts, with 240.

From 1939 to 1941, Bob was the best pitcher in baseball, leading the A.L. in wins, strikeouts, and innings pitched. He averaged more than 25 wins per season and struck out 767 batters in that time.

Bob missed four seasons because of World War II. In all, he won 266 games and threw three no-hitters. He was elected to the National Baseball Hall of Fame in 1962.

INFO-BOX

BIRTHPLACE: Van Meter, Iowa

CAREER: 1936–1956

CLAIM TO FAME: Once a teenage sensation, Bob became one of the greatest fastball pitchers of all time.

CARLTON FISK

Carlton Fisk, who was nicknamed "Pudge" as a boy, grew to be baseball's most durable catcher. He also hit more home runs as a catcher (351) than any other big-league backstop.

A native New Englander, Carlton signed with the Boston Red Sox. In 1972, he was Rookie of the Year. In the 1975 World Series, he homered to win Game 6, one of the Series' greatest games.

In 1981, Carlton joined the Chicago White Sox. He continued to play well even as he grew older. In 1985, at age 37, he hit 37 homers and knocked in 107 runs.

On June 22, 1993, Carlton caught his 2,226th game, breaking the record for most games at catcher. He retired in 1993.

BIRTHPLACE: Bellows Falls, Vermont

CAREER: 1969–1993

CLAIM TO FAME: Carlton played more games at catcher than any other player in baseball history.

BASEBALL

BOXING

GEORGE FOREMAN

In 1994, George Foreman won the heavyweight boxing championship at the age of 45. He was the oldest man ever to wear the crown. It was the second time George had won the heavyweight title; the first time was 21 years earlier!

George was the heavyweight gold medalist at the 1968 Olympics. In 1973, he won the heavyweight title by knocking out defending champion Joe Frazier in the second round! He lost the title to MUHAMMAD ALI by a knockout in 1974.

George left boxing in 1977 to become a Christian minister in Texas. In 1987, he decided to make a comeback. He was 38 and had put on weight. But his punches were powerful, and

INFO-BOX

BIRTHPLACE: Marshall, Texas
CAREER: 1969–77, 1987–present
CLAIM TO FAME: George won the heavyweight championship of boxing twice, 21 years apart.

after 24 fights, he was unbeaten. In 1991, George lost to champion Evander Holyfield. But he won the hearts of many Americans. He endorsed products and got his own TV show.

What he really wanted was another shot at the title. In November 1994, George got his chance. He knocked out Michael Moorer in the 10th round to become champion again!

DICK FOSBURY

Dick Fosbury was one of the world's most successful flops. He was a high jumper with his own way of crossing the high-jump bar — the "Fosbury Flop."

Until Dick came along, most jumpers rolled over the bar with their faces down. Dick threw himself over the bar head-first, with his face up. He then flopped onto the landing cushion on his back.

Dick first worked on the Flop in high school. When he flopped to an Olympic record and the gold medal in 1968, he changed his sport forever. Since 1968, almost every high-jump world record has been set using the Fosbury Flop.

BIRTHPLACE: Portland, Oregon
OLYMPIC CAREER: 1968
CLAIM TO FAME: Dick changed the sport of high jumping by inventing the "Fosbury Flop."

RUBE FOSTER

Andrew "Rube" Foster is called the Father of Black Baseball. Yet people sometimes forget that he was an outstanding pitcher before he became a manager and then founder of the first major baseball league for African-Americans.

In 1902, the 6' 4" tall, 225-pound right-hander may have been the best pitcher in the country. Unfortunately, he was not allowed to play in the major leagues because he was African-American.

Instead, Rube pitched for a team called the Cuban X-Giants. That year, he led them to the championship. Rube was the winning pitcher in four of the team's victories over the Philadelphia Giants in the Black World Series.

INFO-BOX

BIRTHPLACE: Calvert, Texas
CAREER: 1902–1926
CLAIM TO FAME: Rube, a great pitcher and manager, was founder of the first major league for black players, the Negro National League.

DAN FOUTS

Dan Fouts could throw a football as well as any quarterback in NFL history. In 1979, he became the first NFL quarterback to pass for over 4,000 yards (4,082) in a season. He is one of just three quarterbacks to exceed 40,000 career passing yards.

Dan's father was a broadcaster for the San Francisco 49ers, and Dan was a ball boy for the team when he was growing up. Famous San Francisco players stopped by the Fouts home. John Brodie, a 49er quarterback, taught Dan how to throw a spiral.

John taught Dan well. At the University of Oregon, Dan broke 19 school records!

In 1973, Dan joined the San Diego Chargers. In 1978, he led the Chargers to their first winning season in a decade. Dan led the league in passing yards for four consecutive seasons (1979–82) and broke 13 NFL passing records in his career. He even broke his own 1979 record by throwing for 4,715 yards in 1980 and 4,802 yards in 1981. He is third on the list for most yards gained passing (43,040), behind Fran Tarkenton (47,003) and Dan Marino (45,173).

In 1983 and 1986, Dan was named NFL Player of the Year. He was inducted into the Pro Football Hall of Fame in 1993.

INFO-BOX

BIRTHPLACE: San Francisco, California

CAREER: 1973–1987

CLAIM TO FAME: Dan was one of the most productive passers in the history of the NFL.

Amazing Feat

Dan still tops the NFL in most consecutive seasons leading the league in passing (4), most consecutive games with 400 or more yards passing (2), and most games with 300 or more yards passing (51).

On November 22, 1981, in Oakland, California, Dan threw for six touchdowns in a 55–21 rout of the Raiders! He totaled 317 yards passing.

JIMMIE FOXX

Jimmie Foxx started in the major leagues when he was 17, with the Philadelphia Athletics in 1925. His career really took off in 1929. That year, he hit 33 homers, drove in 117 runs, and had a .354 batting average.

For each of the next 11 seasons, the powerful infielder hit at least 30 home runs — a major league record. In 1932, he walloped 58 homers — the fourth-highest season total in major league history.

The next year, Jimmie won the Triple Crown, finishing first in the American League in batting average (.356), homers (48), and RBIs (163). He won the league's MVP award in 1932, 1933, and 1938. In 1938, as member of the Boston Red Sox, he broke the 50-homer mark again!

In all, Jimmie played 20 major league seasons. "Double X" hit a career total of 534 homers, 458 doubles, and 125 triples. He drove in 1,921 runs and batted .325.

Jimmie was elected to the National Baseball Hall of Fame in 1951.

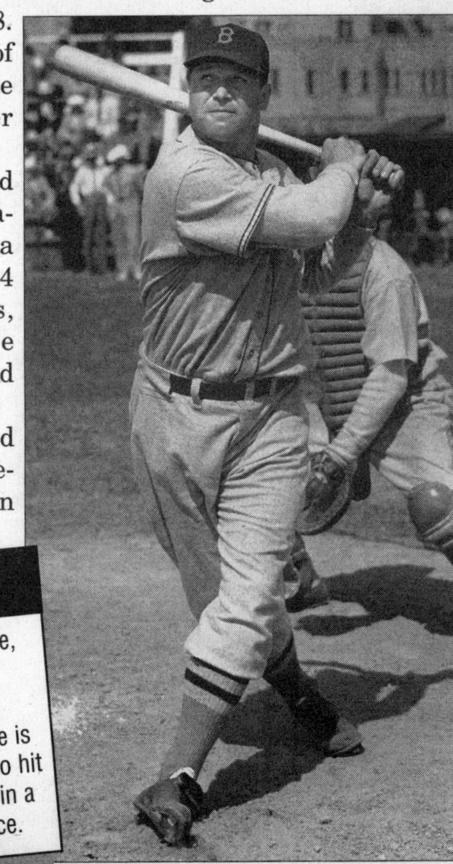

INFO-BOX

BIRTHPLACE: Sudlersville, Maryland

CAREER: 1925–1945

CLAIM TO FAME: Jimmie is one of only five players to hit 50 or more home runs in a season more than once.

A.J. FOYT

It is no surprise that Anthony Joseph (A.J.) Foyt, Junior, grew up to become one of the greatest auto racers in history. He began racing midget cars at age 11. As a teenager, he worked in the family garage.

A.J. was a champion in many types of racing. He was the first driver to win the Indianapolis 500 four times and was Indy-car champion for a record seven times. In 1972, he won the Daytona 500, the biggest event for stock-car racers. In Grand Prix sports cars, he teamed with Dan Gurney to win the tough 24 Hours of LeMans, in 1967. He's the only driver to win all three of those big races.

Unlike most drivers, A.J. was also a good mechanic. Early in his career, he built his own cars. Even when he became a race driver, he still helped to design, modify, or repair his cars, most of which were owned by him and not by sponsors. A.J. became one of the few millionaires on the circuit.

A.J. won the U.S. Auto Club (USAC) championship seven times, scoring the most points on the circuit for those seasons. When he retired, he was the only driver to win more than 100 USAC races. He won more than 20 in each of the four major divisions: sprint, stock, midget, and championship.

INFO-BOX

BIRTHPLACE: Houston, Texas

CAREER: 1957–1993

CLAIM TO FAME: A.J. was the first race-car driver to win the Indianapolis 500 four times.

DAN GABLE

In high school, college, international, and Olympic wrestling competition, Dan Gable suffered only one defeat. That came in 1970, in the final of the NCAA 142-pound championship, which was also the final match of his college career at Iowa State University. That loss ended a string of 176 consecutive victories.

INFO-BOX

BIRTHPLACE: Waterloo, Iowa

CAREER: 1964–1972

CLAIM TO FAME: Pound for pound, Dan was the greatest amateur wrestler in U.S. history.

But Dan didn't let a single defeat stop him. In 1971, he won a gold medal at the Pan American Games, in Cali, Colombia, and took the world championship at 149.5 pounds, in Sofia, Bulgaria. At the 1972 Summer Olympics, in Munich, West Germany (now Germany), competing in the lightweight (149.5-pound) category, Dan became the first wrestler from the U.S. in 12 years to win an Olympic gold medal.

A knee injury forced Dan to retire after the Olympics. He then became one of the greatest wrestling coaches in NCAA history.

Dan's teams at the University of Iowa won nine straight NCAA titles, from 1978 to 1986, and three more in a row from 1991 to 1993.

Dan was elected to the U.S. Olympic Hall of Fame in 1985.

How It Works

"Professional" wrestling is strictly show business. Olympic wrestling is a sport. In international amateur competition, matches consist of two three-minute rounds. A wrestler scores points as a result of successful moves against his opponent. If time runs out without one wrestler having "pinned" the other, the wrestler with the most points is the winner. There are 10 weight classes in Olympic wrestling, ranging from light flyweight to super heavyweight.

BASEBALL

LOU GEHRIG

Lou Gehrig was one of the best — if not *the* best — first basemen in baseball history. Because he played on the same team as Babe Ruth, Lou's great career is often overlooked. The pair were the two greatest hitters ever to play together.

For 12 straight seasons, Lou batted .300 or higher. In 13 straight seasons, he drove in 112 runs or more. And no matter what, Lou played! *(See below.)* For that reason, he was known as "The Iron Horse."

In 1927, Lou won the American League Most Valuable Player Award. He led the league with a then-record 175 RBIs, as well as 52 doubles and 447 total bases. He finished behind the Babe in homers with 47 (that was the year Babe hit 60). Lou's batting average of .373 was also second-best in the league. Many experts consider the 1927 Yankees the greatest baseball team ever.

In 1931, Lou was the leading run producer in the major leagues with 184 RBIs (still an A.L. record) and 163 runs scored. On June 3, 1932, he became the first American Leaguer to hit four homers in a game. In 1934, Lou won the Triple Crown by leading the league in home runs (49), RBIs (165), and batting average (.363).

In spring training of 1939, Lou felt weak and slug-

Amazing Feat

On May 31, 1925, Lou Gehrig began his famous streak of playing in 2,130 consecutive games — as a pinch-hitter. The next day, Yankee first baseman Wally Pipp had a headache. Lou was in the starting lineup! He played so well that Wally lost his job. Lou himself ended the streak almost 14 years later, on May 2, 1939, when he told his manager not to play him because he was tired. (Lou's streak had long before broken the old record of 1,307 consecutive games.) Lou would soon learn that he was very sick. He never played again. CAL RIPKEN, JUNIOR, broke Lou's consecutive-game record in 1995.

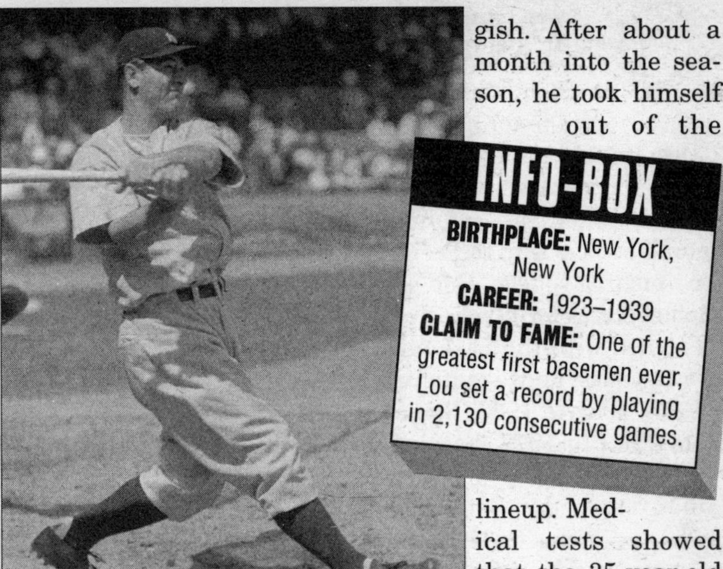

gish. After about a month into the season, he took himself out of the lineup. Medical tests showed that the 35-year-old star had a rare, incurable disease of the nervous system called amyotrophic lateral sclerosis *[ah-my-uh-TROFF-ick LAT-err-uhl skluh-ROW-sis]*. Few people had ever heard of it before, but it soon became known as "Lou Gehrig's disease."

With Lou's baseball career tragically shortened, people marveled at his impressive career statistics: In 2,164 games, Lou had hit 493 homers (the most by a first baseman) and 535 doubles; he had scored 1,888 runs and driven in 1,995 more; and his lifetime batting average was .340. His 23 grand-slam home runs are still a major league record. Lou Gehrig died on June 2, 1941, at the age of 37.

A CLOSER LOOK On July 4, 1939, 61,808 fans came to Yankee Stadium to honor Lou on Lou Gehrig Day. Obviously sick, Lou took the microphone and spoke to the crowd. He said, "Fans, for the past two weeks you have been reading about the bad break I got. Yet, today, I consider myself the luckiest man on the face of the earth." Later that year, Lou was elected to the National Baseball Hall of Fame. There is usually a five-year wait, but it was clear that Lou deserved to be honored as one of baseball's heroes before he died.

BASEBALL

BOB GIBSON

Bob Gibson grew from a sickly child into one of the toughest competitors in baseball.

Despite his many childhood ailments (including asthma and heart problems), Bob was a terrific athlete. He starred in basketball and baseball in high school, and was given a basketball scholarship to Creighton University, in Nebraska. After finishing college, Bob played basketball with the Harlem Globetrotters for a year. In 1957, when he was 21 years old, he signed with the St. Louis Cardinals baseball team. Within two years, he was pitching in the major leagues.

From 1962 to 1966, Bob averaged 230 strikeouts per year; from 1963 to 1972, he averaged 19 wins per season. After breaking his leg in the summer of 1967, the 6' 1" tall fireballer returned in September to win three key games and help the Cardinals win the National League pennant. Then in the World Series he won three complete games.

In 1968, Bob pitched even better. Even though he suffered from pain in his right elbow, he had a 22–9 record (including 15 straight wins), with 13 shutouts, 268 strikeouts, and a 1.12 earned run average (the lowest ever by a pitcher with at least 300 innings pitched).

Bob was elected to the National Baseball Hall of Fame in 1981.

INFO-BOX

BIRTHPLACE: Omaha, Nebraska

CAREER: 1959–1975

CLAIM TO FAME: Bob's 1968 season was one of the greatest ever by a major league pitcher.

ANOTHER SIDE Bob Gibson finished his pitching career with a 251–174 record, 3,117 strikeouts, 56 shutouts, and a 2.91 ERA. He won two Cy Young Awards (1968 and 1970), an MVP award (1968), and nine Gold Gloves (for his fielding). But he could hit, too! Over his career, Bob slugged 24 homers and posted a .206 batting average, which is not bad for a pitcher. In 1970, Bob batted .303 for the season, and was even called on to be a pinch-hitter from time to time.

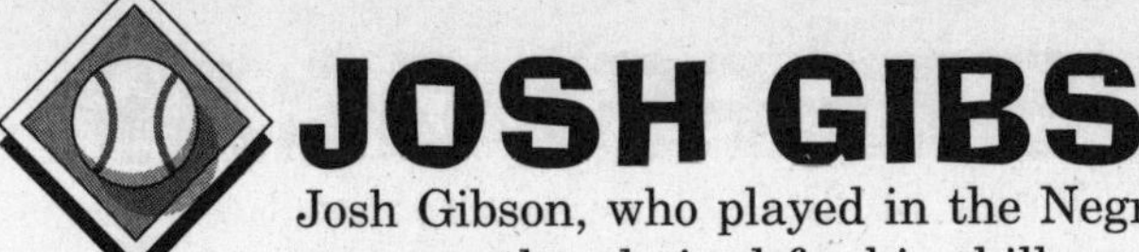

JOSH GIBSON

Josh Gibson, who played in the Negro leagues, was greatly admired for his skills as a catcher. He was called the "Black Babe Ruth" for his home run slugging.

Josh played in an era when African-Americans were not allowed to play major league baseball. He dominated the Negro leagues, beginning in 1930, when he was 18. He never played for a losing team. He also played in Mexico, the Dominican Republic, Puerto Rico, and Cuba.

INFO-BOX

BIRTHPLACE: Buena Vista, Georgia

CAREER: 1930–1946

CLAIM TO FAME: Josh was the greatest hitter — and slugger — in the Negro leagues.

Exact statistics weren't kept, but in 13 full seasons in the Negro leagues, Josh is believed to have won nine home run crowns and four batting titles. His lifetime batting average of .384 was the highest in the Negro leagues' recorded history. In 1931, he reportedly hit 75 homers; in 1934, his homers numbered 69. Estimates give him about 825 home runs for his career!

A Closer Look

On January 1, 1943, Josh Gibson went into a day-long coma, meaning he became unconscious. Josh had been having dizzy spells. He was told by doctors that he had a brain tumor and needed an operation. Josh refused. That season, he won another batting title. Then, from 1944 to 1946, he led the Negro leagues in home runs. On January 20, 1947, Josh told his mother that this was the night he would die. That night Josh had a stroke and died. He was 35 years old.

Josh was known not only for hitting the ball, but for hitting it *long*. He's credited with clouting the longest drive ever hit in Yankee Stadium. People who saw it said that if the ball had cleared a high wall, it would've traveled 700 feet!

Josh died in 1947, the same year that JACKIE ROBINSON broke into the big leagues.

STEFFI GRAF

When Steffi Graf picked up her first tennis racket, she was about 4 years old. She had seen her parents play, and she wanted to be like them. As it turned out, Steffi would not be like her parents. Steffi would turn out to be the Number 1 tennis player in the world.

Steffi's father, who ran a tennis club near their house in Brühl, West Germany, coached Steffi. (West Germany and East Germany were separate countries at that time. They merged to form one Germany in 1990.) When Steffi was 12, she won the West German 14-and-under and 18-and-under competitions, and the European 12-and-under.

INFO-BOX

BIRTHPLACE: Brühl, West Germany (now Germany)
CAREER: 1982 to the present
CLAIM TO FAME: Steffi was ranked Number 1 for 186 straight weeks — the longest time ever!

Steffi turned pro in 1982 at the age of 13 years 4 months. The Women's Tennis Association computer ranked her as the 214th best women's player in the world. In 1984, Steffi competed for West Germany at the Olympics. Tennis was a demonstration sport at the Games, which were held in Los Angeles, California, and Steffi was the youngest tennis player there. Still, she played like a champion and won an honorary gold medal.

Soon thereafter, she put the tennis world on notice. She started 1985 ranked 22nd and finished the year ranked 6th. In 1986, she got her first pro tournament victory by defeating CHRIS EVERT in the finals of the Family Circle Cup. In 1987, she became only the third player ever to beat tennis greats MARTINA NAVRATILOVA and Chris in back-to-back, straight-set matches (she won the best of three sets, two sets to none). That same year, she also became the Number 1 tennis player in the world after beating Chris in the Virginia Slims championships. She then held on to that top spot for 186 weeks — the longest time ever!

When She Was a Kid

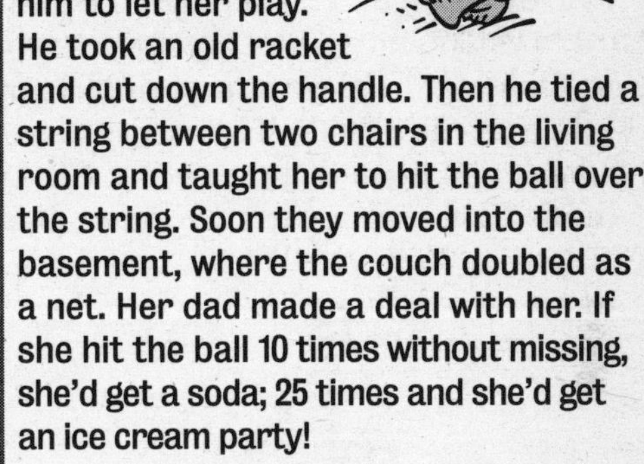

When Steffi was 4, she dragged around her dad's racket, begging him to let her play. He took an old racket and cut down the handle. Then he tied a string between two chairs in the living room and taught her to hit the ball over the string. Soon they moved into the basement, where the couch doubled as a net. Her dad made a deal with her. If she hit the ball 10 times without missing, she'd get a soda; 25 times and she'd get an ice cream party!

On the court, Steffi is totally focused on the game. That concentration helped her, at age 19, to win the tennis Grand Slam *(see page 71)* and a 1988 Olympic gold medal — all in the same year!

Altogether, Steffi has won four Australian Open titles, six Wimbledon titles, four French Open titles, and four U.S. Open titles. That list is likely to grow in the years to come.

DID YOU KNOW?

- Steffi enjoys going to art galleries and museums.
- She considers New York City her favorite city and owns an apartment there.
- Steffi enjoys taking photographs, particularly of people, but not other tennis pros. She knows they get photographed a lot, and she doesn't want to bother them.

FOOTBALL

RED GRANGE

In 1925, a rusty-haired University of Illinois football hero named Harold "Red" Grange shocked America. He became the first college football star to turn pro. He signed with the Chicago Bears. Pro football was a new sport then, and Red's participation made it popular.

Red was called "The Galloping Ghost" because he was so hard to catch and tackle. In four years of high school, he had won four state titles as a sprint champion and scored 75 touchdowns as a football hero. In college, he had starred as a halfback and become a three-time All-America.

In his first season with the Bears, Red played 19 games in 17 cities in 66 days. "It beat practicing," Red said later. He hurt his knee in his second season. In 1926, he played for the New York Yankees football team. In 1929, Red returned to the Bears, and stayed until he retired in 1934.

Red was a charter member of both the college and pro football halls of fame. He died in 1991, at the age of 87.

INFO-BOX

BIRTHPLACE: Forksville, Pennsylvania

CAREER: 1925–1934

CLAIM TO FAME: Red's exciting running helped make professional football a popular sport.

HANK GREENBERG

Hank Greenberg played only about 9½ major league seasons for the Pittsburgh Pirates and Detroit Tigers because of World War II military service. But he was one of the greatest right-handed power hitters ever.

In 1938 Hank hit 58 home runs. In 1,394 career games, the first baseman hit 331 homers, scored 1,051 runs, and batted in 1,276 runs. His career batting average was .313.

Hank, who was Jewish, was also admired for his determination to succeed despite anti-Semitism (discrimination against Jews). He was elected to the National Baseball Hall of Fame in 1956.

INFO-BOX

BIRTHPLACE: New York, New York

CAREER: 1930–1947

CLAIM TO FAME: Hank was one of the greatest right-handed home run hitters of all time.

BASEBALL

JOE GREENE

The Pittsburgh Steeler defensive tackle wasn't called "Mean Joe" for nothing. Joe Greene was tall (6' 4") and big (280 pounds). He was the key to Pittsburgh's "Steel Curtain" defense in the 1970s. That iron defense helped win seven division titles and four Super Bowls.

At North Texas State College, Joe was named the nation's best defensive lineman in 1968. As Pittsburgh's top draft choice in 1969, he was Rookie of the Year and played in the first of 10 Pro Bowls over his 13-year career.

In 1972, in a big win over the Houston Oilers, Joe sacked the quarterback five times, blocked a field goal, forced and recovered a fumble, and made six solo tackles. That season, Pittsburgh won its first division title and Joe was named the NFL's defensive MVP.

INFO-BOX

BIRTHPLACE: Temple, Texas

CAREER: 1969–1981

CLAIM TO FAME: A great defensive tackle, Joe was the key to the Pittsburgh Steeler defense that helped win four NFL championships.

FOOTBALL

WAYNE GRETZKY

Wayne Gretzky is called "The Great One." Why? Because he has scored more points than any other player in the history of the NHL! He also led the Edmonton Oilers to four Stanley Cup championships in five seasons. And he holds more than 60 NHL records.

Wayne played a lot of hockey when he was growing up in Brantford, Ontario, Canada. His dad even built him a rink in the family's backyard. Wayne spent many hours practicing. By the time he was 6, he was good enough to play in a league for 10-year-olds. At 16, Wayne was already a hockey legend. His hero was GORDIE HOWE, and he wore uniform number 99 in honor of Gordie (who wore number 9).

After playing two seasons in the World Hockey Association, Wayne and his team, the Edmonton Oilers, joined the NHL *(see next page)*. The league hasn't been the same since. During his first year in the NHL, Wayne became the youngest player ever to score 50 goals in a season. He also won the first of his 9 Hart (Most Valuable Player) and 10 Art Ross (scoring championship) trophies. That year, Wayne also took home the first of his four Lady Byng Awards, given each season to the most gentlemanly player.

Wayne's fellow players think he's great, too. They voted to give him the Lester B. Pearson Award five times (as the NHL's Most Outstanding Player).

When He Was a Kid

Wayne scored his first goal when he was 2. He shot a sponge ball through the legs of the goaltender, who just happened to be his grandmother. He also began skating at 2. As a teenager, Wayne described his speed on the ice as "brutal," meaning slower than slow. All of the speed in the family must have gone to Wayne's younger sister, Kim. She was an Ontario speed-skating champ!

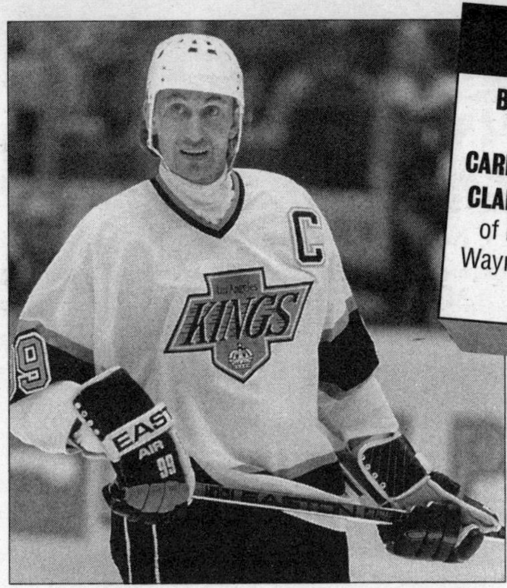

INFO-BOX

BIRTHPLACE: Brantford, Ontario, Canada
CAREER: 1978 to the present
CLAIM TO FAME: The holder of more than 60 records, Wayne is the greatest player in NHL history.

His scoring and unselfish play often inspired his teammates. In 1984, the Great One led his team to greatness — the Oilers beat the New York Islanders in the Stanley Cup finals. It ended New York's championship streak at four, and it started one for the Oilers. Wayne led Edmonton to three more titles. He was named MVP of the playoffs twice.

After winning his fourth Cup with the Oilers, Wayne was traded to the Los Angeles Kings. He led the Kings to their first-ever Stanley Cup appearance in 1993.

Since joining L.A., Wayne has made history in other ways. In 1989, he became the NHL's all-time leading point scorer by breaking Gordie Howe's record (1,850). In 1994, when Wayne scored goal number 802, he broke the record for most career goals. That record had also been held by Wayne's boyhood hero.

HOW IT WORKS Wayne was involved in two giant changes in the NHL. The first was in 1979, when Wayne's team, the Edmonton Oilers, along with the Winnipeg Jets, the Quebec Nordiques, and the Hartford Whalers, joined the NHL. They had been part of the World Hockey Association. The second came when Wayne was traded to Los Angeles. Thanks largely to Wayne, hockey became popular in a warm-weather city for the first time. That opened the door for new teams such as the Tampa Bay Lightning, Florida Panthers, and Mighty Ducks of Anaheim.

BASEBALL

KEN GRIFFEY, JUNIOR

Ken Griffey, Junior, raced to the top of the baseball world as a 19-year-old rookie, and he hasn't looked back.

Unlike most rookies, Ken had plenty of major league experience before the Seattle Mariners made him the first pick of the 1987 draft. Ken's dad, Ken Griffey, Senior, played for the 1975 and 1976 World Series champion Cincinnati Reds. So, before Ken junior spent his first spring training with the Mariners, he had spent many springs with his dad and the various major league teams he played for.

At Archbishop Moeller High School, in Cincinnati, Ohio, Ken hit 20 homers and set a school record with a blistering .478 batting average. Then the Mariners came calling. Junior made it to the majors in 1989, ripping a double in his first at-bat. He also hit a home run in his first at-bat in front of the home crowd.

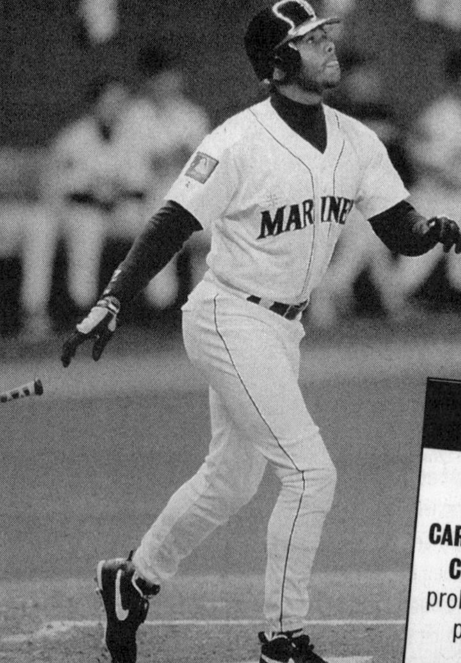

Junior has won five straight Gold Gloves for fielding excellence in center field and once had a streak of 573 chances without an error, which is an American League record. His over-the-wall catches and

INFO-BOX

BIRTHPLACE: Donora, Pennsylvania

CAREER: 1989 to the present

CLAIM TO FAME: Ken is probably the best all-around player in major league baseball today.

diving grabs rob opposing batters of extra-base hits.

By hitting a home run and being named Most Valuable Player at the 1992 All-Star Game, Junior did what his father had done at the 1980 All-Star Game. Most likely, Ken junior will not only better most of his father's achievements, he'll break a few major league records, too. Ken junior tied the record for consecutive games with a home run in 1993, when he went deep in eight straight games. In 1994, he was on a blistering pace to break Roger Maris's single-season home run record, but the season was canceled because of the strike. Ken finished with 40 homers, and they came in only 111 games!

Ken junior is one of the youngest players in history to reach 100 career home runs, hit 20 or more homers in each of his first four years, and drive in 100 runs three times. This "Kid," as Ken junior is nicknamed, is clearly going places.

Family Ties

By making the Mariners' major league club in 1989, Ken junior made history. Ken senior and Ken junior became the first father and son to play in the major leagues at the same time. And one year later, they appeared in the same lineup, when the Mariners signed Ken senior. That day, Senior and Junior got back-to-back hits. They topped that a month later when they hit back-to-back homers!

DID YOU KNOW?

- Ken wears number 24 because, as a teenager, he once hit 24 home runs in a season. It was the first time he hit more homers than his dad.
- In his rookie year, Ken had a candy bar named for him. It was a chocolate bar and it was a big hit in Seattle. The funny thing is, Ken is allergic to chocolate!
- Ken's second-favorite sport is football. He was a star receiver on his high school team. But he gave up the sport after he realized that he'd rather hit than be hit.
- Ken loves cars. Although he owns several real cars, he still likes to pursue his hobby — building model cars.

FOOTBALL

ARCHIE GRIFFIN

Archie Griffin made history at Ohio State University in his hometown of Columbus, Ohio. He was the first player to receive the Heisman Trophy twice, winning in 1974 and 1975.

A running back, Archie gained 5,177 yards in his career, an NCAA record at the time. (The current record-holder is TONY DORSETT.) He rushed for 100 or more yards in 31 straight games, another record. He was a three-time All-America and led Ohio State to four straight Rose Bowls.

Archie wasn't as successful as a pro. He was elected to the College Football Hall of Fame in 1987.

INFO-BOX

BIRTHPLACE: Columbus, Ohio

CAREER: 1976–1983, 1985

CLAIM TO FAME: Archie is the only player to win the Heisman Trophy twice.

BASEBALL

TONY GWYNN

Tony Gwynn, the All-Star right fielder for the San Diego Padres, uses a smaller bat than most players. Yet he's a five-time National League batting champion!

Tony, who grew up in Long Beach, California, is a tough batter to strike out. In 1984, his rookie year, he became the first Padre to reach 200 hits. He also delivered the game-winning RBI that sent San Diego to its first World Series.

During his career, Tony has hit .300 or higher 11 times. He has had eight games with five or more hits. His .370 batting average in 1987 was the N.L.'s best since Stan Musial in 1948. He bettered that with a .394 average in the strike-shortened 1994 season!

Tony is a 10-time All-Star, a 5-time Gold Glove winner, and a career .333 hitter.

INFO-BOX

BIRTHPLACE: Los Angeles, California

OLYMPIC CAREER: 1982 to the present

CLAIM TO FAME: Tony is the best hitter in major league baseball today.

FLORENCE GRIFFITH JOYNER

Florence Griffith Joyner dazzled the track-and-field world in 1988, winning three gold medals and setting two world records.

FloJo, as she is known, began racing when she was 7. In 1979, she had to drop out of college to help support her family. Bob Kersee, then a coach at the University of California at Los Angeles (UCLA), met FloJo when she was working as a bank teller. He helped her get a scholarship to UCLA.

FloJo won silver medals in the 200-meter dash at the 1984 Olympics and at the 1987 world championships. At the 1988 U.S. Olympic Trials (tryouts), FloJo shattered a world record by running the 100-meter dash in 10.49 seconds! She went on to win Olympic gold medals in the 100-meter dash, the 200-meter dash (setting a world record), and the 4 x 100-meter relay.

FloJo retired in 1989. She later became co-chairman of the President's Council on Physical Fitness.

INFO-BOX

BIRTHPLACE: Los Angeles, California

OLYMPIC CAREER: 1984 and 1988

CLAIM TO FAME: FloJo is the fastest female sprinter in track-and-field history.

DOROTHY HAMILL

In 1976, Dorothy Hamill was unbeatable in women's figure skating. She won the U.S. and world championships and an Olympic gold medal. But what Dorothy was also famous for was her hair! Her short dark hair, cut in a style called a "wedge," was copied by girls all over the world.

Dorothy started skating at age 8. She won her first of three straight national titles in 1974. Dorothy won her first world title in 1976.

Dorothy invented a spin, now known as the "Hamill camel." In 1976, she turned professional, and she is a popular attraction at ice shows and pro competitions.

INFO-BOX

BIRTHPLACE: Chicago, Illinois

OLYMPIC CAREER: 1976

CLAIM TO FAME: Dorothy's talent and style turned the heads of skating fans around the world.

JOHN HANNAH

John Hannah stood 6' 3" tall and weighed 265 pounds, but the All-Pro guard was quick and an outstanding run blocker.

Pro football ran in John's family. His father, Herb, played tackle for the New York Giants in the early 1950s. His brother Charlie played tackle for Tampa Bay and the Raiders.

A two-time All-America at the University of Alabama, John joined the New England Patriots in 1973 and made the NFL's All-Rookie team. In 1978, John helped clear the way for the Patriots to rush for an NFL-record 3,165 yards.

John was a five-time NFL Lineman of the Year. He retired in 1986. He was elected to the Pro Football Hall of Fame in 1991.

INFO-BOX

BIRTHPLACE: Canton, Georgia

CAREER: 1973–1986

CLAIM TO FAME: John was one of the best offensive linemen ever to play professional football.

LEON HART

Leon Hart was a 6' 5" tall, 265-pound giant in college and pro football in the 1940s and 1950s.

In college, Leon played offensive and defensive end. On offense, he was a triple threat: He blocked, ran with the ball, and caught passes. During his four years at the University of Notre Dame, the football team went undefeated and won the national championship in 1946, 1947, and 1949. Leon was a three-time All-America. He won the Maxwell Award in 1949 as the nation's top player. He was also the last lineman to be awarded the Heisman Trophy.

Leon joined the Detroit Lions in 1950. He helped the Lions win three NFL championships.

INFO-BOX

BIRTHPLACE: Turtle Creek, Pennsylvania

CAREER: 1946–1957

CLAIM TO FAME: Leon was the last lineman to win college football's Heisman Trophy.

FOOTBALL

JOHN HAVLICEK

John Havlicek was solid in every part of basketball. His shooting, passing, ball-handling, and rebounding skills made this 6' 5" tall forward one of the best ever. He averaged 20.8 points a game over his long career.

"Hondo," as he was sometimes called, played on an NCAA championship team with Ohio State University, then signed with the Boston Celtics. He spent his entire 16-season career with Boston. During his career, the Celtics won eight NBA championships.

John was a team player. During much of his career, he made his important contributions as the "sixth man" — the first non-starting player off the bench.

INFO-BOX

BIRTHPLACE: Martins Ferry, Ohio

CAREER: 1962–1978

CLAIM TO FAME: Coming off the bench, John was one of pro basketball's great "sixth man"players.

BASKETBALL

TONY HAWK

Tony Hawk was 9 years old when he first jumped onto a skateboard. He used it just to get around the neighborhood. About a year later, he began taking it to the park and doing tricks. In 1982, the year he turned 14, he also turned professional.

Tony went on to win six official national championships in a row. But it was his creative moves that helped make the sport popular. Some of his tricks, such as the "air walk" and the "Madonna," are now performed by most pro skaters.

Tony's most famous trick is the "720 aerial." He zooms up the wall of a vertical ramp, launches himself into the air, and turns two somersaults before landing!

INFO-BOX

BIRTHPLACE: San Diego, California

CAREER: 1982 to the present

CLAIM TO FAME: Tony's creative moves on the board helped make skateboarding a popular sport.

ELVIN HAYES

Elvin Hayes was one of the best big men ever to shoot a basketball. A 6' 9" tall, 235-pound center/forward, he could score near the basket or from the outside with his turnaround jump shot. He is one of the leading scorers in NBA history, with a career total of 27,313 points.

Elvin was a three-time All-America at the University of Houston. He was chosen by the San Diego Rockets as the first pick overall in the 1968 NBA draft. In his first season, Elvin averaged 28.4 points a game, becoming one of only two rookies to ever lead the league in scoring average (the other was Wilt Chamberlain).

Elvin moved with the Rockets to Houston in 1971. He played for the Washington Bullets from 1974 to 1981 and helped the Bullets win the 1978 NBA title.

INFO-BOX

BIRTHPLACE: Rayville, Louisiana

CAREER: 1968–1984

CLAIM TO FAME: Elvin was one of the highest-scoring center/forwards in NBA history.

MARQUES HAYNES

Marques Haynes invented the dribbling moves that many NBA backcourt stars use today.

Marques was a star with the Harlem Globetrotters, the Fabulous Harlem Magicians, and several other all-black barnstorming teams. He was advertised as "the world's greatest dribbler." He dribbled the ball behind his back, through his legs, and while sliding on his side. Opponents would swipe at the ball in vain.

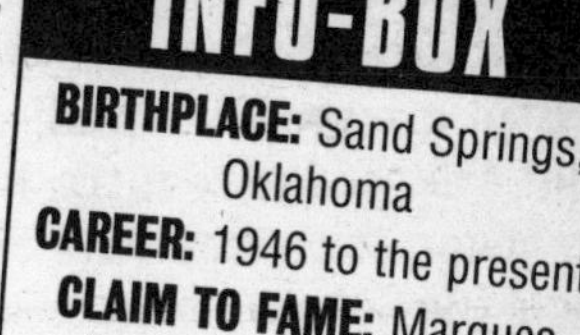

Before 1950, no big-league team would sign a black player. So, African-American players turned to the Globetrotters. The Trotters had been started in 1927 by Abe Saperstein. They were great entertainers, using fancy dribbling, tricky passing, and deadeye shooting to delight crowds.

The first time that Abe saw him, Marques was leading the Langston University (Oklahoma) team to a 74–70 victory over the Globetrotters! The Trotters rarely lost. Abe was impressed enough to sign Marques up.

Marques traveled all over the world with the team. In 1951, the Globetrotters were officially recognized as "ambassadors of good will" by the U.S. State Department.

Fun Fact

In the 1940s and 1950s, pro basketball was trying to attract fans. The Harlem Globetrotters drew big crowds by combining entertainment with basketball. To draw bigger crowds, a new league, the NBA, often scheduled Globetrotter exhibitions before league games. These doubleheaders proved to be very popular. But there was only one problem for the NBA: As soon as the Globies finished, many of the fans left!

ERIC HEIDEN

At the 1980 Winter Olympics, in Lake Placid, New York, Eric Heiden of the U.S. competed in all five of the men's long-track speed-skating races — and won them all! He became the first person ever to win five individual gold medals at one Olympics, winter or summer. (Swimmer MARK SPITZ won seven gold medals in 1972, but three were for relays.) No U.S. Winter Olympic *Team* since 1932 had won five gold medals!

Eric grew up in Madison, Wisconsin. Like many kids in that area of the country, he played ice hockey as a boy. Later, he began to concentrate on speed skating. Luckily, Eric lived near the only 400-meter speed-skating track in the country.

By 1976, when he was 17, Eric competed in the 1976 Winter Olympics. He finished 7th in the 1,500-meter event and 19th in the 5,000 meters. A year later, Eric shocked everyone — even himself — when he won the all-around title at the 1977 world championships. (In the all-around competition, skaters earn points based on their finish in each event.) That win was no fluke: Eric also won the world championship in 1978 and 1979.

Eric trained hard, and by the start of the 1980 Olympics, his legs were so muscular that each of his thighs measured 29 inches around. His waist was only 32 inches around! He was the favorite in all five Olympic events.

Eric won gold medals in his first four events, but his last event of the Games, the 10,000 meters, was proba-

Family Ties

Eric's sister, Beth Heiden, was also a fantastic athlete. A year younger than Eric, Beth was the women's speed-skating all-around world champion in 1979. At the 1980 Olympics, she won a bronze medal in the 3,000 meters. In 1980, Beth also won the world bicycling road-race championship! In 1983, while attending the University of Vermont, she won the NCAA championship in the 7.5 kilometer cross-country skiing event!

bly his most amazing win. The night before, Eric had watched the U.S. hockey team play the Soviet Union in a game that was won by the U.S. in a remarkable upset.

He was so excited after the game that he had trouble falling asleep and ended up oversleeping in the morning. Grabbing just a few pieces of bread, he rushed to the track and calmly skated the grueling 25-lap race. Not only did he win the event, but he beat the second-fastest competitor by a wide margin (eight seconds) and broke the world record!

Eric retired soon after the Olympics. He became a professional bicycle racer and also attended medical school. Eric is now a doctor in Sacramento, California.

A CLOSER LOOK Eric's five Olympic speed-skating gold medals are especially amazing when you consider that he won races at distances ranging from a sprint (500 meters) to a long-distance race (10,000 meters). Try to imagine a runner winning the 100 meters and the marathon, and you have an idea of the achievement. In 1964, Lydia Skoblikova of the Soviet Union won four races in the women's Olympic competition, from 500 meters to 3,000 meters. Eric's and Lydia's feats will probably never be matched. Today, most skaters specialize in either sprint or distance events.

RICKEY HENDERSON

In his first full season in the major leagues (1980), Rickey Henderson became the first American Leaguer — and only the third player in history — to steal at least 100 bases in a season. He hasn't stopped running since.

In 1982, Rickey swiped 130 bases, breaking the single-season record of 112 steals held by Lou Brock. On May 1, 1991, Rickey broke Lou's career record (939). Exactly one year later, Rickey became the first player in major league history to steal 1,000 bases.

In 1989, Rickey won the American League Championship Series MVP award, after leading the Oakland A's past the Toronto Blue Jays with a .400 batting average, eight runs scored, and five runs batted in. He kept it up in the World Series against the San Francisco Giants, topping all batters with nine hits (plus three steals). Playing in three World Series for two teams (the A's and the Blue Jays), Rickey has a career Series average of .339.

INFO-BOX

BIRTHPLACE: Chicago, Illinois

CAREER: 1979 to the present

CLAIM TO FAME: Rickey is the top base stealer and leadoff batter in baseball history.

In 1990, Rickey won the regular-season MVP Award after batting .325 with 28 homers. "The Man of Steal" will surely be a Hall of Famer when his career finally ends.

ANOTHER SIDE Throughout his career, Rickey Henderson has done a lot more than just steal bases. He holds the career record for most home runs leading off a ball game (66, through the 1994 season). He has led the American League five times in runs scored. In 1985, even after missing the first 10 games of the season with a sprained ankle, he scored 146 runs, the most in baseball since Ted Williams scored 150 in 1949. For his hitting and baserunning skills, Rickey is considered the greatest leadoff hitter in major league baseball history.

TED HENDRICKS

FOOTBALL

Ted Hendricks was called "The Mad Stork." What else would you call a 6' 7" defensive player with skinny legs and long arms? When Ted's 15-year NFL career was over, he owned four Super Bowl rings and a spot in the Pro Football Hall of Fame.

INFO-BOX

BIRTHPLACE: Guatemala City, Guatemala

CAREER: 1969–1983

CLAIM TO FAME: "The Mad Stork" was a one-man wrecking crew at linebacker on four Super Bowl teams.

Ted appeared too thin to be a lineman and too tall to be a linebacker. But his height helped him in swatting down passes or field goals. He was one of football's best kick blockers, with 25 blocked field goals and extra points. He recovered 16 fumbles and intercepted 26 passes. He shares the NFL records for most career safeties (4) and most opponents' fumbles recovered in postseason play (4).

An All-America for three years at the University of Miami, in Florida, Ted was drafted by the Baltimore Colts, in 1969. He played linebacker on the Colt team that defeated the Dallas Cowboys in Super Bowl V, in 1971. He joined the Oakland Raiders in 1975 and played on their three Super Bowl title teams.

Ted played in 215 straight games in his pro career, the most ever by a linebacker.

A Closer Look

Ted was a quarterback's nightmare. The Raiders let Ted line up on defense wherever he thought the action would be, and Ted was usually right! Opposing teams had no idea where Ted would show up.

Ted excelled on the blitz. In one playoff game, he sacked Cincinnati Bengal quarterback Ken Anderson four times in a 31–28 Raider victory. In his best season, 1980, Ted had three interceptions, two blocked kicks, a safety, and four forced fumbles.

SONJA HENIE

Sonja Henie *[SOAN-yuh HEN-ee]* of Norway is often called the greatest woman figure skater of all time. She was only 11 years old when she skated in the 1924 Winter Olympics. She finished last in the women's singles event. Two years later, she came in second at the 1926 world championships. After that, Sonja was unbeatable.

Sonja won gold medals at the 1928, 1932, and 1936 Olympics. No other woman has repeated as Olympic singles champion three times. She also won 10 consecutive world singles titles, from 1927 to 1936. Only male skater Ulrich Salchow won more world titles, 11, from 1901 to 1911.

Sonja's personality and figure-skating success made her one of the most popular people in the world. Even though the Olympics were not yet shown on television, newspaper reporters who saw her skate and interviewed her wrote stories telling how charming and beautiful she was. Newsreels (movies of news that were shown in movie theaters before television became popular) showed her graceful and stylish skating and her glamorous outfits, sometimes trimmed with fur. On occasion the police had to be called to

INFO-BOX

BIRTHPLACE: Oslo, Norway
OLYMPIC CAREER: 1924, 1928, 1932, and 1936
CLAIM TO FAME: A three-time gold medalist, Sonja was the most successful female figure skater of all time.

control the crowds at places where she was going to appear.

Skating in the 1920s and 1930s was different from the way it is today. Women did not usually perform jumps or spins, since such moves were considered unladylike. But Sonja was a spectacular skater, and she was among the first to add jumps and other moves from ballet to her programs. And her style of dress, including skirts that ended above the knee *(see below)*, came to be accepted, too.

Time Capsule

Sonja competed in the Olympics from 1924 to 1936. Here are some things that were going on in the U.S. in that time:

- 1924. The first women state governors are elected.
- 1927. Charles Lindbergh becomes the first person to fly from New York to Paris on a non-stop flight.
- 1929. The stock market crashes, leading to the Great Depression.
- 1932. Amelia Earhart becomes the first woman to pilot a plane alone across the Atlantic.
- 1933. President Franklin Delano Roosevelt names the first woman to the Cabinet.

A week after the 1936 Olympics, Sonja won her 10th world title and then retired from competitive skating. But she did not retire from performing. Sonja starred in her own ice show and became a Hollywood actress, making 11 films. She also became a millionaire. In 1969, Sonja died of leukemia, a form of cancer that attacks the blood. She was 57.

A CLOSER LOOK Before Sonja, women had skated in mid-calf-length skirts. When Sonja competed in the Olympics at age 11, she appeared in a short (slightly above the knee) fur-trimmed dress. This was allowed because Sonja was just a kid. But with the shorter skirt came the freedom to try new moves, moves that until then had been tried only by men. Sonja was also the first skater to wear skating boots that matched her outfits. Before, skaters wore only black or neutral (light brown) boots.

GOLF

BEN HOGAN

Ben Hogan concentrated so hard on his golf game that he sometimes wouldn't talk to his playing partner. He won 63 titles over his career to rank third on the Professional Golfers Association (PGA) all-time list.

Between 1948 and 1953, Ben won *eight* major tournaments: the U.S. Open four times, the Masters twice, and the British Open and the PGA Championship one time each. During that time, Ben was nearly killed when a bus hit the car he was driving head-on. He missed a year while recovering!

Ben's best year was 1953. Besides being elected to the PGA Hall of Fame, he won all three majors he played in: the U.S. Open, the Masters, and the British Open.

INFO-BOX

BIRTHPLACE: Dublin, Texas

CAREER: 1931–1970

CLAIM TO FAME: One of golf's all-time greats, Ben nearly won the Grand Slam in 1953.

BASKETBALL

NAT HOLMAN

With his passing and dribbling skills, Nat Holman helped make basketball popular in its early years.

Nat was a member of the first great pro team, the Original Celtics. The Celtics were a team from New York City. The team spent most of its time barnstorming — traveling from town to town to play local teams — and usually winning.

Nat practically invented the point-guard position. But just as important in those days, he put on a show for the fans. He invented plays that have become a part of the game, such as having the center play with his back to the basket as the pivot for the offense.

Nat became a great college coach. In 1950, he led City College of New York to the NCAA and NIT titles in the same season — the only time that has ever been done.

INFO-BOX

BIRTHPLACE: New York, New York

CAREER: 1920–1930

CLAIM TO FAME: A basketball pioneer, Nat helped make basketball the game we know today.

ROGERS HORNSBY

Rogers Hornsby's batting skill was truly awesome. From 1920 to 1925, he won a record six straight batting titles! He's the only right-hander ever to bat .400 or better three times (his .424 average in 1924 is the highest in modern baseball history). He even led the National League in homers twice.

INFO-BOX

BIRTHPLACE: Winters, Texas
CAREER: 1915–1937
CLAIM TO FAME: Rogers had a career .358 batting average and was probably the greatest right-handed hitter in baseball history.

Rogers spent most of his career at second base for the St. Louis Cardinals. He was a difficult person. He argued with teammates, and he never read because he said it hurt his batting eye. But he could hit! He was elected to the National Baseball Hall of Fame in 1942.

PAUL HORNUNG

Paul Hornung was nicknamed "Golden Boy" because of his blond hair, good looks, and sparkling talent. As a quarterback at the University of Notre Dame, he won the Heisman Trophy in 1956. As a halfback for the Green Bay Packers, he sparked the Pack to NFL titles in 1961, 1962, and 1965.

INFO-BOX

BIRTHPLACE: Louisville, Kentucky
CAREER: 1957–1966
CLAIM TO FAME: Paul was one of college and pro football's greatest all-around players.

Paul could run, pass, and kick. He led the NFL in scoring for three seasons. He scored a record 176 points in 1960. In 1961, Paul was in the Army but played on weekends. He was named NFL Player of the Year.

In 1963, Paul was suspended for gambling. He returned in 1964, but his career ended with an injury two years later. He was voted into the Pro Football Hall of Fame in 1986.

GORDIE HOWE

Gordie Howe was a giant in hockey for more than three decades. He played more seasons as a professional athlete (32) than any athlete in any team sport. Gordie was known as "Mr. Hockey" for good reason. He retired holding nearly every NHL scoring record: most goals (801), most assists (1,049), most points scored (1,850), and most games played (1,767). His records seemed untouchable . . . that is, until WAYNE GRETZKY came along.

Gordie was born on March 31, 1928, in Floral, a city in central Canada. He started playing ice hockey when he was 6. As a kid, he would practice as often as he could, even at night under a streetlight. He had little equipment, so he used newspapers for shin pads and old tennis balls for pucks.

By the time he was 18, Gordie was in the NHL, playing for the Detroit Red Wings. He started slowly, scoring only 35 goals in his first three seasons.

In his third season, Gordie suffered a horrible injury during a Stanley Cup playoff game. After a hard check, he crashed headfirst into the boards and suffered a serious brain injury. The doctors didn't know if he would pull through. After surgery, he slowly began to improve.

By his fourth season, Gordie was be-

Time Capsule

During Gordie's long career, the world changed in many ways:

- The Korean and Vietnam wars took place.
- Neil Armstrong was the first person to walk on the moon, in 1969.
- The U.S. population grew by 95 million from 1940 to 1980.
- The first Super Bowl was held, in 1967.
- John Kennedy and Martin Luther King, Junior, were assassinated.
- African-Americans were finally permitted to play major league baseball and pro basketball.
- Seven U.S. Presidents served.
- The NHL expanded from 6 teams to 21 teams.
- President Bill Clinton was born in Hope, Arkansas, in 1946 — the same year Gordie started his NHL career.

coming a great player. He was big and strong, and could skate and shoot. Once he planted himself in front of the net, he was tough to move. He led the league in scoring in three straight seasons, from 1950–51 to 1953–54. He won the Hart Trophy (as MVP) 6 times and played on the All-Star team 21 times.

INFO-BOX

BIRTHPLACE: Floral, Saskatchewan, Canada

CAREER: 1946–1971, 1973–1980

CLAIM TO FAME: For 32 seasons as a pro, Gordie was "Mr. Hockey."

Gordie first retired in 1971. He was elected to the Hockey Hall of Fame one year later. In 1973, he came back to play with his sons for the Houston Aeros in a new league, the World Hockey Association (WHA).

He played in the WHA until 1979, when the league merged with the NHL. By then, Gordie had become a member of the Hartford Whalers. After the 1979–80 season, Gordie called it quits — for good. He was 51 years old and a grandfather.

FAMILY TIES Hockey talent flowed through the Howe family. Gordie's sons, Mark and Marty, played pro hockey side-by-side with their dad on the Houston Aeros of the World Hockey Association. The Howe family took the ice together on September 25, 1973. In the 1974–75 season, Gordie's youngest son, Mark, scored more goals than his dad, but Gordie won the league's MVP award. Gordie said, "It was the most joyous year in my life." Both Mark and Marty went on to follow in their father's footsteps in the NHL.

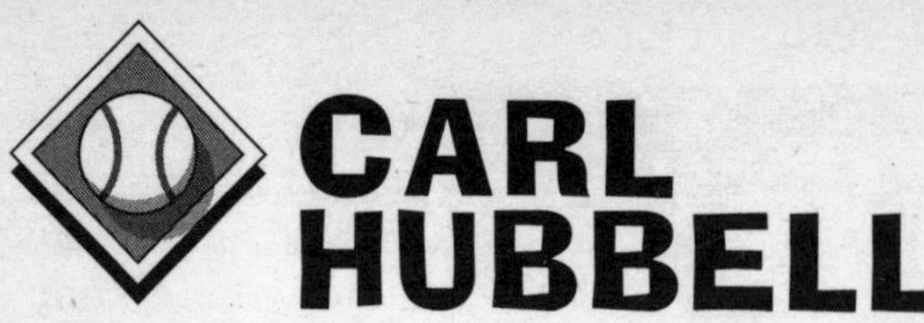

CARL HUBBELL

Carl Hubbell was one of baseball's best pitchers during a period when great sluggers, such as BABE RUTH and JIMMIE FOXX, reigned. Carl won 253 games for the New York Giants in 16 seasons. He won 20 or more games in a season five times.

His career started slowly. Carl had an unusual kind of pitch, and managers were afraid to let him throw it because they feared it would hurt his arm. The pitch was a "reverse curve" or screwball. A screwball breaks the opposite way from a curveball, and throwing it can put a strain on the arm.

Carl struggled for six seasons in the minor leagues and thought about quitting baseball. But the pitcher was at last recommended to Giants manager John McGraw, who turned Carl and his screwball loose.

Carl became known as "King Carl." In 1933, he was National League MVP after posting a 23–12 record with a 1.66 ERA and 10 shutouts. He also won two games to help the Giants win the World Series.

He won another MVP award in 1936. During his career, he led the league in wins and in ERA three times. Carl was elected to the National Baseball Hall of Fame in 1947.

INFO-BOX

BIRTHPLACE: Carthage, Missouri
CAREER: 1928–1943
CLAIM TO FAME: Carl was a great screwball pitcher and one of the National League's best hurlers ever.

AMAZING FEAT For all the great games Carl Hubbell pitched, including a no-hitter in 1929, his greatest moment on the mound may have come during the 1934 All-Star Game. Facing an American League starting lineup of future Hall of Famers, Carl put his screwball to work. After giving up a single and a walk to start the game. Carl struck out five straight All-Stars. He fanned BABE RUTH, LOU GEHRIG, and JIMMIE FOXX to end the first inning. Then he whiffed two more future Hall of Famers, Al Simmons and Joe Cronin, to start the second inning.

BOBBY HULL

Playing goalie was a dangerous job when Bobby Hull was on the ice. With a slapshot clocked at 118 miles per hour, Bobby put the puck into the net 610 times in NHL games! That's the most goals ever made from the left wing position.

Bobby also had amazing speed. He earned the nickname "The Golden Jet" because he could skate almost 30 miles per hour. That speed, combined with his powerful slapshot, made him one of the NHL's top scorers.

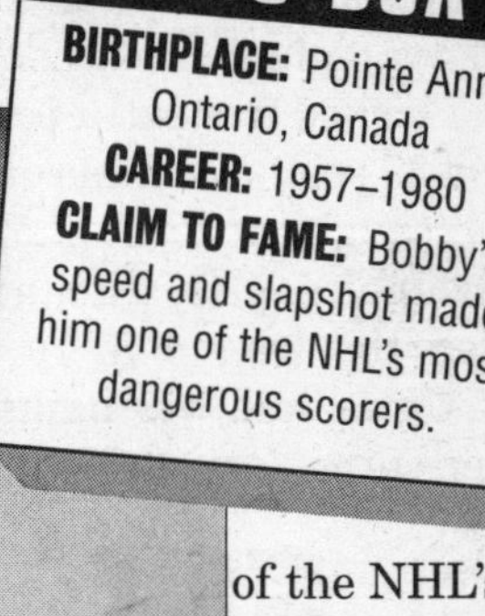

INFO-BOX

BIRTHPLACE: Pointe Anne, Ontario, Canada

CAREER: 1957–1980

CLAIM TO FAME: Bobby's speed and slapshot made him one of the NHL's most dangerous scorers.

Bobby didn't invent the slapshot, but his success helped make the slapshot popular. He was also one of the first players to use a stick with a curved blade. That allowed him to control the puck better.

In 1972, Bobby left the Chicago Black Hawks of the NHL to play in a new league called the World Hockey Association. (The WHA merged with the NHL in 1979.) Bobby played for the Winnipeg Jets for seven and a half years and ended his career on the Hartford Whalers, playing with GORDIE HOWE.

In all, Bobby spent 16 seasons in the NHL. He finished his career with three scoring titles and 12 All-Star appearances. The Golden Jet was voted Player of the Decade for the 1960s in a poll of writers and sportscasters.

Bobby was elected to the Hockey Hall of Fame in 1983. His son, Brett, is now a star player with the St. Louis Blues.

FOOTBALL

DON HUTSON

In the early years of the forward pass, Don Hutson was pro football's greatest pass catcher.

The forward pass was first allowed in the NFL in 1933. Don arrived in the league in 1935 as a member of the Green Bay Packers. He scored a touchdown on his first play in his first pro game. He led Green Bay to the 1936 NFL title. The Pack repeated as champs in 1939 and 1944.

Don could also kick. In a game in 1944, he caught four touchdown passes and kicked five extra points, for a total of 29 points — in one quarter!

Don caught at least one pass in 95 straight games, then a record. He led the league in receiving eight times, and was named NFL Player of the Year in 1941 and 1942.

INFO-BOX

BIRTHPLACE: Pine Bluff, Arkansas

CAREER: 1935–1945

CLAIM TO FAME: The first great NFL wide receiver, Don ranks third all-time in touchdown receptions with 99.

VOLLEYBALL

FLO HYMAN

Flo Hyman didn't start playing volleyball until the 10th grade. But she grew into the best volleyball player in the world. At the University of Houston, she was named the outstanding college player in the country.

Flo stood 6' 5" tall, and was a powerful spiker. As a member of the U.S. national team, she was chosen for the All-World team at the 1981 World Cup Games. She led the U.S. to a silver medal at the 1984 Olympics. Later, she played as a pro in Japan.

Tragically, Flo's life was cut short. In 1986, while in Japan, she collapsed during a game and died. Tests showed that Flo died from Marfan syndrome — a rare illness that affects connective tissue. (Connective tissue holds the body's organs together and gives them shape.) Flo was just 31 years old.

INFO-BOX

BIRTHPLACE: Los Angeles, California

CAREER: 1974–1986

CLAIM TO FAME: Flo was a volleyball legend. An award that honors female pro athletes is named after her.

MIGUEL INDURÁIN

Miguel Induráin *[een-doo-RINE]* is sometimes called "The Extraterrestrial." He is such a good cyclist that opponents swear he must come from another planet.

Miguel actually comes from Spain. But he is best known for his performance in the famed Tour de France bicycle race that takes place every year *(see page 156)*. In the Tour de France, cyclists travel more than 2,400 miles in 23 days, much of it over steep mountains. Miguel won the race *five* years in a row (1991–95). Only two other cyclists ever won it as many as four times in a row.

At 6' 2" tall and 176 pounds, Miguel is one of the biggest and strongest cyclists. He gets more strength from keeping calm during a race. But Miguel has other things going for him. His heart pumps twice as much blood per minute as a normal heart, and his lungs are larger than average.

It's no wonder other cyclists think he's from outer space!

INFO-BOX

BIRTHPLACE: Navarre, Spain
CAREER: 1985 to the present
CLAIM TO FAME: The winner of four straight Tour de France races, Miguel is the top cyclist in the world today.

BO JACKSON

Bo Jackson was the first athlete to start for teams in major league baseball and the NFL in the same year! From 1987 to 1990, Bo played outfield for the Kansas City Royals from April to October and running back for the Los Angeles Raiders from October to January. He was the first athlete chosen to play in both the baseball All-Star Game and the football Pro Bowl.

Even as a kid, Bo was a great all-around athlete. In high school, in Alabama, he set state records in track and field. As a senior, he batted .447 with 20 home runs and was drafted by the New York Yankees. But he decided to accept an athletic scholarship from Auburn University, in Alabama.

At Auburn, Bo played baseball and football. In 1984, he won the Heisman Trophy as the best college football player in the country. He was drafted by the Royals in 1986 and signed with the Raiders in 1987.

While playing baseball in 1989, Bo hit 32 homers, drove in 105 runs, and was named MVP of the All-Star Game. Then he rushed for 950 yards during the 1989 NFL season and was named to the Pro Bowl. Bo

INFO-BOX

BIRTHPLACE: Bessemer, Alabama
CAREER: 1986–1995
CLAIM TO FAME: Bo played in both baseball's All-Star Game and football's Pro Bowl.

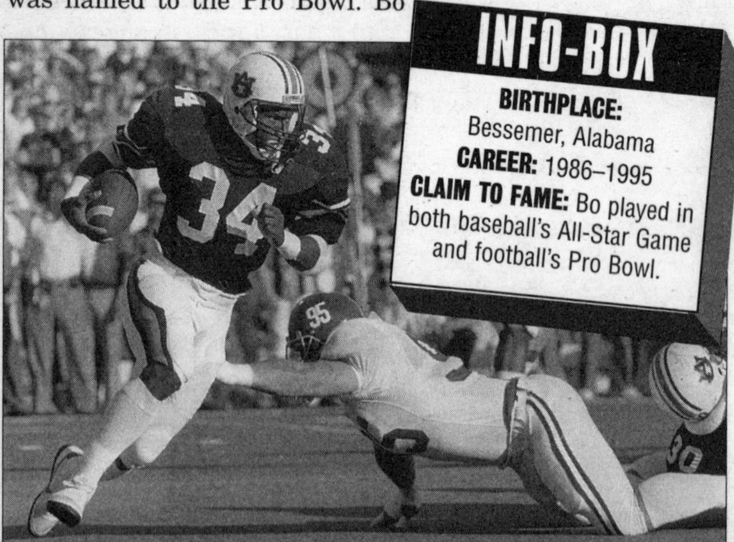

was the first running back in NFL history to run more than 90 yards for a touchdown twice.

In 1991, during a football game, Bo seriously injured his left hip. He had to undergo hip-replacement surgery. His doctors felt that he would never play baseball or football again.

Bo retired from the NFL, and he was released by the Royals. But he was determined to play baseball. After a great deal of rehabilitation, Bo was signed by the Chicago White Sox.

When He Was a Kid

As a kid, Vincent Edward Jackson stuttered when he spoke, and other kids made fun of him. He'd get angry and beat the kids up.

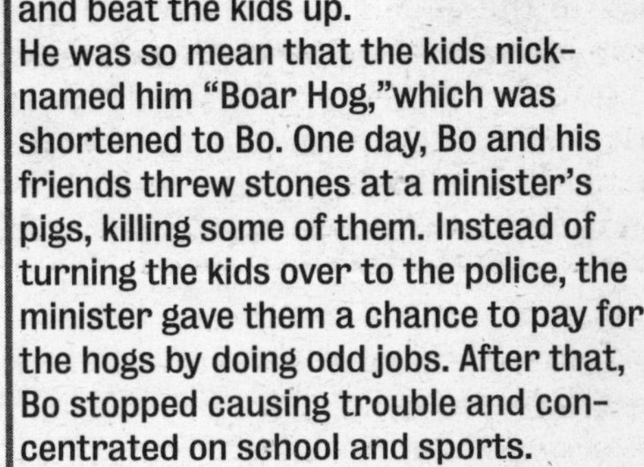

He was so mean that the kids nicknamed him "Boar Hog,"which was shortened to Bo. One day, Bo and his friends threw stones at a minister's pigs, killing some of them. Instead of turning the kids over to the police, the minister gave them a chance to pay for the hogs by doing odd jobs. After that, Bo stopped causing trouble and concentrated on school and sports.

Bo became the first athlete in history to play a major pro sport with an artificial hip. In 1993, he hit 16 home runs for the White Sox and was named Comeback Player of the Year. Bo retired from baseball in 1995 to pursue a career in acting!

ANOTHER SIDE Before Bo's mom died — three weeks after his hip surgery — he promised her that he would play baseball again and that he would give her the ball from his first hit. In his very first post-surgery at-bat, against the Yankees, he hit a homer into the right-field bleachers. Greg Ourednick, age 16, caught it. Some of the fans around him told him he could get money for the ball, but Greg remembered reading that Bo wanted the ball as a gift to his mother. Greg waited outside the clubhouse and gave Bo the ball. Bo was so happy at Greg's kindness that he autographed another ball for Greg and gave him a signed bat. Bo was planning to have the ball bronzed and attached to his mother's tombstone. "I made a promise," he said.

SHOELESS JOE JACKSON

Joe Jackson's slashing swing of his famous bat, "Black Betsy," made him one of the greatest players in baseball, but you won't find him in the National Baseball Hall of Fame.

"Shoeless Joe" — as he was called because he played barefoot in the minors — and seven of his Chicago White Sox teammates were accused of accepting money from gamblers to lose the 1919 World Series. They were tried in court and found innocent, but the baseball commissioner banned them from baseball forever.

Joe could hit! With the Cleveland Indians from 1910 to 1914, his batting average ranged between .331 and a league-leading .408. In 1912, he set an American League record by hitting 26 triples in a season!

During the 1915 season, Joe was traded to the White Sox. In the 1919 World Series — which he was supposed to be trying to lose — he batted .375! His career average of .356 is the third best in history.

Joe could barely read or write. He came from a poor family and had to work instead of attending school. Some people felt this lack of education made it easy for him to be taken advantage of by the gamblers in 1919.

INFO-BOX

BIRTHPLACE: Brandon Mills, South Carolina

CAREER: 1908–1920

CLAIM TO FAME: Joe was one of baseball's great hitters but ended up being banned from the game.

TIME CAPSULE Between 1912 and 1920, Shoeless Joe set some great records in baseball. During those years, news of other kinds was being made in the U.S. and abroad:

- 1912. Woodrow Wilson became the 28th president of the United States, and Boston's Fenway Park opened.
- 1914. An assassin gunned down Archduke Francis Ferdinand of Austria-Hungary, starting World War I.
- 1920. Because African-Americans were barred from playing minor league or major league baseball, Rube Foster founded baseball's first black league — the Negro National League.

REGGIE JACKSON

For his World Series heroics, Reggie Jackson was called "Mr. October." He played on 11 division champions, six pennant winners, and five world champions. His swing produced 563 home runs *and* the most strikeouts in baseball history (2,597).

Reggie played on three World Series champs with the Oakland A's, from 1972 to 1974. He was American League MVP in 1973, when he led the league in home runs (32) and RBIs (117).

Signed by the New York Yankees in 1976, Reggie led New York to three pennants and two world championships. He gave his greatest performance in Game 6 of the 1977 World Series. Reggie hit three home runs in three straight at-bats, each on the first pitch! He was named Series MVP.

A 14-time All-Star, Reggie also played for the Baltimore

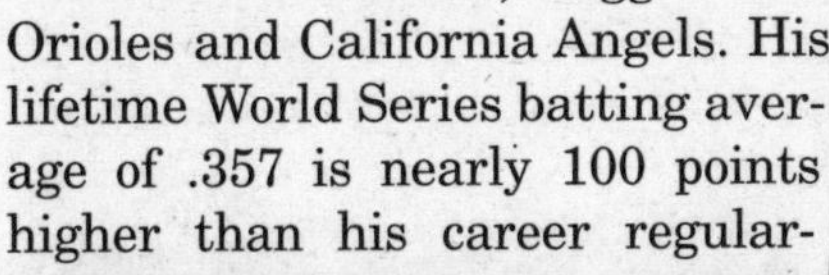

Orioles and California Angels. His lifetime World Series batting average of .357 is nearly 100 points higher than his career regular-season average. He hit more than 30 homers in a season seven times and drove in more than 100 runs six times. He was elected to the National Baseball Hall of Fame in 1993.

INFO-BOX

BIRTHPLACE: Wyncote, Pennsylvania

CAREER: 1967–1987

CLAIM TO FAME: Called "Mr. October," Reggie was one of baseball's greatest World Series performers.

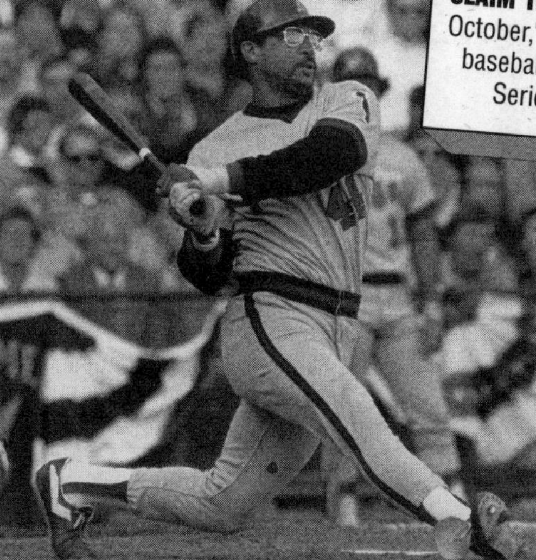

BASKETBALL

MAGIC JOHNSON

His name was Earvin Johnson, Junior, but on the basketball court he was known simply as "Magic." Magic was a 6' 9" guard who could score, pass, rebound, and steal the ball. His skills helped him to become a champion on every level he played. He helped the Los Angeles Lakers win five NBA championships in the 1980's.

As a kid growing up in Michigan, Magic was already an outstanding player. He always scored a lot of points, which annoyed the parents of other kids he played with. To keep everyone happy, Magic begin working on passing the ball to his teammates so that they could shoot. From then on, Magic was known for his unselfish team play.

Magic became a star player in high school, where he led his team to the Michigan state championship in 1977. He then moved on to Michigan State University. In 1979, he led the Spartans all the way to the NCAA championship with a victory over Indiana State Uni-

INFO-BOX

BIRTHPLACE: Lansing, Michigan

CAREER: 1979–1992

CLAIM TO FAME: Magic was one of the greatest passers and most exciting players in NBA history.

versity and its star, LARRY BIRD, in the title game.

The Lakers made Magic the first pick overall in the 1979 NBA draft. Magic responded with one of the best rookie seasons in NBA history. He led the Lakers to the 1980 NBA title, becoming the only rookie ever to be named MVP of the NBA Finals. Magic would lead the Lakers to four more NBA titles. Over his career, he averaged 19.7 points, 7.3 rebounds, and 11.4 assists per game.

Amazing Feat

The Lakers were ahead three games to two in the 1980 NBA Finals. One more win over the Philadelphia 76ers and they would capture the NBA title. But the Laker center, 7' 2" KAREEM ABDUL-JABBAR, was injured and couldn't start in Game 6. Los Angeles made a bold move and started Magic Johnson at center. At 6' 9", Magic was big for a guard, but he was small for a center. Plus, he hadn't played a game at the position since high school. No problem. Magic scored 42 points to go along with 15 rebounds and 7 assists as the Lakers won the game and the championship.

In 1991, Magic retired from the league after he learned he had the HIV virus, which causes AIDS. (He tried to come back for the 1992–93 season but retired again after training camp.) He left as the all-time leader in assists, with 9,921.

But Magic had one more championship to win. As part of the first Dream Team, he won a gold medal at the 1992 Olympics.

ANOTHER SIDE Magic and LARRY BIRD first met on the court at the NCAA championship and joined the NBA the same year. Their teams, Magic's Lakers and Larry's Celtics, competed for the NBA title three times, with the Lakers winning twice. It was an intense rivalry, but over the years, the two players developed a deep respect for each other. Larry cried when he learned that Magic had acquired the HIV virus. After they had both retired, Magic appeared at a ceremony in Boston honoring Larry. Magic opened up his Laker jacket so that Larry could see what he was wearing underneath — a Celtic T-shirt!

BOXING

JACK JOHNSON

Jack Johnson was the first African-American to win the world heavyweight boxing championship. He defeated the champion, Tommy Burns, in Australia, in 1908.

Many white people disliked the fact that a black man had won the title. Former champion James Jeffries, who was white, came out of retirement just to fight Jack in 1910. He was called "The Great White Hope." But James couldn't match Jack's powerful right hand and lost.

In 1915, Jack lost his title to Jess Willard, in Havana, Cuba. He died in a car crash in 1946.

INFO-BOX

BIRTHPLACE: Galveston, Texas

CAREER: 1897–1928

CLAIM TO FAME: Jack was the first African-American to become the heavyweight boxing champion.

BASEBALL

WALTER JOHNSON

Walter "Big Train" Johnson set many pitching records, despite playing for the Washington Senators, a team that often finished near the bottom of the American League standings.

Walter's 1913 season was one of the best in history. He led the A.L. in wins (36), earned run average (1.09), complete games (29), innings pitched (346), and strikeouts (243).

Over his career, Walter threw 110 shutouts, the most in big-league history. His 416 lifetime wins are second only to CY YOUNG's 511.

Walter pitched the Senators to their only World Series championship, in 1924. In 1936, he was one of the first players elected to the National Baseball Hall of Fame.

INFO-BOX

BIRTHPLACE: Humboldt, Kansas

CAREER: 1907–1927

CLAIM TO FAME: A two-time MVP, "Big Train" was the American League's best pitcher for two decades.

BOBBY JONES

Bobby Jones was golf's best amateur player, but he beat professionals, too. Between 1923 and 1930, he won the U.S. Amateur title five times, the U.S. Open four times, and the British Open three times. After becoming the only player ever to win golf's Grand Slam *(see below)*, in 1930, Bobby retired at age 28. He never played professionally.

INFO-BOX

BIRTHPLACE: Atlanta, Georgia

CAREER: 1916–1930

CLAIM TO FAME: An amateur player, Bobby is the only person ever to win the Grand Slam of golf.

Bobby grew up near a golf course, in Atlanta, Georgia. He constantly practiced the game. He won a junior championship at age 9 and broke par (the score a good adult player would shoot for the course) at age 11.

Besides being a sportsman, Bobby was also a fine student. He earned college degrees in literature and law from Harvard and Georgia Tech universities.

Bobby was a star in the Walker Cup, which matches the best amateurs from the United States against the best amateurs from Great Britain. He played 10 matches in the Walker Cup and lost only once.

After he retired, Bobby helped create the Masters tournament and design its golf course, Augusta National, in Georgia. It has become one of the most famous golf courses in the world.

How It Works

The major tournaments of men's golf are the Masters, the U.S. Open, the British Open, and the PGA Championship. A player who wins all four in one year is said to win the Grand Slam. No pro golfer has ever won *that* Grand Slam. In 1930, Bobby won the U.S. Open, the U.S. Amateur, the British Open, and the British Amateur titles. He is considered to have won a Grand Slam. Even though he never played professionally, Bobby is in the Professional Golfers Association Hall of Fame!

MICHAEL JORDAN

Michael Jordan became the greatest basketball player ever by combining natural ability with the drive to work hard.

As a kid, Michael was just an average player. His dad built a basketball court in the backyard so Michael could practice anytime. At first, Michael had to settle for playing on the junior varsity in high school, but that only made him work harder.

The work paid off: Michael made the varsity his junior year. By the time he was a senior, he had grown to 6' 3" and was being recruited by top colleges. He chose the University of North Carolina (UNC). Michael became a starter in his freshman season and hit the winning shot in the 1982 NCAA championship game to give UNC its first national title. At UNC, he was twice named College Player of the Year.

Michael entered the NBA draft after his junior season. He was selected by the Chicago Bulls with the third pick. Before he joined the Bulls, he helped lead the U.S. basketball team to a gold medal at the 1984 Olympics.

Over the course of his NBA career, the 6' 6" guard has been Rookie of the Year, a nine-time All-Star, and a three-time NBA MVP. Along with winning seven straight scoring titles, from the 1986–87 season to the 1992–93 season, Michael set records for most points in a playoff game (63), highest scoring average in the NBA Finals (41.0, in

Another Side

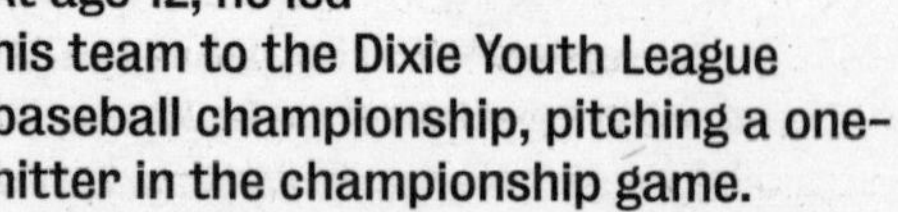

Growing up, Michael's favorite sport was baseball. He played shortstop and pitcher. At age 12, he led his team to the Dixie Youth League baseball championship, pitching a one-hitter in the championship game.

After Michael retired (temporarily, as it turned out) from the NBA, in 1993, the Chicago White Sox signed him to a minor league contract. He played the 1994 season with the Birmingham Barons, as a right fielder. He batted .202, with three home runs, 51 RBIs, and 30 stolen bases.

INFO-BOX

BIRTHPLACE: Brooklyn, New York
CAREER: 1984–1993, 1995 to the present
CLAIM TO FAME: Michael is the greatest pro basketball player ever.

1993), and highest scoring average for a career (32.3).

But Michael's game isn't all scoring. He has made the NBA's All-Defensive team six times and was the Defensive Player of the Year in 1988. He led the Bulls to three straight NBA titles from 1991 to 1993 and was the MVP of the Finals each year. He won a second gold medal at the 1992 Olympics.

Michael's father was murdered after the 1992–93 season. Michael decided to retire from the NBA, saying he "had nothing left to prove." But after a season in baseball *(see page 136)*, Michael returned to the NBA. Despite having been away so long, he led the Bulls to the second round of the playoffs.

DID YOU KNOW?

- In high school, Michael practiced with both the junior varsity and varsity teams every night.
- In the NBA, Michael wears his UNC Carolina Blues shorts under his Bulls uniform for good luck.
- Michael idolized his older brother, Larry, when he played in high school. Larry wore uniform number 45. So, hoping to be half as good as Larry, Michael took 23 as *his* number!

JACKIE JOYNER-KERSEE

Jackie Joyner-Kersee is one of the world's greatest female athletes ever. As a little girl, she dreamed of competing in the Olympics. At the 1988 Olympics, Jackie won her first gold medal, in the seven-event heptathlon, and set a world record by scoring 7,291 points. She then won the gold medal in the long jump five days later. At the 1992 Olympics, she won a gold medal in the heptathlon and a bronze medal in the long jump.

Jackie became interested in sports at a youth center in her hometown of East St. Louis, Illinois. Her training there helped her excel in track and field, basketball, volleyball, and soccer.

After high school, she accepted a basketball scholarship to the University of California at Los Angeles. She starred on the team, but what Jackie really wanted to do was run track. She got permission from her basket-

INFO-BOX

BIRTHPLACE: East St. Louis, Illinois

OLYMPIC CAREER: 1984, 1988, 1992

CLAIM TO FAME: Jackie is the greatest woman athlete of the past 50 years.

ball coach to go out for the track-and-field team.

Track coach Bob Kersee saw Jackie's explosive speed and decided to train her for the heptathlon, a two-day competition in women's track and field in which athletes compete in the 100-meter hurdles, the high jump, the shot put, the 200-meter run, the long jump, the javelin, and the 800-meter run. Jackie won two NCAA heptathlon titles and a silver medal in the event at the 1984 Olympics. A year after graduating from college, she married Coach Kersee.

When She Was a Kid

Even before Jackie took up track and field, she played soccer. She started playing when she was 9. Jackie loved it because it was a sport girls and boys could play together. Between the ages of 10 and 15, she attended summer camp for soccer.

Jackie says her soccer training helped her compete in the heptathlon. She still kicks a ball around with her husband/coach, Bob Kersee. She also gives demonstrations at youth soccer camps.

Besides her Olympic victories, Jackie won the 1987 world championship in the heptathlon and the 1991 world title in the long jump. In 1994, she set a U.S. record with a 24' 7" long jump. She also holds several U.S. records in the indoor hurdles.

Jackie, who turned 33 in 1995, has competed with injuries. She also suffers from asthma, an illness that makes it difficult to breathe. Still, she wants another shot at the Olympics and hopes to make it to the 1996 Games in Atlanta, Georgia.

FAMILY TIES In Los Angeles, California, on August 4, 1984, Jackie and her brother, Al Joyner, became the first brother and sister to win Olympic medals in track and field on the same day. Al won the gold medal in the triple jump, and Jackie won the silver medal in the heptathlon. They are not the only athletes in the family. Al's wife is FLORENCE GRIFFITH JOYNER, and Jackie's husband, Bob, is a coach. Sisters-in-law Jackie and FloJo combined to win five gold medals at the 1988 Summer Olympics.

JOAN JOYCE

During a 20-year career, Joan Joyce pitched 110 no-hitters, including 35 perfect games. Her fastball was clocked at 118 miles per hour, and she struck out more than 6,000 batters. She once pitched 157 scoreless innings in a row! A career .323 hitter, she often led her team, the Raybestos Brakettes of Stratford, Connecticut, in batting, too.

Joan was named an All-America by the American Softball Association for 18 straight seasons. She was MVP of the annual tournament eight times.

A standout basketball player in school, Joan was also good enough at golf to play on the Ladies Professional Golfers Association tour after her softball days were over.

INFO-BOX

BIRTHPLACE: Waterbury, Connecticut

CAREER: 1958–1977

CLAIM TO FAME: With a 507–33 record, Joan was the best women's softball pitcher of all time.

DUKE KAHANAMOKU

Duke Kahanamoku was the son of a policeman. But his name suggested royalty, and he was the king of two sports!

A native of Hawaii, Duke spent his boyhood on the beach, where he swam and surfed. He became the best surfer in Hawaii.

As a swimmer, Duke was the best freestyler in the world for more than a decade. He won gold medals in the 100 meters at the 1912 and 1920 Olympics and in the 4 x 200-meter relay in 1920.

In his travels, Duke visited many beaches and gave surfing demonstrations. He helped popularize the sport in the U.S.

INFO-BOX

BIRTHPLACE: Honolulu, Hawaii

CAREER: 1911–1932

CLAIM TO FAME: Duke was a champion swimmer and is known as "The Father of Surfing."

KIP KEINO

Before Kip Keino, there were no world-famous African runners. Kip started something: Today, many of the world's best distance runners come from Africa.

Kip came from Kenya, a country in eastern Africa. He did most of his training in the mountains, about 6,000 feet above sea level. At high altitude, there's less oxygen and the body has to work harder. That helped Kip get in great shape.

In 1965, Kip set world records in the 3,000-meter and 5,000-meter runs. At the 1968 Olympics, which were held in Mexico City, Mexico (about 7,200 feet above sea level), Kip won a silver medal in the 5,000 meters and a gold in the 1,500 meters.

INFO-BOX

BIRTHPLACE: Kipsamo, Kenya

OLYMPIC CAREER: 1964, 1968, and 1972

CLAIM TO FAME: Kip was the first great runner to come out of Africa.

TRACK & FIELD

JIM KELLY

Jim Kelly is one of the top quarterbacks in the NFL today. He led the Buffalo Bills to a record four straight Super Bowls (all losses) between 1991 and 1994.

Jim played quarterback *and* linebacker for his high school team. He was was recruited to play linebacker for Penn State University! But Jim wanted to pass and enrolled at the University of Miami (in Florida), where he broke a school passing record with 5,228 career yards.

One of six quarterbacks chosen in the first round of the 1983 NFL draft, Jim joined the United States Football League instead. He played with the league's Houston Gamblers before joining the Bills in 1986.

Jim was the top-rated quarterback in the NFL in 1990 and led the league in touchdown passes, with 33, in 1991.

INFO-BOX

BIRTHPLACE: Pittsburgh, Pennsylvania

CAREER: 1984 to the present

CLAIM TO FAME: Jim led the Buffalo Bills to four Super Bowl appearances.

FOOTBALL

BASEBALL

HARMON KILLEBREW

Harmon Killebrew was a soft-spoken, friendly man. But he struck such fear into pitchers that he was called "Killer."

An infielder, Harmon played 21 of his 22 seasons with the Washington Senators–Minnesota Twins (the team moved in 1960). He launched 40 or more home runs in a season eight times and led the American League in home runs six times. In 1969, he was named the league's Most Valuable Player.

Harmon finished his career with 573 homers — fifth on the all-time list. He hit a homer every 14.3 times he came to the plate, third-best in big-league history.

INFO-BOX

BIRTHPLACE: Payette, Idaho
CAREER: 1954–1975
CLAIM TO FAME: A Hall of Famer, "Killer" was one of the greatest home run hitters in American League history.

SKIING

JEAN-CLAUDE KILLY

Jean-Claude Killy equaled an amazing record (set by Austrian skier Toni Sailer, in 1956) when he won all three Alpine skiing events at the 1968 Winter Olympics: the downhill, the slalom, and the giant slalom. (The super-giant slalom and Alpine combined were added later.) The 1968 Games were held in France, and Jean-Claude quickly became a national hero.

Jean-Claude grew up near the French Alps. He won the overall World Cup titles in 1967 and 1968. (The World Cup is a series of international races that make up the winter sports season.)

Jean-Claude later helped organize the 1992 Winter Olympics in Albertville, France.

INFO-BOX

BIRTHPLACE: Saint-Cloud, Seine-et-Oise, France
COLYMPIC CAREER: 1964 and 1968
CLAIM TO FAME: Jean-Claude swept the Alpine races at the 1968 Olympics.

BILLIE JEAN KING

Billie Jean King won 12 Grand Slam singles titles during her career, and was ranked as the world's Number 1 player five times. But more people remember her as the woman who helped women's pro tennis grow.

Billie Jean grew up in California. When she was a kid, she played many sports, including baseball. She discovered tennis when she was 11. In 1961, when she was 17, Billie Jean and Karen Hantze became the youngest team to win the doubles title at Wimbledon. Billie Jean went on to become one of only eight women to win at least one singles title at each of the four Grand Slam events *(see page 71)*.

BIRTHPLACE: Long Beach, California

CAREER: 1966–1983

CLAIM TO FAME: Billie Jean was a Number 1–ranked tennis player and a champion of women's rights in sports.

Billie Jean was a strong voice for women's rights, both on the court and off. In 1973, she beat Bobby Riggs, a great tennis player in the 1930s and 1940s, in a nationally televised match. Bobby had bragged that he could beat any woman. Billie Jean's win helped convince people that women should earn the same amount of money at the sport as men did.

Billie Jean helped found the Women's Tennis Association and was its first president.

VOLLEYBALL

KARCH KIRALY

Karch Kiraly *(ker-EYE)* was the best volleyball player in the world in the mid-1980s, and he's still going strong. Karch led the U.S. to gold medals in the 1984 and 1988 Olympics. He then became a star on the professional two-man beach-volleyball circuit.

Karch's father had been a fine volleyball player, and he pushed his son to excel at volleyball and in school. Karch led Santa Barbara High School (in California) to a state championship. He also graduated third in his class of 800 students.

At the University of California at Los Angeles, Karch led the Bruins to three NCAA championships. He was also on the team that won the world championship in 1986.

INFO-BOX

BIRTHPLACE: Jackson, Michigan

CAREER: 1982 to the present

CLAIM TO FAME: Karch is the greatest U.S. volleyball player of all time.

GYMNASTICS

OLGA KORBUT

Olga Korbut led the way for female gymnasts to be more athletic and acrobatic.

Olga was 17 years old at the 1972 Olympics. She dazzled spectators during the all-around competition, but then fell during a daring performance on the uneven parallel bars. She cried afterward — winning the sympathy of millions who watched in person and on television. Though she came in seventh in the all-around, the 4' 11" tall teenager was the crowd favorite.

Then, during the individual events, Olga shone. She won a silver medal on the uneven parallel bars and gold medals for the balance beam and floor exercise. She was the first person to do a back-flip on the balance beam. She won another gold medal as a member of the winning Soviet team.

INFO-BOX

BIRTHPLACE: Grodno, Soviet Union (now Russia)

OLYMPIC CAREER: 1972 and 1976

CLAIM TO FAME: Olga was a pioneer of athletic moves in women's gymnastics.

JOHANN OLAV KOSS

It's hard to say whether speed skater Johann Olav Koss of Norway will be remembered more for his gold-medal-winning performances at the 1994 Olympics or for his generosity.

Johann was favored to win the three distance events at the 1992 Winter Olympics, but he became sick a week before the Games. He still won the gold medal in the 1,500 meters and the silver medal in the 10,000 meters.

At the 1994 Olympics, in Lillehammer, Norway, Johann won three gold medals, set three world records, and became a national hero. In the 10,000 meters, he broke his own world record by almost 13 seconds!

After winning the 1,500 meters, Johann donated a $30,000 bonus from his sponsors to an organization called Olympic Aid. The organization raises money to buy food, clothing, and other supplies for people in needy countries. Johann also auctioned off his speed skates to raise another $90,000.

For all that he achieved in 1994, *Sports Illustrated* named Johann its Sportsman of the Year.

INFO-BOX

BIRTHPLACE: Oslo, Norway

OLYMPIC CAREER: 1992 and 1994

CLAIM TO FAME: Johann is as well known for his humanitarian efforts as for his four Olympic gold medals.

Another Side

Johann has retired from skating and become a medical student. But he has not retired from being generous. After the Olympics, he asked the children of Norway to donate their used sports equipment to kids in the poor African nation of Eritrea. Johann later traveled to Eritrea to deliver the equipment — about 12 tons' worth! In Norway, Johann also has helped organize the Johann Olav Koss Run, which encourages disabled and able-bodied athletes to participate together.

SANDY KOUFAX

Sandy Koufax once grew so frustrated with playing baseball he considered quitting. But with hard work, the left-hander became an All-Star pitcher for the Los Angeles Dodgers.

Sandy had a blazing fastball, but he had trouble getting it over the plate. In 1961, a Dodger coach noticed that Sandy's windup blocked his view of the strike zone. Sandy fixed that, and for the next six seasons he was the best pitcher in baseball.

From 1961 to 1966, Sandy won 129 games and lost only 47. He won a Most Valuable Player award, three Cy Young Awards, four strikeout titles, and five consecutive ERA titles. In addition, he pitched four no-hitters, including a perfect game. He helped the Dodgers win four pennants and three World Series.

INFO-BOX

BIRTHPLACE: Brooklyn, New York

CAREER: 1955–1966

CLAIM TO FAME: Sandy was the best pitcher in the major leagues for six seasons.

Sandy's arm began to hurt him, and doctors advised him to stop pitching. He retired in 1966. In 1972, at the age of 36, he became the youngest man ever elected to the National Baseball Hall of Fame.

JERRY KRAMER

Jerry Kramer was a three-time Pro Bowl lineman, but he is best remembered for one block. It came in the 1967 NFL Championship Game, known as the "Ice Bowl." The temperature on the field was measured at 46 below zero, with the wind chill.

With 16 seconds left, the Packers trailed the Dallas Cowboys but had the ball on the Dallas 1-yard line. Jerry made a critical block against a bigger opponent, which allowed quarterback Bart Starr to score the winning touchdown.

The Packers won their third straight title and advanced to win their second straight Super Bowl.

INFO-BOX

BIRTHPLACE: Jordan, Montana

CAREER: 1958–1968

CLAIM TO FAME: Jerry was a great offensive lineman on five Green Bay Packer championship teams.

GUY LAFLEUR

Guy Lafleur was a scoring machine for the Montreal Canadiens in the mid-1970s. His goals and assists from the center and right wing positions helped power the Canadiens to five Stanley Cup championships, including four straight from 1976 to 1979. Guy was the centerpiece of a team that symbolized speed, grace, and clean play.

In the 1976–77 season, Guy won the Hart Trophy (as MVP), the Ross Trophy (as top scorer), and the Smythe Trophy (as playoff MVP). Over his career, Guy won three scoring titles and two MVP awards and was selected for the All-Star Game six times.

Guy retired, joined the Hockey Hall of Fame, and made a comeback before he retired for good.

INFO-BOX

BIRTHPLACE: Thurso, Quebec, Canada

CAREER: 1971–1985, 1988–1991

CLAIM TO FAME: Guy led the Montreal Canadiens to five Stanley Cups.

BASEBALL

NAPOLEON LAJOIE

Napoleon Lajoie *[la-JOY]* was the American League's first superstar. He started out with the Philadelphia Phillies of the National League but joined the A.L. in its first season, 1901. He played for the Philadelphia Athletics. The second baseman batted .422 with 14 home runs and 125 RBIs to win the Triple Crown!

The next year, Nap was sold to the league's Cleveland team, the Blues, and he made that franchise a success. For a time the team was known as the Naps. (In 1915, the name was changed to the Indians.)

In 1937, Nap was one of the second group of players elected to the National Baseball Hall of Fame.

INFO-BOX

BIRTHPLACE: Woonsocket, Rhode Island
CAREER: 1896–1916
CLAIM TO FAME: A career .338 hitter, Nap was the American League's first big star.

FOOTBALL

JACK LAMBERT

Jack Lambert was about 20 pounds lighter than most middle linebackers of his time. But he made up for that by becoming one of the best tacklers in football history.

As a rookie in 1974, Jack became the starting middle linebacker for the Pittsburgh Steelers. He quickly became a key part of the team's famed "Steel Curtain" defense. He was named the NFL's Defensive Rookie of the Year that season, and the Steelers won their first Super Bowl. They ended up winning four Super Bowls over a six-year span, and Jack was the defensive captain for two of those teams.

Jack was voted into the Pro Football Hall of Fame in 1990.

INFO-BOX

BIRTHPLACE: Mantua, Ohio
CAREER: 1974–1984
CLAIM TO FAME: Jack was a hard-hitting linebacker on the Pittsburgh Steeler teams that won four Super Bowls.

JOE LAPCHICK

In the early days of pro basketball, Joe Lapchick starred at center for the Original Celtics, a team from New York City.

Joe was playing for money by the time he was 15 years old. At 17, he was 6' 5" tall and was often hired to play against the Original Celtics. When he was 23, the Celtics asked him to join them.

The Original Celtics were one of the great teams in basketball, and Joe and NAT HOLMAN were its biggest stars.

Joe later became an outstanding coach — at St. John's University, in New York, and with the New York Knicks in the NBA.

INFO-BOX

BIRTHPLACE: Yonkers, New York

CAREER: 1915–1936

CLAIM TO FAME: At 6' 5" tall, Joe was the star center on basketball's first great professional team.

BASKETBALL

STEVE LARGENT

Steve Largent wasn't the best athlete ever to play wide receiver in the NFL, but he had great hands, ran precise patterns, and used his head to outwit defenders.

When Steve retired after 14 seasons with the Seattle Seahawks, he held the NFL records for most receptions (819), most receiving yards (13,089), and most receiving touchdowns (100) in a career. All three records have since been broken, but it took three players to do it!

Steve caught at least one pass in 177 straight games, a span of 13 seasons. That was also a record until ART MONK broke it in 1994.

In 1994, Steve was elected to the U.S. House of Representatives by voters in his home state, Oklahoma.

INFO-BOX

BIRTHPLACE: Tulsa, Oklahoma

CAREER: 1976–1989

CLAIM TO FAME: Although not a fast runner, Steve was one of the NFL's all-time great wide receivers.

FOOTBALL

ROD LAVER

Only two male players have ever won the Grand Slam in tennis *(see page 71)*. But only one player, Rod Laver, has won the Grand Slam twice!

In 1962, Rod won the Grand Slam as an amateur. The next year, he turned professional. At that time, pros were not allowed to play in Grand Slam tournaments. In 1968, that rule was changed. A year later, Rod won the Grand Slam again!

Rod grew up in Australia. He was small, but he became very strong by working on his father's cattle ranch. As a tennis player, he was known as "The Rocket." He got the nickname as a joke: Though strong, he was a slow runner, so when he joined the Australian Davis Cup team, the coach decided to tease him a bit! (The Davis Cup is a team tennis competition among countries.)

Despite his size and speed, Rod became one of the most dominant amateur and professional players of his time. In 1962, he won 19 of the 34 tournaments he entered. And in 1969, he won 17 of his 32 tournaments. During his career, he won a total of 47 pro singles tournaments, including 11 Grand Slam singles titles.

The Rocket was inducted into the International Tennis Hall of Fame in 1981.

INFO-BOX

BIRTHPLACE: Rockhampton, Queensland, Australia
CAREER: 1955–1977
CLAIM TO FAME: Rod is the only tennis player to win two Grand Slams — once as an amateur and once as a pro.

TIME CAPSULE Rod won his second Grand Slam in 1969. That was also a big year for some other folks:

- In July, U.S. astronaut Neil Armstrong became the first person to walk on the moon.
- For three days in August, an estimated 300,000 people gathered on a farmer's field in upstate New York to hear many rock bands perform. The concert was known as the Woodstock Music and Arts Festival.
- The "Amazing" New York Mets, the worst team in baseball since the club had been formed in 1962, shocked the baseball world by winning the World Series.

SUGAR RAY LEONARD

"Sugar Ray" Leonard was the most popular boxer of the 1980s. He was a graceful fighter with a handsome smile and a knack for showmanship. Sugar Ray became the first boxer to win titles as a professional in five divisions (welterweight, junior middleweight, middleweight, super middleweight, and light heavyweight), and the first to earn $100 million in purses.

Ray first became popular at the 1976 Olympic Games, in which he won the gold medal as a light welterweight. As a pro, he thrilled fans with his lightning-quick hands and fancy footwork. In 1979, he won his first world title by beating Wilfred Benitez for the WBC welterweight championship.

INFO-BOX

BIRTHPLACE: Wilmington, South Carolina
CAREER: 1976–1991
CLAIM TO FAME: Sugar Ray was the first fighter ever to win titles in five weight classes.

In perhaps his greatest fight, Sugar Ray had to put on weight to fight previously unbeaten middleweight champion Marvelous Marvin Hagler. It was a bruising fight, but Ray won in a decision.

In November 1982, Ray "retired" following an operation to repair an eye damaged by boxing. He would retire and come out of retirement to fight five times. When he retired for good, in 1991, he had a career record of 36–2–1, with 25 knockouts.

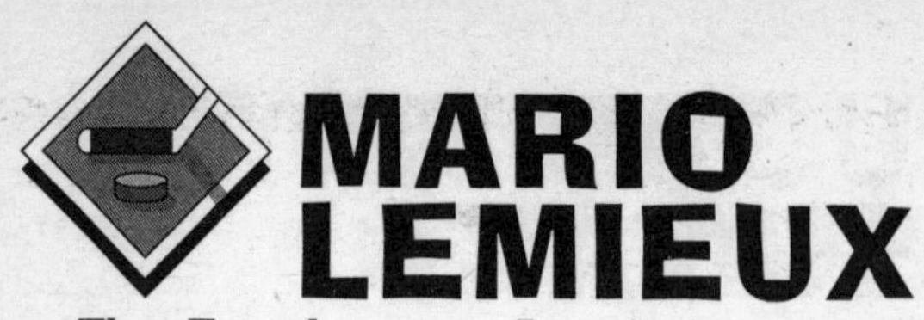

MARIO LEMIEUX

The French name *Lemeiux* means "the best." Mario Lemieux has lived up to his name. The 6' 4" center has been a powerful force in the NHL for 10 seasons.

"Super Mario" led the Pittsburgh Penguins to their first and second Stanley Cup championships. He scored 1,000 career points faster than anyone in NHL history besides Wayne Gretzky, and he won four NHL scoring titles. Mario's career has been interrupted by injuries and illness, but not before he had made his mark as one of the best players ever.

Mario grew up in Montreal, Canada. He loved ice hockey. When he was very young, Mario taught himself to skate by holding on to a chair and pushing it around a rink near his house. His dad helped him when he grew a little older: He would pack the front hallway of their house with snow so Mario and his two brothers could practice skating indoors!

By the time Mario was old enough to play in the Quebec Major Junior Hockey League, he had become a local legend. He played three seasons for the Laval Voisins team, where his point total was the highest in league history.

The Penguins chose Mario with the first pick of the 1984 NHL draft. In his first game, Mario scored a goal on the first shot he took! That year, he scored 100 points (43 goals and 57 assists), won the All-Star Game's MVP award, and was named NHL Rookie of the Year.

A Closer Look

For the Canada Cup series in 1987, Mario and Wayne Gretzky played together for Team Canada. Wayne played center and Mario right wing. They led Canada to the Cup.

During the series, Wayne helped Mario understand just how good he could be. "He gave me a lot of confidence in myself," Mario said. "Super Mario" scored a tournament-high 11 goals. Nine of them were set up by "The Great One," Wayne Gretzky.

In 1988, Mario won his first scoring title. He also won the Hart Trophy as the NHL's MVP. In 1991, he led the Penguins to their first Stanley Cup championship. The Pens repeated in 1992, and Mario was super once again. He won the Conn Smythe Trophy as the MVP of the playoffs in both championship runs.

INFO-BOX

BIRTHPLACE: Montreal, Quebec, Canada
CAREER: 1984 to the present
CLAIM TO FAME: Until illness and injury slowed him, Mario was the NHL's best player.

Mario was slowed by injuries (mostly to his back). He missed a lot of games but still led the Penguins in scoring year in and year out. In 1993, Mario learned he had Hodgkin's disease, a form of cancer. He finished the 1993–94 season, but then decided to sit out the 1994–95 season to recover from the disease and his injuries.

AMAZING FEAT In January 1993, Mario learned he had Hodgkin's disease, a form of cancer that attacks the lymph nodes in the body and stops the body's ability to fight infection. Surgeons removed the cancer, and Mario had two months of radiation treatment to kill off leftover cancer cells. Radiation can make a person feel weak and tired. Mario was not expected to play any more games in 1993. But he returned to the ice on March 2, 1993, just 12 hours after his final treatment. He played 20 minutes, and had one goal and one assist.

CARL LEWIS

Carl Lewis is the most successful track-and-field athlete of all time. He has won 18 United States, world, and Olympic championships.

Carl, who grew up in Willingboro, New Jersey, came from a family of athletes. Both his mother and father ran track in college and became teachers and track coaches. His sister, Carol, was an Olympic long jumper. Carl's sports hero was JESSE OWENS.

Carl himself started competing in track-and-field events when he was 8. In high school, he set a U.S. high school long-jump record of 26' $8\frac{1}{4}$". He attended the University of Houston (Texas) on a track scholarship.

At the 1983 world championships, Carl won gold medals in the 100-meter dash, the 400-meter relay, and the long jump. At the 1984 Olympics, Carl won four gold medals — in the 100-meter and 200-meter dashes, the 400-meter relay, and the long jump. That matched the feat that Jesse Owens had achieved at the 1936 Olympics.

But Carl didn't stop there. At the 1988

BIRTHPLACE: Birmingham, Alabama

CAREER: 1980 to the present

CLAIM TO FAME: With eight Olympic gold medals, Carl is the greatest track-and-field athlete in U.S. history.

Olympics, he won a gold medal in the long jump, becoming the only man to win two Olympic golds in that event. He won a silver medal in the 200 meters, and he finished second in the 100 meters — but was awarded the gold medal after the first-place finisher, Ben Johnson, of Canada, was found to have used illegal drugs to help him run faster.

Another Side

He sprints. He jumps. He sings. Carl Lewis has sung the national anthem at sporting events and even recorded an album, in 1985, called *The Feeling That I Feel.* His single "Break It Up" was such a hit in Sweden it earned him a gold record. The album was also successful in Japan. Carl recorded another album, in 1987, that also did well in Europe. It seems that everything Carl touches turns to gold.

At the 1991 world championships, Carl was 30 years old, older than most sprinters. But he blazed through the 100 meters to set a new world record of 9.86 seconds. (That record was lowered to 9.85 by U.S. sprinter Leroy Burrell, in 1994.)

Carl was golden again at the 1992 Olympics, winning in the long jump and the 400-meter relay. At the 1993 world championships, he won a bronze medal in the 200 meters.

Will Carl run and jump at the 1996 Olympics? He isn't talking about quitting. "I'll retire when the moment comes when I run my best race and can't win anymore," he says.

DID YOU KNOW?

- Although he never played football or basketball in high school, Carl was drafted by the NFL's Dallas Cowboys and the NBA's Chicago Bulls.
- Carl's sister, Carol, was a world-class long-jumper. In 1983, she ranked Number 1 in the U.S. and third in the world. Carol was a member of three U.S. Olympic Teams.
- When Carl was young, the kids in the neighborhood didn't think he was much of an athlete. When they chose teams on the playground, "everybody else would be picked first," recalls an old friend. "Then it would be, 'Okay, you get Carl.'"

GREG LEMOND

Greg LeMond won the prestigious Tour de France cycling race three times between 1986 and 1990.

Greg began cycling when he was 14 years old, taking long bicycle trips with his father. A year later, he rode in his first race. In 1984, he entered his first Tour de France and finished third. He was the first non-European competitor ever to finish in the top three. He won the race for the first time in 1986.

In 1987, Greg broke his wrist in a pileup in a European race. He was about to return to competition when he was accidentally shot by his brother-in-law while hunting. Greg suffered severe internal injuries. When he finally recovered, he had to undergo an emergency appendectomy, and then was sidelined by an infection in his right shin.

INFO-BOX

BIRTHPLACE: Lakewood, California

CAREER: 1980–1994

CLAIM TO FAME: A three-time winner of the Tour de France, Greg was the best cyclist in U.S. history.

He was back for the Tour de France in 1989. Nobody expected him to win, but he did. A few weeks later, Greg won the world championship to become one of only five cyclists to win a Tour de France and a world title in the same year.

Greg continued his success in 1990 by winning the Tour de France for the second year in a row. Two years later, he won the Tour DuPont in the United States. He retired in 1994.

A CLOSER LOOK The Tour de France is more than 2,000 miles long and takes 23 or 24 days to complete. It is a "stage" race. In a stage race, each day there is a new race, or stage. The overall winner of the race is the person who rides all the stages in the least time. The course, which is different every year, is dangerous and exhausting. The riders must go up and down mountain terrain and, at times, they can reach dangerous speeds of 70 miles per hour. The Tour always finishes in Paris, but past races have crossed into Belgium, Switzerland, Spain, Italy, and England.

NANCY LIEBERMAN

Nancy Lieberman was one of the best women basketball players ever. She grew up playing against boys on the outdoor courts of New York City. As a 16-year-old high school student, she was the youngest member of the U.S. Olympic women's basketball team that won a silver medal at the 1976 Games.

At Old Dominion University, in Virginia, Nancy was a 5' 10" forward and point guard. Averaging 18.1 points and 7.2 assists per game during her college career, she led the team to national titles in 1979 and 1980. In both years she was named the Collegiate Woman Athlete of the Year.

After college, Nancy played in two pro leagues — the Women's Professional Basketball League and the Women's American Basketball Association — but both quickly folded. In 1986, she played briefly in a game in the United States Basketball League, a men's minor league. She was the first woman ever to play in a men's pro game.

INFO-BOX

BIRTHPLACE: Brooklyn, New York

CAREER: 1976–1986

CLAIM TO FAME: Nancy was one of the all-time greats — and a pioneer — in women's basketball.

NANCY LOPEZ

Nancy Lopez burst onto the professional golf scene in 1978. In her first pro season, she won nine tournaments, including a record five in a row and the Ladies Professional Golf Association (LPGA) Championship. She was Rookie of the Year and Player of the Year. She brought a lot of attention to her sport.

Nancy learned the game from her father, Domingo, and picked it up easily. She won the New Mexico Women's Amateur Championship at the age of 12, and at 15, she won the first of her two United States Golf Association (USGA) Junior Girls titles. The next year, she entered the U.S. Women's Open as an amateur and finished second.

INFO-BOX

BIRTHPLACE: Torrance, California

CAREER: 1977 to the present

CLAIM TO FAME: Nancy's exciting — and winning — play helped make women's golf a major sport.

Nancy turned pro at the age of 20 and won 17 of the first 50 tournaments she entered. Entering 1995, Nancy had won 47 tournaments, including three LPGA titles. She has been Player of the Year four times. In 1987, at age 30, she became the youngest member of the LPGA Hall of Fame *(see box at right)*.

Nancy's husband, Ray Knight, is a former professional baseball player. Playing for the New York Mets, Ray was World Series MVP in 1986.

How It Works

Players are not *voted* into the LPGA Hall of Fame. They have to win entry. You must be a member of the LPGA for at least 10 straight years. You also have to win a combination of two major tournaments and 30 regular tour events, one major and 35 regulars, or no majors and 40 regulars. The majors are the U.S. Women's Open, the Mazda LPGA Championship, the du Maurier Classic, and the Nabisco Dinah Shore.

GREG LOUGANIS

With gold-medal performances in 1984 and 1988, Greg Louganis became the first male diver to win both the springboard and platform events in two Olympics in a row. (Female diver Patty McCormick, of the U.S., did it in 1952 and 1956.)

Greg's Olympic highlight film actually begins in 1976. At age 16, he earned a silver medal. At the 1984 Olympics, he won the springboard by the largest margin in Olympic history. In 1988, he won the springboard even after hitting his head on the board early in the event and receiving stitches.

Had it not been for the U.S. boycott of the 1980 Olympics, in Moscow (the U.S. did not compete to protest the Soviet Union's attack on Afghanistan), Greg might have won medals in four consecutive Olympics. He did win five world titles.

In 1995, Greg revealed that he had the HIV virus, which causes AIDS (and that he had had the virus while competing at the 1988 Olympics). Greg said he wanted to show people who have the AIDS virus that they could still lead productive lives.

INFO-BOX

BIRTHPLACE: San Diego, California

OLYMPIC CAREER: 1976, 1984, and 1988

CLAIM TO FAME: Graceful and acrobatic, Greg was the greatest diver of all time.

BOXING

JOE LOUIS

Joe Louis was heavyweight champion of the world longer than any other boxer. He ruled the division for 11 years, 8 months, and one week, from June 1937 to March 1949. "The Brown Bomber," as he was called, was the first African-American to become a sports hero to both black and white people in the United States.

Joe fought Max Schmeling of Germany in two of the biggest fights in boxing history. Their first fight took place in 1936. In that contest, Max knocked Joe out in the 12th round.

The following year, Joe won the heavyweight title from James Braddock. But he never forgot that frustrating defeat by Max. "I won't be champion until I get that Schmeling," he said.

In 1938, Joe and Max fought a rematch. A lot of tension surrounded this fight because World War II was about to begin — and Germany and the United States would be on opposite sides. When Joe knocked out the German fighter in the first round, he became a national hero!

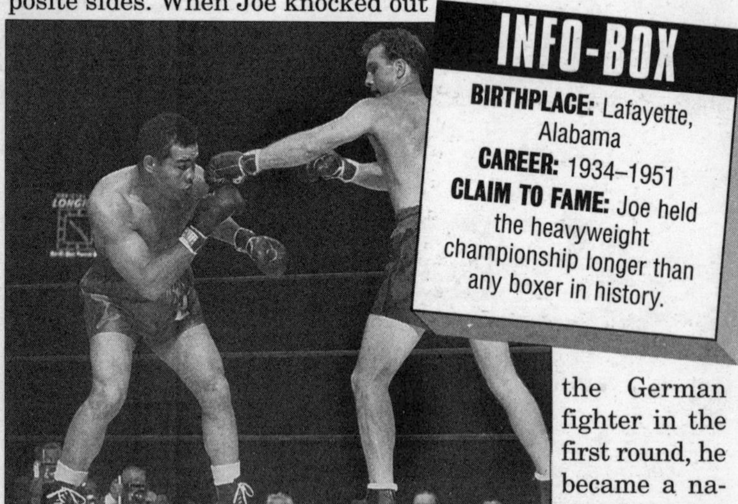

INFO-BOX

BIRTHPLACE: Lafayette, Alabama

CAREER: 1934–1951

CLAIM TO FAME: Joe held the heavyweight championship longer than any boxer in history.

In all, Joe fought a record 25 successful title defenses. He retired as champion in 1949, but he later attempted a comeback. In the comeback he was 8–2. He finally retired for good with a record of 63–3, with 49 of those victories by knockout.

RONNIE LOTT

What quarterback JOE MONTANA did for the offense of the great San Francisco 49er teams of the 1980s, Ronnie Lott did for the defense. With Ronnie protecting against the pass, the 49ers won four Super Bowls.

Ronnie, who had been an All-America at the University of Southern California, became the heart and soul of the 49er defense as a rookie, in 1981. Ronnie returned three interceptions for touchdowns that season, and the 49ers won their first Super Bowl.

INFO-BOX

BIRTHPLACE: Albuquerque, New Mexico

CAREER: 1981 to the present

CLAIM TO FAME: Ronnie is one of the NFL's hardest hitters and all-time best defensive backs.

While roaming the defensive backfield for the 49ers, and later for the Los Angeles Raiders and New York Jets, Ronnie has been a leader by example. He is known for making bone-crunching tackles that make wide receivers think twice about catching the ball in his territory.

But Ronnie's reputation as a hard hitter should not take away from the fact that he is also a great pass defender. He has led the league in interceptions twice (in 1986 and 1991), and his 63 career interceptions (through 1994) rank fifth on the NFL's all-time list. He joined the Kansas City Chiefs in 1995.

HOW IT WORKS Ronnie Lott has been voted to the Pro Bowl 10 times, the first four times as a cornerback and the next six as a safety. Both positions are parts of a team's defensive backfield, which is made up of two cornerbacks, a free safety, and a strong safety. The cornerbacks cover the opposition's two main wide receivers. The free safety is a team's "center fielder." He lines up behind the rest of the defense, free to cover a third receiver or help the cornerbacks. His job is to go to where he thinks the ball will be going. The strong safety lines up on the strong side of the field (the side that the tight end lines up on). He sometimes covers the tight end, sometimes covers wide receivers, and sometimes moves up to help stop the running game.

FOOTBALL

HANK LUISETTI

Angelo "Hank" Luisetti popularized the one-handed push shot, using one hand at the side of the ball to guide it and the other hand behind the ball to shoot it — the way players shoot today. Until the mid-1930s, the two-handed set shot had been the only accepted way to shoot.

Hank began using the new shot as a kid. He wore leg braces and couldn't squat to take a set shot, so he pushed the ball to the basket.

He perfected his shooting at Stanford University, where he was twice named Collegiate Player of the Year. Eventually, everyone began using Hank's way of shooting.

INFO-BOX

BIRTHPLACE: San Francisco, California

CAREER: 1934–1938

CLAIM TO FAME: Hank never played pro ball, but his shooting style changed the game of basketball.

JOHN MACKEY

As a Baltimore Colt in the 1960s, John Mackey changed the way tight end was played.

Before John came along, tight ends were used mostly to block. Few caught passes. But not only could John catch the football, he was also as strong as a bull. It almost always took more than one player to tackle him.

John was also a fast runner who could catch long passes. In Super Bowl V, in 1971, he caught a 75-yard touchdown pass that helped the Colts beat the Dallas Cowboys!

As head of the players association in the 1970s, John led the battle for free agency, which today gives players who qualify the right to sign with the team of their choice. In 1992, he became the third tight end ever elected to the Pro Football Hall of Fame.

INFO-BOX

BIRTHPLACE: Queens, New York

CAREER: 1963–1972

CLAIM TO FAME: John helped make tight end into an important offensive position.

PHIL MAHRE

Phil Mahre was the first U.S. skier to win an Olympic gold medal in Alpine skiing and the first to win a World Cup title *(see page 142)*.

Phil and his twin brother, Steve, grew up in the Cascade Mountains of Washington. Both began skiing when they were very young. Phil went on to win seven U.S. championships.

About a year before the 1980 Olympics, Phil injured his left ankle. He competed in the Olympic slalom with a three-inch metal plate and four screws in his ankle, and still won a silver medal!

From 1981 to 1983, Phil was World Cup Alpine champ. He won his Olympic gold medal in 1984, with brother Steve taking the silver.

INFO-BOX

BIRTHPLACE: Yakima, Washington
OLYMPIC CAREER: 1976, 1980, and 1984
CLAIM TO FAME: Phil was the most successful Alpine skier in U.S. history.

KARL MALONE

Karl Malone is known as "The Mailman" because he always delivers. In his first 10 seasons with the Utah Jazz, the powerful 6' 9" tall, 255-pound forward averaged 26 points and 11 rebounds per game.

Karl played his college ball at Louisiana Tech, a small school. But he still became an NBA first-round draft pick. In Utah, Karl teamed up with point guard JOHN STOCKTON to form one of the most productive offensive duos in basketball history.

Karl was among the league leaders in scoring and rebounding in nine of his first 10 seasons. He played on the Dream Team, which won the gold medal at the 1992 Olympic Games. In 1993, Karl and John became the first players from the same team ever to share the All-Star Game MVP Award.

INFO-BOX

BIRTHPLACE: Summerfield, Louisiana
CAREER: 1985 to the present
CLAIM TO FAME: An awesome scorer and rebounder, "The Mailman" is the top power forward in the NBA today.

GREG MADDUX

Atlanta Brave pitcher Greg Maddux has been almost unhittable on the mound. The right-hander won a record three straight Cy Young Awards, from 1992 to 1994!

Greg is not an overpowering pitcher, but he understands how to pitch. He relies on his control and knows how to mix up his breaking ball, change-up, and fastball.

Greg was a hotshot as a teenager coming out of Las Vegas Valley High School, in Las Vegas, Nevada. He was an all-state baseball first-teamer in his junior and senior seasons. And when he wasn't on the mound baffling batters, he was playing center field.

The Chicago Cubs selected Greg with their number two pick in the 1984 amateur draft. Greg decided to sign with the Cubs instead of accepting a baseball scholarship to college. After nearly three years in the minor leagues, he got the chance to pitch for the Cubs. In 1986, he won two games and lost four.

The 1988 season was a breakout season for Greg: He won 18 games! He followed it up with a 19-win season in 1989 and led the Cubs to the National League East pennant.

Greg had 15 victories in 1990 and in 1991. He also won a Gold Glove award for his fielding, and set a major league record for most putouts by a pitcher in a nine-inning game, with seven.

With a 20–11 record in 1992, Greg won the first of his three Cy

When He Was a Kid

If anyone had had a hint that Greg would become a baseball superstar, it was his older brother, Mike. Greg used to tag along when Mike went to play baseball games with his friends. Greg was so good that the older kids would ask him to play with them. That happened back when Mike (who later pitched for the Philadelphia Phillies and the New York Mets) was 11 years old and Greg was only 6!

Young Awards. He signed with the Atlanta Braves as a free agent after the 1992 season, and his winning ways continued. Greg won another 20 games and a second straight Cy Young Award that season. He also led the Braves to their third straight appearance in the National League Championship Series. But his best was yet to come.

INFO-BOX

BIRTHPLACE: San Angelo, Texas

CAREER: 1986 to the present

CLAIM TO FAME: Greg is the best pitcher in baseball today.

In 1994, Greg had a great season, even though it was shortened by the strike. He had 16 wins, a league-leading 1.56 ERA, 10 complete games, 3 shutouts, and 156 strikeouts. The National League honored him with the Cy Young Award for the third straight season.

FAMILY TIES Greg and Mike Maddux actually faced each other in a major league game in 1986. Greg was pitching for the Cubs, and Mike for the Philadelphia Phillies. Greg's team won, 8–3. Mike gave up only three earned runs but still got the loss. It was the only time in major league baseball history that two brothers faced each other as rookie starting pitchers.

When was the previous time Greg and Mike pitched against each other? "The last time I faced him was in the backyard, playing Wiffle ball," Mike said. "We both hit about .700 that day."

MICKEY MANTLE

Few players in the history of baseball had as much talent as Mickey Mantle. The New York Yankee centerfielder was a powerful switch-hitter. Before he was slowed by leg injuries, he was also one of the fastest runners in baseball.

"The Mick" played his first major league game when he was 19 years old, and he went on to play 18 seasons with the Yankees. He hit 536 home runs (more than any switch-hitter in baseball history) and played for eight World Series champions. He was a 16-time American League All-Star and was named the league's MVP in 1956, 1957, and 1962.

Mickey's greatest year was 1956, when he became one of only 14 players to hit for the Triple Crown — he led the league in home runs (52), RBIs (130), and batting average (.353).

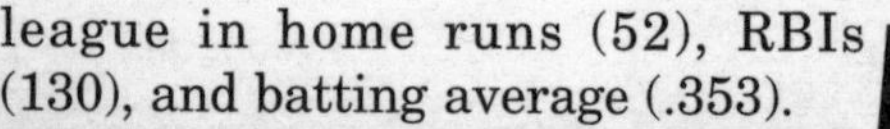

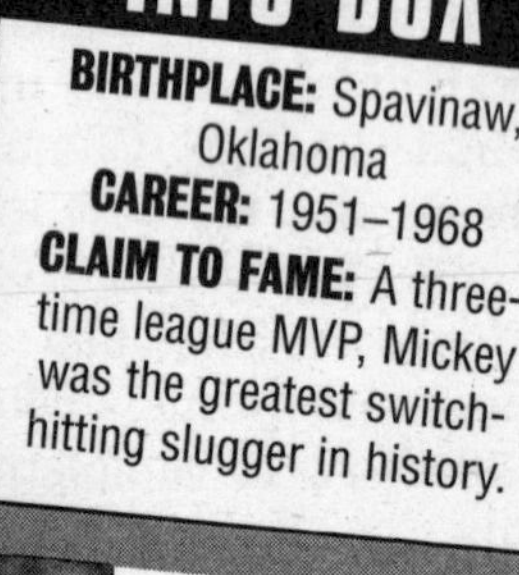

INFO-BOX

BIRTHPLACE: Spavinaw, Oklahoma
CAREER: 1951–1968
CLAIM TO FAME: A three-time league MVP, Mickey was the greatest switch-hitting slugger in history.

In 1974, Mickey was elected to the National Baseball Hall of Fame. He later said that he might have been a better player if he had not drank so much alcohol. He developed liver disease, and died of cancer in 1995.

DIEGO MARADONA

Diego Maradona is one of the world's greatest soccer players. People have often compared him to PELÉ.

At age 19, he led Argentina to victory in the 1979 Junior World Cup. Seven years later, he scored five goals and led his country to the World Cup championship. In 1990, with Diego on the field, Argentina again reached the finals of the World Cup, but they were beaten by Germany, 1–0.

In 1994, Diego was found guilty of taking an illegal drug during the World Cup. He was banned from competition for 15 months. He hoped to make a fresh start by rejoining his old club in Argentina.

INFO-BOX

BIRTHPLACE: Buenos Aires, Argentina
CAREER: 1976 to the present
CLAIM TO FAME: A brilliant playmaker, Diego has led Argentina to the World Cup finals twice.

PETE MARAVICH

Nobody in college basketball history has ever scored like Pete Maravich. He averaged 44.2 points a game for his career!

Pete grew up with a basketball spinning on his finger. He attended college at Louisiana State University, where he set the three highest marks in NCAA Division I history for most points scored in a season and scored more points in his career than anyone else (3,667).

In 10 NBA seasons, Pete averaged 24.2 points a game. In 1976–77, with the New Orleans Jazz, he led the league with 31.1 points per game.

Pete retired in 1980. He died of a heart attack in 1988 while playing pickup basketball in a church gym. He was 40 years old.

INFO-BOX

BIRTHPLACE: Aliquippa, Pennsylvania
CAREER: 1970–1980
CLAIM TO FAME: "Pistol Pete" is college basketball's single-season and all-time scoring champion.

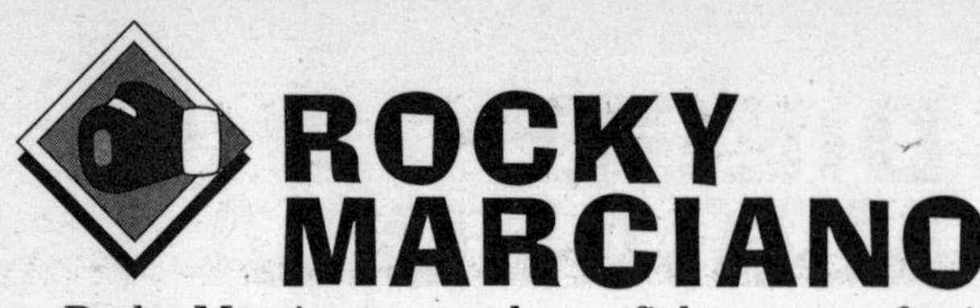

ROCKY MARCIANO

Rocky Marciano never lost a fight as a professional boxer. He was knocked down — but never out — only twice in his career. Although small for a heavyweight (5' 10", 185 pounds), he was one of the division's most powerful punchers.

Known as "The Brockton Blockbuster," Rocky wasn't a fancy fighter. He would take a punch from an opponent just to land a harder one. As a winner, Rocky never gloated. When he knocked out JOE LOUIS, ending that great champion's career, Rocky called it "the saddest punch of my life."

Rocky won the heavyweight championship from Jersey Joe Walcott, in 1952. It was Rocky's 43rd fight, and in it he was dropped to the canvas for the first time in his career. Still, he got up to knock out Jersey Joe in round 13.

During his pro career, Rocky won all 49 of his fights, 43 by knockout. It is still the longest winning streak by any heavyweight boxer ever!

After he KO'd Archie Moore, in 1955, Rocky retired. He was still at the top of his career, but he wanted to spend time with his family.

Tragically, Rocky died in an airplane crash in 1969.

DAN MARINO

In his 13th year as the Miami Dolphins' quarterback, Dan Marino is still treasured for his golden arm, his sharp eyes, and his quick release when throwing the ball. He's had a record-breaking career and earned himself a sure spot in the Pro Football Hall of Fame.

Dan played college football in his hometown of Pittsburgh, Pennsylvania. He led the University of Pittsburgh Panthers to three 11–1 seasons and into a major bowl game four times. As a junior, he was MVP of the Sugar Bowl.

He was drafted by the Dolphins in 1983. Dan was named NFL rookie of the year and became the only rookie quarterback ever to start in the Pro Bowl.

The next season, Dan set records for touchdown passes in a season (48), most passing yardage (5,084), most completions (362), and most games with 300 or more passing yards (9). He led the Dolphins to the Super Bowl (they lost to the San Francisco 49ers) and was named NFL Player of the Year.

Dan has kept on firing! By the time he retires, he is likely to hold every major NFL career passing record.

INFO-BOX

BIRTHPLACE: Pittsburgh, Pennsylvania

CAREER: 1983 to the present

CLAIM TO FAME: Dan is on track to finish his career as the greatest passer in NFL history.

MORE STARS! Dan couldn't have broken all of those NFL records if not for a great offensive line protecting him. From 1983 to 1990, the Dolphins gave up the fewest sacks in the NFL. Richmond Webb, the Dolphin left tackle, has been a Pro Bowl player in each of his five NFL seasons. The left tackle is the most important lineman for a right-handed quarterback such as Dan. He keeps defenders such as Reggie White and Bruce Smith from tackling Dan from behind, where Dan can't see them. Dan's other great linemen have included Pro Football Hall of Famers Bob Kuechenberg and Dwight Stephenson and Pro Bowl players Ed Newman, Roy Foster, and Keith Sims.

WILLIE MAYS

On a baseball field, Willie Mays could do it all: He could hit for average, hit for power, run, throw, and play great defense. He has been called the most complete player of all time.

In high school, Willie starred in baseball, basketball, and football. In 1948, at the age of 17, he was playing in the Negro leagues (major league baseball did not start accepting black players until 1947) and showing off his many skills.

In 1950, the New York Giants baseball team bought Willie's contract. He was called up from the minors in 1951. Although he started his major league career with an 0-for-22 slump, Willie's first hit in the majors was a home run off pitcher WARREN SPAHN, who became a Hall of Famer! Willie was named Rookie of the Year, and the Giants went on to win the National League pennant that season.

Willie served in the U.S. Army in 1952 and 1953 but returned to baseball and an amazing career. In 1954 and 1965, he was named the league's Most Valuable Player. He was elected to 20 All-Star teams during his 22-year career. His 660 home runs are the third most in major league history.

Known as the "Say Hey Kid" because he would greet his teammates with "Say hey," Willie was spectacular not only at the plate and in the field but also on the bases. He won four straight stolen-base titles, from 1956 to 1959.

Willie loved playing in New York City and became a folk hero in the streets of Harlem, a

Amazing Feat

Willie made one of the greatest fielding plays in baseball history. In Game 1 of the 1954 World Series, with the Giants playing the Cleveland Indians, the score was tied, 2–2. With two men on in the eighth, the Indians' Vic Wertz hit a fly to deep center field. Willie made an over-the-shoulder "miracle catch" nearly 440 feet from home plate. The Indians' threat was stopped, and the Giants went on to sweep the Series.

neighborhood in the borough of Manhattan. He often visited there to play stickball in the streets with kids. When the Giants moved to San Francisco in 1958, Willie's fans were heartbroken.

BIRTHPLACE: Westfield, Alabama
CAREER: 1951–1952, 1954–1973
CLAIM TO FAME: Willie may have been the most complete baseball player ever.

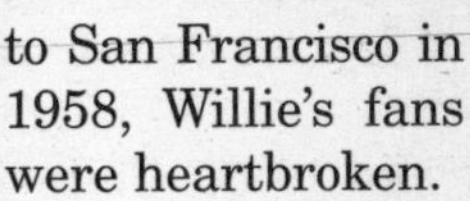

In the outfield, Willie could make even the hardest plays look easy. His famous "basket catch," in which he caught a ball at his waist with his glove turned up and open, became his trademark. His 7,095 putouts are a major league record for an outfielder.

In 1972, Willie was traded to the New York Mets and received a hero's welcome back to New York City. He helped the Mets into the World Series in 1973, where they lost to the Oakland Athletics. He retired after that season and was elected to the National Baseball Hall of Fame in 1979.

MORE STARS! From 1951 to 1957, New York City was home to three of the greatest center fielders of all time: Willie Mays of the New York Giants, MICKEY MANTLE of the New York Yankees, and Duke Snider of the Brooklyn Dodgers. All three hit more than 400 career home runs each and became Hall of Famers. In the time they all roamed New York City outfields, their teams met in the World Series five times. Two of the three teams moved to California in 1958: the Giants to San Francisco and the Dodgers to Los Angeles.

CHRISTY MATHEWSON

Christy Mathewson was one of the great pitchers of the early 1900s. He won 373 games, tying him with Grover Cleveland Alexander for third all-time.

In college, Christy starred in three sports. He was a member of the literary society and class president.

With the New York Giants, he won at least 30 games in a season four times. In 1908, he won 37 games!

In 1925, Christy died from a lung disease caused by poison gas he had inhaled during World War I. In 1936, he was one of the first group of players elected to the National Baseball Hall of Fame.

INFO-BOX

BIRTHPLACE: Factoryville, Pennsylvania
CAREER: 1900–1916
CLAIM TO FAME: "Matty the Great" was one of the best pitchers and best-loved players of the early 1900s.

BOB MATHIAS

In 1948, at age 17, Bob Mathias became the youngest person ever to win the Olympic decathlon. He went on to become the first person to win two straight Olympic decathlons.

Before reaching his first Olympics, Bob won the national decathlon championship. Just three months earlier, he had never competed in most of the decathlon events! (The decathlon has 10 events: the 100-meter dash, 110-meter hurdles, 400-meter run, 1,500-meter run, shot put, discus throw, javelin, pole vault, long jump, and high jump.)

In 1952, Bob beat the second-place finisher in the decathlon by the largest margin in Olympic history. He later appeared in four movies and served as a U.S. congressman for eight years.

INFO-BOX

BIRTHPLACE: Tulare, California
OLYMPIC CAREER: 1948 and 1952
CLAIM TO FAME: Bob was the first athlete to win two Olympic decathlons.

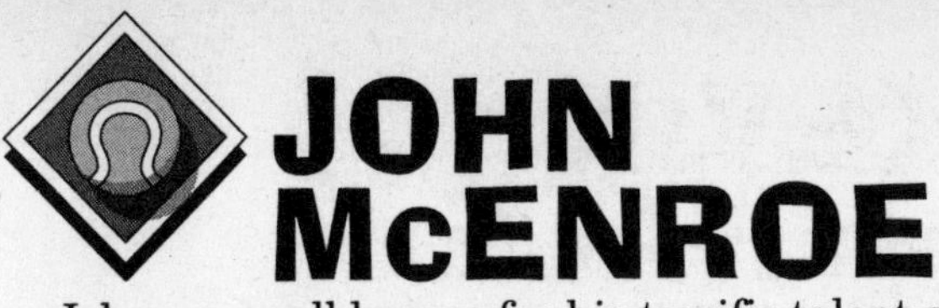

JOHN McENROE

John was well known for his terrific talent and his terrible temper on the tennis court. He grew up in Queens, New York. In 1977, when he was 18, John and his childhood friend, Mary Carillo, won the mixed doubles title at the French Open. Later that year, he became the youngest male to reach the semi-finals at Wimbledon.

John was a genius on the tennis court. Though not a natural athlete, he had a great serve, was a crafty shotmaker, and was fearless about rushing the net. Those skills helped him win three Wimbledon titles and four U.S. Open titles. During his career, John won 77 tournaments; only JIMMY CONNORS and Ivan Lendl *(see page 187)* won more.

But John also had his flaws. He demanded perfection of himself and those around him, and when he didn't get it, he screamed at officials and threw temper tantrums on the court. John was often fined for his behavior, and at the 1990 Australian Open, he became the first player ever to be thrown out of a Grand Slam event.

John retired in 1992 and no longer plays official tournaments. He works as a tennis analyst on television.

INFO-BOX

BIRTHPLACE: Weisbaden, West Germany (now Germany)

CAREER: 1977–1991

CLAIM TO FAME: John was probably the best shotmaker in tennis history.

BASKETBALL

KEVIN McHALE

Kevin McHale was one of the key players on the great Boston Celtic teams of the 1980s. At 6' 10" tall, with amazingly long arms, Kevin was a great rebounder and shot blocker. Close to the basket, he could score almost at will. He had a career average of 17.9 points per game.

With his barrel chest and long arms, Kevin was awkward-looking as a boy. But he became a star at the University of Minnesota. The Celtics drafted him third overall in 1980. Led by Kevin, LARRY BIRD, and Robert Parish, Boston made the NBA Finals five times in the 1980s and won three times.

INFO-BOX

BIRTHPLACE: Hibbing, Minnesota

CAREER: 1980–1993

CLAIM TO FAME: Kevin was one of the best inside players in pro basketball history.

HOCKEY

MARK MESSIER

Mark Messier has played on six Stanley Cup champion teams, five times with the Edmonton Oilers. The sixth came in 1994, when the 6' 1" center guided the New York Rangers to their first Cup in 54 years. Mark is the first player ever to be captain of two different Stanley Cup championship teams.

Mark was 17 years old when he turned pro, with the World Hockey League. At 18, he was drafted into the NHL by the Edmonton Oilers. By the end of the 1983–84 season, he had his first championship ring.

Mark was traded to the New York Rangers at the beginning of the 1991–92 season. That season, he was named league MVP.

INFO-BOX

BIRTHPLACE: Edmonton, Alberta, Canada

CAREER: 1979 to the present

CLAIM TO FAME: Mark has been a key member of six Stanley Cup champion teams.

GEORGE MIKAN

BASKETBALL

George Mikan was the NBA's first star and its first big player. At 6' 10" and 245 pounds, he might not seem that big by today's standards. But in the 1940s and 1950s, the average player was much smaller.

George wasn't a natural athlete. As a high school player in Joliet, Illinois, he was cut from his school team. When he entered DePaul University, his coach helped him develop his basketball skills. George then became a three-time All-America! As a junior and senior, he was College Player of the Year.

George played nine years of pro basketball, averaging 22.6 points per game. He led the Minneapolis Lakers to five championships between 1949 and 1954. (The team moved to Los Angeles in 1960.) In 1950, an Associated Press poll named George the greatest player of the first half of the 20th century.

George retired when he was just 29 years old. He coached the Lakers for part of a season and was later the first commissioner of the American Basketball Association.

INFO-BOX

BIRTHPLACE: Joliet, Illinois

CAREER: 1946–1956

CLAIM TO FAME: A dominating big man, George was the first star attraction of the newly formed NBA.

SHANNON MILLER

When Shannon Miller started gymnastics classes at the age of 5, who knew she would become the Number 1 gymnast in the world? Shannon won five medals at the 1992 Olympics and the world all-around championships in 1993 and 1994.

Shannon first learned how good she could be when she was 8 years old. She and her mom traveled to Russia, where she met and trained with some of the world's best gymnasts and coaches. One coach told Shannon's mom that Shannon had the potential to be a champion if she got the proper coaching.

Back home, in Oklahoma, Shannon began training with coach Steve Nunno, who had been an assistant to legendary coach Bela Karolyi *(see pages 70 and 213)*. Coach Nunno drove Shannon hard. She trained six days a week.

But all that hard work paid off. In 1991, Shannon became the national balance beam champion. At the 1991 World Gymnastic Championships, she helped the U.S. team win the silver medal.

About six weeks be-

INFO-BOX

BIRTHPLACE: Rolla, Missouri

CAREER: 1990 to the present

CLAIM TO FAME: A two-time world champion, Shannon is the most successful gymnast in U.S. history.

fore the 1992 U.S. championships, Shannon injured her elbow and needed surgery. It didn't keep her from competing, though.

Shannon made the U.S. Olympic Team and went on to compete at the 1992 Games, in Barcelona, Spain. Although she wasn't expected to be the U.S. star, she won five medals — two silvers and three bronzes — more than any other U.S. athlete at the Barcelona Olympics.

Did You Know?

- At the 1992 Olympics, Shannon was the shortest and lightest U.S. athlete. She was 4' 6" tall and weighed 69 pounds. She is now 4' 11" tall and weighs 93 pounds.
- Shannon gets more than 100 fan letters a week. Her dad, Ron, sorts the mail and makes sure she answers all the requests for autographs, pictures, and information.
- In her free time, Shannon likes to play with Dusty, her golden retriever. Dusty's picture is in the gold locket she wears.

Shannon continued her winning ways at the world championships in 1993. She won gold medals in the all-around competition and two individual events (floor exercise and uneven bars), becoming the only U.S. woman to win three gold medals at a world championship. At the 1994 worlds, Shannon won the all-around competition again and the balance beam individual event.

Shannon has won five Olympic and seven world championship medals, more than any other U.S. gymnast, male or female. She hopes to make the 1996 Olympic team.

ANOTHER SIDE When Shannon is away from gymnastics, she says she is quiet and shy. But the fierce dedication she brings to competition also applies to her schoolwork. Shannon maintains a straight-A average and is a member of the Oklahoma and National honor societies. In 1994, she won the Dial Award as the nation's top female student-athlete.

CHERYL MILLER

Cheryl Miller was probably the most talented player in women's basketball history. She won the Naismith Award, as college basketball's Player of the Year, every year from 1984 to 1986.

Cheryl grew up playing basketball against her younger brother, Reggie — the same Reggie Miller who currently stars for the NBA's Indiana Pacers. But Cheryl was famous first. She starred at Riverside Poly High (in California), where she became the first player, male or female, to be named a four-time high school All-America.

INFO-BOX

BIRTHPLACE: Riverside, California
CAREER: 1983–1986
CLAIM TO FAME: Cheryl was probably the most talented player in women's basketball history.

The 6' 4" scoring sensation was also a four-time All-America at the University of Southern California, from 1983 to 1986. She led the Women of Troy to two national titles, in 1983 and 1984, and was the Final Four MVP both years.

In international competition, Cheryl was the leading scorer on the gold-medal-winning U.S. team at the 1984 Olympic Games.

Cheryl became head coach of the USC women's basketball team in 1993. In her first season, she led the team to a 26–4 record and a conference championship.

More Stars!

Cheryl set a high school record by scoring 105 points in a single game. But in 1990, that record was almost broken. Lisa Leslie, a 6' 5" senior at Morningside High (in Los Angeles) scored 101 points — in the first half! — of a game against South Torrance. But when the South Torrance team quit at halftime, it kept Lisa from breaking Cheryl's record. Lisa later played basketball at USC, where her coach was . . . Cheryl Miller!

JOE MONTANA

If you had to choose one quarterback for your football dream team, chances are Joe Montana would be the guy. Joe led the San Francisco 49ers to four Super Bowl victories in the 1980s and also became the only player ever to be named Most Valuable Player of the Super Bowl three times.

Joe wasn't the biggest quarterback and he didn't have the strongest arm, but he usually found a way to win. His leadership ability helped make his teammates better, and he was at his best when the odds were against him. In Super Bowl XXIII, in 1989, Joe threw the game-winning touchdown pass with 34 seconds left to play!

INFO-BOX

BIRTHPLACE: New Eagle, Pennsylvania

CAREER: 1979–1995

CLAIM TO FAME: Joe was probably the greatest clutch quarterback in football history.

Joe led many last-minute comebacks in both pro football and in college, where he played for the University of Notre Dame. But perhaps his greatest comebacks were from injuries. Joe hurt his back in 1986 and his elbow in 1991. Both times, doctors said he might never play football again. But Joe fought his way back.

NFL quarterbacks are rated according to how well they pass. Joe, who played for the Kansas City Chiefs from 1993 to 1995, has the second-highest career rating in NFL history.

FUN FACT Joe Montana grew up in Monongahela, a small city in western Pennsylvania, near Pittsburgh. Six of the greatest quarterbacks in football history (including Joe) are from this region.

The other western Pennsylvania passers are George Blanda (from Youngwood), Jim Kelly (Pittsburgh), Dan Marino (Pittsburgh), Joe Namath (Beaver Falls), and Johnny Unitas (Pittsburgh). Maybe it has something to do with the water. More likely, however, it is because football is very popular in this area and kids start playing the game at a young age.

ART MONK

In 1984, Art Monk caught 106 passes for the Washington Redskins. At the time, it was the most receptions in one season in NFL history. (Cris Carter of the Minnesota Vikings now holds the record — 122.) But Art didn't stop there. Through the 1994 season, Art had 934 career receptions — also the most in league history.

Art didn't start out as a wide receiver. He had been a running back in high school and started out at that position at Syracuse University (New York). But Art had been a national-champion hurdler in high school. The Syracuse coaches thought Art's leaping ability and his height (6' 3", tall for a running back) would allow him to catch passes that most other players couldn't reach.

They were right. Art became one of the top college receivers in the country. As a pro, he helped the Redskins win three Super Bowls before signing with the New York Jets in 1994. At 37 years of age, Art is no longer tops, but he remains consistent. In 1994, he increased the number of consecutive games in which he made at least one catch to 180, also an NFL record.

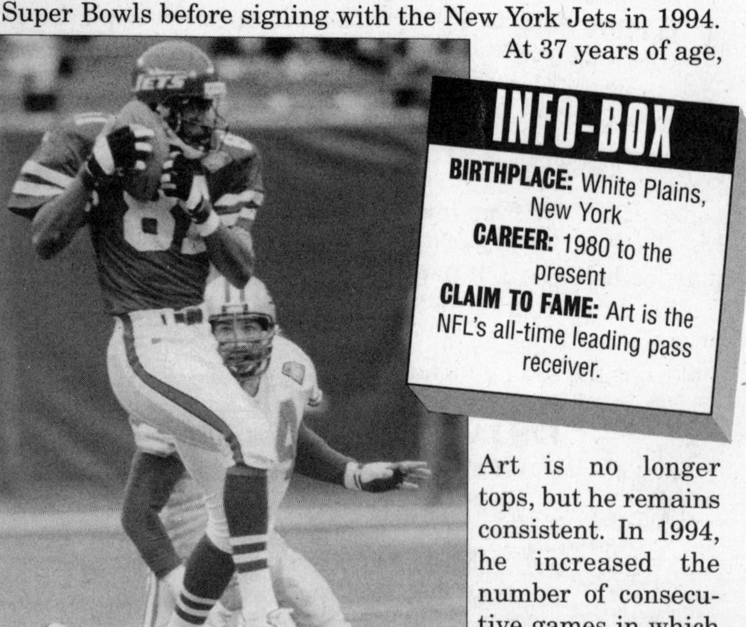

INFO-BOX

BIRTHPLACE: White Plains, New York

CAREER: 1980 to the present

CLAIM TO FAME: Art is the NFL's all-time leading pass receiver.

WARREN MOON

Warren Moon was not at first considered good enough to play in the NFL. So he played pro football in Canada and became one of the best quarterbacks in two different leagues. If you combine his Canadian Football League (CFL) and NFL statistics, Warren has passed for more yards than any quarterback in pro football history.

Warren played for the Edmonton Eskimos from 1978 to 1983 and helped the Eskimos win five Grey Cups (Canada's Super Bowl). He then signed with the NFL's Houston Oilers and helped them make the playoffs. Warren now plays for the Minnesota Vikings.

INFO-BOX

BIRTHPLACE: Los Angeles, California

CAREER: 1978 to the present

CLAIM TO FAME: Warren has been an outstanding quarterback in Canada and in the NFL.

HOWIE MORENZ

Howie Morenz helped hockey become known as "the fastest game on earth." A member of the Montreal Canadiens, he was best known for racing down the ice and faking out defensemen with lightning-fast moves. Howie won the Hart Trophy (as MVP) three times and the Art Ross Trophy (as scoring leader) twice. At a time when fewer goals were scored, he once scored 40 in 44 games!

Hockey lost one of its finest when Howie suffered an injury that led to his death at age 35. (He broke a leg and then developed blood circulation problems.) Howie was one of the first 12 players inducted into the Hockey Hall of Fame, in 1945.

INFO-BOX

BIRTHPLACE: Mitchell, Ontario, Canada

CAREER: 1923–1937

CLAIM TO FAME: Howie was a great goal-scorer in the early years of the NHL.

BASEBALL

JOE MORGAN

Joe Morgan was only 5' 7" tall and 150 pounds, but he combined speed and power to become the only second baseman ever to win two MVP awards in a row (1975 and 1976). He stole more than 40 bases in a season nine times and is the National League's all-time leader in walks. He earned five straight Gold Glove awards for fielding.

"Little Joe" played for five teams, but his best years were with the Cincinnati Reds, which he joined in 1972. He became an important piece of the "Big Red Machine" that won the World Series in 1975 and 1976, the year he drove in 111 runs and hit 27 homers.

Joe was elected to the National Baseball Hall of Fame in 1990.

INFO-BOX

BIRTHPLACE: Bonham, Texas
CAREER: 1963–1984
CLAIM TO FAME: A home run hitter, base stealer, and slick fielder, Joe was one of the best second basemen in baseball history.

BILLIARDS

WILLIE MOSCONI

Willie Mosconi ruled the sport of pocket billiards, or pool, from 1941 through 1957. During that time he won 15 world championships.

Willie got his first taste of pocket billiards at the age of 6. His father, Joseph, owned a boxing gym and billiard parlor. But Joseph did not want his children playing billiards, so he locked up the balls and cue sticks. Willie would sneak down to the table at night and practice with a broomstick and potatoes.

Willie won his first tournament at age 19. In 1941, Willie won his first world title. After that, he was the best in the world for 17 years!

INFO-BOX

BIRTHPLACE: Philadelphia, Pennsylvania
CAREER: 1933–1957
CLAIM TO FAME: The greatest pool player ever, Willie won 15 world championships.

EDWIN MOSES

Between 1977 and 1987, Edwin Moses won 122 straight 400-meter hurdles races. That's the longest winning streak in any event in track-and-field history!

Edwin attended Morehouse College, in Georgia, on an academic scholarship. The track coach at Morehouse convinced Edwin to train for the 1976 Olympic Games, where he set his first world record and won the gold medal in the 400-meter hurdles.

At the 1984 Olympics, he won another gold. When he retired, he owned 13 of the 19 fastest 400-meter hurdle times in history.

INFO-BOX

BIRTHPLACE: Dayton, Ohio
OLYMPIC CAREER: 1976 and 1984
CLAIM TO FAME: A champion 400-meter hurdler, Edwin put together the longest winning streak in track history.

MARION MOTLEY

Marion Motley was one of the first black athletes to play modern professional football. At 6' 2" tall and 235 pounds, Marion was a big man who preferred to run over tacklers rather than around them.

As a member of the Cleveland Browns, Marion was the leading rusher in the All-America Football Conference, a league that existed from 1946 to 1949. In 1950, the Browns joined the NFL, and Marion led that league in rushing, too. He once rushed for 188 yards on just 11 carries in a game. It is still an NFL record.

In 1968, Marion became the first African-American player inducted into the Pro Football Hall of Fame.

INFO-BOX

BIRTHPLACE: Leesburg, Georgia
CAREER: 1946–1955
CLAIM TO FAME: A powerful running back, Marion was the first great African-American pro football star.

ANTHONY MUÑOZ

Offensive lineman Anthony Muñoz was known to some of his teammates on the Cincinnati Bengals as "The Eraser." Why? Because when Anthony blocked somebody, that player disappeared from the play!

Anthony, 6' 6" tall and 290 pounds, was the anchor for the Bengal offensive line in the 1980s. (The Bengals won three division titles and went to the Super Bowl in 1982 and 1989.)

Anthony was named to 11 straight Pro Bowls. His work helping children and charities earned him the NFL Man of the Year award in 1991.

INFO-BOX

BIRTHPLACE: Ontario, California

CAREER: 1980–1992

CLAIM TO FAME: Anthony is considered to be the best offensive lineman ever to play professional football.

TY MURRAY

Even before he started kindergarten, Ty Murray wanted to be a rodeo cowboy. His father, mother, and uncle all competed. Ty became one of the greatest of all time at bronco riding, bull riding, and bareback riding.

Ty was 2 years old when his father put him on a calf for the first time. When he was 18, he joined the Professional Rodeo Cowboys Association (PRCA). That year, 1988, Ty was named Rookie of the Year!

In his second year in the PRCA, Ty became the youngest person ever to win the World Champion All-Around Cowboy title. (He beat his uncle to do it!) He won six straight all-around titles from 1989 to 1994. No one in the 66-year history of the PRCA has ever won more than six all-around titles.

INFO-BOX

BIRTHPLACE: Phoenix, Arizona

CAREER: 1988 to the present

CLAIM TO FAME: Ty is one of the greatest rodeo cowboys of all time.

STAN MUSIAL

Stan Musial of the St. Louis Cardinals was such a good hitter that over his 22-year career, he was known in the National League as "Stan the Man."

Stan learned baseball from his father, a semi-pro player. At age 15, Stan was playing on his dad's team!

In 1943, just his second full big-league season, Stan was named National League MVP. He would lead the Cards to four pennants and three World Series titles.

Stan retired with seven batting titles, a .331 lifetime average, and 3,630 hits. He is the only man to play 1,000 games each at first base and in the outfield. Stan was elected to the National Baseball Hall of Fame in 1969.

INFO-BOX

BIRTHPLACE: Donora, Pennsylvania

CAREER: 1941–1944, 1946–1963

CLAIM TO FAME: Stan was one of the National League's best hitters for 22 years.

BASEBALL

BRONKO NAGURSKI

Bronko Nagurski was one of the toughest players in football history. He starred on offense and defense for the Chicago Bears, and was among the first players elected to the Pro Football Hall of Fame, in 1963.

As a fullback, Bronko was so strong, it was said, that he didn't need blockers! On defense, he played linebacker. He helped the Bears win back-to-back NFL championships in 1932 and 1933.

Bronko retired in 1937 and became a pro wrestler. But he returned to the Bears in 1943 (at age 35), when younger players had been drafted to fight in World War II. He scored the go-ahead touchdown in that year's NFL title game!

INFO-BOX

BIRTHPLACE: Rainy River, Ontario, Canada

CAREER: 1930–1937, 1943

CLAIM TO FAME: Bronko was a great fullback and linebacker in the early days of pro football.

FOOTBALL

MARTINA NAVRATILOVA

Martina Navratilova won more tournaments (167) than any other player, male or female, in tennis history. She won 18 Grand Slam singles titles and 55 Grand Slam titles overall (including singles, doubles, and mixed doubles championships), second only to Margaret Court. Martina finished a year ranked Number 1 in the world seven times.

Martina grew up in Czechoslovakia, a country in Central Europe that in 1993 divided into two countries. She played in her first tournament there when she was only 8 years old. She reached the semi-finals. At 14, Martina won her first national title, in the 14-and-under division.

In 1973, when she was just 16, Martina came to the U.S. for the first time to play in a tournament. She decided she wanted to live in the U.S. because the people had more freedom than the Czechs did. (Czechoslovakia was ruled by a Communist dictator.) Martina had to defect, or run away, from Czechoslovakia, which she did in 1975. She had to leave her family and friends behind. She became a U.S. citizen in 1981.

It was hard for a teenager to be on her own in a strange country. Martina gained a lot of weight. She lost some big matches, and her confidence fell. Even though she won Wimbledon in 1978 and 1979, some tennis watchers felt that she wasn't living up to her potential. When Martina got serious about getting in shape and began concentrating on her game,

Another Side

Martina wasn't just the best singles player in history, she was the best doubles player, too. During her career, she won 163 doubles titles, including 31 Grand Slam doubles titles. From 1981 until 1984, Martina and her partner, Pam Shriver, won 42 of the 50 doubles tournaments they entered. They once won 109 consecutive matches. Overall, they won eight straight Grand Slam titles and 79 tournaments together.

she became the best women's player ever.

Between 1981 and 1985, Martina won 12 Grand Slam singles titles, including 6 in a row between June 1983 and September 1984. She won six consecutive Wimbledon titles (1982–1987), something no other woman has ever done. In 1983, she finished the year with an 86–1 record, the best winning percentage (.988) in tennis history. And in 1984, Martina won 74 straight matches!

INFO-BOX

BIRTHPLACE: Prague, Czechoslovakia (now the Czech Republic)
CAREER: 1973–1994
CLAIM TO FAME: A great athlete, Martina was the best female tennis player ever.

Martina was a great serve-and-volley player *(see page 72)*. Her powerful play in the early 1980s forced her rivals to get into better shape, too. Martina retired in 1994. The $20 million in prize money she won in her career is the second-highest of all time, behind Ivan Lendl *(see below)*.

MORE STARS! Martina wasn't the only Czechoslovakian tennis player to become famous in the U.S. Ivan Lendl did, too. Like Martina, Ivan defected to the U.S. (1984) and became an American citizen (1992). And like Martina, he was a great champion. Between 1980 and 1994, Ivan won 94 tournaments, including eight Grand Slam titles. Only JIMMY CONNORS of the U.S. won more tournaments (107). And Ivan won more prize money than anyone — slightly more than $20 million!

JOE NAMATH

"We're going to win Sunday. I'll guarantee you." With those words, the legend of Joe Namath was born. Joe was a great quarterback whose strong arm and leadership ability helped him become a Pro Football Hall of Famer. But he is best known for his bold promise that the New York Jets would beat the highly favored Baltimore Colts in Super Bowl III (1969). Joe didn't lie: The Jets won, 16–7.

Joe had been a star quarterback at the University of Alabama before joining the Jets, a team that played in the old American Football League (AFL). Badly injured knees made it sometimes difficult for Joe to walk, never mind run, but his rifle arm and lightning-quick release made him the most dangerous passer in football. He was AFL Rookie of the Year in 1965 and Player of the Year in 1968. He took the Jets to the AFL championship and then to the Super Bowl.

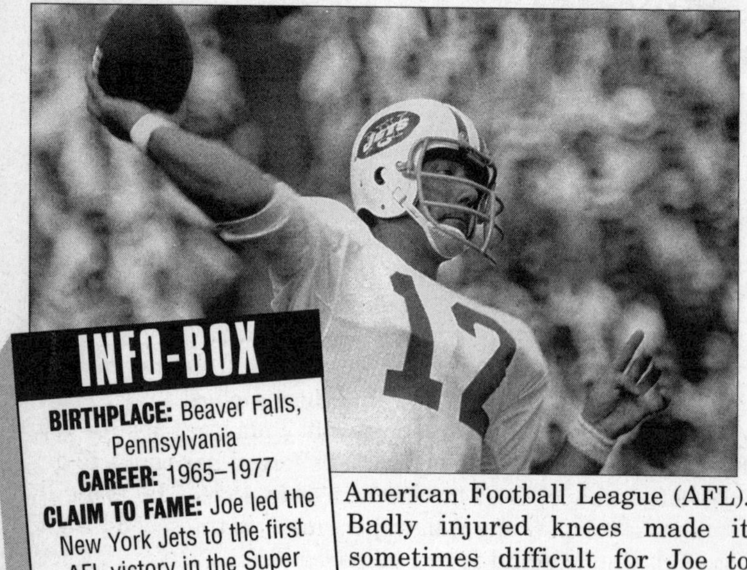

INFO-BOX

BIRTHPLACE: Beaver Falls, Pennsylvania

CAREER: 1965–1977

CLAIM TO FAME: Joe led the New York Jets to the first AFL victory in the Super Bowl.

At that time, the Super Bowl was a showdown between the champions of the AFL and the older, more established NFL. The Jets' victory earned respect for the newer league and eventually led to the two leagues combining to form one larger league — the NFL we know today.

JACK NICKLAUS

In a career of more than 30 years, Jack Nicklaus has won 18 major championships *(see below),* more than any other golfer. And he finished second in majors 19 times!

INFO-BOX

BIRTHPLACE: Columbus, Ohio

CAREER: 1961 to the present

CLAIM TO FAME: Jack has won more major tournaments than any other golfer in history.

Jack is the only golfer ever to win all four majors at least three times. He won six Masters tournaments, five Professional Golfers Association (PGA) tournaments, four U.S. Opens, and three British Opens. Jack has won 70 tournaments and been named Player of the Year five times.

"The Golden Bear," as Jack is known, first lumbered onto the golfing scene as a teenager. He got his nickname because of his blond hair and stocky build. As a 19-year-old, Jack won the U.S. Amateur Championship in 1959, and he won it again in 1961. He then turned pro and won his first major at the 1962 U.S. Open, defeating ARNOLD PALMER.

Jack won his most recent major, his sixth Masters, in 1986. At age 46, he was the oldest player ever to win the event.

Today, Jack plays on the Senior PGA Tour (for golfers age 50 or over). The Golden Bear won the U.S. Senior Open in 1991 and 1993.

How It Works

Four tournaments make up the Professional Golfers Association (PGA) major tournaments. They are the Masters, the British Open, the United States Open, and the PGA Championship. Except for the Masters, which is always played at Augusta National Golf Club, in Georgia, the majors are played at different golf courses each year. The British Open is played on various courses in Great Britain, including Scotland. Scotland is considered the birthplace of golf.

PAULA NEWBY-FRASER

At 5' 6" and 115 pounds, Paula Newby-Fraser doesn't look tough enough to compete in the triathlon. But Paula has won 20 of 29 competitions. She was voted the top female athlete of the 1980s by *The Los Angeles Times*.

INFO-BOX

IRTHPLACE: Harare, Rhodesia (now Zimbabwe)

CAREER: 1985 to the present

CLAIM TO FAME: Paula is one of the world's greatest female athletes.

Paula was born in the British colony of Rhodesia (now an independent nation called Zimbabwe), in Africa, and moved to South Africa with her parents when she was 4 years old. She was a good swimmer and might have made the Olympics, but South Africa was barred from competing because the country discriminated against black people.

Paula didn't take up the triathlon until after college, and then only as a way to stay fit. But she was a natural at it. In her first competition, just weeks after she had started training, she won the women's event and set a course record. She won the next four triathlons she entered that year.

Soon after, Paula decided to make the sport her career. She now lives in San Diego, California, and trains up to 10 hours a day for 10 months a year.

Amazing Feat

Some triathlons are tougher than others, but the Ironman Triathlon World Championship is the toughest of all. It takes place in Hawaii, and consists of a 2.4 mile rough-water swim, a 112-mile bike race, and the 26.2-mile Honolulu Marathon. In her first year of competing in triathlons, Paula tackled the Ironman. With hardly any training, she finished third! Through 1994, she has won the women's competition in the Ironman seven times.

GREG NORMAN

"The Shark," as Greg Norman is known, is in the hunt for tournament titles more often than any other golfer today. He led the Professional Golfers Association (PGA) in winnings in 1986 and 1990 and has won the Vardon Trophy (for the season's lowest scoring average) twice.

Greg has won the British Open twice, but is better known for his heartbreaking defeats. He has lost each of the four majors *(see page 189)* in a playoff.

In 1986, Greg was the leader going into the final round of all four major tournaments, but he won only the British Open. He won his second major in 1993, with a British Open record low score of 267. His 64 was the best-ever final round by a champion.

INFO-BOX

BIRTHPLACE: Queensland, Australia
CAREER: 1983 to the present
CLAIM TO FAME: Greg has been the most consistent player in golf in the 1980s and 1990s.

PAAVO NURMI

Paavo was known as "The Flying Finn" with good reason. At the 1920, 1924, and 1928 Olympics, he won a total of nine gold medals — more than anyone ever has — and three silver medals. During his career, he set 29 world records at distances from 1,500 to 20,000 meters!

Paavo didn't like crowds, which might help explain why he ran away from his competitors. And he carried a stopwatch with which he paced himself.

His greatest year was probably 1924. Three weeks before the Olympics, he set two world records on the same day, in the 1,500 meters and the 5,000 meters, with only an hour to rest between races. At the Olympics, he again had to run the two races within an hour. He won both, setting an Olympic record in each.

INFO-BOX

BIRTHPLACE: Turku, Finland
OLYMPIC CAREER: 1920, 1924, and 1928
CLAIM TO FAME: Paavo was one of the greatest distance runners in Olympic history.

MATTI NYKANEN

Matti Nykanen got his first pair of jumping skis when he was 9 years old. By age 17, he was the world junior champion. In 1983, at 19, he won the overall World Cup title *(see page 142)* for the first of four times.

At the 1984 Olympics, Matti won a silver medal in the normal hill and a gold medal in the large hill (a third event is the large-hill team).

But Matti had problems. He drank a lot and got into fights. He was twice kicked off the Finnish team. By the 1988 Olympics, he had matured — and become unbeatable. He became the first ski jumper to win three golds at one Olympics.

INFO-BOX

BIRTHPLACE: Jyväskylä, Finland
OLYMPIC CAREER: 1984 and 1988
CLAIM TO FAME: Matti was the world's greatest ski jumper.

DAN O'BRIEN

Dan O'Brien went from a "disaster" at the 1992 U.S. Olympic Trials to establishing himself as the world's greatest athlete.

The title of World's Greatest Athlete usually goes to the world or Olympic champion in the decathlon *(see page 172)*. Dan had had the second-highest decathlon score in history in 1991, and was favored to win the decathlon gold medal at the 1992 Summer Olympics. At the U.S. Olympic Trials (tryouts), Dan was on world-record pace after seven events. But he missed all three attempts in the pole vault, finished in 11th place, and didn't even make the U.S. team!

Dan was crushed. But he bounced back quickly. One month after the Games, Dan set a new world record at a meet in France.

INFO-BOX

BIRTHPLACE: Portland, Oregon
CAREER: 1990 to the present
CLAIM TO FAME: Dan is the world record-holder in the decathlon, with 8,891 points.

AL OERTER

Al won the discus throw at four straight Olympics and set an Olympic record each time. He was also the first person to throw the discus more than 200 feet.

INFO-BOX

BIRTHPLACE: Astoria, New York

OLYMPIC CAREER: 1956, 1960, 1964, and 1968

CLAIM TO FAME: Al is the only Olympian to win his event four straight times.

In 1954, when he was a high school student, in West Babylon, New York, Al set a national high school discus record. He earned a scholarship to the University of Kansas. Following his sophomore year, in 1956, he qualified for his first Olympic team.

Al won gold medals at the 1956 and 1960 Games, but his most amazing Olympic performance came in 1964. He suffered extreme back pain, and less than one week before the Olympics, he tore some rib cartilage. (Cartilage is elastic skeletal tissue.) Doctors advised him to rest for six weeks, but Al decided to compete anyway. On his first throw in the preliminary round, he set an Olympic record, which he promptly broke in the final. Al won his fourth Olympic gold medal in 1968.

Al retired from discus competition in 1969. He missed the 1972 and 1976 Olympics. But then he decided to come out of retirement. He resumed competition and set personal bests of 221' 4" in 1978 and 227' 11" in 1980. In 1980, Al was 43 — and he still finished fourth at the national championships!

HOW IT WORKS Throwing a discus is a lot different from throwing a Frisbee. For one thing, it's much heavier. The men's discus weighs 4 pounds 6.55 ounces, while the women's discus weighs 2 pounds 3.27 ounces. The thrower holds the discus flat on the palm of his hand and curls his fingertips over the edge. He holds the discus with a straight arm and spins around. As he spins, he swings the arm away from the body and then releases the discus.

SADAHARU OH

Sadaharu Oh was the king of Japanese baseball. The lefthanded-hitting slugger, whose last name means "king" in Japanese, hit 868 career home runs, setting an all-time professional baseball record.

Sadaharu, the son of a Chinese father and a Japanese mother, was not always liked by the Japanese fans because he wasn't a full-blooded Japanese. But after he helped lead the Tokyo Yomiuri Giants to 12 Japan Series championships (including nine in a row!), he became the most popular sports figure in Japanese history.

Not a very big man at 5' 10" and 175 pounds, Sadaharu generated power by lifting his front leg into the air just before striking the ball.

Sadaharu started as a pitcher. Later he moved to first base. He was amazingly consistent.

INFO-BOX

BIRTHPLACE: Tokyo, Japan
CAREER: 1959–1981
CLAIM TO FAME: The legendary Japanese baseball star hit more home runs than any other player in professional baseball history.

During one 13-year stretch, he averaged 45 home runs and won the home run title each year. His best home run season came in 1965, when he hit a record 55 homers.

After retiring, Sadaharu went on to manage the Yomiuri Giants.

HAKEEM OLAJUWON

Hakeem Olajuwon is the best center playing professional basketball today. Not bad for a guy who grew up in the African country of Nigeria and didn't play competitive basketball until he was 15 years old!

INFO-BOX

BIRTHPLACE: Lagos, Nigeria
CAREER: 1984 to the present
CLAIM TO FAME: Although he didn't play basketball until he was 15, Hakeem has become the best center in the NBA today.

Hakeem impressed coaches with his natural ability. He even received a scholarship to play basketball at the University of Houston, in Texas.

In just two years, Hakeem became one of the best big men in college basketball. "The Dream," as he was called, was both a great defensive player and a good offensive player who averaged 13.3 points and 10.7 rebounds per game.

In 1984, the Houston Rockets made Hakeem the first pick in the NBA draft. He led them to the NBA Finals in the 1985–86 season, in which they lost to the Boston Celtics. In the 1988-89 season, Hakeem became the first NBA player to have 200 blocks and 200 steals in the same season. In 1993–94, he was the NBA's regular-season MVP and Defensive Player of the Year.

Hakeem led the Rockets to back-to-back NBA titles, in 1994 and 1995. He was named Finals MVP both times.

For his career, Hakeem has averaged 24.0 points, 12.4 rebounds, 3.6 blocks, and 1.9 steals per game. Maybe his name explains his greatness. *Olajuwon* means "always being on top."

When He Was a Kid

Hakeem's first game was team handball — a sport like soccer. He played on his region's team at Nigerian sports festivals. The quickness he developed in that sport helped him with basketball.

SHAQUILLE O'NEAL

In his short time in the NBA, Shaquille O'Neal has emerged as the one of the most dominant players in the game and one of its most popular stars. In the 1994–95 season, the Orlando Magic center led the league in scoring, and for the third straight season, he was among the league leaders in rebounds, blocked shots, and shooting accuracy. At 7' 1" and 310 pounds, Shaquille often looks unstoppable on the court.

Born in Newark, New Jersey, Shaquille traveled a lot as a kid. His father was a sergeant in the U.S. Army and was often transferred from base to base.

Shaquille was tall but awkward as a kid. It wasn't until he was in 10th grade (while his family was living in Germany) that Shaquille learned how to use his size and strength on the basketball court.

After his father was transferred back to the U.S., Shaquille spent two years at Cole High School, in San Antonio. There he led the basketball team to a 68–1 record and a state championship in his senior year.

After graduation, Shaquille attended Louisiana State University. Even though he was big, Shaquille was still a raw talent compared to other college players. He worked hard to improve.

In only his second year of college ball, Shaq averaged 27.6 points, 14.7 rebounds, and 5 blocked shots per game. That season, he was voted College Player of the

When He Was a Kid

LSU coach Dale Brown first met Shaquille while giving a basketball clinic at the U.S. Army base in Germany where Shaq's dad was stationed.

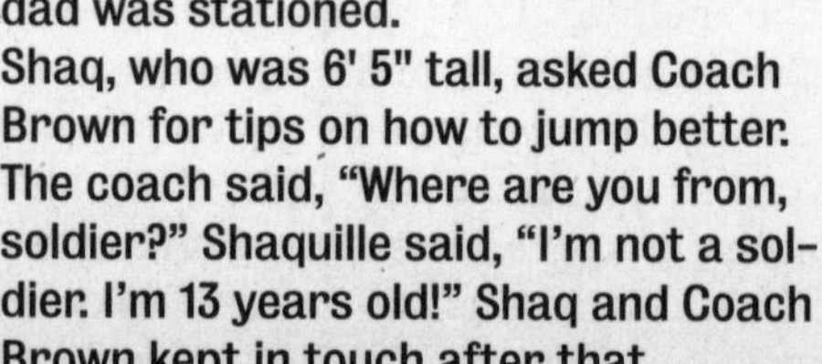

Shaq, who was 6' 5" tall, asked Coach Brown for tips on how to jump better. The coach said, "Where are you from, soldier?" Shaquille said, "I'm not a soldier. I'm 13 years old!" Shaq and Coach Brown kept in touch after that.

Year. For his career at LSU, he averaged 21.6 points and 13.5 rebounds and was a two-time All-America.

Shaquille entered the NBA draft following his junior season at LSU and was selected by the Orlando Magic with the first pick. After the "Shaq Attack" arrived in Orlando, the Magic won 20 more games than it had won the season before!

INFO-BOX

BIRTHPLACE: Newark, New Jersey
CAREER: 1992 to the present
CLAIM TO FAME: Shaquille is the biggest young talent in professional basketball today.

Shaquille has gotten better and better. In his second season, 1993–94, Shaquille finished second in the NBA in scoring and led the Magic to its first playoff appearance. In 1994–95, he led the NBA in scoring (with 29.3 points per game) and took his team to the NBA Finals — all at the age of 23!

DID YOU KNOW?

- Shaquille's full name is Shaquille Rashaun O'Neal. Shaquille Rashaun means "little warrior" in Arabic.
- Shaq has already acted in a movie, *Blue Chips*, and rapped on two solo albums: *Shaq Diesel* and *Shaq-Fu: da Return.*
- Shaq's career bests are 53 points, in a game against the Minnesota Timberwolves, in April 1994; 28 rebounds, in a game against the New Jersey Nets, in November 1993; and 15 blocked shots, in that same game against the Nets. All are Magic team records.

BOBBY ORR

Bobby Orr was one of the best defensemen ever to play hockey. He was a pioneer at his position — a defenseman who scored! Bobby was the first defenseman to score more than 40 goals and more than 100 points in a season, and the first to win a league scoring title. His efforts helped turn his team, the Boston Bruins, into NHL champions.

The Bruins recognized Bobby's talents unusually early. They acquired the rights to sign Bobby and placed him on their protected list when he was only 12 years old! The Bruins brought him into the NHL in 1966, when he was 18. He won the Calder Memorial Trophy (given to the best rookie) in 1966–67.

INFO-BOX

BIRTHPLACE: Parry Sound, Ontario, Canada

CAREER: 1955–1978

CLAIM TO FAME: Bobby was the first NHL defenseman also to play outstanding offense.

In the 1969–70 season, Bobby won four individual awards — the Art Ross Trophy, for scoring (an award that most people thought would never go to a defenseman); the Norris Trophy, for top defenseman (an award he would win a record eight times in a row); the Hart Trophy, for league MVP; and the Conn Smythe Trophy, for playoff MVP.

Bobby capped off his award-winning season by scoring the winning goal in the last game of the 1970 Stanley Cup finals. He led the Bruins to another Stanley Cup championship in 1972.

Bobby was elected to the Hockey Hall of Fame in 1979.

MEL OTT

When people think of home run hitters, they think of big, burly men. At 5' 9" and 170 pounds, Mel Ott was hardly that. But for 22 seasons, he was one of the most feared sluggers in baseball and became the first National Leaguer to hit 500 home runs.

Besides awesome power, the left-handed hitter brought a unique batting style to the plate. With his feet planted wide apart, he would approach a pitch by raising his front leg in the air, dropping it quickly, and lashing at the ball. It obviously worked, because Mel was wearing a major league uniform by the time he was 17.

INFO-BOX

BIRTHPLACE: Gretna, Louisiana
CAREER: 1926–1947
CLAIM TO FAME: The left-handed-hitting slugger was the first National Leaguer to hit 500 home runs.

As a member of the New York Giants, Mel led the league in home runs six times. In 16 World Series games, he batted .295, with four home runs and 10 RBIs. He homered in the 10th inning of Game 5 of the 1933 World Series to give the Giants the championship.

Groomed as a catcher, Mel was switched to the outfield by Giants manager John McGraw. He finished his career with a .304 average and 511 home runs. Mel, who was elected to the National Baseball Hall of Fame in 1951, was killed at age 49 by a drunk driver.

ANOTHER SIDE After his playing days were over, Mel managed the Giants for about six and a half seasons, during which the team had a 464–530 record. Mel had been considered one of the nicest men in baseball. Some people felt Mel's pleasant personality kept him from becoming a winning manager. In fact, Dodger manager Leo Durocher once said of Mel's Giants, "The nice guys over there are in last place." (Leo later titled his autobiography *Nice Guys Finish Last.*) Mel tried to change his image, and in 1946 he became the first manager ever to be thrown out of both games of a doubleheader.

JESSE OWENS

In 1936, Jesse Owens became the first track-and-field athlete to win four gold medals at one Olympics. He won the 100-meter and 200-meter dashes and the long jump, and ran the first leg on the U.S. winning 4 x 100-meter relay team.

Jesse was born in Alabama. His grandparents had been slaves, and his parents were sharecroppers (people who farm other people's land, usually because they can't afford land of their own). Jesse worked in the fields picking cotton. When he was 9, Jesse, his nine older brothers and sisters, and his parents moved to Cleveland, Ohio. After school, Jesse delivered groceries and worked in a shoe-repair shop.

At Fairmount Junior High School, Jesse set the first of many track-and-field records. In 1928, he high-jumped 6' and long-jumped 22' $11\frac{3}{4}$" — both were national junior high school records. By the time he graduated from high school, in 1933, he had won 74 of 79 sprint races he had entered.

Jesse attended Ohio State University. At a meet in his sophomore year of college, Jesse set or equaled six world records in one day!

INFO-BOX

BIRTHPLACE: Decatur, Alabama

OLYMPIC CAREER: 1936

CLAIM TO FAME: Before Carl Lewis came along, Jesse was the greatest track-and-field athlete in history.

He set records in the 220-yard dash, the long jump, and the 220-yard hurdles, and equaled the record in the 100-yard dash. (The records in the 220-yard dash and the 220-yard hurdles also counted as records in the 200-meter dash and the 200-meter hurdles.) His record in the long jump lasted for more than 25 years!

In 1936, Jesse set two Olympic records — in the long jump and the 200-meter dash. He tied the Olympic record in the 100 meters.

A Closer Look

The 1936 Olympics were held in Berlin, Germany. Germany was ruled by Adolph Hitler, a dictator who wanted to rule the world. Hitler believed that certain Germans, called Aryans, were superior to all other people, and that people who were not white Christians should be eliminated. As he conquered Europe, Hitler ordered the mass murder of millions of Jews and other people. Hitler wanted to use the 1936 Olympics to show the world that German athletes were the best in the world. But Jesse Owens, an African-American, helped ruin Hitler's Olympic vision.

After the Olympics, Jesse could not continue running and jumping. At the time, athletes were not allowed to take money for competing. Jesse earned a living by racing against horses, dogs, and automobiles in front of live crowds.

Late in the 1940s, Jesse helped organize sports programs on the state and city levels. He also worked for the U.S. government and traveled the world making speeches. Jesse, who smoked cigarettes, died of lung cancer in 1980.

WHEN HE WAS A KID Jesse's real name was James Cleveland Owens. When he was young, his family moved up north and James had to go to a new school. On his first day of school, in Cleveland, Ohio, the teacher asked his name. James said it was "J.C." (the initials standing for James Cleveland). He spoke with a thick Southern accent. Because of that, the teacher misunderstood him and thought his name was "Jesse." The name stuck for all time.

SATCHEL PAIGE

In a career spanning five decades, Leroy "Satchel" Paige pitched in the Negro leagues and in the major leagues. It is said he won more than 2,000 games in Negro league play.

Satchel got his nickname when he worked carrying bags, or satchels, at a bus depot. He pitched for several Negro league teams but is best known for his time with the Kansas City Monarchs. (Blacks were not allowed to play in the major or minor leagues at the time.)

Satchel was a great strikeout pitcher and showman. Between seasons, he barnstormed (traveled with all-star teams) around the U.S. playing local teams. Sometimes he would have his fielders sit down while he struck out the side. He also played on several Negro league all-star teams that played exhibition games against major league all-stars. The Negro leaguers won more than half of those games.

In 1948, the year after baseball was integrated, Satchel joined the Cleveland Indians. At 42, he was the oldest rookie ever. His six wins helped the Indians win the pennant.

In 1971, Satchel became the first player elected to the National Baseball Hall of Fame for his play in the Negro leagues.

INFO-BOX

BIRTHPLACE: Mobile, Alabama
CAREER: 1926–47, 1950, 1955 (Negro leagues); 1948–49, 1951–53, 1965 (major leagues)
CLAIM TO FAME: Satchel was the greatest pitcher in the Negro leagues.

ARNOLD PALMER

Arnold Palmer's many fans were called "Arnie's Army," and they cheered his every shot. Arnie won 60 titles during his career (fourth on the all-time list) and became the first golfer to earn $1 million.

INFO-BOX

BIRTHPLACE: Latrobe, Pennsylvania
CAREER: 1954 to the present
CLAIM TO FAME: Arnie won 60 titles during his career and was probably the most popular golfer ever.

Arnie's father was a club pro at a golf course, and by age 4, Arnie was playing golf with a club cut down to his size. At age 25, in 1954, he won the U.S. Amateur Championship. He joined the Professional Golfers Association (PGA) tour in 1955.

Before Arnie came along, golf was considered a game played only by rich, sometimes snobby people. But Arnie was not like that at all. His clothes were sloppy, his hair messy. And he played boldly, with emotion.

From 1958 to 1964, Arnie was on top of the golf world. He won the Masters four times, the British Open twice, and the U.S. Open once. He won the Player of the Year award twice during that span. Arnie joined the PGA Hall of Fame in 1980.

Although he has said he is retired, he still competes on the Senior Tour and in some PGA events.

Amazing Feat

At the 1960 U.S. Open, Arnie made one of golf's most amazing comebacks. As in most pro tournaments, U.S. Open golfers play four rounds of 18 holes each. Arnie was seven shots behind the leader going into the final round. But then he began his charge. He made six birdies on the first seven holes. (Par is the number of shots a hole is expected to be played in. A birdie is one under par.) Arnie shot a 65 for the round and won the title!

JIM PALMER

Jim Palmer wasn't the hardest-throwing pitcher in the major leagues, but he was one of the smartest. With a high leg kick as his helper, he would mix up his fastball, curveball, and slider to keep batters off-balance.

During his 19 seasons with the Baltimore Orioles, Jim won 20 games in a season eight times. He led the league in wins three times and in earned run average twice. His 2.86 career ERA is fourth-best in major league history among pitchers with more than 3,000 innings pitched

A three-time Cy Young Award winner, Jim helped lead the Orioles to six pennants and three World Series titles. He was a great clutch pitcher — he never gave up a grand slam home run, and he recorded a post-season record of 8–3.

INFO-BOX

BIRTHPLACE: New York, New York

CAREER: 1965–1984

CLAIM TO FAME: Jim won 20 or more games in a season eight times and three Cy Young Awards.

One of his best assets was his intensity during every game. Earl Weaver, his former manager, knew that was a big part of Jim's success. "Palmer isn't a pitcher who works every four days," Earl once said. "He's in the ball game nine innings every night, sitting on the bench studying pitchers' motions and watching how teams hit."

Jim now works as a TV broadcaster. He was elected to the National Baseball Hall of Fame in 1990.

Another Side

In 1966, Jim was 20 years old and new to the major leagues. He developed an odd superstition. One day, his wife, Susie, made pancakes for breakfast. That night, Jim pitched and won. The next three times he was scheduled to pitch, Susie made pancakes — and Jim won each time. One day, he skipped the pancakes. That night he pitched — and lost! Jim won every game he pitched after a pancake breakfast that year. Jim's old friends still call him "Cakes."

WALTER PAYTON

Walter Payton was nicknamed "Sweetness" for his sweet moves carrying the football. But Walter, who played for the Chicago Bears, was probably the toughest running back around. He earned 16,726 yards during his 13-year career, becoming the NFL's all-time leading rusher.

Walter had a perfect mix of lightning speed and sledgehammer strength. He played 10 seasons in which he rushed for at least 1,200 yards. He was a great blocker and receiver. In his career, he caught 492 passes (more than any running back in history at the time he retired) and scored 125 touchdowns.

Even after he became a star, Walter stayed in great shape with a strenuous off-season training program. He missed only one game in his career!

In 1977, Walter rushed for 275 yards in a single game — a record that no one has matched.

In 1985, Walter led the Chicago Bears to a 15–1 record and their first NFL title in 22 years.

Walter's feats on the field earned him a place in the Pro Football Hall of Fame, in 1993.

INFO-BOX

BIRTHPLACE: Columbia, Mississippi

CAREER: 1975–1987

CLAIM TO FAME: Walter rushed for more yards in a game and a career than any other NFL running back.

PELÉ

There is a handful of people who are so famous they are known by only one name. One of these is Pelé. (His real name is Edson Arantes do Nascimento.) During his sensational 20-year career, he scored 1,282 goals (in 1,355 games, nearly a goal a game), led Brazil to three World Cup championships, and earned the title "The King of Soccer."

As a kid, Pelé *[pay-LAY]* always had a natural talent for soccer. His father was a professional soccer player who taught him the game. But at that time, pro soccer players made very little money. Since Pelé and his friends couldn't afford a real soccer ball, they made their own from rags and old socks and played barefoot in the streets.

One day while playing, 11-year-old Pelé was noticed by a retired soccer player, Waldemar de Brito. Waldemar was impressed by Pelé's ability and became his coach for the next four years. Afterward, Pelé was ready to join Santos, a club team that played professionally. Waldemar believed Pelé would be the greatest athlete in the world someday.

Pelé quickly began to prove him right. He scored four goals in his first game with Santos juniors, in 1955. Three years later, he was on Brazil's national team.

At the age of 17, Pelé became an international star. His ability to whirl around defenders and score goals helped Brazil win its first World Cup championship, in 1958. Brazil won the title in Sweden, becoming the only South American country to win the World Cup in Europe. In 1962 and 1970, Pelé led Brazil

A Closer Look

Pelé's native country of Brazil has a proud soccer history. Of the 15 World Cup championships that have been played, Brazil has won four (1958, 1962, 1970, 1994). That's more than any other country! In 73 World Cup matches, Brazil has 49 wins, 11 losses, and 13 ties. Brazil is also the only nation to participate in every World Cup championship tournament. In 1994, the Brazilian team defeated Italy to win the championship.

to two more World Cup championships.

Pelé scored a total of 97 goals for Brazil in international competitions. He scored an amazing 1,088 goals while he led his Santos team to nine league titles.

After 18 years with Santos, Pelé joined the New York Cosmos of the North American Soccer League (NASL), in 1975. He and the NASL wanted soccer to become as popular in the U.S. as it was in the rest of the world. Pelé made dazzling plays with his head, chest, thighs, and feet. During his three years with the Cosmos, he was named the league's MVP (in 1976) and led the team to the NASL title (in 1977).

Pelé played his last game on October 1, 1977, before 75,646 fans at Giants Stadium, in East Rutherford, New Jersey. The game was an exhibition match in his honor between the Cosmos and Santos. He played the first half for the Cosmos and the second half for Santos.

INFO-BOX

BIRTHPLACE: Três Corações, Minas Gerais, Brazil
CAREER: 1956–1977
CLAIM TO FAME: Pelé was the greatest soccer player in history and a worldwide ambassador for the sport.

ANOTHER SIDE Even though he's retired, Pelé is still very active in soccer. He runs soccer camps and clinics around the world. He also serves as the sport's goodwill ambassador. In 1986, Pelé tried to convince world soccer organizations to hold the World Cup tournament in the United States. They didn't listen to him then, but his influence helped bring the World Cup to the United States in 1994. In 1995, Pelé was named Brazil's new minister of sports.

BASKETBALL

BOB PETTIT

Bob Pettit was one of the great forwards in the early years of the NBA. He was the first NBA player to score more than 20,000 career points.

A center at Louisiana State University, Bob averaged 31.4 points per game as a senior. When he joined the NBA, with the Milwaukee Hawks, he switched to forward. He was named Rookie of the Year in 1954–55. The next season, Bob and the Hawks moved from Milwaukee to St. Louis. (They moved to Atlanta in 1968.)

In 1958, Bob scored 50 points in the final game to help the Hawks win the NBA title. Over his 11-year career, he averaged 26.4 points and 16.2 rebounds per game and was named MVP twice.

INFO-BOX

BIRTHPLACE: Baton Rouge, Louisiana

CAREER: 1954–1965

CLAIM TO FAME: Bob was the first NBA player to score more than 20,000 points in a career.

AUTO RACING

RICHARD PETTY

Richard Petty followed in the footsteps of his father, Lee, and became a champion stock-car racer. During his career in the National Association of Stock Car Auto Racing (NASCAR), he won 200 races — nearly twice as many as any other driver.

Richard won his first NASCAR driving title in 1964. (Drivers receive points for the order in which they finish. The driver with the most points at season's end wins the title.) Richard was NASCAR Winston Cup champion seven times. He also won the Daytona 500 race seven times.

"King" Richard, as he was known, retired in 1992. Now his son Kyle is one of the top drivers on the NASCAR circuit.

INFO-BOX

BIRTHPLACE: Level Cross, North Carolina

CAREER: 1958–1992

CLAIM TO FAME: "King" Richard won more stock-car races than any other driver in history.

JACQUES PLANTE

Jacques Plante changed the game of hockey. He was the first goalie to regularly wear a face mask in a game and the first to leave the net to play the puck.

Goalies didn't wear face masks in games before the 1960s.

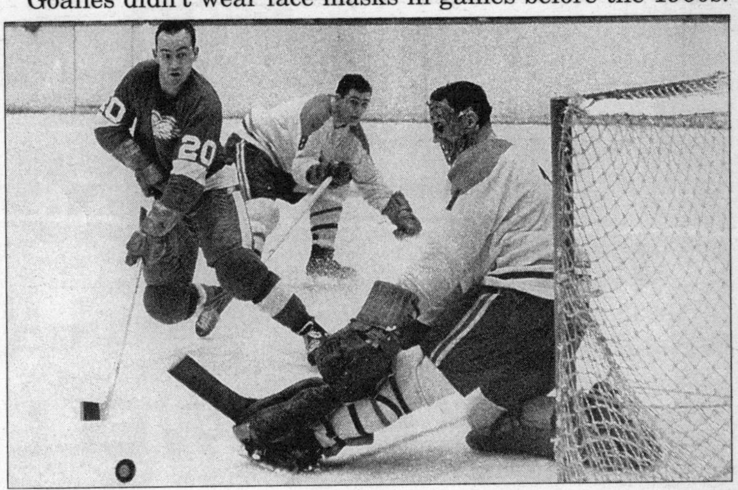

But during a game on November 1, 1959, a slapshot hit Jacques in the face. He returned to the game with a face mask. Soon all goalies in the league were wearing them.

In the early days, goalies usually stayed close to their nets during a game. But not Jacques. He often sped out of the net to pass the puck to a teammate. Now it's common for goalies to leave the net to help start plays.

Jacques played for five NHL teams but spent most of his career in Montreal. In 10 seasons, he helped the Canadiens win six Stanley Cups, including five in a row (1956–60)! He won the Vezina Trophy (for the lowest goals-against average) seven times. In 1962, he won the Hart Trophy as the league's MVP.

INFO-BOX

BIRTHPLACE: Mont Carmel, Quebec, Canada
CAREER: 1952–1965, 1968–1975
CLAIM TO FAME: Jacques changed the way hockey goalies play.

DENIS POTVIN

Denis Potvin combined scoring with crushing checks that left opponents crumpled on the ice. A defenseman, he scored 310 goals and 1,052 points, breaking the records of BOBBY ORR. (Paul Coffey would later top Denis's marks.)

By age 14, Denis was already a famous player in Canada. In 1973, the New York Islanders made him the first pick in the NHL draft.

Denis was Rookie of the Year, and he went on to win the Norris Trophy (best defenseman) three times. As team captain, Denis led New York to four Stanley Cups. In 1991, he was elected to the Hockey Hall of Fame.

INFO-BOX

BIRTHPLACE: Ottawa, Ontario, Canada
CAREER: 1973–1988
CLAIM TO FAME: When Denis retired, he was the NHL's highest-scoring defenseman.

MIKE POWELL

When Mike Powell won the long jump at the 1991 world track-and-field championships, he broke one of the most amazing records in the sport.

In 1968, Bob Beamon of the United States won the Olympic gold medal when he jumped 29' 2½". That jump broke the record held by Ralph Boston of the U.S. by nearly two feet!

For years, Mike had jumped in the shadow of CARL LEWIS. Carl had beaten him all 15 times they had competed, including the 1988 Olympics (Carl won the gold, Mike the silver). But at the 1991 worlds, Mike uncorked a jump of 29' 4½" — and the record was his.

Mike won a silver medal at the 1992 Olympics, and was undefeated in 25 meets in 1993. He was the top-ranked long-jumper in the world in 1993–94.

INFO-BOX

BIRTHPLACE: Philadelphia, Pennsylvania
CAREER: 1988 to the present
CLAIM TO FAME: Mike broke Bob Beamon's 23-year-old, "unbreakable" record in the long jump.

THE PROTOPOPOVS

In 1964, Ludmila Belousova *[bell-ew-SO-va]* and Oleg Protopopov *[pro-toe-POP-off]* became the first skating pair from the Soviet Union to win an Olympic gold medal. Since then, the Soviets and now the Russians *(see page 54)* have won every gold medal in pairs skating.

INFO-BOX

BIRTHPLACE: Leningrad (Oleg) and Ulyanovsk (Ludmila), Soviet Union (now Russia)
OLYMPIC CAREER: 1960, 1964, and 1968
CLAIM TO FAME: They were pioneers in Olympic pairs.

Ludmila and Oleg met at a skating rink, and were married in 1957. In 1960, they placed ninth at the Winter Olympics. But their ballet-like movements and emotional routines soon made them giants in figure skating — and helped them win world and European championships four years in a row, 1965–68. They won Olympic gold medals in 1964 and 1968.

The Protopopovs invented the death spiral, a move in which Oleg held Ludmila with one hand and spun her around the ice, face-up, in a big circle. Ludmila's body spun parallel to the ice. The death spiral is now required in pairs skating.

In 1969, the Protopopovs lost their European and world titles to a younger Russian pairs team. After that, they turned professional and performed in ice shows.

MORE STARS! The next great Soviet pairs skaters after the Protopopovs were Irina Rodnina and Aleksander Zaitsev. Although Irina won the 1972 Olympic pairs competition with Aleksei Ulanov, they split up after the Games. Irina found a new partner, Aleksander. They fell in love and were married in 1975. The next year, they won the gold medal at the Olympics. In 1978, Irina won her 10th straight world championship (four with Aleksei, six with Aleksander). She took the next year off to have a baby, but the parents made a blazing comeback at the 1980 Olympics. They skated perfectly, and all nine judges placed them first! Irina had won her third Olympic gold medal.

KIRBY PUCKETT

At 5' 9" tall and 215 pounds, Kirby Puckett may not look like a professional athlete. But he is one of baseball's true superstars. During his career with the Minnesota Twins, he has won six Gold Gloves for fielding and a batting title, and he has helped the Twins win two World Series.

Kirby grew up in a tough neighborhood in Chicago, Illinois. He attended Triton Junior College (near Chicago) and led his team to the Junior World Series. He eventually signed with the Twins.

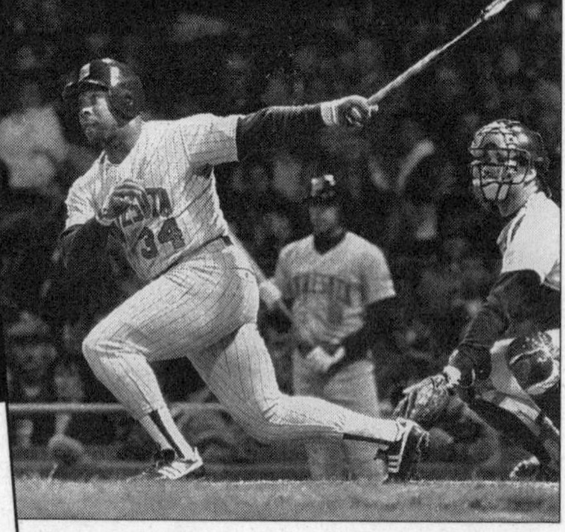

Kirby got four hits in his first major league game, but he went his whole first season without a home run. His bat came alive in 1985, though. He hit 31 homers that year, becoming the first player to hit no homers in one season and 30 in another.

INFO-BOX

BIRTHPLACE: Chicago, Illinois
CAREER: 1984 to the present
CLAIM TO FAME: Kirby has used his bat and glove to lead the Minnesota Twins to two World Series titles.

Kirby has batted .300 or more seven times. In 1987, he hit .332, with 207 hits, and made eight catches that robbed opposing teams of home runs. In the World Series that season, he led all batters with 10 hits.

In 1988, Kirby batted .356 and had 121 RBIs. The following season, he led the league in batting with a .339 average — becoming only the second right-handed batter to do so in 20 years! In 1994 he led the American League with 112 RBIs.

In a survey by the newspaper *Baseball America,* Kirby was voted baseball's Best Role Model and Friendliest Player.

MARY LOU RETTON

Mary Lou Retton was 8 years old when she watched NADIA COMANECI score the first perfect 10 in Olympic gymnastics, at the 1976 Games. Nadia's score appeared on the scoreboard as a 1.0, to show a 10. When Mary Lou got a 1.0 in her first competition, she was very excited. Unfortunately, her score really was a 1.0.

INFO-BOX

BIRTHPLACE: Fairmont, West Virginia

OLYMPIC CAREER: 1984

CLAIM TO FAME: Mary Lou was the first U.S. gymnast to win a gold medal in the Olympic all-around event.

At the 1984 Olympics, 16-year-old Mary Lou — a muscular 4' 9" — was ready to turn her 1.0 into a 10. This was her first major international competition. She had the same coach as Nadia, Bela Karolyi.

After the first two events in the all-around competition, Mary Lou was in second place. During the floor exercise, she scored the first 10 of the competition. Then came her final event, the vault. Mary Lou needed to score a perfect 10 to win the gold medal — and she did it!

Mary Lou became the first U.S. gymnast to win the Olympic gold medal in the all-around event. She also earned a silver and two bronze medals in individual events.

A Closer Look

Athletes from the U.S. were very successful at the 1984 Summer Olympics, in Los Angeles, California. They won more medals (174) than athletes from any other country. But a large part of the Americans' success was due to the Soviet Union's boycott of those games.

In 1980, the Olympics had been held in the Soviet Union. To protest a Soviet invasion of the country of Afghanistan, the U.S. and a few other countries did not send athletes to those Olympics. When the Olympics were held in the U.S. in 1984, the Soviet Union boycotted them, in an act of political revenge.

JERRY RICE

Jerry Rice is the best wide receiver in the NFL today — and of all time! He has played 10 years with the San Francisco 49ers and set some amazing records along the way. No other player in the NFL has scored 139 touchdowns in his career. Jerry is also the all-time leader in touchdown catches, 116, and holds the record for most consecutive games catching a touchdown pass, 13. He has helped the San Francisco 49ers win three Super Bowls.

Jerry's skill with his hands came from working with his father, who was a bricklayer. When he was young, Jerry would stand on a scaffold (a high platform) and catch bricks tossed by his five brothers as they helped their father on the job during the summers. The training paid off for Jerry when he played football at B.L. Moore High School, in Mississippi. He caught 35 touchdown passes and won a scholarship to Mississippi Valley State University.

The college was not well known for football, but NFL scouts heard about Jerry's performance at Mississippi Valley State. During his four years there, Jerry caught passes for 4,693 yards and set 18 NCAA Division I-AA records.

INFO-BOX

BIRTHPLACE: Starkville, Mississippi

CAREER: 1985 to the present

CLAIM TO FAME: Jerry is the best wide receiver in NFL history.

Jerry was chosen by the 49ers in the first round of the NFL draft, in 1985. In his rookie year, he caught 49 passes for 927 yards, and was named NFC Rookie of the Year.

He hasn't let up yet! In 1987, Jerry led the NFL in scoring with 138 points on 23 touchdowns. It was the most points ever scored by a wide receiver. He caught 65 passes for 1,078 yards in that strike-shortened season and helped the 49ers win the NFC West. Jerry was voted Player of the Year by the NFL, *Sports Illustrated,* and *The Sporting News.*

During Super Bowl XXIII, in 1989, Jerry gained 215 receiving yards on 11 catches (both records) and was named MVP. Jerry holds several career Super Bowl records, too *(see below)*, as well as the mark for most touchdown passes caught in post-season play (17).

When He Was a Kid

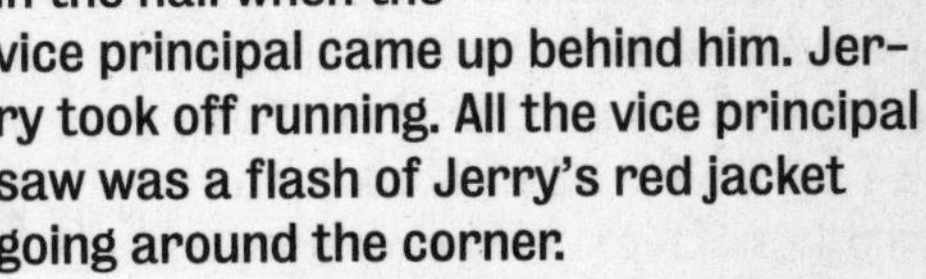

Jerry Rice never really planned to play football. But one day in high school, he decided to skip class. He was hanging out in the hall when the vice principal came up behind him. Jerry took off running. All the vice principal saw was a flash of Jerry's red jacket going around the corner.

The vice principal did catch up with him, though. But instead of punishing Jerry, he gave him a choice: go to detention or try out for the school football team. (He didn't want that great speed to go to waste!) Jerry chose football.

AMAZING FEAT In January 1995, at Super Bowl XXIX, in Miami, Florida, Jerry helped the 49ers beat the San Diego Chargers, 49–26. He caught 10 passes for 149 yards. He also had three touchdowns, to tie his record set in the 1989 Super Bowl (49ers Roger Craig and Ricky Watters share the mark). Jerry holds five Super Bowl career records. He has the most Super Bowl receptions (28), points (42), touchdowns (7), receiving touchdowns (7), and receiving yards (512).

MAURICE RICHARD

Maurice Richard was called "Rocket" because of his tremendous skating speed. In his 18-year career, he helped the Montreal Canadiens win eight Stanley Cups.

In the 1944–45 season, Maurice became the first player to score 50 goals in 50 games. By the time he retired, he had scored 544 regular-season goals and 82 playoff goals.

In 1955, Maurice's younger brother, Henri ("Pocket Rocket"), joined the Canadiens. Together, they helped Montreal win five straight Stanley Cups.

Maurice was elected to the Hockey Hall of Fame in 1961.

INFO-BOX

BIRTHPLACE: Montreal, Quebec, Canada

CAREER: 1942–1960

CLAIM TO FAME: "Rocket" was one of the NHL's fastest skaters and greatest goal scorers.

JOHN RIGGINS

John Riggins, a 6' 2", 240-pound fullback, was called "The Diesel." He would run down the field like a truck!

John played his first five seasons with the New York Jets. But he really made his mark with the Washington Redskins.

In January 1983, the Redskins faced the Miami Dolphins in Super Bowl XVII. With his team trailing, John took a handoff on fourth down and ran 43 yards for the go-ahead touchdown! John set what was then a record by rushing for 166 yards, and was named MVP.

In the 1983 season, John scored a record 24 touchdowns. He scored 116 touchdowns in his career.

John was elected to the Pro Football Hall of Fame in 1992.

INFO-BOX

BIRTHPLACE: Seneca, Kansas

CAREER: 1971–1979, 1981–1985

CLAIM TO FAME: John ran like a truck — all the way to a Super Bowl MVP and an NFL touchdown record.

CAL RIPKEN, JUNIOR

Cal Ripken, Junior, grew up playing baseball. His dad was Cal Ripken, Senior, a former coach and manager of the Baltimore Orioles.

INFO-BOX

BIRTHPLACE: Havre de Grace, Maryland
CAREER: 1981 to the present
CLAIM TO FAME: Cal is baseball's modern iron man and one of the best slugging shortstops in history.

After he graduated from high school, Cal signed with the Orioles. During his early career in the minor and major leagues, his playing time was divided between shortstop and third base. At 6' 4" tall and 220 pounds, Cal was considered big for a shortstop. That didn't slow him down, though. In 1982, he was American League Rookie of the Year.

The next season, Cal became a full-time shortstop. He hit .318, with 27 home runs and 102 RBIs, and led the Orioles to a World Series title. Cal was named American League MVP.

Cal had another MVP year in 1991. First he was MVP of the All-Star Game (he has been named to every All-Star team since 1983). Then he was honored as American League MVP. He batted .323, with 34 homers and 114 RBIs.

In 1993, Cal broke the record for career home runs by a shortstop, 287. On September 6, 1995, Cal broke LOU GEHRIG's record by playing in his 2,131st consecutive game.

FAMILY TIES In 1987, the Orioles feathered their nest with Ripkens. Cal was at shortstop, his dad was hired as the Oriole manager, and Cal's younger brother, Billy, came up from the minors to play second base. Cal and Billy made a great double-play combination. In 1990, the duo committed only 11 errors — the fewest in major league history by a second-shortstop combination. That same year, both homered in the fifth inning of a game against the Toronto Blue Jays, becoming only the fifth pair of brothers to go deep in the same inning. Billy is now with the Texas Rangers.

BASKETBALL

OSCAR ROBERTSON

Oscar Robertson was the NBA's first great all-around basketball player. He mastered every phase of the game: shooting, dribbling, passing, rebounding, defense, and teamwork.

"The Big O" grew up in Indiana, where he led Crispus Attucks High School, an all-black school, to two state titles. No all-black school had won the state title before.

At the University of Cincinnati, Oscar led the NCAA in scoring and was Player of the Year in 1958, 1959, and 1960. When he graduated, the 6' 5" guard was the all-time college scoring champ.

In 1960, Oscar co-captained the U.S. Olympic basketball team to a gold medal. He was drafted into the NBA by the Cincinnati Royals (now the Sacramento Kings). He led the league in assists and was named Rookie of the Year. Three seasons later, he was league MVP.

BIRTHPLACE: Charlotte, Tennessee
CAREER: 1960–1974
CLAIM TO FAME: Oscar was one of the greatest guards and all-around players in basketball history.

Cincinnati traded Oscar to the Milwaukee Bucks early in the 1969–70 season. There he teamed up with KAREEM ABDUL-JABBAR to lead the Bucks to the NBA title.

Oscar is the highest-scoring guard of all time (with 26,710 points) and retired as the assists leader, too (with 9,887). He was elected to the Naismith Memorial Basketball Hall of Fame in 1979.

Fun Fact

A basketball player gets credit for a triple-double when he posts double figures in three statistical areas (usually points, rebounds, and assists) in one game. The triple-double wasn't kept as an official stat until 1980 — long after Oscar played. But during the 1961–62 regular season, Oscar *averaged* a triple-double: 30.8 points, 12.5 rebounds, and 11.4 assists per game!

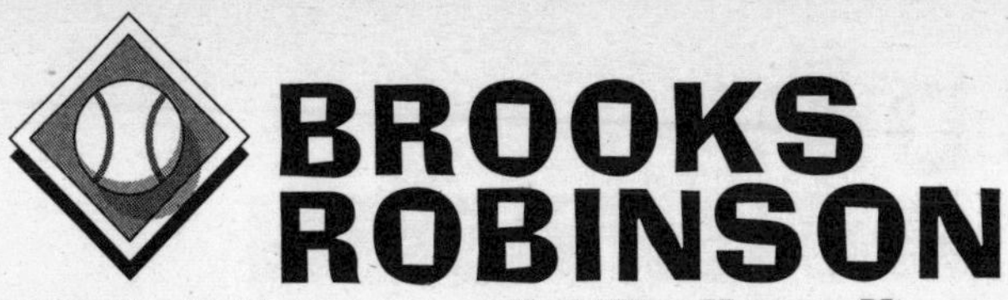

BROOKS ROBINSON

Brooks Robinson was called "The Human Vacuum Cleaner" because he scooped up any ball hit near him. The third baseman picked up 16 Gold Gloves during his 23 years with the Baltimore Orioles. He played in 15 straight All-Star Games.

Brooks had his best season in 1964. That year, he batted .317, led the league with 28 homers, and knocked in 118 runs. He was voted the American League MVP.

Brooks played in five American League Championship Series and in four World Series. In 1966, with teammate FRANK ROBINSON (no relation), the "Frank and Brooks Show" helped lead the Orioles to their first World Series championship.

In the 1970 World Series, Brooks hit .429 and made one great fielding play after another. He dove to his left and then to his right to rob Cincinnati Red batters of sure base hits. Brooks was the Series MVP, as Baltimore won the Series in five games.

INFO-BOX

BIRTHPLACE: Little Rock, Arkansas

CAREER: 1955–1977

CLAIM TO FAME: "The Human Vacuum Cleaner" was the best fielding third baseman in baseball history.

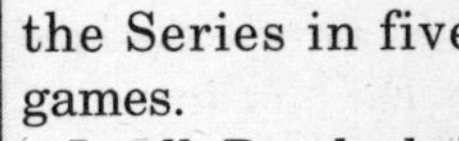

In all, Brooks led the league in assists 8 times and in fielding percentage 11 times.

He was elected to the National Baseball Hall of Fame in 1983.

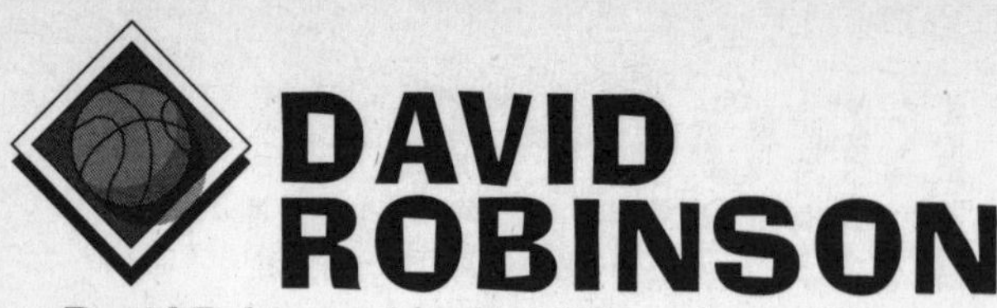

DAVID ROBINSON

David Robinson is called "The Admiral" because he attended college at the U.S. Naval Academy. He also has the kind of great all-around talent that allows him to take over a basketball game just as an admiral runs a fleet of ships.

When he was a kid, David enjoyed playing baseball, and he played just one year of high school basketball at Osbourn Park High School, in Manassas, Virginia. He went on to the Naval Academy, where he was almost not accepted because of his height. He was 6' $7\frac{1}{2}$" at the time and just made it under the height limit. By the end of his sophomore year, David had grown another five inches!

David was an All-America basketball player in his junior and senior years at the Naval Academy. He was named College Player of the Year his final season, averaging 28.2 points, 11.8 rebounds, and 4.5 blocks in 32 games. He led the NCAA in blocks, was third in scoring, and was fourth in rebounding. David became the first player to finish his college career with more than 2,500 points and 1,300 rebounds while shooting over 60 percent from the field.

The San Antonio Spurs chose David with the first pick of the 1987 NBA draft. He did not report to the team until two years later. He had to serve in the U.S. Navy first.

In his first year in the NBA, David was named to the All-Star team and won Rookie of the Year honors. He helped the Spurs go

Another Side

Basketball is not the only thing David plays. He also plays the piano, the saxophone, and the synthesizer!

David is a serious musician. He has played with famous saxophonist Branford Marsalis. If he weren't a basketball player, David says, he would like to be a professional musician. If that failed, he would be a scientist. David has a degree in civil engineering and helped build a submarine base while he was in the Navy.

from a losing team to a playoff team.

David has led the NBA in blocks (1992) and scoring (1994). In 1992, he became the third player in NBA history to finish the season in the Top 10 in five different categories — scoring (23.2), rebounding (12.2), blocks (4.49), steals (2.32), and field goal percentage (55.1). David clinched his 1994 scoring title on the final day of the season by scoring 71 points against the Los Angeles Clippers. That was the seventh-highest game total in NBA history.

INFO-BOX

BIRTHPLACE: Key West, Florida
CAREER: 1989 to the present
CLAIM TO FAME: David is one of the leading scorers, rebounders, and shot-blockers in the NBA.

In 1995, David did even better. He had another great all-around season, and was named the league's MVP! In the playoffs, he led the Spurs to the Western Conference finals, where they lost to HAKEEM OLAJUWON and the Houston Rockets.

A CLOSER LOOK During David's two-year stint in the Navy, he didn't play much basketball. The only competitive basketball he played was with the 1988 U.S. Olympic Team. The team came in third in the Olympic competition, taking the bronze medal. David was a little rusty, and he averaged only 12.8 points and 6.8 rebounds per game. David also played for the gold-medal-winning U.S. Olympic Dream Team at the 1992 Olympics.

FRANK ROBINSON

Frank Robinson was the first player to win the Most Valuable Player Award in both leagues and the first African-American to manage a major league baseball team. For 21 seasons, he was one of the toughest competitors in all of baseball.

Frank made the National League All-Star team as a Cincinnati Red outfielder in 1956, his first season in the majors. He was also named Rookie of the Year. In 1961, the Reds won the National League pennant and Frank was the league's MVP.

After 10 years with the Reds, Frank was traded to the Baltimore Orioles. He helped lead the O's to four pennants and two World Series championships. In 1966, he won the Triple Crown, leading the league in batting average (.316), home runs (49), and RBIs (122). He also led the Orioles to the 1966 World Series, where they swept the Dodgers in four games. That season, Frank was the American

INFO-BOX

BIRTHPLACE: Beaumont, Texas

CAREER: 1956–1976

CLAIM TO FAME: Before he became baseball's first black manager, Frank was a champion on the diamond.

League MVP and the World Series MVP.

Frank was not the fastest runner on the base paths, but he had great running instincts. He reached double figures in stolen bases for nine straight years. As a hitter, he crowded the plate, daring pitchers to drive him back. (As a rookie, he was hit by a pitch 20 times — a rookie record.) He was tough in the field, too, earning a Gold Glove in 1958.

In 1970, Frank hit two grand slams in the same game! That year, he and the Orioles went on to become world champions again — taking the World Series from the Cincinnati Reds in five games.

In 1975, Frank became player-manager of the Cleveland Indians *(see above)*. He retired as a player in 1976, and was elected to the National Baseball Hall of Fame in 1982.

Another Side

Frank's baseball know-how and fierce competitiveness led to the job of player-manager with the Cleveland Indians in 1975. In 1976, Frank's Indians had an 81–78 record, their best finish since 1968. Frank, who later managed the San Francisco Giants and the Baltimore Orioles, was voted Manager of the Year in both leagues — in 1982 with the Giants and in 1989 with the Orioles.

AMAZING FEAT In 1966, Frank was named the Most Valuable Player of a World Series dominated by pitchers. That year, the Dodgers and the Orioles played in the lowest-scoring World Series in history. Both teams had great pitching staffs. The Orioles had Jim Palmer, who would be a Hall of Famer, and the Dodgers had Sandy Koufax and Don Drysdale, also future Hall of Famers. Yet the star of the series was Frank Robinson.

Frank hit .286 for the Series, with a triple, two homers, and three runs batted in. That may not sound like a lot, but Frank's three RBIs were more runs than the Dodgers scored in the whole series! The O's held Los Angeles to just two runs in a four-game sweep. Frank hit a home run in the final game, giving the Orioles a 1–0 win and their first world championship.

JACKIE ROBINSON

Jackie Robinson was the first African-American to play major league baseball in the 20th century. He was also the first to win the Most Valuable Player Award and to be elected to the National Baseball Hall of Fame. Before Jackie broke the color barrier in 1947, African-Americans had not been allowed to play in the major leagues since 1887.

Jackie made history as a student, too. He was the first athlete to win varsity letters in four different sports at the University of California at Los Angeles.

After college, Jackie played baseball for the Kansas City Monarchs, a Negro league team. In 1945, he signed with the Brooklyn Dodgers. He played a season with a Dodger minor league team and then moved to the big leagues. Jackie had to face racism from players and fans, but he was determined to succeed.

At the end of the 1947 season, Jackie was named Rookie of the Year. In 1949, he was the National League MVP. In his 10-year career, he was a six-time All-Star.

Jackie was elected to the Hall of Fame in 1962. Ten years later, the Dodgers retired his number, 42.

INFO-BOX

BIRTHPLACE: Cairo, Georgia

CAREER: 1947–1956

CLAIM TO FAME: With his courage and great talent, Jackie opened the door for African-Americans to play major league baseball.

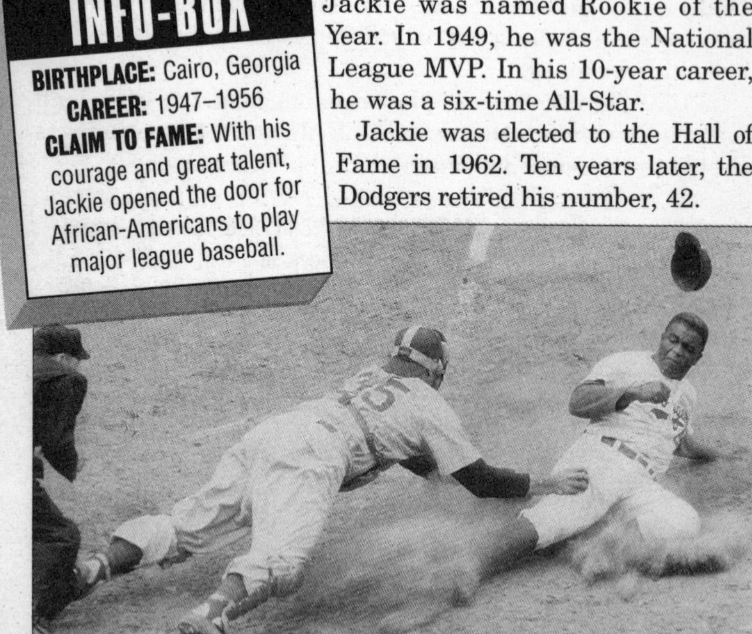

SUGAR RAY ROBINSON

"Sugar Ray" Robinson was a hero to generations of Americans who admired his fancy style. He was the welterweight boxing champion from 1946 to 1951. He moved on to the middleweight division and won that title five times.

INFO-BOX

BIRTHPLACE: Detroit, Michigan

CAREER: 1940–1952, 1955–1965

CLAIM TO FAME: The original "Sugar Ray" won six titles in two weight classes.

In his 26-year boxing career, Sugar Ray won 174 times and lost 19. He recorded 109 knockouts but was knocked out himself only once.

As an amateur fighter, Sugar Ray won two Golden Gloves titles and 85 straight bouts. In 1940, he turned professional. He was undefeated in his first 40 pro bouts, until he lost a decision to Jake LaMotta, in 1943.

Between 1943 and 1951, Sugar Ray was undefeated in 91 straight fights, ruling the welterweight (up to 147 pounds) division. He gave up that title to go after the middleweight (160 pounds) crown. He won it for the first time in 1951.

Sugar Ray was such an entertainer in the ring that he retired for a while to try to become a singer and dancer. But he soon returned to boxing to win more titles.

Amazing Feat

Sugar Ray suffered only one knockout defeat in his entire career. The KO came in 1952, during a bout at Yankee Stadium, in New York City. It was a hot summer night, and Sugar Ray was fighting champion Joey Maxim for the light heavyweight (175 pounds) title.

By the 13th round, Sugar Ray was far ahead on the judging cards against his much larger opponent. But in the extreme heat, Sugar Ray collapsed after the 13th round. Joey Maxim was credited with a knockout victory.

PETE ROSE

Pete Rose was one of baseball's greatest hitters. He holds the major league record for career hits with 4,256. As a switch-hitter, he collected more than 200 hits in a season a record 10 times! He's also the only player to play 500 games at each of five different positions.

Pete's nickname was "Charlie Hustle" because he often ran to first on a walk and slid into bases head first.

His playing career spanned 24 years. He played with the Cincinnati Reds, Philadelphia Phillies, and Montreal Expos, but is best remembered with the Reds, his hometown team. Pete joined them in 1963 and was Rookie of the Year.

Pete had his best season in 1973. He won his third batting title, hitting .338, and was named National League MVP. He helped the Reds win back-to-back World Series in 1975 and 1976 (Pete was Series MVP in 1975). In 1980, Pete led the Phillies to a Series title.

Pete returned to the Reds in 1985, first as player-manager and then as manager. In 1989, while he was manager of the Reds, Pete was banned from major league baseball because of gambling activities. The ban has kept Pete from being elected to the National Baseball Hall of Fame.

INFO-BOX

BIRTHPLACE: Cincinnati, Ohio

CAREER: 1963–1986

CLAIM TO FAME: Pete made more hits than any other player in major league baseball history.

Amazing Feat

The 1978 season was a memorable one for Pete Rose. During June and July, he attempted to break the record 56-game hitting streak set by Joe DiMaggio. Pete got a hit in 44 straight games! But the streak ended on August 1, in Atlanta, when Pete went hitless. Pete's streak tied an 81-year-old National League record set by Willie Keeler of the Baltimore Orioles. Pete batted .385 during the streak!

WILMA RUDOLPH

In 1960, Wilma Rudolph became the first United States woman ever to win three gold medals in track and field at one Olympics.

Wilma's success on the track came after a long struggle as a child, when a disease called polio left her unable to use her left leg. When she was 6, she learned to walk with a brace on the leg. Her family massaged her leg often, and by age 11, Wilma was walking normally. Soon she was running and jumping, too!

INFO-BOX

BIRTHPLACE: Bethlehem, Pennsylvania

CAREER: 1956–1964

CLAIM TO FAME: Wilma overcame polio as a child to become an Olympic champion.

In high school, Wilma was named to the state all-star basketball team all four years. She won high school state track titles in the 50-yard, 75-yard, and 100-yard dashes. In 1956, when she was 16 years old, Wilma won her first Olympic medal, a bronze, as a member of the U.S. 4 x 100 relay team.

The three gold medals Wilma won in 1960 were in the 100-meter and 200-meter sprints and as a member of the 4 x 100 relay team. She also set a world record in the 100 meters.

Wilma later worked as a teacher and coach. In 1974, she was elected to the National Track and Field Hall of Fame.

BILL RUSSELL

After Bill Russell started playing pro basketball, the game was never the same. The center dominated the sport in the 1960s by playing intense defense. No one had ever done that before. During the 13 seasons he played for the Boston Celtics, they won 11 NBA titles!

Bill was the first player to take over a game without scoring much. For a long time, teams tried to win games by sinking as many baskets as possible. But Bill showed that rebounding and shot-blocking could win games, too.

Bill, who grew up in Oakland, California, attended the University of San Francisco. With Bill anchoring the middle of the San Francisco defense, the team won 55 straight games between 1954 and 1956. They won back-to-back NCAA titles in 1955 and 1956. Bill was the tournament MVP in 1955.

After winning a gold medal as a member of the 1956 Olympic basketball team, Bill was drafted by the Celtics. He led Boston to the NBA championship in his first season! They were also champs in every year from 1959 through 1966 — eight seasons in a row!

Bill was an All-Star 12 times and the NBA's Most Valuable Player five times. He scored 14,522 points during his 13-year career, an average of 15.1 points per game.

In a typical game, Bill would grab at least 20 rebounds. He once had 51 re-

A Closer Look

Wilt Chamberlain may have been a more dominant offensive center, but Bill Russell surely had his number. Bill was shorter than Wilt and he didn't score nearly as many points, but the two big men had a great rivalry. Their teams met two times in the NBA Finals, and Bill's Celtics won both times. The first time, in 1959, Bill grabbed 35 rebounds in one game! During the 1960–61 season, Wilt averaged 50.4 points per game, but Bill was named the NBA's Most Valuable Player.

INFO-BOX

BIRTHPLACE: Monroe, Louisiana

CAREER: 1956–1969

CLAIM TO FAME: As the greatest defensive player in pro basketball, Bill led the Celtics to 11 NBA titles.

bounds in a single game! In all, he grabbed 21,620 rebounds, for an average of 22.5 per game. Only Wilt Chamberlain has more career rebounds.

Bill was a great shot-blocker, too. He had long arms and he studied the shooting routines of other players. When an opponent took a shot, Bill was there to block it. He didn't try to swat the ball out of bounds. Instead, he looked to gain control of the ball or tap it over to a teammate to start the Celtics off on a fast break and an easy basket.

He was voted into the Naismith Memorial Basketball Hall of Fame in 1974. In 1980, a group of pro basketball writers voted him the greatest player in NBA history.

ANOTHER SIDE When Boston coach Red Auerbach retired after the 1966 season, Bill took over the Celtics as a player-coach. He was the first African-American to coach a major league professional team in any sport. In 1968 and 1969, Bill guided the Celtics to two NBA championships. He later served as general manager and coach of the Seattle SuperSonics and head coach of the Sacramento Kings.

BABE RUTH

George Herman "Babe" Ruth was baseball's first great home run hitter, and fans flocked to see him play. He changed the game of baseball.

Babe learned to play ball from a priest at St. Mary's Industrial School, in Baltimore, Maryland. He had been sent there at age 7 by his parents, who couldn't control him.

Babe developed into an outstanding baseball player and was signed as a pitcher by the Baltimore Orioles, which was then a minor league team. Many of his teammates called the 19-year-old "Babe" because he was so young. In the middle of the 1914 season, Babe joined the Boston Red Sox. He quickly became one of the best pitchers in the major leagues. He also turned out to be a powerful hitter.

In 1918, Babe started playing some games in the outfield. He led the league in home runs with 11 that year. In 1919, the Red Sox made Babe a starter in the outfield, as well as a pitcher. The next year, he was traded to the New York Yankees.

INFO-BOX

BIRTHPLACE: Baltimore, Maryland
CAREER: 1914–1935
CLAIM TO FAME: Babe was baseball's first great home run hitter and became its most famous player.

Babe and his home run production were helped by several rule changes in 1920. The ball became livelier when its rub-

BASEBALL

ber center was replaced by cork. Spitballs were no longer allowed, and baseballs used in games were changed regularly instead of being used until they fell apart, as had been the practice.

Another Side

Babe's lifetime record as a pitcher was 94 wins and 46 losses! In 1916, he led the league with a 1.75 earned run average, helping the Red Sox win a world championship. Two years later, Babe led the Red Sox to another World Series title. In World Series play, Babe's ERA was 0.87 — a record that still stands.

In 1920, Babe hit 54 home runs! No one had hit more than 29 in a season before (Babe himself had done that in 1919). From 1926 through 1931, he averaged more than 50 home runs a year. He hit 60 home runs in 1927 and 714 home runs in his career, both records that stood for a long time. (Roger Maris hit 61 home runs in 1961, and HANK AARON hit his 715th home run in 1973.) In all, Babe led the American League in home runs 12 times and in RBIs 6 times.

"The Sultan of Swat" led the Yankees to seven World Series. Yankee Stadium was built to hold the crowds that came to see him. It was known as "The House That Ruth Built."

Babe retired in 1935. In 1936, he became one of the first players elected to the National Baseball Hall of Fame.

AMAZING FEAT Babe's most famous homer was his "called shot" against Chicago Cub Charlie Root in Game 3 of the 1932 World Series. The Yankees led the Series two games to none, and were in Chicago for Game 3. With the scored tied, 4–4, in the top of the fifth, the Babe stepped up to the plate. With the count at 2–2, Babe pointed toward the bleachers in center field — and hit the next pitch there for a home run. Did he "call" his home run? No one knows for sure. He might have been pointing to the pitcher, he might have been showing the crowd that he still had one more strike, or he might have been pointing at the Cub bench, filled with players who were razzing him. But one thing's for sure: It makes a good story.

NOLAN RYAN

Nolan Ryan was one of the toughest pitchers to hit in the history of baseball. Nolan is baseball's all-time strikeout leader (with 5,714). His fastball was once clocked at 100.9 miles per hour! The right-hander pitched a record seven no-hitters in his career!

From the time he was a high school pitcher in Alvin, Texas, Nolan was famous for his blistering fastball. He started his major league career with the New York Mets, and worked as a starter and a reliever on the "Miracle" Mets team that upset the Baltimore Orioles in the 1969 World Series.

Nolan struggled with his control early in his career. (He would lead the league in walks eight times.) The Mets grew frustrated with him and traded him to the California Angels in 1971.

With the Angels, Nolan became a star. He led the American League in strikeouts 11 times, fanning a record 383 in 1973. He later joined the Houston Astros and then finished his career with the Texas Rangers. Nolan won 20 games twice, led the league in shutouts three times, and won the ERA title twice.

Nolan pitched for a record 27 big-league seasons. He had 324 career victories, 11th on the all-time win list.

INFO-BOX

BIRTHPLACE: Refugio, Texas

CAREER: 1966, 1968–1992

CLAIM TO FAME: Nolan struck out more batters and pitched more no-hitters than any pitcher in the history of baseball.

Amazing Feats

Nolan pitched a record seven no-hitters. Here are the highlights:

- Nolan pitched his first no-hitter on May 15, 1973 and his seventh on May 1, 1991 — nearly 18 years later!
- On July 15, 1973, Nolan became only the fifth pitcher to throw two no-hitters in a season.
- On June 11, 1990, Nolan, at age 43, became the oldest pitcher ever to throw a no-hitter — until he threw another one (his last) a year later.

PETE SAMPRAS

In 1990, at age 19, Pete Sampras became the youngest men's U.S. Open champion in history! He has since won six more Grand Slam titles *(see page 71)* and was the world's Number 1–ranked men's player in 1993 and 1994.

Pete is a great all-around player who can serve, volley, and hit winners from the backcourt. In 1992, he competed for the U.S. in the Summer Olympic Games, in Barcelona, Spain. In 1993, he had victories at the Japan Open, in Tokyo; Wimbledon; and the U.S. Open. He became the first American to win Wimbledon and the U.S. Open in the same year since JOHN MCENROE did it in 1984. He also became the first player to record more than 1,000 aces in a year (an ace is a serve that the opponent can't get his racket on).

INFO-BOX

BIRTHPLACE: Washington, D.C.

CAREER: 1988 to the present

CLAIM TO FAME: Pete is one of the best male tennis players competing on the tour today.

Success hasn't spoiled Pete. He is quiet and laid-back. Pete, who grew up in California, stays calm during matches, making shots that keep opponents hopping.

Pete won two more Grand Slam events in 1994: Wimbledon and the Australian Open. That year he won tournaments on all four surfaces: carpet, clay, grass, and hard court. In 1995, Pete won Wimbledon for the third straight year and the U.S. Open for the third time.

WHEN HE WAS A KID Ever since Pete was 7, he wanted to be a professional tennis player. His idol was ROD LAVER, a tennis star from Australia. Rod won 11 Grand Slam titles in the 1960s. Pete studied tapes of Rod's playing to learn how to improve his own game. When Pete was 11, he met Rod and even got the chance to hit a few balls with him. Pete was so excited and nervous that he barely hit any over the net!

FOOTBALL

BARRY SANDERS

Barry Sanders isn't the biggest running back in the NFL. But what he lacks in size — being only 5' 8" tall and 203 pounds — he makes up in lightning speed and surprising power. Just when he appears to be cornered by tacklers, his tree-trunk legs shift into overdrive. Many players on opposing teams shudder with fear when they have to face him.

Barry led the NFL in rushing in 1990 and 1994. He has rushed for more than 1,000 yards in each of his first six seasons in the league.

Despite his awesome record and all the attention he receives, Barry is very shy and soft-spoken. His father taught him to stay modest and believe in himself.

Barry learned those lessons early. At North High School, in Wichita, Kansas, Barry played wide receiver and defensive back because his older brother Byron was a tailback and Barry didn't want to compete with him. Even after Byron had graduated, the coaches were afraid that because of his size, Barry might get hurt. He didn't become the starting tailback until the fourth game of his senior season! Then Barry made up for the lost time. He rushed for 274 yards in that

INFO-BOX

BIRTHPLACE: Wichita, Kansas

CAREER: 1989 to the present

CLAIM TO FAME: Barry rushed for 1,000 or more yards in each of his first six NFL seasons.

game and for more than 1,000 yards over the five remaining games, to finish the season with a school-record 1,417 yards.

In his first two seasons at Oklahoma State University, Barry played second fiddle to teammate (and current Buffalo Bill) Thurman Thomas. But during his junior year, in 1988, Barry made his mark. He set 13 NCAA records, including most rushing yards (2,628) and most touchdowns (39) in a season. He won the Heisman Trophy as the top college football player of the year.

When He Was a Kid

When Barry was growing up, he spent his summer months working in his father's roofing business. One of Barry's jobs was to climb ladders and haul hundreds of pounds of asphalt strapped to his back. That's hard work! Maybe that's why today Barry can carry linebackers on his back as he runs for touchdowns!

Barry was the Detroit Lions' first-round draft pick in 1989. In his first year in the NFL, he ran for 1,470 yards and was Rookie of the Year. In 1990, he led the league in rushing with 1,304 yards. Barry was NFL rushing champion again in 1994, when he ran for 1,883 yards, tying JIM BROWN for the fourth-highest single-season total in NFL history.

In his first six NFL seasons, Barry rushed for 8,672 yards, scored 67 touchdowns, and made six straight trips to the Pro Bowl. The modest Barry has reason to be proud.

DID YOU KNOW?

- In 1988, Barry averaged 295.5 yards per game rushing, receiving, and returning kicks for Oklahoma State. That broke college football's oldest record, which had been set in 1937 by Byron "Whizzer" White of the University of Colorado. (Byron was later an associate justice on the U.S. Supreme Court.)
- Barry has great speed and strength. He has run the 40-yard dash in 4.27 seconds, has squat-lifted 557 pounds, and has jumped 41½ inches straight up from a standing start!
- A religious man, Barry gives 10 percent of his salary to his church in Kansas.

DEION SANDERS

Whether Deion Sanders is high-stepping into the end zone with an interception for the Dallas Cowboys or stealing bases for the San Francisco Giants, he can light up a ball game.

As an outfielder for the Atlanta Braves, the Cincinnati Reds, and the Giants (he also played for the New York Yankees), Deion has become one of the National League's top leadoff hitters. In 1992, he hit 14 triples in spite of playing in fewer than 100 games. During the 1992 World Series, with the Braves, he batted .333 and stole four bases.

Deion's record in football is even more impressive. He was a two-time All-America cornerback at Florida State University. He won the 1988 Jim Thorpe Award as the nation's top defensive back and was a first-round draft pick of the Atlanta Falcons in 1989.

One of the fastest men in the NFL, Deion has often been among the league leaders in interceptions and punt and kickoff returns. He has even played a little wide receiver. In his first game in 1992, Deion returned a kickoff 99 yards for a touchdown. He has played in three Pro Bowls in six seasons.

INFO-BOX

BIRTHPLACE: Fort Myers, Florida

CAREER: 1989 to the present

CLAIM TO FAME: Deion is the only player today who stars in both professional baseball and football.

Deion would play baseball until the season ended in October and then join the Falcons to play football. The Falcons wanted Deion full-time or not at all, but Deion refused to give up baseball. Before the 1994 season, the Falcons made him a free agent, and he signed with the San Francisco 49ers.

Amazing Feat

In 1989, his rookie year, Deion made history. On September 5, while playing for the New York Yankees, Deion hit a home run. On September 10, in the first quarter of his first game with the Falcons, Deion returned a punt for a touchdown. He was the first athlete to hit a home run in the major leagues and score a touchdown in the NFL in the same week!

In his only season with the 49ers, Deion was a defensive force. He intercepted six passes and returned three of them for touchdowns. He became the first player in NFL history to have two interception returns for touchdowns of more than 90 yards in one season. The 49ers won the Super Bowl, and Deion was named the NFL's Defensive Player of the Year. In September 1995, he joined the Cowboys.

Deion likes to be called "Prime Time." Some people think he has a big ego because of the things he does. But Deion says he's nothing like his razzle-dazzle image. In fact, when he was growing up, he was shy and sensitive. He even cried when his teams lost and got headaches before and after games because he was so focused on winning.

Now Deion is the one giving other teams headaches.

DID YOU KNOW?

- Deion wears rubber bands on both wrists. He started doing it in college for good luck.
- Deion collects cars. He owns 11, and every one is black.
- Deion's mom says that her son has always been afraid of the dark. "He still sleeps with the lights on," she says.
- Deion wants to be a rap star. He has released an album called *Prime Time.* He also raps on the soundtrack to the movie *Street Fighter.*

FOOTBALL

GALE SAYERS

Gale Sayers was such a great running back he was nicknamed "The Kansas Comet." Unfortunately, knee injuries forced him to retire after just seven seasons in the NFL.

After playing college football at the University of Kansas, Gale joined the Chicago Bears, in 1965. In just his third game, he scored four touchdowns. Later that season, he tied a record by scoring *six* touchdowns in a game! Gale set a rookie record by scoring 22 touchdowns in 1965 and was named Rookie of the Year.

Gale led the NFL in rushing in 1966 and 1969. He averaged 5.0 yards per carry for his career and a record 30.6 yards per kick return.

INFO-BOX

BIRTHPLACE: Wichita, Kansas

CAREER: 1965–1971

CLAIM TO FAME: Gale was one of the most exciting running backs in football history.

BASKETBALL

DOLPH SCHAYES

At 6' 8", Dolph Schayes was basketball's first modern forward — fast and willing to drive to the basket. He retired as the leading scorer in NBA history, with 19,249 points.

Dolph played his first pro season for the Syracuse Nationals of the National Basketball League. He was Rookie of the Year. (The next season, Syracuse became part of the NBA. The team later moved to Philadelphia and became the 76ers.)

The 12-time All-Star was always among the leaders in scoring and rebounding. He led the Nats to the NBA title in 1955.

Dolph is the father of Danny Schayes, who plays for the Phoenix Suns.

INFO-BOX

BIRTHPLACE: New York, New York

CAREER: 1948–1964

CLAIM TO FAME: Dolph was professional basketball's first modern, high-scoring forward.

MIKE SCHMIDT

In 18 seasons with the Philadelphia Phillies, Mike Schmidt hit 548 home runs and was National League MVP three times. He led the league in home runs eight times and in RBIs four times.

Early on, Mike struck out often and made many errors. But he learned to judge pitches and improved his defense. He then won 10 Gold Glove awards for fielding.

Mike led his team to a World Series win in 1980 and was the MVP. He hit more home runs (509) than any other third baseman. In 1995, he was voted into the National Baseball Hall of Fame.

INFO-BOX

BIRTHPLACE: Dayton, Ohio
CAREER: 1972–1989
CLAIM TO FAME: A great slugger and a solid fielder, Mike was the best all-around third baseman in baseball history.

TOM SEAVER

Tom Seaver was known as "Tom Terrific." For 20 seasons, he was one of the most talented pitchers in the major leagues.

A right-hander, Tom was Rookie of the Year in 1967 for the New York Mets and eventually won the Cy Young Award three times. In 1969, he won 25 games and helped the Mets win their first World Series. Tom also pitched for the Cincinnati Reds, the Chicago White Sox, and the Boston Red Sox. He had many great games, including a no-hitter and a 19-strikeout game. He fanned a major-league-record 10 batters in a row to end that game!

Tom set another record by striking out 200 or more batters in each of 10 seasons. He won 311 games, and was inducted into the National Baseball Hall of Fame in 1992.

INFO-BOX

BIRTHPLACE: Fresno, California
CAREER: 1967–1986
CLAIM TO FAME: Tom was one of the most consistent winners in National League history.

BASEBALL

SECRETARIAT

Secretariat was a horse, but his appeal went beyond racing and touched people in a special way. Even people who did not normally follow racing knew of the exploits of the chestnut-colored stallion known as "Big Red."

Trained by Lucien Lauren and regularly ridden by jockey Ron Turcotte, Secretariat was the greatest thoroughbred of the last 40 years. Other horses compiled better records than Secretariat's 16 victories in 21 career starts. Other horses won more money than Secretariat's $1,316,808. But no horse could dominate a race as he could.

Secretariat lost his first race, on July 4, 1972. But he won seven of his next eight starts and was named Horse of the Year in his first racing season. He was the first 2-year-old ever to achieve that honor. As a 3-year-old, in 1973, he won the title again and set new standards of excellence.

No horse since Citation in 1948 had won the Triple Crown (the Kentucky Derby, the Preakness Stakes, and the Belmont Stakes). On May 5, 1973, Secretariat won the Kentucky Derby in 1:59$\frac{2}{5}$, a track record for the 1$\frac{1}{4}$-mile classic that still stands. Two weeks later, he won the 1$\frac{3}{16}$-mile Preakness Stakes, at Pimlico racetrack, in Baltimore, Maryland. His time of 1:54$\frac{2}{5}$ was hotly disputed. He may have set a record, but the official clock had not worked properly.

He had only to win the Belmont three weeks later to win the Triple Crown. Before the Belmont Stakes, Secretariat's picture appeared on the cover of *Time,*

More Stars!

In a poll conducted in 1988 by *Racing Action,* a weekly newspaper, to determine the greatest thoroughbreds of this century, Secretariat finished second behind a horse called Man O' War.

Man O' War never won the Triple Crown because his owner didn't enter him in the Kentucky Derby. Man O' War did win the Preakness and the Belmont Stakes in 1920. He raced 21 times during his career and won 20 times.

INFO-BOX

BIRTHPLACE: Doswell, Virginia

CAREER: 1972–1973

CLAIM TO FAME: Secretariat was one of the greatest racehorses in thoroughbred racing history.

Sports Illustrated, and *Newsweek* magazines. He didn't let anyone down. Secretariat's run in the Belmont Stakes is widely regarded as the greatest performance in horse-racing history. He covered the mile and a half in 2:24 and won by an astounding 31 lengths. His time shattered the track record by 2 3/5 seconds and still stands.

After winning four of his next six races, Secretariat was retired. He was sold for $6.08 million to a group of horsemen, who used him to breed other racehorses. Secretariat spent the last 16 years of his life at Claiborne Farms, in Kentucky. He received many fan letters, and people made special trips just to watch him graze in the pasture.

A CLOSER LOOK To win the Triple Crown, a 3-year-old horse must win the three biggest races of the year: the Kentucky Derby, the Preakness Stakes, and the Belmont Stakes. Besides Secretariat, only 10 horses in history have won the Triple Crown: Sir Barton (in 1919), Gallant Fox (1930), Omaha (1935), War Admiral (1937), Whirlaway (1941), Count Fleet (1943), Assault (1946), Citation (1948), Seattle Slew (1977), and Affirmed (1978).

WILLIE SHOEMAKER

Willie Shoemaker grew up to be only 4' 11" and 100 pounds. But he did not let his size prevent him from succeeding. Willie became the winningest jockey in horse-racing history, compiling 8,833 victories over a 41-year career.

Born in Texas, Willie moved with his family to California when he was 10. He was a boxer and a wrestler in high school. When he was 16, he got a part-time job working with horses at a ranch.

Willie went to San Francisco to learn to become a jockey. He made his riding debut in 1949 and continued to ride until he was 58. He rode more mounts (40,350) and won more stakes races (1,009) than any other jockey. He once won a record 485 races in a season! Willie won the Kentucky Derby four times, the Preakness twice, and the Belmont Stakes five times.

Although Willie survived many falls as a jockey, his worst injury came after he had quit riding. He was paralyzed from the chest down when the car he was driving ran off the road and crashed. Now confined to a wheelchair, he still loves to be around racing and works training horses.

INFO-BOX

BIRTHPLACE: Fabens, Texas
CAREER: 1949–1990
CLAIM TO FAME: In his 41-year career, Willie won more races (8,833) than any other jockey in horse-racing history.

When He Was a Kid

Willie Shoemaker was born a month earlier than he was supposed to be and weighed only two and a half pounds at birth. This was before hospitals had special equipment to help premature babies. In fact, most babies were born at home. The doctor doubted the baby would live through his first night. But Willie's grandmother wrapped him in blankets and put him on the oven door to keep warm. Miraculously, Willie survived.

O.J. SIMPSON

FOOTBALL

O.J. Simpson is one of America's most recognizable people. Before he was in movies or on television or in the headlines, he was a football player — one of the best running backs of all time.

O.J., which stands for Orenthal James, was one of the most graceful football players ever. He spun and danced his way down the field to avoid would-be tacklers. While playing for the University of Southern California in 1968, O.J. won the Heisman Trophy, which is given to the best player in college football.

Later, with the Buffalo Bills of the NFL, "Juice," as O.J. was called, became the first player ever to run for more than 2,000 yards in one season, which he did in 1973. He finished that season with 2,003 yards in 14 games. O.J.'s great career with the Bills and San Francisco 49ers earned him a spot in the Pro Football Hall of Fame.

INFO-BOX

BIRTHPLACE: San Francisco, California

CAREER: 1969–1979

CLAIM TO FAME: O.J. was the first NFL running back to rush for more than 2,000 yards in a season.

After he retired, O.J. worked as a sports announcer and actor in movies and commercials. O.J.'s fame turned to infamy in 1994, however, when he was accused of killing his ex-wife and a male acquaintance. Now O.J. Simpson is famous for being perhaps the most well-known American ever to go on trial for murder.

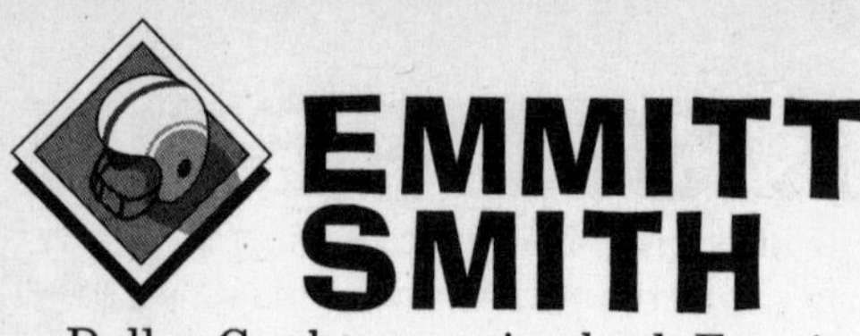

EMMITT SMITH

Dallas Cowboy running back Emmitt Smith has done a lot in a short time. He has won three rushing titles in just five NFL seasons. He is the first running back to win a rushing title and play in the Super Bowl in the same season. He is also the first running back to win a rushing title, the regular- season Most Valuable Player Award, and the Super Bowl MVP trophy in the same season!

It seems that Emmitt has been on a fast track for a long time. In his four years at Escambia High School, in Pensacola, Florida, Emmitt gained 8,804 career yards. He is third on the all-time rushing list in the National High School Sports Record book. In his senior year, he was named Player of the Year by both *USA Today* and *Parade* magazine.

INFO-BOX

BIRTHPLACE: Pensacola, Florida

CAREER: 1990 to the present

CLAIM TO FAME: Emmitt won three rushing titles in his first five seasons in the NFL.

Emmitt attended college at the University of Florida. There, in just the seventh game of his freshman year, he passed the 1,000-yard mark in rushing. That was the fastest anyone had rushed for 1,000 yards in the history of college football. In his three seasons at Florida (he left after his junior year), Emmitt became the fifth-leading rusher in the history of the Southeastern Conference, with 3,928 yards, and set 58 school records.

Many pro football scouts didn't think Emmitt would make it in the NFL because of his height (he's only 5' 9" tall, short for the pros) and average speed. Sixteen NFL teams passed on him in the 1990 draft, until the Dallas Cowboys selected him.

Another Side

In his first year in the NFL, Emmitt started collecting football cards — of himself! He got to be quite a collector and, in 1991, opened his own sports-card shop in Pensacola. Today, his store has more than one million cards in stock — no, they're not all Emmitt Smith cards! The store, named Emmitt, Inc., Trading Cards and Collectibles, sells different kinds of sports cards, helmets, caps, jerseys, and jackets. Emmitt's family helps run the shop. During football's off-season, you might even run into Emmitt himself there!

With the Cowboys, Emmitt won three straight rushing titles (1991–93). He became the first player to have back-to-back seasons of 1,500 yards or more since WALTER PAYTON. In Super Bowl XXVII, in 1993, Emmitt rushed for 108 yards on 22 carries and scored one touchdown, helping the Cowboys win 52–17. In Super Bowl XXVIII, in 1994, Emmitt rushed for 132 yards, scored two touchdowns, and was named the game's MVP.

Although he has achieved a lot already, Emmitt has big plans for the future. He hopes to break the NFL's career rushing record of 16,726 yards, held by Walter Payton.

DID YOU KNOW?

- Emmitt's favorite subject in school was math. He loved fractions and geometry.
- In addition to collecting cards, Emmitt likes to collect model trains and play video games.
- When he's not playing football, Emmitt's favorite places to be are at home or on the golf course.

OZZIE SMITH

Ozzie Smith has been called the greatest shortstop ever to play baseball. His defensive play is often so spectacular that he was given the nickname "The Wizard of Oz." His 13 Gold Gloves for fielding are the most ever earned by a National Leaguer.

Ozzie has been a major league player since 1978, when he started with the San Diego Padres. A 13-time All-Star, Ozzie began as a weak hitter but eventually made himself into a dangerous offensive player. He rarely strikes out, and he draws a high number of walks.

His best offensive season came in 1987, when he batted .303, with 75 RBIs and 89 walks. He also steals a lot of bases — 569 through 1994.

In 1982, Ozzie set a World Series record for most putouts by a shortstop in a seven-game series — 22. His performance helped the St. Louis Cardinals defeat the Milwaukee Brewers in the World Series.

Ozzie holds the single-season (621) and career records for most assists by a shortstop.

INFO-BOX

IRTHPLACE: Mobile, Alabama

CAREER: 1978 to the present

CLAIM TO FAME: Ozzie, nicknamed The Wizard of Oz, is the finest fielding shortstop in baseball history.

BASEBALL

WARREN SPAHN

With 363 victories, Warren Spahn is the winningest left-handed pitcher of all time. He won 20 or more games in a season 12 times, and led the National League in wins eight times.

Because of Army service, Warren didn't play his first full season until 1946, when he turned 25. He became the ace of the Milwaukee Braves' staff for 17 seasons. (The Braves moved to Atlanta in 1966.)

In 1957, Warren won the Cy Young Award and helped the Braves win the World Series. In 1963, at the age of 42, he won 23 games! Warren was elected to the National Baseball Hall of Fame in 1973.

INFO-BOX

BIRTHPLACE: Buffalo, New York

CAREER: 1942, 1946–1965

CLAIM TO FAME: Warren was the winningest left-handed pitcher in baseball history.

TRIS SPEAKER

His combination of excellence in the field and at the plate made Tris Speaker one of the best center fielders in baseball.

Tris batted .344 for his career, and nobody has been able to approach his record of 792 career doubles. He also holds the outfield records for most career assists (448) and double plays, and is second on the all-time putout list (6,791). A daring defender, he often played shallow, making plays in the infield and chasing down short flies.

Tris helped the Boston Red Sox win two World Series and the Cleveland Indians win their first World Series. In 1937, he was inducted into the National Baseball Hall of Fame.

INFO-BOX

BIRTHPLACE: Hubbard City, Texas

CAREER: 1907–1928

CLAIM TO FAME: Tris, a career .344 hitter, was one of the greatest center fielders in baseball history.

MARK SPITZ

In 1968, Mark Spitz boasted that he would win six gold medals in the swimming events at the Summer Olympics. Mark was way off. He won only two gold medals — both in relays — as well as a silver and a bronze. Even worse, he came in last in the 200-meter butterfly. That was a big disappointment because Mark held the world record in that event.

But four years later, at the 1972 Olympics, Mark's prediction came true. By the end of the swimming competition, he had collected seven gold medals and set world records in each event. His medals came in the 100-meter and 200-meter freestyle events, 100-meter and 200-meter butterfly, 400-meter freestyle relay, 800-meter freestyle relay, and 400-meter medley relay. Mark was the first swimmer ever to win more than five gold medals and the first athlete ever to win seven gold medals in a single Olympics!

Mark was born in California. His family moved to Hawaii when he was 2. He learned to swim at the world-famous Waikiki Beach, in Honolulu, Hawaii. He swam there every day from the time he was 2 until his family moved back to the mainland when he was 6.

By then, Mark was an excellent swimmer for his age. He started swimming competitively at the age of 8. When he was ready to go to college, he chose to attend Indiana University, where he won eight NCAA ti-

More Stars!

Matt Biondi was the best U.S. male swimmer since Mark Spitz. Matt's best strokes were also freestyle and butterfly. He won his first Olympic medal, a gold, in the 4 x 100-meter relay at the 1984 Games. At the 1988 Olympics, Matt won seven medals: five gold (in the 50-meter and 100-meter freestyles, the 400-meter and 800-meter freestyle relays, and the 400-meter medley relay), a silver, and a bronze. In 1992, Matt won three more medals — bringing his Olympic total to 11 — to tie Mark Spitz!

INFO-BOX

BIRTHPLACE: Modesto, California
OLYMPIC CAREER: 1968 and 1972
CLAIM TO FAME: Mark won a record seven gold medals at the 1972 Olympics.

tles from 1969 to 1972. In 1971, Mark won the Sullivan Award, which is given each year to the country's best amateur athlete.

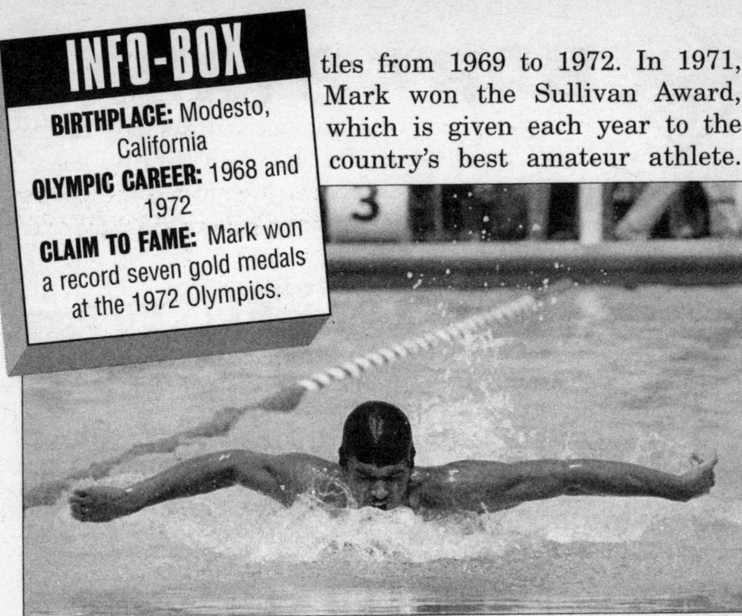

His best strokes were the freestyle and the butterfly.

Soon after the 1972 Olympics, Mark retired. But in 1991, at the age of 41, he launched a comeback. He tried to qualify for the 1992 Summer Olympics in the 100-meter butterfly. He didn't make the U.S. team, but he couldn't really complain. After all, he had already won 11 Olympic medals!

TIME CAPSULE In 1972, Mark Spitz made Olympic history by winning seven gold medals. Here are some things that were going on in the rest of the world that year:

- U.S. President Richard Nixon visited China. The two countries agreed to improve their relationship.
- After a four-year calm, the U.S. resumed heavy bombing in North Vietnam after the North Vietnamese attacked the demilitarized (or neutral) zone.
- President Nixon became the first U.S. President to visit Moscow, in the Soviet Union (now Russia). There he met with Soviet leaders and completed a military arms agreement.
- Five men were arrested for breaking into the offices of the Democratic National Committee in the Watergate office complex in Washington, D.C. The men were trying to steal information that could damage the Democratic party and help President Nixon get re-elected. This action led to the resignation of President Nixon.

FOOTBALL

BART STARR

Bart Starr was the quarterback for one of the NFL's great teams. But he wasn't always a success. Bart wasn't drafted until the 17th round, and he was taken by a losing team, the Green Bay Packers. (In 1958, the Packers won only one game!)

But with Bart and coach Vince Lombardi, the Packers turned it around. Beginning in 1961, they won five NFL titles in seven years.

Bart led the league in passing three times and was NFL Player of the Year in 1966. He was MVP of the first two Super Bowls ever played — both won by Green Bay.

Bart is one of nine players from the Packers of the 1960s to be elected to the Pro Football Hall of Fame.

INFO-BOX

BIRTHPLACE: Montgomery, Alabama

CAREER: 1956–1971

CLAIM TO FAME: Bart was the quarterback for the great Green Bay Packer teams of the 1960s.

FOOTBALL

ROGER STAUBACH

Although he got a late start, Roger Staubach had a big impact on the Dallas Cowboys. He led them to four Super Bowls!

Roger attended the U.S. Naval Academy, where he won the Heisman Trophy. He then served in the Navy for four years.

Roger led the Cowboys to a Super Bowl win in 1972 and was named the game's MVP. (He and Marcus Allen are the only two players to win a Heisman Trophy, NFL Player of the Year award, and Super Bowl MVP.)

In 1979, at age 37, Roger led the NFL in passing. But a series of head injuries forced him to retire at the end of the season. He was elected to the Pro Football Hall of Fame in 1985.

INFO-BOX

BIRTHPLACE: Cincinnati, Ohio

CAREER: 1969–1979

CLAIM TO FAME: Roger quarterbacked the Dallas Cowboys to four Super Bowls.

JAN STENERUD

FOOTBALL

When Jan *[yahn]* Stenerud moved to the U.S. from Norway at age 19, he had never even seen a football game. His sport was ski jumping, and he had earned a scholarship to Montana State University. But Jan quickly got into football. With a kicking style he learned from playing soccer, he went on to become one of the best place-kickers ever in the NFL.

Jan played 19 seasons, mostly with the Kansas City Chiefs. He kicked a record 373 field goals and is second all-time in points scored.

In Super Bowl IV, in 1970, Jan kicked three field goals to help the Chiefs win the championship.

INFO-BOX

BIRTHPLACE: Fetsund, Norway

CAREER: 1967–1985

CLAIM TO FAME: Jan is the only player in the Pro Football Hall of Fame for his place-kicking alone.

JOHN STOCKTON

BASKETBALL

John Stockton is the best point guard in the NBA today and one of the best in history. On February 1, 1995, he broke Magic Johnson's career assist record with his 9,922nd assist.

John had a great college career at Gonzaga University in Washington. The Utah Jazz made him their first pick in the 1984 NBA draft.

Since then, John has set many assists records. After 11 seasons, he was averaging more than 11.6 assists per game. That's the highest career average ever! He has led the NBA in assists for eight seasons in a row.

John was a member of the 1992 U.S. Olympic basketball Dream Team, which won the gold medal in Barcelona, Spain.

INFO-BOX

BIRTHPLACE: Spokane, Washington

CAREER: 1984 to the present

CLAIM TO FAME: John has passed for more assists than any other player in NBA history.

NAIM SULEYMANOGLU

Naim Suleymanoglu may be only 5' tall and 132 pounds, but he is one of the strongest men in the world. He was the second weightlifter ever to lift more than three times his body weight and the youngest world-record holder in weightlifting history. At age 15, he set records by lifting a total of 629.8 pounds and 353.6 pounds in the clean and jerk.

Naim was born in Bulgaria, when it was under Communist rule. In the 1988 and 1992 Olympics, he competed for Turkey, his parents' homeland. He won three gold medals each time. In 1988, he set six world records on the same day!

INFO-BOX

BIRTHPLACE: Ptichar, Bulgaria
OLYMPIC CAREER: 1988, 1992
CLAIM TO FAME: "The Pocket Hercules" was the youngest world-record holder in weightlifting history.

JOHN L. SULLIVAN

John L. Sullivan was boxing's last bare-knuckle champion. He reigned from 1882 to 1892. One of the first American sports idols, John L. had a popular song and a poem written about him!

In boxing's early days, fighters did not wear gloves. The last bare-knuckle heavyweight title bout took place in 1889. The undefeated John L. beat Jake Kilrain in a fight that lasted 75 rounds!

Boxing adopted a new set of rules in the late 1800s. One of those rules said that boxers had to wear padded gloves. In 1892, John L. fought for the title under the new rules. He was knocked out in the 21st round by "Gentleman" JIM CORBETT. It was John L.'s only fight wearing boxing gloves.

INFO-BOX

BIRTHPLACE: Roxbury, Massachusetts
CAREER: 1878–1905
CLAIM TO FAME: John L. was a heavyweight boxing champion before there were boxing gloves.

LYNN SWANN

Lynn Swann was one of the best wide receivers in the NFL in the 1970s. His amazing talent and acrobatic catches helped the Pittsburgh Steelers win four Super Bowls.

During his career, Lynn made 51 touchdown receptions and was named to three Pro Bowls. In four Super Bowls, he caught passes for a total of 364 yards. That was an NFL record until it was broken by JERRY RICE.

INFO-BOX

BIRTHPLACE: Alcoa, Tennessee

CAREER: 1974–1982

CLAIM TO FAME: Lynn was a great wide receiver for the Pittsburgh Steeler teams that won four Super Bowls.

One of Lynn's greatest moments came during Super Bowl X, in 1976. Two weeks before the game, he suffered a head injury in a playoff game. But it didn't stop him from playing in the Super Bowl.

During the game, Lynn made four spectacular catches and gained 164 yards. He caught the fourth pass off his fingertips, then zoomed into the end zone for a 64-yard touchdown. That play made the score 21–10 over the Dallas Cowboys. The Steelers won the game, 21–17, and Lynn was named the Super Bowl's Most Valuable Player.

MORE STARS! Lynn Swann was part of a Pittsburgh Steeler offense that sometimes was overshadowed by the team's awesome defense. The "Steel Curtain," as the defense was called, got most of the attention when Pittsburgh won four Super Bowls, but the offense was a powerhouse, too.

Lynn and John Stallworth formed a dynamic duo at wide receiver. John averaged a record 40.3 yards per catch in Super Bowl XIV, in 1980. Quarterback TERRY BRADSHAW was a two-time Super Bowl MVP and earned a spot in the Pro Football Hall of Fame. Running back Franco Harris, also a Hall of Famer, is the Super Bowl's all-time leading rusher. In four games, he rushed for 354 yards on 101 carries, both records. Center Mike Webster was one of the best offensive linemen in football history.

FRAN TARKENTON

After 18 seasons in the NFL, Fran Tarkenton had completed more passes (3,686) for more yards (47,003) and more touchdowns (342) than any other quarterback in league history. But he is better known for his legs than his throwing arm!

Fran had a style all his own. Instead of dropping straight back before passing the football, Fran would take the snap from center and often run all over the field before finding a receiver to throw to. Sometimes he would just take off and run with the ball himself. This is called "scrambling." Though other players had done it before him, Fran was the first player to be described as a scrambler.

INFO-BOX

BIRTHPLACE: Richmond, Virginia

CAREER: 1961–1978

CLAIM TO FAME: Fran was a great scrambling quarterback and the NFL's all-time leading passer.

After starting his pro career with the Minnesota Vikings, Fran then played five years for the New York Giants. He returned to Minnesota in 1972. He led the Vikings to the Super Bowl three times, but they lost each time.

Fran was named the NFL's Most Valuable Player in 1975, when he led the league in touchdown passes and led the National Football Conference in passing.

Amazing Feat

Fran played in his first NFL game on September 17, 1961, at Metropolitan Stadium, in Bloomington, Minnesota, against the Chicago Bears. Fran came off the bench to lead the Vikings to five touchdowns, four passing and one rushing (by himself). The Vikings won, 37–13, in a big upset. Why was it such an upset? Not only was it Fran's debut, it was also the Vikings' first game ever!

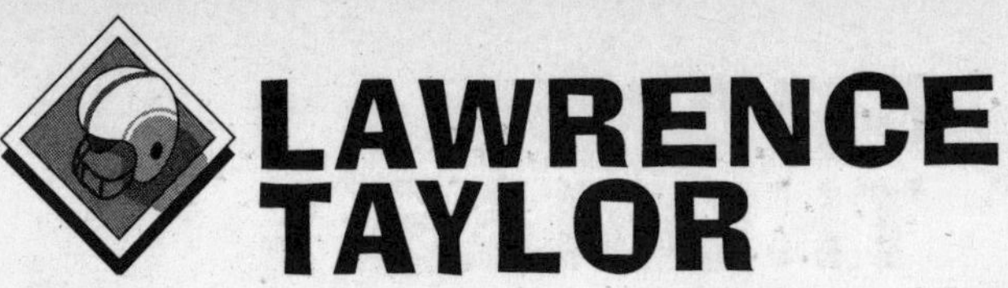

LAWRENCE TAYLOR

Who was the best linebacker in NFL history? It just might have been Lawrence Taylor. As a New York Giant, Lawrence was so hard to stop that some players called him "Superman."

His combination of speed, power, aggressive play, and talent for being all over the field — sacking the quarterback, stopping running backs, and breaking up pass plays — changed the way football was played in the 1980s. Offensive linemen, who weighed as much as 50 pounds more than Lawrence, couldn't do anything to stop him. Sometimes teams playing the Giants had to change their whole strategy just to try to control Lawrence!

INFO-BOX

BIRTHPLACE: Williamsburg, Virginia

CAREER: 1981–1993

CLAIM TO FAME: Lawrence could win games almost single-handedly from the linebacker position.

Lawrence finished his career with 132.5 sacks. That's the most sacks ever recorded by a linebacker (and it doesn't even include the 9.5 sacks he had before sacks became an official statistic, in 1981). He led the Giants to two Super Bowls and helped them win it each time!

"LT," as he was called, played in 10 Pro Bowls — an NFL record. He was a three-time NFL Defensive Player of the Year. In 1986, he became the first linebacker — and just the second defensive player ever — to be named league MVP.

FRANK THOMAS

Frank Thomas is called "The Big Hurt" because his play with his bat and his glove hurts opposing teams. But Frank knew his own share of hurt on his way to the major leagues.

The first year Frank tried out for his high school baseball team, he was cut. He worked hard to make the team the next season, batted .472, and led Columbus (Georgia) High School to its first state title.

Frank had a great high school career, but not one major league team selected him in the 1986 amateur draft. So he accepted a football scholarship to Auburn University (in Alabama). He made the baseball team after a tryout, and set school records for home runs in a career (49) and in a season (21). He was the Southeastern Conference's MVP in 1989.

Frank starred for the U.S. team at the Pan American Games in 1987. But he was cut from the 1988 U.S. Olympic baseball team.

The Chicago White Sox took notice of

INFO-BOX

BIRTHPLACE: Columbus, Georgia

CAREER: 1990 to the present

CLAIM TO FAME: "The Big Hurt" is probably the most feared hitter in baseball today.

Frank and made him the seventh pick overall in the 1989 draft. One year later, Frank was called up from the minors to give the Sox some punch in their pennant drive. Frank did the job, batting .330 with 31 RBIs and 7 home runs in 60 games. He has been a big man in the Sox lineup ever since.

Another Side

Frank was a three-sport star at Columbus High School, in Georgia, and went to the University of Auburn to play football as a tight end. He played little his freshman year, catching three passes for 45 yards. But playing a little football turned out to be a big part of Frank's decision to pursue baseball full-time. After spraining his knee in practice, Frank decided there was too much risk of injury in football. He concentrated only on baseball.

But Frank wasn't finished being hurt. People questioned his defensive skills. So, Frank lifted weights more and took extra fielding practice. In 1993, he was the starting first baseman for the American League All-Star team, a feat he repeated in 1994.

In his first four full seasons, Frank became only the fifth major leaguer in history to bat over .300, hit 20 home runs, drive in 100 runs, score 100 runs, and walk 100 times in three consecutive seasons. He won the league's MVP Award two years in a row, in 1993 and 1994. He batted .353 with 38 home runs and 101 RBIs in the strike-shortened 1994 season.

Frank is a modest man. After a homer, he'll circle the bases quickly, with his head down. The Big Hurt wants to beat the other team — but he doesn't want to hurt the pitcher's feelings.

A CLOSER LOOK Above his locker in the White Sox clubhouse, Frank has stuck three strips of white athletic tape. He has written on each strip. They read: RELAX, HAVE SOME FUN; RELAX, STAY WITHIN YOURSELF; and D.B.T.H. The first two are reminders to stay loose and focused at the same time. The third stands for DON'T BELIEVE THE HYPE. Even as a star, Frank wants to be a humble and hard-working player.

ISIAH THOMAS

The 6' 1" tall, 185-pound Isiah Thomas proved that a little man can succeed in a big man's game. The point guard and captain of the Detroit Pistons led his team to NBA championships in 1989 and 1990 (when he was Finals MVP).

In college, Isiah led Indiana University to the NCAA championship in 1981 and was voted the Most Outstanding Player of the tournament. He turned professional after his sophomore season.

Isiah was selected by Detroit as the second overall pick in the 1981 NBA draft. He proved to be a great clutch performer who could shift his play into a higher gear when a game was on the line.

INFO-BOX

BIRTHPLACE: Chicago, Illinois

CAREER: 1981–1994

CLAIM TO FAME: Isiah was an explosive scorer and one of the greatest passers in NBA history.

Isiah played 13 seasons with the Pistons. He is the team's all-time leader in points, assists, steals, and games played. His 9,061 career assists (an average of 9.3 per game) is the fourth-highest total in NBA history. He was named to the All-Star team in each of his first 12 seasons, and twice won the game's MVP Award (1984 and 1986).

Now, Isiah is vice president of the Toronto Raptors, a new NBA team that began play with the 1995–96 season.

Amazing Feats

Isiah was awesome in the playoffs. In the 1988 NBA Finals, he scored 25 points in the third quarter of Game 6 against the Los Angeles Lakers, a record for points in a quarter of a Finals game. He had 24 points in the third quarter of a playoff game against the Atlanta Hawks in 1987. In a playoff game against the New York Knicks, in 1984, Isiah scored 16 points in 94 seconds!

JIM THORPE

At the 1912 Olympics, in Stockholm, Sweden, the King of Sweden called Jim Thorpe "the greatest athlete in the world." Jim had won two gold medals. But, in fact, his sports career was only beginning.

Born in Oklahoma in 1888, Jim was part Irish, part French, and part Native American. He was a standout athlete in college at the Carlisle Indian School, in Pennsylvania. At the 1912 Olympics, he won the decathlon and the pentathlon, both multi-event competitions.

Jim played major league baseball for six seasons. In 1915, he also signed to play pro football with a team called the Canton Bulldogs for $250 a game. Jim was a star in the early days of pro football. In 1920, while he was still a player, he was president of a new league that became the NFL in 1922.

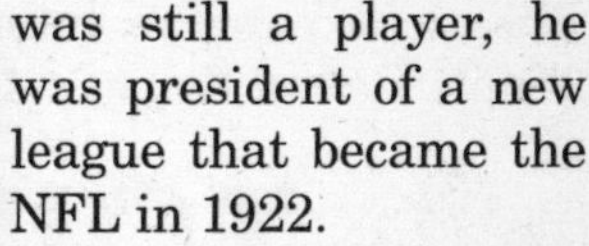

Jim was voted the greatest athlete of the first half of the 20th century in an Associated Press sportswriters poll. He was the first player inducted into the Pro Football Hall of Fame.

INFO-BOX

BIRTHPLACE: Prague, Oklahoma

CAREER: 1912–1928

CLAIM TO FAME: A standout in three sports, Jim was perhaps the greatest athlete who ever lived.

BILL TILDEN

Bill Tilden used his powerful serve to dominate international tennis from 1920 until 1925. During that time, he was 66–0 in singles matches and won the U.S. National Championships (now known as the U.S. Open) six times. At a height of 6' 2", he was known as "Big Bill."

In 1920, at age 27, Bill became the first U.S. player to win Wimbledon. He went on to win Wimbeldon twice more, in 1921 and 1930.

Bill turned professional in 1930. (In those days, the most famous tournaments — *see page 71*— were open only to amateurs.) Bill went on to win the U.S. professional singles title in 1931 and 1935. He was elected to the International Tennis Hall of Fame in 1959.

INFO-BOX

BIRTHPLACE: Philadelphia, Pennsylvania

CAREER: 1913–1945

CLAIM TO FAME: "Big Bill" was the king of men's tennis in the 1920s and one of its earliest professionals.

TORVILL AND DEAN

Jayne Torvill and Christopher Dean changed ice dancing with their precise moves and imaginative routines.

Jayne and Christopher, who were both from Nottingham, England, became partners in 1975. In 1978, they won the first of a record six straight British titles. They won the first of four straight world titles in 1981.

But it was their performance at the 1984 Olympics that made them famous. They received a perfect 6.0 score in artistic impression from all nine judges.

Jayne and Christopher turned professional and became a popular attraction at ice shows. They returned to the Olympics in 1994, and won a bronze medal.

INFO-BOX

BIRTHPLACE: Nottingham, England (both)

OLYMPIC CAREER: 1980, 1984, and 1994

CLAIM TO FAME: Jayne and Christopher helped make ice dancing a popular sport.

VLADISLAV TRETIAK

Vladislav Tretiak was once known as the best goaltender in the world. He appeared for the country that was known as the Soviet Union *(see page 54)* in four different Olympic Games, winning three gold medals and one silver.

For 14 years, Vladislav was the goalie for the Red Army team, which was the Soviet Union's national team. When the Soviets toured North American cities to play NHL teams, Vladislav shut out the Montreal Canadiens and the Quebec Nordiques in back-to-back games.

His greatest Olympic performance was at the 1984 Games. Vladislav allowed only five goals, while his teammates scored 48! The Soviets shut out the teams from Canada and Czechoslovakia to win the gold medal. The Soviet goalie's goals-against average was just 0.67!

Vladislav's outstanding play earned him the respect of his country and the world. However, his government would not allow him to leave the Soviet Union to play in the NHL, as some Russian players do now. Vladislav was elected to the Hockey Hall of Fame in 1989.

INFO-BOX

BIRTHPLACE: Moscow, Soviet Union (now Russia)

CAREER: 1969–1984

CLAIM TO FAME: A three-time Olympic gold medalist, Vladislav was one of the best hockey players in history.

BRYAN TROTTIER

From his second game in the NHL, in 1975, 19-year-old Bryan Trottier was a hockey sensation. That night, he scored three goals and earned five points to tie the club's single-game scoring records. Bryan went on to set new rookie records for assists (63) and points (95), and won the Calder Trophy as the NHL's best rookie!

INFO-BOX

BIRTHPLACE: Val Marie, Saskatchewan

CAREER: 1975–1994

CLAIM TO FAME: Bryan was one of the greatest all-around centers in NHL history.

After that, things kept getting better for Bryan. In the 1978–79 season, he scored 134 points. That year Bryan won the Art Ross Trophy (as the league's leading scorer) and the Hart Trophy (as the NHL's Most Valuable Player). His abilities to excel on both offense and defense made him one of the most successful centers in the league.

Bryan, who grew up in Canada, holds the NHL's record for most points in one period, with six! He played on six Stanley Cup champion teams, helping the New York Islanders win four Cups in a row and helping the Pittsburgh Penguins win two in a row.

More Stars!

With the Islanders, Bryan played on the same line as MIKE BOSSY and Clark Gillies. This trio was the perfect mix of speed, precision, and power. Mike was the sharpshooter, Bryan was the passer, and Clark, the biggest of the three, was the muscle. A hard-hitter, he would wrestle the puck away from opposing players and pass it to his linemates. While this threesome —and defenseman DENIS POTVIN — played together, the Islanders won three Stanley Cups in a row, from 1980 to 1982. The Isles added a fourth in 1983, with Anders Kallur replacing Clark.

JOHNNY UNITAS

Johnny Unitas's intelligence, confidence, and leadership ability helped him become one of the greatest quarterbacks of all time. But things did not start out easy for him.

Drafted in 1955 by the Pittsburgh Steelers, Johnny was cut before the season started because the team didn't think he was good enough. The Baltimore (now Indianapolis) Colts signed him a year later to be their backup quarterback. But when the starter was injured in the fourth game of the season, Johnny took over. He quickly became a star.

Johnny led the Colts to NFL championships in 1958 and 1959, and was named the NFL Player of the Year three times (1959, 1964, and 1967). The 1958 NFL Championship Game, in which Johnny helped the Colts beat the New York Giants in sudden-death overtime, has been called the greatest football game ever played.

Johnny retired in 1973. He still holds one record that may stand forever: 47 straight games with at least one touchdown pass. The closest anyone has ever come to that record was 30 games, by DAN MARINO.

In 1979, Johnny was inducted into the Pro Football Hall of Fame.

INFO-BOX

BIRTHPLACE: Pittsburgh, Pennsylvania
CAREER: 1956–1973
CLAIM TO FAME: Johnny was one of the greatest quarterbacks in NFL history.

WES UNSELD

Wes Unseld was one of the best rebounders ever to play basketball. He was only 6' 7" tall (short for a center), but he weighed 245 pounds and knew how to use his size to box out opponents.

Wes played in college for the University of Louisville, in Kentucky. In his three varsity seasons, he averaged 20.6 points and 18.9 rebounds per game and was twice named to the All-America team.

The Baltimore Bullets selected Wes as the second overall pick in the 1968 NBA draft. In his first season, he ranked second in the league with 18.2 rebounds per game and was named Rookie of the Year and Most Valuable Player. Wes and WILT CHAMBERLAIN are the only NBA players to receive those two honors in the same season.

INFO-BOX

BIRTHPLACE: Louisville, Kentucky
CAREER: 1968–1981
CLAIM TO FAME: Although he was only 6' 7" tall, Wes was one of basketball's best centers.

Before Wes joined the Bullets, the team had never had a winning season. He played 13 years for the Bullets (first in Baltimore, then in Washington) and the team reached the playoffs 12 straight times. The Bullets won the 1978 NBA championship and Wes was voted the MVP of the Finals.

Wes's 13,769 career rebounds currently rank him ninth on the NBA's all-time list. He was elected to the Naismith Memorial Basketball Hall of Fame in 1988.

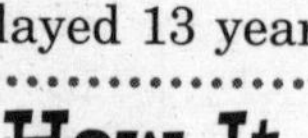

The Bullets were known as a fast-breaking team (moving the ball upcourt for the score before the opposing team has a chance to set up its defense). Wes was the man who got it started. When the ball bounced off the rim, Wes would jump up with his elbows pointed outward (to keep his opponents away) and grab the ball. Then, with his famous passing style — holding the ball with two hands over his head — he would whip off an outlet pass to start a fast break for an easy Bullet basket.

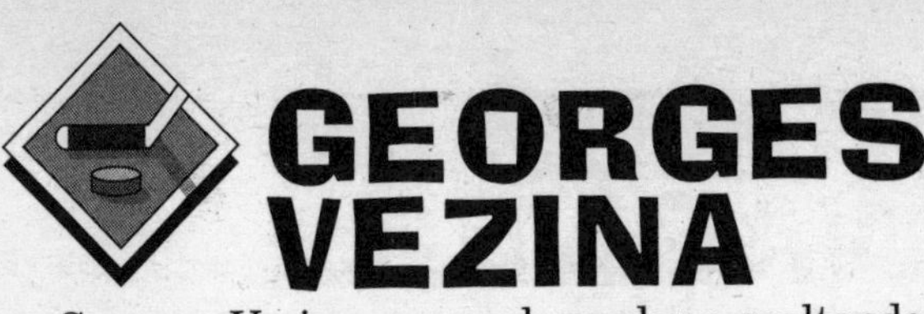

GEORGES VEZINA

Georges Vezina was a legendary goaltender who led the Montreal Canadiens to two Stanley Cup championships.

He was called "The Chicoutimi Cucumber" because he was born in Chicoutimi, Quebec, Canada, and he always kept his cool in big games (he was as "cool as a cucumber").

Georges didn't learn to skate until he was 18 years old. He started out playing goal while wearing boots!

> **INFO-BOX**
>
> **BIRTHPLACE:** Chicoutimi, Quebec, Canada
>
> **CAREER:** 1910–1925
>
> **CLAIM TO FAME:** Georges's great play as a goaltender inspired the NHL to name an important award after him.

During the Stanley Cup playoffs for the 1923–24 season, Georges had a 1.00 goals-against average (that means he gave up an average of just one goal per game). He once played in 366 games in a row, including playoff games.

Georges never missed a professional game until he became sick from tuberculosis, a disease that affects the lungs. He died on March 24, 1926, from the disease. He was 39 years old.

Each year the NHL's best goaltender receives the Vezina Trophy *(see below)*, in honor of Georges's accomplishments. Georges was elected to the Hockey Hall of Fame in 1945.

HOW IT WORKS The Vezina Trophy is given each year to the best goaltender in the NHL, as voted by the league's general managers. But it wasn't always that way. Before 1981, the award was given to all the goaltenders on the *team* that allowed the fewest goals in a season.

The first goalie to win the Vezina Trophy was George Hainesworth, who had been Georges Vezina's replacement in the Montreal goal, after the 1926–27 season. George also won the award the next two seasons. In fact, Canadien goalies dominate the list of the award's winners. Three goalies for the team have won the award five or more times: Bill Durnan, JACQUES PLANTE, and KEN DRYDEN.

HONUS WAGNER

Honus Wagner was the best player in the National League in the early 1900s. He was a Pittsburgh Pirate for 37 years — 18 as a player and 19 as a coach.

Honus was discovered when he was 18 by a scout for the Louisville Colonels, then a National League team. The scout was there to watch Honus's brother. Legend has it that the scout saw Honus throwing rocks across a wide river. He thought Honus had a great arm and signed him on the spot!

INFO-BOX

BIRTHPLACE: Carnegie, Pennsylvania

CAREER: 1897–1917

CLAIM TO FAME: Honus was probably the greatest shortstop in major league baseball history.

During his career, Honus starred at shortstop, but he played every position except catcher. His lifetime batting average was .327. His 3,418 hits put him seventh on the all-time list.

Honus was quick on the base paths. He stole 722 bases in 20 seasons! In the 1909 World Series, he stole six bases and batted .333 to lead the Pirates to their first championship.

As a fielder, he was known for his big, steam-shovel hands. He would often scoop up a handful of dirt with the ball and throw them both to first base.

In 1936, Honus became one of the first five players inducted into the National Baseball Hall of Fame.

Fun Fact

In 1909, Honus Wagner's picture was printed on one of the first baseball cards ever made. The cards were made by a tobacco company. Honus didn't like that. He didn't want people to think he approved of smoking. So he asked the company to stop selling the cards. Honus's cards were pulled off the shelf and destroyed, after fewer than 100 of the cards had been sold. Today, those cards are extremely valuable. Any of the original cards that survived is now worth between $100,000 and $500,000 — depending on its condition. One of those cards is owned by hockey great Wayne Gretzky!

GRETE WAITZ

Without Grete Waitz, there might not be a marathon race for women at the Olympics. Grete showed that women could compete at long-distance running. In 1975, she set a world record in the 3,000-meter run. But at the 1976 Olympics, the longest women's race was the 1,500-meter run!

INFO-BOX

BIRTHPLACE: Oslo, Norway
CAREER: 1978–1990
CLAIM TO FAME: Grete proved to the world that women can run marathons and other long-distance races.

Grete, who is from Norway, began running track when she was 12. In those days, she ran shorter races, but she knew she was better at the longer distances. Grete won a bronze medal in the 1,500-meter run at the 1974 European championships. She won another bronze medal in the 3,000 meters at the 1978 championships. But Grete really made her mark in the marathon.

In 1978, Grete ran the New York City Marathon, her first marathon (26.2 miles). Not only did she win, but she ran the fastest time ever for a woman, 2:32:50. Grete won again in 1979 and 1980, and set a world record each time!

During her career, Grete won the New York City Marathon a record nine times.

In 1984, the women's marathon was included in the Olympics for the first time. Grete won the silver medal in the event.

More Stars!

Like Grete Waitz, Ingrid Kristiansen is from Norway. And like Grete, Ingrid changed the way people thought about female runners. In 1986, Ingrid became the only runner, male or female, to hold records in the 5,000-meter and 10,000-meter runs and have the fastest time in the marathon — all at the same time. Ingrid is also the only athlete to hold world titles in track, cross-country, and road racing.

FOOTBALL

HERSCHEL WALKER

Herschel Walker's blend of size and speed has made him one of the best running backs in football. He broke records in college and helped kick off a brand-new league in the pros!

At the University of Georgia in 1982, Herschel won the Heisman Trophy. In 1983, he left college early to play professional football. (He got his degree in criminal justice in 1984.) Herschel did not sign with the NFL, though. Instead he signed with New Jersey Generals, of the United States Football League (USFL).

Herschel was the USFL's biggest star. In 1985, the last year the USFL existed, Herschel rushed for 2,411 yards! That season total has never been matched by a pro in any league.

Herschel joined the NFL with the Dallas Cowboys in 1986. He later played for the Minnesota Vikings and the Philadelphia Eagles.

During the 1994 season, with the Eagles, Herschel became the only NFL player ever to log a 90-yard-plus reception, a 90-yard-plus run from scrimmage, and a 90-yard-plus kickoff return in one season. He joined the New York Giants before the 1995 season.

INFO-BOX

BIRTHPLACE: Wrightsville, Georgia

CAREER: 1983 to the present

CLAIM TO FAME: Herschel rushed for more yards in a pro season than any other running back in history.

Another Side

Herschel is a man of many talents. He was a track star in high school and college, and he represented the United States at the 1992 Winter Olympics in the two-man bobsled event. He studies martial arts and has a second-degree black belt in Tae Kwan Do. Herschel has even made his own fitness video for children. He can also hold his own when it comes to ballet. Herschel danced with the Fort Worth Ballet in Fort Worth, Texas, in 1988.

BILL WALTON

Bill Walton was an outstanding center who didn't have to score a lot of points for his team to win. He was an excellent passer, rebounder, and shot-blocker.

While in college at the University of California at Los Angeles (UCLA), Bill averaged 20.3 points and 15.7 rebounds a game. He helped UCLA win 88 straight games. The 6' 11", 235-pound center was the college Player of the Year from 1972 through 1974.

INFO-BOX

BIRTHPLACE: La Mesa, California

CAREER: 1974–1987

CLAIM TO FAME: A great all-around center, Bill led his teams to championships in college and in the NBA.

UCLA won the NCAA title in 1972 and 1973, and Bill was the tournament's Most Outstanding Player both times. In the 1973 championship game, Bill took 22 shots and made 21 of them!

Bill was the Portland Trail Blazers' first pick in the 1974 NBA draft. By 1977, the Trail Blazers were NBA champions and Bill was MVP of the Finals. He led the league in rebounding and blocked shots per game that year. In 1978, Bill was voted league MVP despite missing 24 games with a foot injury.

Bill played with the San Diego Clippers (now the Los Angeles Clippers) from 1979 to 1982. He joined the Boston Celtics for the 1985–86 season and helped them win the NBA championship. The following season, another injury forced him into retirement.

Bill was elected to the Naismith Memorial Basketball Hall of Fame in 1993.

PAUL WARFIELD

What made Paul Warfield such a terrific wide receiver was that he was a great all-around athlete. In high school, he earned varsity letters in football, basketball, and track. In college, he played football and ran track.

At Ohio State University, Paul didn't miss a game in three years. He played on offense as a halfback and on defense as a safety. He was an All-America as a senior. He was also an all-Big 10 sprinter, broad jumper, and hurdler.

In 1964, Paul was drafted in the first round by the Cleveland Browns. He played in Cleveland until he was traded to the Miami Dolphins after the 1969 season. There Paul and quarterback Bob Griese helped the team go undefeated for the 1972 season and win the Super Bowl.

Paul caught 427 passes for 8,565 yards and 85 touchdowns in his NFL career. He led the NFL in touchdown receptions twice and was named to the Pro Bowl seven times. He was inducted into the Pro Football Hall of Fame in 1983.

INFO-BOX

BIRTHPLACE: Warren, Ohio

CAREER: 1964–1977

CLAIM TO FAME: A fine all-around athlete, Paul was one of the NFL's first great acrobatic wide receivers.

Fun Facts

In 1974, Paul Warfield signed a contract to play with a new league, the World Football League (WFL). The WFL hoped to make football more exciting by changing some NFL rules. For example, balls for kickoffs were placed at the 30-yard line instead of the 35 so there would be fewer touchbacks and more kick returns. A fifth quarter was added to break ties. Fair catches weren't allowed on punts. Receivers needed to have just one foot inbounds for a pass to be complete.

The WFL folded in 1975, but some of its ideas were later adopted by the NFL.

DONNA WEINBRECHT

Olympic mogul champion Donna Weinbrecht played a lot of sports as a kid in New Jersey. She tried everything from swimming to riding a unicycle. She didn't give moguls skiing a try until she was 10, but when she did, she was hooked!

After graduating from high school in 1983, Donna went to art school. When the school closed, she decided to focus on skiing. She moved to Vermont and got a job as a waitress. She practiced skiing whenever she could.

INFO-BOX

BIRTHPLACE: West Milford, New Jersey

OLYMPIC CAREER: 1992 and 1994

CLAIM TO FAME: Donna was the first women's Olympic champion in moguls skiing.

In 1986, Donna placed 16th at the national championships. The next year, she placed fourth and made the U.S. team. In 1988, Donna became the national champion in women's moguls. She held on to that title for the next five years! In 1990, she was the World Cup champion *(see page 142)* for the first of three years.

Moguls skiing was an Olympic medal event for the first time in 1992, and Donna won the gold medal! Later that year, she injured her knee and missed the 1992–93 season. She came back to compete at the 1994 Olympics, in Lillehammer, Norway, and finished seventh.

HOW IT WORKS Moguls skiing is one of the four competitions in freestyle skiing. The others are aerials, ballet, and combined. Only moguls and aerials are Olympic events.

- Moguls. Moguls are snow bumps. In moguls competition, skiers ski down a steep course filled with moguls (bumps). The have to perform two jumps during the run. Skiers perform a variety of jumps with funny names, such as daffies, zudniks, and kosaks. They are judged on how fast they ski, how well they turn and go over the moguls, and how well they do their jumps.
- Aerials. Each skier takes two jumps off a platform and does flips, stunts, or acrobatic moves. It's a lot like diving with skis on!

JOHNNY WEISSMULLER

Johnny Weissmuller is famous for starring in Tarzan movies, but before his movie career, he was an awesome swimmer.

Johnny was born in 1904 in Europe, in an area that is now part of Romania. His family moved to the United States when he was 4 years old.

In 1922, Johnny made history when he became the first person to swim 100 meters in less than a minute. He competed in his first Olympics in 1924, winning three medals in one day! He won golds in the 100-meter freestyle and 4 x 200-meter freestyle relay and a bronze in water polo. Two days earlier, he had won a gold medal in the 400-meter freestyle.

At the 1928 Olympics, Johnny again won the 100-meter freestyle and anchored the gold-medal-winning 200-meter relay team. That gave him a total of five Olympic gold medals.

Johnny was training for the 1932 Olympics when he got his start in motion pictures. He was asked to audition for the part of Tarzan. He became the first of four Olympic medalists to play Tarzan in the movies.

INFO-BOX

BIRTHPLACE: Freidorf, Hungary (now part of Romania)

OLYMPIC CAREER: 1924 and 1928

CLAIM TO FAME: Johnny won five Olympic gold medals in swimming.

HANNI WENZEL

In 1976, Alpine skier Hanni Wenzel became the first person from the tiny European country of Liechtenstein to win a medal at the Winter Olympics. It was a bronze medal in the slalom. Four years later, she did even better. She made history by winning three medals in Alpine skiing at one Olympics.

> **INFO-BOX**
>
> **BIRTHPLACE:** Staubirnen, Germany
>
> **OLYMPIC CAREER:** 1976 and 1980
>
> **CLAIM TO FAME:** Hanni won three Alpine skiing medals at one Olympics.

Hanni was born in Germany, but her family moved to Liechtenstein when she was 1. In 1974, after winning the slalom at the world championships, she became a citizen of Liechtenstein. Hanni won the overall World Cup title in 1978 and 1980 *(see page 142)*.

At the 1980 Winter Olympics, in Lake Placid, New York, Hanni skied in all three Alpine skiing events. She won a silver medal in the downhill. Then she won gold medals in the giant slalom and slalom. Hanni joined Rosi Mittermaier *(see right)* as the first women to win three Alpine medals at one Olympics.

Hanni's brother, Andreas, won a silver in the giant slalom, too!

More Stars!

At the 1976 Olympics, Rosi Mittermaier of West Germany (now Germany) became the first woman to win three medals in Alpine skiing at one Olympics. Rosi won gold medals in the slalom and downhill and a silver medal in the giant slalom.

Vreni Schneider of Switzerland joined the club at the 1994 Olympics. Vreni won a gold medal in the slalom, a silver in the Alpine combined, and a bronze in the giant slalom. At the 1988 Olympics, Vreni added two more gold medals, in the slalom and the giant slalom.

JERRY WEST

Jerry West was called "Mr. Clutch" because he had a knack for sinking the last shot to win a game. He averaged 27 points per game over his NBA career and led the Los Angeles Lakers to the NBA Finals nine times.

INFO-BOX

IRTHPLACE: Cheylan, West Virginia
CAREER: 1960–1974
CLAIM TO FAME: Jerry was one of the greatest clutch shooters and defensive players in NBA history.

Jerry had also been a clutch player at East Bank Consolidated High School, in West Virginia. He led the East Bank team to the state basketball title in 1956.

As a student at West Virginia University, Jerry was a college All-America twice. He was on the team that won a gold medal at the 1960 Olympics.

In 1960, the Minneapolis Lakers drafted Jerry into the NBA. (The team moved to Los Angeles with the 1960–61 season.) He teamed up with ELGIN BAYLOR and, later, WILT CHAMBERLAIN.

Jerry was at his best during the playoffs, averaging 29.1 points per game. He was named MVP of the 1969 playoffs, although his team lost. In 1972, he led the Lakers to the NBA title.

Jerry was named to the NBA All-Defensive Team four times. He was voted into the Naismith Memorial Basketball Hall of Fame in 1979.

Did You Know?

- To celebrate the state championship that Jerry helped the school win, East Bank Consolidated High School used to change its name to *West* Bank Consolidated one day a year!
- Jerry's form on the court was picture perfect. For proof, check out the NBA logo. The player dribbling straight at you is none other than Jerry West! The NBA has used Jerry's silhouette on its logo for the past 25 years.
- After he retired, Jerry coached the Lakers and then became their general manager. While Jerry has been general manager, the Lakers have won three NBA championships.

RANDY WHITE

For 14 seasons, 6' 4" tall, 265-pound Randy White played defensive tackle for the Dallas Cowboys. He was named to the Pro Bowl nine years in a row.

Randy played football, basketball, and baseball in high school. At the University of Maryland, he won the Outland Trophy and the Vince Lombardi Award as college football's top lineman. He was the second player chosen in the NFL draft.

At the end of his first season as a Dallas starter, the Cowboys defeated the Denver Broncos in Super Bowl XII. Randy was co-MVP of the game.

Randy had a career total of 114 sacks and more than 1,100 tackles. He was elected to the Pro Football Hall of Fame in 1994.

INFO-BOX

BIRTHPLACE: Wilmington, Delaware

CAREER: 1975–1988

CLAIM TO FAME: The anchor of a great Dallas Cowboy defense, Randy was one of the best defensive tackles ever.

KATHY WHITWORTH

Kathy Whitworth won 88 tournaments in her career. That's more than any other golfer in history!

Kathy was amazingly consistent. She won tournaments in each year between 1962 and 1978! Between 1963 and 1969, she won 51 titles. She also won tournaments in three decades: the 1960s, 1970s, and 1980s.

By 1982, Kathy had broken the Ladies Professional Golf Association (LPGA) record of 82 career wins. The men's record was 84. Kathy tied that record in 1983 by winning the Women's Kemper Open with a 40-foot putt on the final hole.

Kathy won Player of the Year honors seven times and entered the LPGA Hall of Fame in 1975.

BIRTHPLACE: Monahans, Texas

CAREER: 1959–1992

CLAIM TO FAME: Kathy is the all-time leading tournament winner in professional golf.

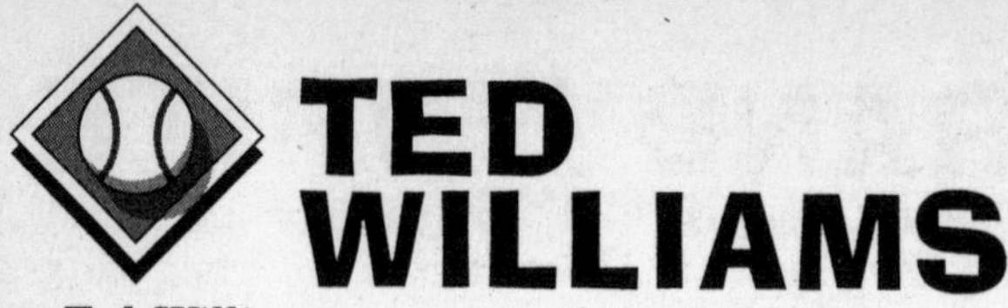

TED WILLIAMS

Ted Williams was one of the best hitters there ever was. His batting average for the 1941 season was .406! No major leaguer has batted .400 since.

He was a powerful hitter, too, smacking 521 homers in his career. He won the Triple Crown twice (leading the league in batting average, RBIs, and home runs), in 1942 and 1947.

Ted joined the Boston Red Sox when he was 20 and stayed for his entire career. In 1941, his third season, he came into a doubleheader on the last day of the season with his batting average at .39955. His manager told him he could sit out, and his average would have been rounded up to a perfect .400. But Ted wanted to play. He went on to get six hits in eight at-bats to raise his average six percentage points!

Over his 19-season career, Ted's batting average dipped below .300 only once. His career average was .344. And if he hadn't missed almost five seasons (he was a Marine Corps pilot in World War II and in the Korean war), Ted might have broken Babe Ruth's home run record before Hank Aaron did.

Ted ended his pro career with a home run in his final at-bat. He was elected to the National Baseball Hall of Fame in 1966.

INFO-BOX

BIRTHPLACE: San Diego, California

CAREER: 1939–42, 1946–60

CLAIM TO FAME: Ted hit more than 500 homers and was the last player to bat more than .400 in a season.

DAVE WINFIELD

Dave Winfield is one of only three players ever to have more than 3,000 hits, 450 home runs, and 200 stolen bases in a career.

In college, Dave was drafted by teams in baseball, basketball, and football! He chose baseball and went right to the majors with the San Diego Padres.

In 1980, Dave joined the New York Yankees. That season, he helped them win the American League East. Dave had at least 100 RBIs for five straight seasons with the Yankees. He joined the Toronto Blue Jays for the 1992 season and helped them win the World Series. Dave has played for a total of six big-league teams.

INFO-BOX

BIRTHPLACE: St. Paul, Minnesota

CAREER: 1973 to the present

CLAIM TO FAME: Dave has been one of baseball's great all-around outfielders for more than 20 seasons.

KELLEN WINSLOW

Kellen Winslow had great size (6' $5\frac{1}{2}$" tall, 250 pounds), speed, and hands. He could make acrobatic catches and run over defenders. Those talents made him an awesome tight end.

Kellen did not start playing football until his senior year in high school. But by the time he was at the University of Missouri, he was an All-America.

Kellen played 10 seasons for the San Diego Chargers. In that time, he caught 541 passes for 6,741 yards. He led the NFL in receptions two years in a row. Between 1980 and 1984, he caught more passes than any other NFL receiver. In 1981, Kellen set an NFL record with five touchdown receptions in one game!

INFO-BOX

BIRTHPLACE: St. Louis, Missouri

CAREER: 1979–1988

CLAIM TO FAME: A big man who was also a great athlete, Kellen was pro football's best tight end.

KATARINA WITT

Katarina Witt grew up in East Germany (which is now part of Germany). In 1981, she won the first of her eight national figure-skating titles. She was just 15 years old! Katarina went on to win six straight European titles, four world championships, and two Olympic gold medals.

Katarina discovered skating when she was in kindergarten. After her class visited a training center, she begged her parents for skating lessons. Katarina showed great talent. She started training as much as six hours every day.

In 1984, Katarina won her first Olympic gold medal. She repeated her success in 1988. Until then, SONJA HENIE was the only female skater ever to repeat as singles champion.

After the 1988 Games, Katarina turned professional. Pro skaters were not allowed to compete in the Olympics. But that rule was changed in 1993.

Katarina competed in the 1994 Olympics and finished seventh. She dedicated her program to the people of war-torn Sarajevo, the city that hosted the 1984 Winter Olympics.

INFO-BOX

BIRTHPLACE: Karl-Marx-Stadt, East Germany (now Germany)

OLYMPIC CAREER: 1984, 1988, and 1994

CLAIM TO FAME: Katarina won two gold medals.

CARL YASTRZEMSKI

Carl Yastrzemski had some big shoes to fill when he joined the Boston Red Sox in 1961. TED WILLIAMS had just retired after playing left field for the Red Sox for nearly 20 years. But "Yaz" filled Ted's shoes comfortably for the next 22 years.

In 1967, Carl became one of only 14 major leaguers to win the Triple Crown. He led the majors in home runs (44), batting average (.326), and RBIs (121). He also led the Red Sox to the American League pennant!

During his career, Carl was named to 18 All-Star teams. He was elected to the National Baseball Hall of Fame in 1989.

INFO-BOX

BIRTHPLACE: Southampton, New York

CAREER: 1961–1983

CLAIM TO FAME: Carl is the only American Leaguer ever to have more than 3,000 hits with 400 home runs.

CY YOUNG

Long before there was a Cy Young Award, there was a Cy Young — the winningest pitcher ever. Cy is baseball's all-time career leader in wins (511), innings pitched (7,356), and complete games (750). He also *lost* more games (315) than anyone else.

In 1903, Denton "Cy" (for Cyclone) Young pitched in major league baseball's first World Series. He won two games and helped the Boston Pilgrims defeat the Pittsburgh Pirates for the title.

Cy is the only pitcher to win 200 games in both the National and American leagues. Since 1956, major league baseball has honored its best pitchers by presenting them with the Cy Young Award. Cy himself was honored with a place in the National Baseball Hall of Fame, in 1937.

INFO-BOX

BIRTHPLACE: Gilmore, Ohio

CAREER: 1890–1911

CLAIM TO FAME: Cy won more games than any other pitcher in the history of major league baseball.

BASEBALL

STEVE YOUNG

Steve Young is one of the most talented quarterbacks in NFL history. He can throw with the best passers, and he can run like a running back.

Steve grew up in Greenwich, Connecticut, and played football, basketball, and baseball in high school. He accepted a football scholarship to Brigham Young University, in Utah. After serving as a backup, he was an All-America quarterback by his senior year and led the NCAA in total offense (passing and running).

After graduation, Steve signed with the Los Angeles Express of the new United States Football League. He became the only player in pro football history to throw for 300 yards and run for 100 yards in one game.

When the USFL folded, Steve joined the Tampa Bay Buccaneers. During his time with the Bucs, the team was only 3–18.

But the San Francisco 49ers saw Steve's potential. They traded for him in 1987, so that he could back up their quarterback, Joe Montana. Steve got his chance to start when Joe was injured for the 1991 season, and he led the NFL in passing! In 1992, with Joe still hurt, Steve led the league in passing again, and was named league MVP. Joe was traded to the Kansas City Chiefs.

Steve would top the NFL in passing for four straight seasons. In 1995, he led the 49ers to a Super Bowl win and was the game's MVP.

INFO-BOX

BIRTHPLACE: Salt Lake City, Utah

CAREER: 1984 to the present

CLAIM TO FAME: Steve is the highest-rated passer and the most dangerous quarterback in the NFL today.

When He Was a Kid

As the quarterback of the junior varsity football team in high school, Steve once threw seven interceptions — in one game! But Steve didn't let that setback stop him. By his senior year in high school, he was captain of the football, basketball, and baseball teams and had won a scholarship to BYU.

BABE DIDRIKSON ZAHARIAS

Any sport that Babe Didrikson Zaharias tried, it seemed, she played better than anyone else.

Babe, whose real first name was Mildred, began playing basketball in elementary school, and scored 104 points in a high school game. After high school, she worked for a company in Texas. She competed on the company's basketball and track teams.

INFO-BOX

BIRTHPLACE: Port Arthur, Texas

CAREER: 1932 (Olympics); 1935–1943, 1947–1954 (golf)

CLAIM TO FAME: Babe was one of the greatest athletes of all time.

At the 1932 Amateur Athletic Union's women's track-and-field championships, 18-year-old Babe won six events, set four world records (in the 80-meter hurdles, high jump, long jump, and javelin), and won the team competition — all by herself! At the 1932 Olympics, Babe won two gold medals and a silver.

Babe took up golf, and in 1947, she became the first U.S. woman to win the British Amateur. Between 1935 and 1954, she won 82 tournaments, including a record 17 in a row.

In 1950, Babe helped found the Ladies Professional Golf Association. That year, she was voted the top woman athlete of the first half of the 20th century by the Associated Press.

EMIL ZATOPEK

Emil Zatopek *[zah-TOE-pek]* is the only runner ever to win the 5,000-meter and 10,000-meter runs and the marathon — all at the same Olympics!

INFO-BOX

BIRTHPLACE: Koprivnice, Moravia, Czechoslovakia

OLYMPIC CAREER: 1948, 1952, and 1956

CLAIM TO FAME: Emil was the greatest long-distance runner in history.

During his career, Emil set 18 world records. At the 1948 Olympics, he won the gold medal in the 10,000 meters and the silver in the 5,000. Four years later, he became the first runner in 40 years to win the gold in both the 5,000-meter and 10,000-meter runs at the same Olympics.

But that wasn't enough for Emil, and he decided to try the marathon, too. The fact that he had never run a marathon before didn't matter to him.

Midway through the 26.2 mile race, Emil asked Jim Peters of Great Britain a question. Jim, who was favored to win the race, was running alongside Emil. Emil asked Jim if he thought they were running too slowly.

Jim said yes, and that was all Emil needed to hear. He simply took off! Emil cruised to the gold medal and set an Olympic record.

More Stars!

Abebe Bikila of Ethiopa was the first black African to win an Olympic marathon and the first runner to win two consecutive Olympic marathons.

At the 1960 Games, in Rome, Italy, the 28-year-old Abebe was an unknown. Still, Abebe, who liked to run barefooted, ran the fastest marathon ever and took the gold.

In 1964, Abebe ran the Olympic marathon again. Just 40 days before the Olympics, he had had his appendix removed. Abebe still won the marathon in the fastest time ever! Only this time, he wore shoes.

INDEX

Photo Credits UPI/Bettmann: 8, 11, 17, 22, 24, 29, 35, 39, 41, 45, 49, 53, 56, 63, 66, 68, 70, 73, 75, 79, 81, 85, 88, 90, 93, 94, 97, 100, 102, 105, 109, 115, 118, 123, 125, 127, 128, 131, 132, 137, 138, 143, 146, 151, 153, 154, 159, 160, 165, 166, 168, 171, 173, 175, 176, 186, 188, 194, 198, 200, 202, 205, 207, 209, 212, 214, 219, 221, 222, 224, 227, 229, 230, 236, 241, 243, 244, 246, 249, 259, 263, 269, 272, 276, 278, 281; AP/Wide World: 13, 106, 157, 180, 196, 234, 255, 261

Contributors

Darice Bailer: Marcus Allen, Lance Alworth, Sammy Baugh, Chuck Bednarik, Raymond Berry, George Blanda, Terry Bradshaw, Jim Brown, Dick Butkus, Earl Campbell, Larry Csonka, Eric Dickerson, Tony Dorsett, John Elway, Dan Fouts, Red Grange, Joe Greene, Archie Griffin, John Hannah, Leon Hart, Ted Hendricks, Paul Hornung, Don Hutson, Jim Kelly, Jerry Kramer
Susan Brody: Brian Boitano, Dick Button, Nadia Comaneci, Kornelia Ender, Janet Evans, Dorothy Hamill, Eric Heiden, Sonja Heinie, Jean-Claude Killy, Olga Korbut, Greg Louganis, Phil Mahre, Matti Nykanen, Johan Olav Koss, The Protopopovs, Mary Lou Retton, Mark Spitz, Torvill and Dean, Donna Weinbrecht, Johnny Weissmuller, Hanni Wenzel, Katarina Witt, Paul Warfield, Randy White, Kellen Winslow
Robert Campbell: Hobey Baker, Jean Beliveau, Mike Bossy, Ken Dryden, Phil Esposito, Gordie Howe, Bobby Hull, Guy Lafleur, Mark Messier, Howie Morenz, Bobby Orr, Jacques Plante, Denis Potvin, Maurice Richard, Vladislav Tretiak, Bryan Trottier, Georges Vezina, Warren Spahn, Tris Speaker, Honus Wagner, Ted Williams, Dave Winfield, Carl Yastrzemski, Cy Young, Roger Clemens
Craig Ellenport: Jack Lambert, Steve Largent, Ronnie Lott, John Mackey, Art Monk, Joe Montana, Warren Moon, Marion Motley, Anthony Muñoz, Bronko Nagurski, Joe Namath, Walter Payton, John Riggins, Gale Sayers, O.J. Simpson, Bart Starr, Roger Staubach, Jan Stenerud, Lynn Swann, Fran Tarkenton, Lawrence Taylor, Jim Thorpe, Johnny Unitas, Herschel Walker
David Fischer: Muhammad Ali, Julio Cesar Chavez, Jim Corbett, George Foreman, Sugar Ray Leonard, Joe Louis, Rocky Marciano, Sugar Ray Robinson, John L. Sullivan, Cheryl Miller, Bob Pettit, Oscar Robertson, Bill Russell, Dolph Schayes, John Stockton, Isiah Thomas, Wes Unseld, Bill Walton, Jerry West, Patty Berg, JoAnne Carner, Ben Hogan, Bobby Jones, Nancy Lopez, Jack Nicklaus, Greg Norman, Arnold Palmer, Kathy Whitworth
Sherie Holder: Andre Agassi, Pete Sampras, Oksana Baiul, Bonnie Blair, Steffi Graf, Jackie Joyner-Kersee, Carl Lewis, Shannon Miller, Troy Aikman, Bo Jackson, Dan Marino, Jerry Rice, Barry Sanders, Deion Sanders, Emmitt Smith, Flo Hyman, Tony Gwynn, Joe Jackson
Gregg Mazzola: Carl Hubbell, Reggie Jackson, Walter Johnson, Harmon Killebrew, Sandy Koufax, Nap Lajoie, Mickey Mantle, Christy Mathewson, Willie Mays, Joe Morgan, Stan Musial, Sadaharu Oh, Mel Ott, Satchel Paige, Jim Palmer, Kirby Puckett, Brooks Robinson, Frank Robinson, Jackie Robinson, Pete Rose, Babe Ruth, Nolan Ryan, Mike Schmidt, Tom Seaver, Ozzie Smith
Fred McMane: Mark Allen, Mario Andretti, Earl Anthony, Jeff Blatnick, Susan Butcher, Don Carter, A.J. Foyt, Dan Gable, Tony Hawk, Miguel Induráin, Joan Joyce, Duke Kahanamoku, Karch Kiraly, Greg LeMond, Diego Maradona, Willie Mosconi, Ty Murray, Paula Newby-Frasier, Pelé, Richard Petty, Secretariat, Willie Shoemaker, Naim Suleymanoglu
Michael Northrop: Kareem Abdul-Jabbar, Nate Archibald, Rick Barry, Elgin Baylor, Larry Bird, Carol Blazejowski, Bill Bradley, Wilt Chamberlain, Sweetwater Clifton, Bob Cousy, Dave Cowens, Bob Davies, Julius Erving, John Havlicek, Elvin Hayes, Marques Haynes, Nat Holman, Magic Johnson, Joe Lapchick, Nancy Lieberman, Hank Luisetti, Karl Malone, Pete Maravich, Kevin McHale, George Mikan
Lee Schreiber: Hank Aaron, Ernie Banks, Cool Papa Bell, Johnny Bench, Yogi Berra, George Brett, Lou Brock, Roy Campanella, Rod Carew, Steve Carlton, Roberto Clemente, Ty Cobb, Dizzy Dean, Joe DiMaggio, Bob Feller, Carlton Fisk, Rube Foster, Jimmie Foxx, Lou Gehrig, Bob Gibson, Josh Gibson, Hank Greenberg, Rickey Henderson, Rogers Hornsby
Donald Stohrer: Charles Barkley, Michael Jordan, Hakeem Olajuwon, Shaquille O'Neal, David Robinson, Barry Bonds, Ken Griffey Junior, Greg Maddux, Cal Ripken Junior, Frank Thomas, Wayne Gretzky, Mario Lemieux, Michelle Akers
Stephen Thomas: Roger Bannister, Sergei Bubka, Dick Fosbury, Florence Griffith Joyner, Kip Keino, Bob Mathias, Edwin Moses, Paavo Nurmi, Dan O'Brien, Al Oerter, Jesse Owens, Mike Powell, Wilma Rudolph, Grete Waitz, Babe Didrikson Zaharias, Emil Zatopek, Arthur Ashe, Bjorn Borg, Maureen Connolly, Jimmy Connors, Margaret Court, Chris Evert, Billie Jean King, Rod Laver, John McEnroe, Martina Navratilova, Bill Tilden

Additional reporting and writing by **David Sabino** and **Alex Bhattacharji**